PRAISE FOR THE BESTSELLING

ANGEL

"Heart-stopping romance."

"Wonderful, original." *The Sun*

"Packed with suspense and drama." *The Daily Mail*

"Sparkling." *Books for Keeps*

"Awesome." *Once Upon a Bookcase*

"Will leave you breathless." *Daisy Chain Book Reviews*

"Stunning." *Book Angel Booktopia* for *Chicklish*

"Made me laugh, smile and cry." *Open Book Society*

"Fresh, imaginative...highly addictive." *Empire of Books*

"Will suck you in and take you on a thrill ride."
Feeling Fictional

"Pure perfection." *Dark-Readers*

"Unmissable." *Jess Hearts Books*

"Mind-blowing, spine-tingling, absolutely brilliant."
Book Passion for Life

Powys

37218 00526228 7

L.A. WEATHERLY was born in Little Rock, Arkansas, USA. She now lives with her husband and their cat, Bernard, in Hampshire, England, where she spends her days – and nights! – writing.

L.A. Weatherly is the author of over forty books, which have been published in over ten different languages.

www.leeweatherly.com
www.angelfever.com

ANGEL FEVER

ANGEL FEVER

L.A. WEATHERLY

USBORNE

To the memory of my father, Jack Weatherly.
FF, I wouldn't have traded you. So much of me is you.
Thank you.

First published in the UK in 2013 by Usborne Publishing Ltd., Usborne House,
83-85 Saffron Hill, London EC1N 8RT, England. www.usborne.com

Copyright © L.A. Weatherly, 2013

The right of L.A. Weatherly to be identified as the author of this work has been asserted
by her in accordance with the Copyright, Designs and Patents Act, 1988.

Cover photographs of boy (left) and girl by Pawel Piatek.
Cover photograph of boy (right) © Edgardo Contreras/Getty Images

The name Usborne and the devices ♀ ⊕ are Trade Marks of
Usborne Publishing Ltd.

All rights reserved. No part of this publication may be reproduced, stored in a retrieval
system or transmitted in any form or by any means, electronic, mechanical,
photocopying, recording or otherwise without the prior permission of the publisher.

This is a work of fiction. The characters, incidents, and dialogues are products of the
author's imagination and are not to be construed as real. Any resemblance to actual
events or persons, living or dead, is entirely coincidental.

A CIP catalogue record for this book is available from the British Library.

ISBN 9781409522393   JFMAMJ ASOND/13 02172/3

Printed in Reading, Berkshire, UK.

PROLOGUE

"*HOLD STILL,*" *SAID ALEX.*

"*I can't!*" *Willow gasped. She was leaning over the stream, her long blonde hair a slithering mass of shampoo. She shrieked, half laughing, as Alex poured a canful of water over it. "Oh! That is so cold!"*

Alex started laughing too. "You're the one who wanted to wash it."

"*I had to; it was getting disgusting... Is all the shampoo out?"*

He grinned as he scooped more chilly water from the stream. "Nope. Not even close."

As Alex woke up, Willow's laughter faded into silence.

There was no stream, no ramshackle cabin nearby. He was lying in a sleeping bag in a tent, its nylon walls a deep blue in the predawn light. Even Willow was different. The girl asleep in his arms had short red-gold hair now; it framed her face in untidy spikes.

A dream. Alex smiled as he stretched, remembering that day up at the cabin – and then everything came slamming back and his smile vanished. Christ, no wonder he'd been dreaming about the cabin: back then their biggest problem had been hiding out from the Church of Angels. Now…Alex let out a breath and rubbed his temples with one hand.

Now things were a little different.

The uncertainty was the worst part, he thought grimly. If they just knew what the hell was going on, they could start to deal with it. But it had been three days – *three days* – and he and the rest of his team still had no clue.

They were finally almost out of the Sierra Madre; their journey north through Mexico had been spent mostly on mountain back roads so they could keep out of sight. Three days of the truck lurching over rough terrain; three days of dust and plummeting views. Three days of sending Seb, the only native Spanish speaker, ahead to high, isolated farms to purchase gas.

"They don't know yet that something has happened," Seb had reported each time he returned, lugging enough gas to keep them going – along with food pressed on him by the farmers' wives. "All they know is that the TV stations aren't working and the internet is down."

Alex had felt his team's tension increase with every rendition of this. The words didn't begin to tell them what they were all so desperate to know. Homes up here had generators; it meant nothing that the farms still had electricity. What was going on everywhere else?

Did dead TV and internet mean that more of the world than just Mexico City was gone?

With a soft rustle, Willow stirred in his arms. As her green eyes flickered open, they at first held only sleepy confusion – and then Alex saw her remember.

She swallowed and shifted so that her arms were folded across his chest. She rested her chin on them. "Morning," she whispered.

"Morning." Alex stroked her spiky hair, smoothing it from her face. "Did you sleep okay?"

"Not really." She pressed her cheek against his palm. "I – I still can't stop seeing it," she admitted in a small voice. "Every time I close my eyes."

"I know. Me too," Alex said roughly. The sight of Mexico City as it had gone down – buildings shuddering into nothing; cars and people tumbling into gaping cracks

– was one that would never leave him.

Willow's eyes were haunted. "And I just keep thinking… if Mexico City was the only place affected, then we should be seeing helicopters heading down there to help. The Red Cross or the army or…" She trailed off. She didn't need to add how silent the skies had been.

Alex gripped her hand hard. "The US could still be okay," he told her. "If only one or two cities were hit there, they'll be focusing relief efforts on those for now – not here." He'd been saying the same thing for days, trying to keep his team calm. Besides – please, god – it could actually be true.

Willow's gaze was steady. If she'd psychically sensed his jumble of hope and dread, she didn't comment. Looking down, she trailed a finger across his chest. Finally she cleared her throat.

"So…tell me something about you I don't know," she said.

Surprise touched him; it was a game they'd played back at the cabin. "You already know everything about me," he said softly. He pulled her fully on top of him and wrapped his arms around her.

Her voice was strained. "Oh, I bet there are still one or two mysteries left, if you try… Please?" she added.

Alex knew she was trying to take his mind off what had happened – and her own, for that matter. "Okay, give me a time frame," he said at last.

"Preteen," suggested Willow. "Say, between nine and twelve."

His father's training camp in the New Mexico desert: cement buildings, burning white in the sun. Alex thought, stroking Willow's spine. "Have I told you that I broke my arm when I was ten?"

She shook her head. "No, how?"

"I crashed Juan's motorcycle. He'd just taught me how to ride it, and I thought it'd be cool to go for a night drive through the desert."

Willow's body relaxed a little. "You mean you stole his bike?"

Alex nodded, remembering. "Yeah, pretty much. There was a full moon, and I was doing donuts in the sand – and then these two headlights came at me out of nowhere, and I skidded and hit my arm on a rock."

"Your dad?"

"Yeah – and, man, he was pissed. Especially since he had to take me to Alamogordo to the hospital."

Silence fell. With an effort, Alex kept his thoughts from what might have happened to the world. *Your turn*, he started to say, and then they heard the echo of a truck door closing.

Willow glanced up. "Someone else must be awake."

"We'd better get moving," said Alex.

Their eyes met. Once they were out of the mountains,

the plan was to return to the main highways; with luck they'd be back in the US by noon. The question was, what would they find?

Willow licked her lips. "So…how long do you think it'll take us to reach Nevada once we cross the border?"

"Normally less than a day," Alex said. "Now, though – I guess it depends."

Willow started to say something else but didn't. She nodded tensely, and sat up and reached for their tangle of clothes.

Watching her get dressed, there was suddenly so much Alex wanted to say: that no matter what had happened, their group of Angel Killers would somehow be all right. That as long as the two of them were together, they'd get through anything. The words felt hollow, even to him.

At least Raziel's gone, he reminded himself harshly. The angel's fiery death above Mexico City had been the one positive in all this.

Willow pulled on her blue hoodie; her tousled head emerged. Alex touched her face, caressing her cheekbone with one thumb. "You are so beautiful, you know that?" he said in a low voice.

Abruptly, Willow looked close to tears. She clutched his hand. "It'll be okay," she said. "Oh god, Alex, it just has to be."

He had no answer. He cradled her face and kissed her

deeply, and for a few seconds lost himself in the feel of their lips together.

The low, worried buzz of voices came from outside. Seb, Liz and Sam were all up. He and Willow drew apart, and Alex let out a breath.

"We'd better go," he said.

The journey to Nevada took three more days.

On his first glimpse of the small brick building in the middle of the desert, Alex was so tired that all he could think was, *Oh, shit, we're in the wrong place.* Then his brain cleared a little, and he realized this was it after all.

"What the hell?" Sam demanded from the back. "This is just an electricity substation!" They could see pylons clustered in the building's yard, stabbing at the sky.

"That's all it's supposed to look like," Alex said sharply as he steered the 4 × 4 over the uneven dirt road.

Willow glanced at him from the front passenger seat but didn't say anything. They were all exhausted, on edge…and hardly any wiser about what had happened to the world. *Though the signs don't look great so far,* thought Alex grimly. The fact that there'd been no border control was kind of a tip-off.

As they'd neared the United States, they'd heard people shouting gleefully about the abandoned border. If true, the ramifications were chilling, but Alex had decided to try it for the sake of speed. And when they'd reached Ciudad Juárez, it had been true all right: people swarming over the fence into El Paso, dropping into the US unchallenged; cars cruising straight through the unmanned gates, honking joyfully.

"*Dios mío* – they still think there's something better here," Seb had murmured.

No one had paid attention to their dusty 4 × 4. They'd drawn their guns anyway. Willow had been driving; she'd sped them across the border, knuckles white on the wheel – and then they were home again.

It was nothing at all like the place they'd left.

Even without the border chaos, it was obvious there'd been major earthquakes in the US too. Whole swathes of the nation's electricity grids had been knocked out – the night-time portion of the drive had been shrouded in an eerie darkness, without a single light showing. Things were even worse in daylight, with panicked looting going on everywhere they passed, until Alex had decided to stick to back roads again.

How much? he kept thinking. The question pounded at his brain. *How much of the world has been destroyed?*

They'd almost reached the brick building now. It looked as if it had crouched undisturbed here in the desert for decades. *DANGER OF ELECTROCUTION. KEEP OUT!* read the weathered sign.

A CIA agent had tipped them off about this place back in Mexico City. The code that she'd given them worked; the gate gave a jerk and slid open. A garage door raised up, leading into the building itself, and inside there was a light. Of course, realized Alex, the place must really be a substation, which meant it had its own power supply. The door slid shut as they drove inside.

The small room contained only a desk with a display of video monitors. On the wall facing them were two elevators: one car-size and the other smaller.

No one spoke as they got out of the truck. Alex drew his pistol. He'd done a scan for energy and knew there wasn't anyone inside – but he still felt better armed.

They took the smaller elevator down. After nearly a minute, its doors opened onto a large garage. A dozen shiny 4 × 4s were parked, waiting. At one end stood a pair of gasoline pumps, like a miniature gas station.

They stepped out and stared. "Do you think there's actually *gas* in those?" Liz asked finally.

"Yeah, definitely." Alex gave a short, humourless laugh. "Ever wonder where your tax dollars went?"

Their footsteps echoed down gleaming corridors as they explored the bunker. The details they'd been given had done nothing to prepare Alex for actually being here. The vast underground base could support a thousand people for up to two years. It just went on and on: a fully stocked armoury, an industrial-size kitchen, closets piled high with sheets and pillowcases. The silence got to you after a while; Alex kept bracing himself with every door he opened, not knowing what he was about to see.

But there was no sign that anyone had been here recently. And no sign of their missing teammates, Kara and Brendan – last seen in Mexico City.

Willow stood peering into a closet full of cleaning supplies. She gave Alex a worried glance as the others went on ahead.

"Kara definitely knows where this place is, right?" she asked in an undertone.

Alex nodded, not surprised that she'd picked up on his thoughts. Kara had seen the specs on the base. If she and Brendan had made it out, this was where they'd have come.

Willow touched his arm. "Alex, they could still show up."

She didn't add that the odds of them having made it through the lurching Mexico City streets in Juan's old van were infinitesimal…if they'd managed to escape the Church of Angels mob at all. Alex saw again the hundreds of bloodthirsty people, all intent on killing the AKs, and his jaw tightened.

"Yeah, they could still show up." He heard his voice shut a door on the conversation. How many people he cared about had he now lost to the fight with the angels?

Silently, Willow stepped close and slipped her arms around him. Alex let out a breath and held her, dropping his head down to her shoulder.

"Hey, we've found something," said Sam, coming back to them.

Alex glanced up. "What?"

"Shortwave radio." The big, muscular Texan still wore the same rumpled clothes he'd had on when they escaped Mexico City. "And it works," he added.

Alex's pulse leaped. Shortwave radios could broadcast worldwide – they were the one way the planet could still communicate even if other systems were gone. They followed Sam quickly to what was clearly a communications room, where a curved metal desk held a gleaming radio.

Seb stood with his hands propped on the desk; Liz sat frowning as she twiddled the dial. A few times she paused, fine-tuning. Each time there was only static.

She shook her head. "I don't think anyone's—"

And then the speakers burst into life.

"...this terrible catastrophe. But do not despair, because I am stepping forward to offer my leadership..."

Alex froze at the male voice with its English lilt. Oh *Christ*, no – it couldn't be.

"What the hell?" Sam yelped. "But Raziel's dead! We saw him die!"

"Quiet," Alex said tersely.

Willow's face had drained at the sound of her father's voice; she clutched the desk. Alex turned up the volume; without looking up, he gripped her hand.

"…those who do not know what has happened, I am deeply sorrowed to announce that the Seraphic Council has been assassinated in Mexico City. This vile deed was carried out by Willow Fields and her gang of Angel Killers, knowing full well that the Council had put down roots of energy in your world. She *knew* their assassination would cause the very earth to grow unstable."

Oh, the bastard. And people will believe it too, Alex thought. The world already believed that Willow was a terrorist – and of course Raziel left out the fact that *he* was the one who'd wanted the Council dead and had manipulated the unknowing AKs into doing it for him.

Raziel sounded aggrieved, sincere: "She is a deranged individual who hates the angels. *She* is the reason for the earthquakes that have devastated so much of your world."

So much of the world? Alex swallowed and glanced at Willow. Her eyes had grown too big for her face. The others stood stricken and waiting.

A faint rustle of paper. "In the US, the following cities have been destroyed: New York, Chicago, Los Angeles, Seattle, New Orleans, Dallas…"

Alex's mind reeled as the list went on and on, over a dozen, each city name a death knell. How could New York

City be *gone*? And Chicago. It was his hometown. He had a fuzzy memory of walking along the lakeside with his mother – of her laughing and calling ahead to his brother Jake to slow down.

Liz was crying. "Is he…is he lying, maybe?"

"No," Seb said faintly, staring at the radio. "I think he is telling the truth."

Sam's broad face was slack. "Dallas…" he murmured, pushing a helpless hand through his hair.

Willow had gone deathly pale. Alex's hand tightened on hers. "Okay, we already knew it was bad," he said from between gritted teeth. He glared at the others. "This is not going to break us. Do you hear me? This is *not* going to break us."

"…worldwide, the news is also dire. We have confirmed accounts of the destruction of London, Paris, Tokyo, Madrid…"

Finally the terrible litany came to an end.

"There are no words for what has happened," said Raziel. "Cities have been levelled. Millions have died. And Willow Fields is at fault. *She* has done this to your world."

With a small whimper, Willow pressed a hand to her mouth; her shoulders crumpled as if she'd been punched.

"No!" Alex straightened quickly and pulled her away from the others. "You do not believe this," he said fiercely.

"You are *never* to believe this crap. Do you hear me? *It was not your fault.* It was him – Raziel. *He's* the one who's done this."

Willow had a hand over her face, crying. "I should have known – I should have figured out sooner what he was up to. Oh god, all those people…"

Alex folded Willow into his arms as she began to sob. "How could you have known?" he demanded. "You were trying to *save* the world. Raziel knew that – he used it!" Alex drew back, stroked her hair from her face with both hands. "Willow, don't believe him! Tell me you know it wasn't your fault."

"I…" Willow struggled to speak against the tears. "Maybe not completely my fault, but—"

"It wasn't your fault *at all*!"

"Of course it was! I had a role in it, Alex. How can I get away from that – *how*?"

"You had a role like a pawn in a chess game has a role, *querida*," Seb said vehemently from behind them. "That's all."

Over Willow's shoulder, Alex could see the expression on Seb's stubbled face, his love for Willow clear. "And you weren't the only one who didn't know Raziel was spying on us," Seb added. "I checked too; I found nothing!"

"I know that!" Willow cried. "But if I'd just figured it out sooner—"

"How?" broke in Alex. "You didn't know he was in your head in the first place!" He gripped her hands. He thought he'd do anything, pay any price, if he could take this anguish away from her. "Willow, there was no way you could have stopped it – none. This was all him, okay? Not you. Never you."

She clung to his hands, her face tormented. Finally she gave a faint moan and leaned forward onto Alex's chest. He wrapped his arms around her, cradling her.

No one spoke. In the background Raziel's voice was reciting the list of cities again. *On a loop,* Alex thought, his own shock and grief pulling at him.

When Willow at last raised her head, she looked as if she'd aged a decade. "Okay," she said woodenly. "I'll – try not to blame myself." Her eyes were locked on his; her voice lowered to a whisper. "And…I love you, by the way."

He kissed her, not caring about the others standing there. He knew, though, that this would haunt her for ever, and inwardly he cursed Raziel even more. The destruction of half the world was still too much to take in; his mind kept skittering away from the reality of it. But what the angel had done to his own daughter made Alex want to rip Raziel's halo apart with his bare hands.

Liz cleared her throat, her cheeks damp. "He's – he's still talking."

Willow let out a breath and nodded; they returned to the others.

Raziel's voice had become reassuring. "But you don't need to be afraid! I have a plan that will save us all."

Alex stiffened. No matter how bad things were already, he had a feeling Raziel was about to make them worse.

"As you know, you currently have no power," the angel continued. "Sadly, reinstating it everywhere is not an option – we must conserve our resources from now on. And so selected cities are going to be transformed into bountiful Edens, where life will continue as before! There you will have warmth and electricity, food and comfort."

Alex frowned. *Selected cities?* But if they bypassed the damaged stations on the grid until they were repaired, bringing back the electricity shouldn't be that difficult. There was no reason to permanently ration power.

No, no reason…except to gain control.

"…meanwhile, emergency camps are being set up. The military is providing assistance. Make your way to one of the temporary camps, and soon there will be glorious Edens for all!"

Great. So Raziel now had control of the military too. Alex could practically see the angel's feigned sad smile as he finished: "These are dark times, but a new dawn is coming. I will take care of you. That is my promise."

After a pause the message began once more.

Seb's jaw was taut. "These Edens will be—"

"A trap," finished Alex flatly. "Yeah, I *bet* he wants to conserve his resources; he's just knocked off half the angels' food supply. So now he'll lure people to live in a few centralized places where he can control everything."

"Like fish in a fish farm," whispered Liz.

On the radio, Raziel was denouncing Willow again.

"Oh, man." Sam's voice was bleak. "How is he even still alive? *How?*"

Alex shook his head; he had no idea. Raziel had been battling rival angels above the lurching streets of Mexico City – there'd been a flash of light they'd all thought had meant his death.

Yeah, right. They should have known better – beings like Raziel stuck around until the bitter end. Alex grimaced and moved to snap off the radio; Willow's hand flew out to stop him.

"No, wait," she murmured. "I can almost…" She trailed off, staring at the speakers as Raziel said again, "But you don't need to be afraid! I have a plan that…"

"Afraid," Willow echoed. Abruptly, her face cleared. "There's something we haven't thought of!" she gasped. "Alex, remember on top of the Torre Mayor, when my mind linked with Raziel's? I sensed that half the angels had died – because *he* knew it. But there was something else."

Alex saw again their altercation atop the highest building in Mexico – Raziel running after the AKs with a howling Church of Angels mob just behind. "Go on," he said.

Willow took a breath. "He was scared. He still is; I can hear it in his voice. Because with so many angels dead, the survivors are vulnerable too now."

Harsh excitement swept over Alex. *Of course.* The angels were creatures of energy, all linked. If you killed one, they each felt it.

And if enough died, the rest would follow.

He gripped Willow's hand urgently. "How many more have to die?"

"Not many." Willow's expression went distant again; Alex could practically feel her studying the brief encounter with her father. "The number was almost right there in his head... I think we're talking hundreds, not thousands. More like *one* hundred, even."

A hundred angels. Alex didn't move as electricity sizzled through him.

Liz looked dazed. "But...that means we've almost defeated them."

Her words seemed to rouse Sam. "A *hundred*?" he yelped. "Hell, we could do that in a week!" He slapped the desk. "Okay, who's with me? I say we leave here right now and go kill us some angels!"

"No," Alex said sharply. "We've got to plan this carefully – *really* carefully."

"You want a plan?" retorted Sam. "Okay, here's one: we go out there, start shootin', and don't get caught! Now, come on!"

Alex's voice rose. "There are only five of us! The second we kill one, they'll all feel it; they'll know we're still around! If they wipe us out before we finish them off, then that is *it*, for ever." He rapped a fist against his palm, his mind ticking as he considered options, then discarded them.

"We need a bigger team," he muttered. "A lot bigger. We've got to lie low for a while – months, a year even – let Raziel think we died in Mexico City. And then when there are enough angels gathered in one place, we'll *strike* – get rid of them all at once."

"But what about the Edens?" protested Liz. "If we wait too long, he'll fill the whole world with those places!"

"Let him," said Alex curtly. "The angels would still be feeding from humans anyway. The important thing is to get rid of them. No mistakes, no screw-ups – just get *rid*, for good."

The others exchanged glances...and Alex knew he'd convinced them. Even Sam. Willow's eyes were steady on his; he could feel her love for him – her support. He let out a breath, daring to imagine a world without the angels.

"Oh Christ, babe," he murmured. "I can't tell you how much I hope you're right about this."

"She's right." Seb was sitting on the desk, fiddling with a paper clip. He looked up, his gaze on Willow. "I can sense what she's getting very easily."

The tips of Willow's ears reddened, and Alex knew that Seb meant the psychic link he and Willow shared: the only two half-angels in the world.

Willow had told Alex everything that had happened between her and Seb – the way they'd kissed that night in Mexico City. Though Alex hadn't enjoyed hearing it, he'd known it was his own stupid fault. He and Willow had fought over her friendship with Seb, and he'd been too stubborn to make up with her before the terrorist attack that had separated Willow and Seb from the others. The weird thing was that he couldn't bring himself to dislike Seb any more. The half-angel was a good guy – his only crime was being in love with Willow.

Liz cleared her throat. "Listen, I think we should…not *celebrate,* but… Well, I mean, we're all still alive, and it looks like we might really have a chance again, and…" She tried to smile, her eyes still red. "Besides, I found what has to be the biggest pantry in the universe. The food's mostly military issue, but there's a whole mountain of it."

Alex touched her shoulder. "That's the best idea I've heard all day."

They sat up planning for hours in the base's rec room: a too-large space that felt almost cosy with the mood that had gripped them all. Their new knowledge made the air crackle with hope – gave them something to think about instead of all the destruction.

Eventually, though, the long, fraught journey caught up with them. One by one, they dropped off where they sat, until only Alex and Willow were still awake, lying curled up on one of the sofas, holding each other.

"Are you okay?" he asked in an undertone, stroking his thumb across her cheekbone.

She let out a breath. "Kind of numb. But, yeah… You?"

Alex nodded. "Now I am."

He had no intention – none – of making his strike against the angels until they were ready. Because if he did this right, his plan would work. Then not only would what was left of the world be saved, but he and Willow could have the long life together that they both wanted.

The crystal pendant he'd given her glinted around her neck. He touched it gently, feeling its warmth from her skin. Willow swallowed and reached out to trace his eyebrow with her finger. The motion was full of wonder, as if she were discovering him for the first time.

Nothing will stop us this time, Alex vowed to himself,

and to her. *We're going to defeat them.*

As he kissed her, he felt something close to joy, despite the shattered world that lay above.

CHAPTER *One*

SOMETIMES WHEN I LOOKED BACK on my old life I could hardly believe it.

My old life: that was the one where I lived in Pawntucket, New York (population 19,000), and thought I was just a normal teenage girl. Or at least as normal as someone nicknamed "Queen Weird" could hope to be. I went to Pawntucket High, drove an old Toyota, skipped as many classes as I could get away with. And it never, not even once, occurred to me that I might not be completely human.

In some ways, I hadn't changed much since then. I still loved tinkering with engines; my favourite colour was still purple. But in other ways, I was a million miles apart from that girl. Once I'd combed vintage clothing stores for the bizarre and wonderful; now I usually just threw on jeans and a T-shirt. They were easy to run in – and with the life we led now, you kind of had to take that into consideration.

I guess the biggest change of all, though – apart from realizing the truth about myself – had to be guns. I'd always hated them. Sometimes boys at my high school would talk about going hunting, and it would make me shudder: the idea of actually stalking a living creature; of aiming at it and pulling a trigger; of seeing it crumple in front of you, so that it ceased to exist any more – I couldn't understand how anyone, ever, could bring themselves to do it.

That was before I knew we were at war.

I crouched on the ground with the cold weight of a rifle in my hands. I wielded it expertly, aiming and shooting like a machine as explosions seared overhead: white petals that fell, glittering, against the darkness, as angel after angel was killed.

In the unearthly glow, I could see the outline of Salt Lake Eden with its barbed-wire fence. Around me were the shadowy figures of other Angel Killers, the echoes of gunfire, muffled shouts.

"Man, that's gotta be almost it," muttered Sam next to

me. Another explosion lit his broad face, showing it gleaming with sweat. "It has *got* to be."

I started to reply, then broke off at a sudden flash of white. "Sam, look out!" I cried. I flipped onto my side, quickly tracking the angel.

He scowled as he saw it corkscrewing down at us; we both shot at once. A second later, shards of light were drifting on the air. I let out a shaky breath as Sam and I glanced at each other. Just on my own, I'd already shot, what – four, five? *That's got to be way over a hundred by now,* I thought feverishly.

The words had barely formed in my mind when a dozens-strong flock soared at us out of nowhere, their pale, glorious figures etched against the stars. My veins chilled. How could they even still be alive now – *how?*

I pushed the thought away – not helpful. As the angels plunged into an attacking dive, I squeezed the trigger and shot. Fervent gunfire was going off all around me; I could hear people swearing. Above, three angels burst into nothing, but there were still way too many. We weren't going to make it this time—

No. We were.

Still shooting, I reached within for my own angel: the shining winged twin with my face. Some distance away I saw that Seb's angel was already flying, fending off an attacker with quick, strong thrusts of his wings.

In my angel form, I paused only long enough to make myself tangible so I could grab the sensor from my pack; then I was hurtling through the air too. Wings spread, I darted in front of one of the approaching angels, and it veered off wildly; another appeared, and I did the same, swooping back and forth.

"It's Willow! Get them while she holds them off!"

Even with adrenalin surging through me, I was still amazed at the accuracy of the detail: every angelic feather was outlined in blue-white light; the faces were all individual, all enraged as they screeched at me.

Don't think. Defend. Around me came a series of explosions so fast and furious that I was flying in a hailstorm of light. Time shifted to slow motion – a long scream that echoed in my ears; a halo bursting so close by that I could see every dot of light, spiralling off into the darkness. Finally there was only one angel left – and then someone shot, and that one was gone too.

"That's it!" shouted Alex's voice. The night-time vanished as the room's lights burst on, leaving us blinking. "We've done it!" he called. "All the angels in the world are *gone!*"

My human self exhaled as cheers from almost a hundred people echoed through the cavernous underground room.

We had rid the world of the angels. Again.

"Good one, angel chick," Sam said with a grin, giving

me a one-armed hug as we got to our feet. His short blond hair stood up in gel-coaxed spikes. "Man, I thought that last bunch was gonna get us."

"You and me both," I admitted. Some of my own hair had escaped its shoulder-length ponytail and I quickly pulled the unruly brown waves into place. I hated its current colour, but Raziel had plastered posters of me everywhere – if I went back to my natural blonde I'd be endangering all of us every time I stepped outside. Fortunately there was no shortage of hair dye in abandoned stores.

Reaching up, I took the sensor from my angel as she glided back down to me, her snowy wings outspread.

At one time, seeing a half-angel in action would have brought sidelong stares from the other AKs; now no one paid any attention. The group knew by now that I was nothing like the angels we were trying to defeat. My angel self didn't have a halo, and she didn't feed – not from human energy or anything else. I hadn't even known I *was* half-angel until I was sixteen.

With a quick flutter, my angel merged into my human self, leaving just "me" standing there. Distantly, I could sense Seb's angel merging with him too, far across the training room. At my automatic awareness of Seb – the familiar feel of his energy, so like my own – a pang of sadness went through me. I ignored it.

"Okay, guys – take five while we get this stuff turned off," called out Alex.

I looked over as he started to roll a holograph machine back into place, his shoulders flexing through his T-shirt. He sensed me watching and glanced up. The corners of his mouth lifted as his blue-grey eyes locked with mine. Then someone asked him a question, and he turned back to his work, motioning to a cable snaking across the floor.

I smiled. Alex and I had been together for over a year now, but it didn't seem to matter – just a look from him could still melt me.

People were standing around the training room, talking in small clusters. Occasionally a burst of laughter floated towards me. It was a relief that people still *could* laugh – when we'd first found out the extent of the destruction ten months ago, I'd wondered if anyone would ever laugh again.

But the human race is resilient, I guess. Down here, nobody wanted to dwell too much on what had happened to the world; conversations about it were practically taboo. The whole base knew that we had to focus on defeating the angels – not waste our energy grieving over the past.

I sighed. Good advice. So why was it so hard for me to follow it sometimes?

Liz made her way over to Sam and me, her sharp-featured face slightly flushed. "Good thing we've gotten so much better lately," she said. "I cannot *believe* that we have less than two months left before the attack."

Sam stretched, looking like a quarterback relaxing at half-time. "Yeah, I can't wait for the real thing," he drawled. "'Bout time we kicked those angels' asses for ever."

"*If* we succeed," Liz pointed out testily. "It's not guaranteed, you know."

"I'm with Liz; we need all the practice we can get," I said. I glanced at the centre of the hangar-like room, where an elaborate set rose up – a depressingly accurate representation of what used to be Salt Lake City, right down to the coils of barbed wire and perky sign: *WELCOME TO SALT LAKE EDEN, A BASTION OF THE ANGELS' LOVE!*

A bolt of hatred for my father went through me. His Edens were everywhere now; hardly a week went by that a new one wasn't announced on the shortwave. And we suspected that the places were even worse than we'd first thought, though we didn't have any information from someone who'd actually been inside of one. The barbed wire glinting on top of the set's fence said it all: once you entered an Eden, you didn't come out again.

The strange thing was how much the Edens had helped us.

Because while most people were only too happy to flock to them, a tiny minority didn't. They stayed on in the devastated cities or in the thousands of "dark towns" across the country, scavenging to survive. Raziel's Edens didn't just lure millions with their ease and electricity – they also made it clear exactly who the scrappy rebels without angel burn were. As a result it'd only taken us a couple of months to put together a good-size team of ninety-four recruits. I just really hoped that Raziel could take a moment to appreciate the irony when we finally made our move.

So I guess that was another way I'd changed: the Willow Fields of just over a year ago hadn't been a vengeful person. But then, she hadn't had my memories.

Liz started to chew a fingernail and caught herself. "Willow, are you sure you can't get *anything* psychically about Founding Day?" she asked anxiously. "Not even a tiny hint?"

I pushed my thoughts away; I knew better than to dwell on all this. "No, I'm way too emotionally involved," I said, managing a smile. "Sorry – psychic drawback number five."

To be honest, I was getting tired of people asking me that, though I couldn't really blame them, with the attack drawing so close. Salt Lake City had been the first Eden; in two months they'd be holding a massive Founding Day celebration, with thousands of angels circling overhead.

And we'd be right there waiting for them.

Everyone's attention went to the centre of the room, where Alex was clambering onto one of the crates that made up our mock Salt Lake Eden. I smiled as I watched him, my tensions easing. I seriously didn't think I'd ever seen anything quite as sexy as the sight of Alex wearing camouflage trousers and a black T-shirt. Unless it was the sight of him not wearing them.

He jumped on top of the crate; as he faced the team, he looked relaxed and confident, his dark hair tousled. "Okay, listen up!" he shouted. "That was excellent work, everyone. I've just got a couple of things to say—"

A chorus of good-natured groans. Alex grinned and swung himself down to a sitting position, legs dangling. I could see the toned outline of his chest against the T-shirt.

"Yeah, I know; I'm never satisfied, right? So, first of all – everyone still needs to work on disguising their auras. I saw a lot of you forgetting as the simulation went on." Alex's eyes met mine – Seb and I taught the classes for the energy work – and I nodded. The team was trying hard, but it just didn't come easily to most humans.

"They'll get there," I said for us both.

"Good. And in terms of everyone's shooting…" Alex paused, scanning the crowd before he smiled. "Guys, that was *awesome*. Your time was eight minutes twelve; that's better than it's ever been." He scratched the back of his neck as he added casually, "Oh, and by the way – the program was set for two-fifty."

Excitement rustled through the room; there were scattered cheers. Sam, Liz and I exchanged a jubilant glance. *Two hundred and fifty angels.* And we only needed to kill about half that many.

"So even with the aura work, we're not in bad shape already – you can all be damn proud of yourselves," Alex said firmly. "But what you *cannot* do is start getting cocky. Like I've said, shooting real angels is different. You've got to be aware of what the simulation can't mimic."

There were grim nods from around the room as he talked about angel burn, describing the ease with which an angel could link minds with you – how you'd only have seconds to break away before they started feeding from your life force, and then you'd be theirs for ever, worshipping and damaged. My fingers tightened on my rifle as I thought of my mother, sitting lost in her dreams.

"I don't want to lose any of you, okay?" Alex's voice was low, but it carried to every corner of the room. "Not a single one – and if we do this thing the way we've been planning, then I won't."

Emotion gripped me, recalling the dozens of nights Alex had lain awake beside me, going over the plan. *They trust me,* he'd said once, rubbing his forehead tiredly when I'd urged him to get some sleep. *I've got to make sure they're right to.*

On top of the crate, Alex gave a sudden grin. "Okay,

enough of that," he said. His gaze picked out a tall guy with brown hair. "Paul, dude – you do realize that if these weren't laser rifles, you'd have taken Chloe's head off, right? You want to explain what happened?"

And as Paul winced and attempted a response, I smiled dryly – because I wasn't the only one who'd been affected by Alex's grin lighting up his strong, regular features. I could sense the fluttering pulses around me like a flock of hummingbirds. Even if I'd had no psychic skills whatsoever, I'd have known that half the girls down here had a crush on my boyfriend – it wasn't hard to figure out, if blushes and admiring sideways glances were anything to go by.

The other half all had a thing for Seb.

I held back a sigh; covertly, I found myself studying Seb's face as he stood across the room. You wouldn't have guessed he was Mexican from looking at him; his mother's family had been European immigrants. From Italy, Seb always claimed – and he looked it, with his hazel eyes and loose chestnut curls. Though I always thought what he really looked like was a rock star, with the light stubble that usually coated his jaw.

Next to Alex, Seb was the best-looking boy I'd ever seen. I could understand why so many of the girls were attracted to him, even *without* the fact that he was half-angel – which only seemed to make him that much more intriguing to them.

I just wished he could feel intrigued by one of them in return.

In a sudden flash, I realized that Seb was aware I was thinking about him. From across the room, he gave me a quick, almost irritated glance, eyebrows raised; I felt a shutter slam down over his thoughts, blocking me out.

I crossed my arms tightly and looked away. I hated the distance between us, in every sense of the word. There was a time when Seb and I would have gravitated to stand next to each other as naturally as two magnets.

"Looks like we got another member of the CCC," Sam muttered in my ear.

The Carrera Crush Club. Reluctantly, I glanced back and saw who Sam meant: a tall, leggy girl named Meghan was standing near Seb. She was eighteen, with auburn hair that spilled past her shoulders and a sort of girl-next-door face, so that I could never decide whether she was simply pretty or completely beautiful. But whenever I sensed her energy, it felt like bouncing rays of sunshine.

"No, they've been friends for a while; she's part of that group he hangs out with," I murmured back. Paul was still explaining, protesting that his rifle wasn't working. Alex, looking like he seriously doubted it, had jumped down to go take a look.

"Yeah, but check out the way she's looking at him." Sam's blue eyes narrowed. "I'm telling you, she's got it *bad.*"

Across the room, Meghan said something to Seb. His reply looked teasing; her cheeks tinged pink as she smiled.

Sam shook his head – half jealous, half admiring. "Man, that guy's the biggest flirt on the planet. Wonder if he's keeping track? He could be going for a world record of crushees here."

I made a face and looked away. It was true that Seb didn't seem to mind being the base's most eligible bachelor. He wasn't vain, but there was no way he could be unaware of the effect he had on girls – and I guess he wouldn't even have been *half* human if he didn't enjoy the attention.

But when Seb and I had first met, our minds had touched and explored each other effortlessly, our half-angel connection transcending normal things like getting to know each other. I'd seen then how much of an extrovert he could seem with his teasing charm – when really, he was anything but that.

He'd told me once that I was the only person who'd ever really known him.

The problem was, no matter how many "crushees" Seb had, I knew that our time down here had done nothing to lessen his feelings for me. In fact, as the months had passed, the only change had been in his growing reluctance to be around me. And, okay, it wasn't like I didn't *understand* it – but I hated that things had come to this. I hated not being close to him any more.

I missed my friend.

"I'm not sure," I said, fingering a flowing pink sleeve. It was later that afternoon, and I was standing on Liz's bed in my bare feet, straining to see all of myself in the mirror over her dresser drawers.

"It looks great," Liz said in surprise.

"Yes, but it's *pink.*" I was already taking it off.

"Pink's got such a bad rep. Okay, forget that one." Liz went rummaging through her closet again. Back when we'd been recruiting people, she'd always managed to snag lots of expensive clothes from abandoned stores. I hadn't seen the point since we didn't have anyplace to wear them, but I guess that was just me.

"Here, try this." Liz tossed something black and flashing at me: a sleeveless top made of shiny black sequins. I pulled it on; it slithered down my torso like chain mail.

She whistled. "Oh, *sexy.* That one, definitely. Alex won't be able to keep his hands off you."

I gazed at the plunging draped neckline. The black sequins moved when I did, glittering and alive. "No, it's not right."

"Willow! Honestly, if you don't wear that one I'm going to – wait, what are you doing?"

I was taking off the short black skirt I was wearing,

struggling to keep my balance on the bed as I stepped out of it. "It's too much with the skirt – it looks like I should be thirty years old and drinking cocktails." I pulled on my jeans again. The contrast with the faded denim made the black top even sexier.

There was a pause as Liz studied me. She nodded.

"You're right," she said. "*That* is perfect. Now, jewellery."

"I've got this," I said in surprise, touching my crystal teardrop pendant. Alex had given it to me almost exactly a year ago, on my seventeenth birthday. I'd barely taken it off ever since.

"What about earrings, though? Look." She brandished a sparkly pair.

"I don't have pierced ears."

"You don't have pierced ears *yet*," she corrected.

I opened my mouth to say, *Whoa, hold it right there –* and stopped with a gasp. A cold fog of fear had swamped me from out of nowhere, settling icily over my heart. I shivered at its intensity…and then it was gone, along with the words from my throat.

"Hey, don't look so freaked out! Fine, we won't pierce your ears if you're going to be *that* much of a wuss," Liz said, laughing.

I shook my head; in the mirror, my eyes looked wide and uncertain. "It wasn't that. I thought I felt—" I broke off. Remembering how Raziel had psychically spied on me, I quickly searched my mind. I knew how to do it now; if he'd realized I was still alive and was somehow back again, I'd feel him. But there was nothing.

Liz was staring. "Are you all right?"

"I'm fine," I said finally. And it seemed true. The fear was gone as completely as if it had never been there at all.

"Sure?"

"Yeah, I'm okay." My voice sounded more confident this time – I'd probably just had some kind of weird fast-forward to the attack. *I'll ask Seb if he felt anything too, just to make sure,* I decided. He'd be out on the firing range now; I'd collar him as soon as he finished. Then I sighed, thinking of the guarded quality that would come over his energy the second he saw me.

There was a knock on the door, and Meghan poked her vivid head in. "Liz, do you have a— Oh, wow!" Her blue eyes widened; she came into the room, grinning and looking me up and down. "Willow, you look great!"

I'd almost forgotten what I was wearing. "Thanks," I said, touching the sequinned top. Meghan wasn't really a friend of mine, but I liked her. She was one of those rare people who just always managed to be happy. Before the quakes, she'd been training to be a dancer and had apparently had a promising career ahead of her, before the world became so devastated – yet you never got even a hint of her feeling sorry for herself.

"She won't let me pierce her ears," grumbled Liz as I jumped off the bed.

Meghan stared at her. "Seriously? You want to stick a needle through her earlobes?"

"See?" I said to Liz.

"*You've* got pierced ears," Liz pointed out to Meghan.

Meghan fingered one of her dangly gold hoops. "Well, yeah, but I got them done at a shop. But, hey, what about shoes?" she added brightly. "Do you want to borrow a pair? I've got the perfect ones!" She darted out of the room, her rich hair glinting like autumn.

Liz laughed. "No one does 'enthusiasm' better than Meghan."

"How come I'm the only one down here who doesn't have a dressy wardrobe?" I said, gazing after her.

"The rest of us got our priorities right, that's all."

Meghan reappeared with a pair of shiny high-heeled shoes and crouched down gracefully on her long legs. "Oh, good – looks like we're the same size." As she began angling one of the shoes onto my bare foot, I started to protest, then just let her do it – it would have been like trying to halt a force of nature. Besides, I was too busy drinking in the shoes. They were a deep wine colour and almost old-fashioned: a chunky heel and rounded toe; a big button perched on the strap. But somehow they looked just…

"Amazing," said Liz. "Meghan, you're a genius."

I turned my ankle this way and that. The shoes gleamed like fresh paint. "These are just…absolutely gorgeous. Thank you so much."

Meghan sank back on her heels, regarding my feet with a small, wistful smile. "I love these shoes," she said. "I always think they bring me luck." She glanced up with a sudden grin. "And you're going to be the birthday girl, so you get *extra* luck. That's the rule. Anyway, I got distracted," she went on, jumping to her feet. "What I came in here for was to ask if you've got iPods. I'm going to make a playlist for the party."

Officially, the upcoming party next week was to celebrate Alex's and my birthdays – I'd be turning eighteen, and he'd be nineteen. But really, it was just to give people a chance to let off steam and relax. After months of intense training, everyone was more than ready to.

I shook my head. "Sorry, I was still playing CDs back in Pawntucket."

"I've got one," said Liz. "Wait, I think I left it in the kitchen. Back in a sec."

After Liz had gone, a silence stretched out between Meghan and me. I glanced at Liz's clock. I needed to go talk to Seb soon, but it seemed rude to just leave Meghan there. Turning to her, I started to make some comment about the party – and caught her giving me a sideways glance, lips pursed.

"What?" I said in surprise.

Her milky skin flushed. "Sorry. It's just that – I mean… you're half-angel, aren't you?"

She blurted the words out, and I blinked. Meghan *knew* I was half-angel. Everyone in the base knew, because Seb and I used our angels to help train people.

Before I could respond, Meghan shook her head. "God, don't even answer that. I just wanted to know…well… what's it like?" Her voice was soft, hesitant.

Strangely enough, in all our time here, no one had ever asked me that. I sank down onto Liz's bed as I tried to gather my thoughts.

"I don't know," I said finally. "I only found out a year ago, so it's still pretty new to me. A lot of times, even now, I'm not really conscious of my angel; I just feel human. And then other times, I'm so completely aware of this other self inside me."

Meghan had lowered herself into Liz's desk chair, listening intently. She glanced down, trailing her finger back and forth across the desk. "Do you think – do you think maybe it's because you didn't know what you were for so long that you're with Alex now? I mean, Alex is *gorgeous,* and he's a great guy," she added hastily. "But if you'd known that you were half-angel all your life, then…well, do you think you could ever fall in love with a human?"

Suddenly it was all too clear what this was about.

"I can't really answer that," I said slowly. "I mean, I can only look at it from my own experience."

Meghan nodded, her blue eyes disappointed. "Okay," she said after a pause. "Thanks. I was just curious."

All at once her emotions swept over me. Usually I had to hold someone's hand to get something, but this was so strong – an aching sweetness that caught at my throat. *This isn't just a crush,* I thought in a daze. *She's really in love with Seb.*

I swallowed, shaken by the depth of her feelings – and wondered if I should warn her against caring so strongly for Seb, who'd always been adamant that he could never get seriously involved with a human girl. But Seb had to already know how she felt; he could read auras like other people read comic books. He'd be careful not to hurt her.

Even so, I couldn't help saying, "Um, Meghan – listen, I'm not sure if—"

I didn't know whether I was disappointed or relieved when Liz came back just then – I'd had no idea how I was planning on finishing that sentence.

"Here you go." Liz handed Meghan the iPod. "I think Sam's got one too."

Meghan had been watching me with a slight frown; coming back to herself, she took the iPod and fiddled with its dial. She brightened. "Ooh, good, lots of indie stuff. There's not much point in asking Sam Houston, though, is there? I bet he's got both kinds of music – country *and* western."

Liz grinned. "I think they sometimes listen to classic rock in Texas too."

"A night of the Eagles and Chicago? Willow and Alex would never forgive me. Okay, laters, gators," said Meghan, tucking the iPod in her jeans pocket. She glanced at me. "And, Willow – thanks," she added in an undertone.

For what? I had a feeling that I hadn't exactly succeeded in warning her away from Seb. I made a mental note to get her alone sometime soon and try again. "Thank you for the shoes," I replied.

"Hey, I want those back, you know," she said, laughing. "Your present is that you get to *borrow* them."

CHAPTER *Two*

THAT NIGHT I LAY IN bed staring at the shadows on the ceiling, while Alex sat at our desk, working on his laptop. The strange moment of fear from that afternoon hadn't come back, but I couldn't get it out of my head. For something that had only lasted a second, it had been so incredibly intense.

When I'd asked Seb whether he'd also felt it, he'd said no – and I'd sensed his concern for me, along with his flash of irritation at himself for feeling it. I'd wanted to mention Meghan too, but it had felt pretty impossible. The days when Seb and I talked about anything and everything were gone.

Pushing my problems with Seb aside, I frowned as I thought again about that icy dread. *Had* it been a fast-forward to the attack, or something else? My psychic senses were usually pretty reliable – if I'd had a feeling, then something was probably going on.

"You're still worrying about this, aren't you?" Alex said, glancing over at me. We'd discussed it and agreed I should try to forget about the feeling unless I got something more specific.

"I can't help it," I admitted. "I just wish I could figure out what it meant."

There was a *click* as Alex shut his laptop. "Come on," he said. "Let's get out of here and go for a walk."

"A what?" I blinked as Alex grabbed his jeans and pulled them on over his boxers. The tattoo on his left bicep flexed: an *AK* in black gothic letters. "But it must be—" I glanced at the clock. "Alex, it's after midnight!"

"Yeah?" He scooped up my jeans from the floor. "Perfect – there's a full moon tonight; it'll have risen by now." He dropped onto the mattress on his knees. "Come on, time to get dressed."

"Alex—" I broke off as I started to laugh. He was crouched on the edge of the bed manoeuvring my feet into the jeans, his expression intent as the muscles of his chest and shoulders moved.

"You look so serious," I said, propping myself up to watch.

He shook his dark head. "You know, this isn't exactly easy when you're not helping. Here, lift up."

Smiling now despite myself, I angled my midsection upwards. "Have you actually ascertained yet that I want to go on this walk?"

"Of course you do. A romantic walk in the moonlight with your boyfriend?" Alex tugged my jeans up the rest of the way and fastened them; with a grin, he kissed me. Then, more serious, he touched my face. "Come on. Really. It'll do you good; you can't just lie here worrying all night."

I still found myself getting lost in his blue-grey eyes sometimes – the way they contrasted so sharply against his black lashes. "Okay, you win." I climbed out of bed and pulled on a sweater over my white camisole – the desert gets cold at night.

Alex had put on a long-sleeved T-shirt; he took his pistol from the dresser, checked it, and stuck it in the back of his jeans. As we stepped out into the corridor, he eased the door closed behind us. The thick walls were pretty soundproof, but the one noise guaranteed to penetrate was a door banging shut.

Suddenly I was almost giggling at the furtiveness of it all. "Why don't we do this more often?" I whispered.

Alex's lips twitched. "Oh, yeah, because you took no persuading at all. 'A walk!' you said, springing out of bed. 'Great, let me get dressed!'"

As we reached the garage, we were both stifling laughter. Once we were on ground level, we said hi to Matt, the recruit on guard duty, and then stepped out into the yard. Alex had been right; there was a full moon. Its light glinted on the chain-link fence. He punched in the code for the gate, and a moment later we were walking hand in hand down the gritty dirt road.

I was glad to see he'd shifted his aura. Like mine, it now appeared a sickly grey that clung close to his body – completely unappealing to a hunting angel. "You've gotten really good at that," I said, studying him.

He squeezed my hand. "Had a good teacher."

At first we'd thought that only Seb and I could change our auras, but then we'd found out humans could do it too; it just took them a lot longer to grasp. Alex, Sam and Liz hadn't found it nearly as difficult as the rest of the team, though. They'd all been trained in energy work – Alex, since he was a child in his father's AK camp, where he'd learned to scan the ethereal level for angels.

There was a rocky outcrop not far away, its rounded shape dark against the stars. We started up it, shifting from hiking to gentle climbing as it steepened. The moonlight was so bright it was actually casting shadows.

On the other side was a six-foot drop. Alex jumped lightly to the ground. "Come on, I'll catch you," he said, holding his arms out.

I sat down, legs dangling. "Are you sure about this?"

"Hey, don't you trust me?" Alex took my hand with a grin and tugged; as I launched myself off the edge, he caught me solidly. Slowly, I slid down his body as he lowered me to the ground.

The feel of him so close was very…distracting. For a second I found myself wondering why we hadn't brought a blanket, then rolled my eyes. I was really starting to develop a one-track mind. It was kind of hard not to – Alex was like a drug I could never get enough of.

"Good catch," I said. Somehow my voice was normal.

I could tell Alex's thoughts had been travelling in the same direction. He shook his head as if to clear it. "Well, it helps when the person you're catching is extremely cute."

We sat on the ground with our backs against the rock, stretching our legs out and gazing up at the stars. They glittered coldly across the night sky. I pointed to a small, bright zigzag. "Cassiopeia, right?"

Alex put his arm around me. "I've taught you well, grasshopper."

I tickled him just under his armpit: the one place he was ticklish. "Maybe, but *you* still can't fix an engine."

He gave a yelp of laughter, twisting away. "No fair, you know all my weak spots. Yeah, guilty as charged."

As I settled against him, the desert lay vast and still

around us. It was so desolate, as if we were up on the surface of the moon. As if no one else even existed.

Yet barely a hundred miles away lay the ruins of Las Vegas – and like in all the ruined cities, people still lived there, somehow, in shelters made from collapsed buildings. A helpless anger touched me. It was the same all over, for anyone who didn't go to an Eden. Across the country were thousands of "dark towns" with buildings still intact, but no electricity – all people could do was scavenge and try their best to survive. Not all of them did.

The quakes had changed everything, for ever.

Stop. Don't go there, I warned myself. It was too late; I was already reliving the earthquake that had flattened Mexico City. I shivered as I recalled that groaning roar. And a lot of our recruits had been through even worse. When I'd first held their hands to make sure we could trust them, I'd seen so much sorrow – so much pain.

I looked up to find Alex studying me. "What are you thinking?" he asked softly.

I swallowed. "Just…wondering what we'll do if we actually succeed. Where would you want to go? Someplace up in the mountains, maybe, like back to the cabin?"

One of his eyebrows rose sceptically. "A, anywhere as long as it's with you, and, B, why do I have the feeling that you're sitting there blaming yourself again?"

I stared out at the desert and couldn't answer.

"Stop," Alex said in a low voice. He cupped my face in his hands, gently forcing me to look at him. "Listen to me. It wasn't your fault."

I managed a tiny smile. "Are you turning psychic now?"

"Yeah, I wonder how I can possibly manage to know what you're thinking, when you're such a total enigma."

I choked out a laugh. "Pretty predictable, huh?"

"When it comes to this? Just a little." He rested his forehead against mine. He didn't say anything else. He didn't have to – we'd already had this conversation more times than I could count.

"You know what I really want to do if we win?" said Alex finally.

"No, what?"

He hesitated, his gaze searching mine. "I want to find your mother," he said. "I want that for you more than anything, Willow. I don't care if we have to spend years looking for her – if we can, then we're going to do it."

My throat went tight. I checked on my mother psychically every day. It was always such a relief to feel that she was still okay – even though I had no idea where she was or who was keeping her safe. And just the fact that Alex wanted that for me…it meant everything.

"Thank you," I said.

I stretched upwards, brushing his lips lightly with my own. Then again, more lingeringly. Much more lingeringly.

Alex wrapped his arms around me, pulling me onto his lap. His lips were so familiar – warm, slightly rough, as intoxicating as the first time we'd ever kissed. When we finally came up for air, I felt dizzy.

"Maybe one of these years, I'll get used to how amazing that feels," I whispered, stroking his warm back under his shirt.

"Really?" Alex said huskily. "I never will – not if we live to be a hundred." His heartbeat pounded against mine. "Willow, listen – do you really feel like staying out here? Maybe we could—"

"Go back to our room instead?" I finished for him. I kissed his nose. "Yes, you are definitely reading my mind," I said solemnly.

Suddenly we were both laughing. My laugh turned to a squeal as Alex scooped an arm under my knees and lurched up with me in his arms. He nibbled at my earlobe. "So I guess this is our walk biting the dust."

I twined my arms around his neck. "Yeah, Matt's going to be laughing at us. We've hardly been gone any time at all."

"You know what, that is so far down on my list of priorities right now that it's practically nonexistent." Grinning, Alex gave me a boost and I scrambled onto the boulder. With a quick jump, he braced himself against the top and began to lift himself up.

Admiring the motion of his muscles, I smiled and crouched down, stretching a hand out to help…and then terror slammed into me like a fist of ice.

I gasped and rocked backwards, stunned by its intensity. It was the same fear I'd felt that afternoon, times about a thousand. My stomach knotted, adrenalin surging through me.

Something was going to happen soon. Oh god, something terrible was going to happen—

Alex was beside me, clutching my shoulders. "What's wrong? What is it?"

"Something…I don't…something bad…" My mouth felt thick and clumsy.

His fingers tightened. "Willow, come on, talk to me!"

The primal fear released its grip a fraction, leaving dread as thick as swamp water. "Something's going to happen!" I burst out. "We've got to go – we've got to stop it!"

I turned and ran, stumbling over the uneven rock and then skidding down the other side. I was pounding towards the base when Alex caught up, darting in front of me and grabbing my arms again. "Willow, *wait*! What's going on?"

"I don't know!" I cried. "But we've got to go – we've *got* to!"

"Go *where*?"

I realized I had no idea. I looked around wildly, as if the

answer might be lying somewhere on the desert ground. There was nothing.

I reached quickly inside myself; I could sense that my angel was just as worried as I was. Shifting my consciousness to hers, I lifted out of my human body and soared up into the stars.

The fear hit me again, full force. Fighting against panic, I glided, reaching out with everything I had.

"Are you getting anything?" Alex asked. In my human form, I was aware of his hands, warm on my arms. He stood peering up at my angel's bright form.

No, I started to say…but instead my voice came out in a ragged whisper: "The east."

Because all at once I could sense it: something dark was waiting to be unleashed on the eastern horizon. In the air my wings went cold as I realized the angels were waiting too – they were all gathering. Getting ready.

"How far away; can you tell?" Alex said urgently.

I was shivering. "I don't know!" Feeling suddenly frightened and too exposed, my angel returned to me in a rush. "But, Alex, we've got to try and stop it! There's some kind of powerful force – the angels are all waiting for something—"

His face hardened. "Come on." Grabbing my hand, we took off at a run back to the gate. A wide-eyed Matt was already there, swinging it open for us.

"I saw you on the cameras. What's going on?"

"Willow's seen something," Alex said shortly.

Matt paled; the whole base knew what "seen something" meant. We rushed back into the building, Matt jogging along beside us. "You want me to sound the alarm?"

Alex shook his head. "No, not yet." As we stepped into the elevator, he half turned, throwing the words over his shoulder: "Wake up Sam, Liz and Seb; tell them I need to give them a quick briefing."

As the elevator whirred downwards, I tried to convince myself that I'd overreacted – that whatever was going to happen wasn't *that* bad. Any comfort from this vanished once we'd left the elevator behind and reached the hub of the base. Seb was running towards us from one of the dorm corridors wearing only a pair of jeans, his bare feet slapping at the floor…and somehow I knew it wasn't because of Matt's alarm.

Seb's eyes were fixed on mine as he reached us. I got a jolt of tension from him – and, despite my panic, realized how long it had been since we'd shared our thoughts so fully.

"Willow!" he gasped. "Something is happening—"

I licked dry lips. "I know. I feel it too."

Alex grabbed his arm. "What did you get?"

Looking frustrated, Seb shoved his hands through his curls. "I'm not sure, but it woke me up. There is something coming, something big—"

"Something *coming*?" Alex repeated sharply.

Prickles ran over my scalp. This was different from what I'd gotten, and not in a good way.

Liz and Sam appeared, looking rumpled and jerked awake. "What's goin' on?" demanded Sam. He had on striped pyjama bottoms and a white T-shirt. Liz was fumbling with the tie to her bathrobe.

Alex quickly explained. "Come on, let's get into the war room." He glanced at Seb and me. "I want to get you both near a map, see what you can pick up."

Urgency was pounding at me. "Alex, we don't have much time—"

"Ten minutes of planning might save us time," he said shortly.

Seb glanced at me; I could tell he was feeling the same thing I was. Though I knew Alex was right, my every instinct was screaming, *Run, move, hurry!*

"Yes, okay," Seb said for us both.

He stayed beside me as we all headed quickly down the corridor. Despite the fear, on some level it just felt good to be in tune with him again – though I realized that I was a shade too aware of his bare chest, with its dusting of golden-brown hair. Alex's chest was almost completely hairless. I shoved the thought away impatiently. Why was I *comparing* them?

"So, wait. Is all we've got to go on a psychic feeling?"

asked Liz once we were in what we called the war room – a gleaming conference space with a U-shaped table and maps on the wall.

"It's a pretty strong psychic feeling," I told her wryly.

Sam shrugged. "Well, I know y'all are like the Psychic Twins, but if that's *all* we've got, then maybe—"

"Our entire plan is based on psychic information, remember?" said Alex. He turned on the light over the largest map. The United States burst into brightness. Tiny red flags peppered its surface, showing the locations of all known Edens.

"Okay, can you get anything more specific?" Alex asked, looking back at Seb and me.

Conscious of everyone watching, I went over to the map, Seb following close behind. It was so large that I couldn't have touched Canada without craning on my tiptoes. Shutting my eyes, I took a deep grounding breath and focused, trying to pinpoint the fear.

For a moment nothing happened – and then my hand lifted of its own accord and started moving across the map, skimming over the tops of stickpin flags as if I was stroking the heads of a field of flowers. I walked with it, letting it guide me, aware of Seb doing the same.

Slowly, my hand came to a stop. My index finger pointed. I opened my eyes to see Seb's finger a millimetre from my own – so close I could feel its warmth.

Both our fingers were pointing to Denver, Colorado.

I stared at the map as memories came crashing over me: the Church of Angels cathedral in Denver, with its broad white dome and stained-glass windows. Myself trying to stop the Second Wave and failing; thousands of people cheering the flood of incoming angels as I almost died in that place.

Seb hadn't been in Denver that day, but he knew what had happened. His expression tensed as he glanced at me. "*Dios mío,*" he murmured.

"Oh, shit – *Denver?*" Sam exclaimed behind us. "Is there another Wave coming?"

Liz's voice quavered. "But...no, wait, that doesn't matter, does it? I mean, even if there is, if we kill a few, we still kill them all. So we can just ignore this, right?"

"No!" I cried. I sank into one of the chairs, clutching my head. "We can't ignore it. Alex, we've got to go there. We *have* to."

He sat beside me and gripped my hand. "Who's 'we'?"

"You and me." The words came instantly, chilling me even though I knew, instinctively, that they were right.

Seb's jaw tightened; before he could protest, Sam was talking again.

"*What?* Oh, man, no way; that's completely insane. Denver's an Eden now! *Raziel's* there, for Chrissake. You could be walking right into a trap!"

"It's not a trap," I murmured, still rubbing my temples. "It's too big – it's all of them."

"Yeah, that's reassuring, when 'all of them' would love to kill us," Sam retorted.

Liz dropped into a chair opposite, nervously twisting a strand of hair. "Not to mention the *humans* who want us dead. You're still public enemy number one, Willow. All we've got going for us is that no one knows whether we're still alive. If anyone captured you, that'd be it for all of us."

Alex had been sitting silently, looking deep in thought. "We're going to have to do it," he decided, squeezing my fingers and releasing them. He shoved his chair back as he rose.

"No!" Seb's fists clenched; the knife scar on his forearm gleamed in the harsh light. "There's no reason for Willow to go. I'll go instead – I'm just as psychic as she is. And much better with auras."

Though I knew Seb was only trying to protect me, I was stung. "Not any more," I protested.

"Oh, yes, I am," he insisted. "You still don't think to check them half the time."

Liz bit her fingernail. "But look, if there's another Wave coming, then we can't stop it, so why should *any* of us go? Why don't we just stay here and keep training?"

"That's why only Willow and I are going – so the rest of you can do exactly that," said Alex. "But, yes, we do have to go. We don't know for sure that it's another Wave; it could be something else. We've got to find out in case it affects our plans."

"But why must it be Willow?" pressed Seb again. "Alex, *hombre,* you don't want her to go any more than I do—"

"No, but that's what she's seeing psychically, so I'm going with it." Alex propped his hands on the back of a chair and studied Seb, his gaze intense. "What about you? Leave your feelings out of it – can you honestly tell me you're getting something different?"

An anguished expression crossed Seb's face.

"No, I didn't think so," said Alex after a pause. "Okay, everyone, that's it. Sam, you're in charge until I get back. Seb, keep training everyone on the aura work, and, Liz, I want you helping out on the firing range as much as possible."

"When are you leaving?" she asked.

Alex's eyes met mine. "As soon as we're packed."

"You're taking one of the sat phones, at least." Sam's face was stony; it wasn't a question. The sat phones we'd found in the comms room were probably the only non-Eden phones in the country that still worked.

"Yeah, we'll check in every few hours." Alex glanced at Seb again; lowering his voice, he said something in Spanish. Seb gave a grim smile; Alex clapped him briefly on the shoulder and headed out of the room, moving with a loose, quick confidence.

As the others followed, Seb took my arm, holding me back. "Willow—"

"Seb, it's all right – I'll be okay," I said softly.

I was painfully aware of the gulf yawning between us. And now, with his emotions raw on his face, I saw just how much Seb needed to keep himself distant from me if he could. And as much as I hated it, I couldn't blame him. For him to have to sense, every day of his life, how deeply I was in love with Alex... I swallowed, imagining it.

"I'll be fine," I repeated, trying to keep my voice light. "Don't work the recruits too hard. Or flirt with too many of them. You know that half of them would already throw themselves over a cliff for you."

Seb didn't even smile. As if unable to stop himself, he bent down and kissed my cheek, his lips warm against my skin. Our minds touched again, no barriers at all for a change, and my throat clenched as his naked thought came clearly:

I love you, querida.

My eyes pricked with sudden tears. "Don't," I said. "Please, Seb, don't." And whether I meant *Don't be in love with me* or *Don't say the words,* I didn't even know. Both, I guess. Both were tearing my heart out.

I longed to hug him but realized it wouldn't be fair. Instead I gripped his hand blindly for a second – and then hurried from the room.

Chapter *Three*

RAZIEL STOOD IN THE EMPLOYEE parking lot of the Denver Church of Angels. The building's high, curved wall rose before him – so similar to its physical counterpart in the angels' dimension, yet wholly different.

Thinking of his home world, Raziel gave a private smile and gazed up at the sky, where he could sense the gate he'd prepared so painstakingly. It was a thrill to realize just how many secret things about it could be sensed by no other angels…mainly because none of them would ever imagine that he might do such a thing.

Bascal was with him: an angel who was shorter than

average, with solid muscles and a shaved head. Raziel had never figured out whether the shaved head was meant to be ironic. Not that "irony" was a word he'd expect Bascal to know.

"Double whammy tomorrow," Bascal said, his tone heavy with satisfaction. "They're not even going to know what's hit them."

Raziel's mouth twitched. "No, probably not," he said.

Bascal stood braced, arms behind his back as he squinted upwards. "Well, if there's any trouble, we'll be ready."

Raziel had a feeling there might be. Thankfully, most angels were still stunned from the deaths of the Council members ten months ago. None seemed to have noticed that he'd been unobtrusively putting together a small army for months now, made up of Bascal and his other angel cronies.

Bascal gave Raziel a sideways look. "So, anyway…once it's all over with, we can talk about a reward, yeah?"

Raziel held back a sigh at the bluntness, thinking of Charmeine with her crystal wit and subtle mind. The energy wave that had slammed into them above Mexico City had stunned them both; Raziel, recovering first, hadn't hesitated to do away with his scheming former collaborator – but he'd be lying if he said he didn't miss her. Still, at least Bascal was strictly a right-hand man and knew it.

Raziel raised an eyebrow. "A reward?" he repeated, as if such an idea had never entered his head.

Bascal scratched the back of his neck. "Yeah. I was thinking maybe…better classifications for me and my friends."

How predictable. Raziel nodded, bored already. "Don't worry – you'll get them."

He kept gazing upwards, enjoying the gate's intricate feel. It had taken almost a year of preparation, both here and in the angels' world – much of it covert and made far more difficult by the execrable timings he had to worry about now. This was a new thing since the quakes: irritatingly, the destruction of the Council's roots of energy had also affected the ethereal world – things had become jarred between the two dimensions, throwing them out of sync. He'd have been ready months ago otherwise.

But now, finally, the moment was nearly here.

With a shimmer, Bascal shifted to his angel form. "See you tomorrow, boss," he said as he lifted into the air. "And don't forget about that reward, huh?"

"Never," Raziel promised, deadpan.

Once Bascal was gone, Raziel scanned the gate a final time, then extended his scan to include the earth's energy field. This cloaked the planet on the ethereal level like a human's aura, its vast presence constantly shifting like wind currents.

As Raziel concentrated, his brow furrowed. There it was again. That strange sense that he'd picked up on a few times since the earthquakes: a feeling like a deep core of gravity, separate from the earth's energy field but weaving through it. Something strong yet unaware, which everything else in the world was straining towards.

The sensation was fleeting; he was left frowning and uncertain. *Unaware* – well, naturally; energy wasn't *sentient.* Yet when he searched again, the unknown force was gone.

He shook his head impatiently. Didn't he have enough on his plate without imagining things? Though he was ready for what would happen tomorrow, he wasn't looking forward to it. No angel would be.

Yet it was needed – just like the angels needed his leadership, even if they didn't admit it. Especially since most of them were convinced that the Angel Killers were dead now. Raziel saw again his daughter's green eyes locked on his as she coolly stepped off the Torre Mayor – and knew it would have taken more than the destruction of one of the largest cities in the world to kill her.

Why hadn't there been even a hint of her and her assassin boyfriend since, though? *Ten months* without a single angel death. Either they really were dead or they were hiding out somewhere, planning something. He was beginning to feel paranoid for suspecting the latter, but knew his own capacity for deceit too well to underestimate his daughter's.

No, tomorrow was necessary. Very necessary.

Raziel shifted to his angel form and lifted up in a brilliant glimmer of wings, leaving his black BMW below – he felt like flying through the bright coolness of the autumn day. Leaving the cathedral behind, he soared south over Denver Eden. From this height, he could take in at a glance what he'd accomplished: the different zones that now dissected the mountain city like graph paper; the high, imposing walls that rose in the distance.

Gazing down, he could see hundreds of people, their life energies on display as they shopped, wandered through the parks, drove cars. All so beautifully ordinary. He took good care of his cattle; no one could say otherwise. When you stepped into an Eden, you stepped into bliss – just like he'd promised.

Raziel couldn't hold back a smirk as the wind whispered past his wings. Yes, bliss: he doubted that any resident of his Edens would describe life otherwise. Certainly not once they'd known the angels' feeding touch…which never took very long.

He glided high; below, other angels hunted in small, lazy circles. There'd been complaints at first about the need to keep to assigned zones, but by now most seemed resigned to it. Raziel suspected that many angels actually *liked* the order imposed by his new regime, especially now the Council was gone. What was it about the angelic mind that craved something definitive to cling to?

A green-tinted glass building rose up above the others, reflecting mountains and clouds. Raziel swooped in through its highest window and shifted back to his human form. The penthouse apartment was a symphony of high windows and polished wood, with the Rockies rearing up to the north.

He tossed his suit jacket onto the sofa and settled into a broad leather armchair. As if on cue, a pair of beautiful young women appeared: one blonde, the other brunette – both dressed in tight clothes that it took little imagination to picture coming undone.

"Would you like anything?" asked the brunette, her eyes wide and hopeful. They used to call him "sir", until he decided that familiarity was more enticing.

Unbuttoning his shirt collar, Raziel hardly looked up. As he reached for the remote control and turned on the TV, he said, "Just a drink, perhaps. Do we have any Evian?"

"Of course." As the brunette hurried off, the blonde settled at his feet, leaning her head against his knee. She was named Summer and had been a world-renowned model; it amused Raziel when he remembered seeing her image on magazine covers.

He idly stroked her hair as an old rerun of *I Love Lucy* came on. They hadn't gotten around to creating new TV shows yet, but this was in the works: every time an actor entered an Eden, they were whisked here to Denver, where writers were busy preparing several new programmes. One, *Angel Avengers,* was sure to be a hit: it featured a small group who spent their lives hunting down Angel Killers, destroying them in new and inventive ways each week.

"I love this one," murmured Summer, as Lucy cavorted in a vat of grapes. She tilted back her perfect head to gaze adoringly at Raziel. "It's so funny."

"I'm delighted you're enjoying it, my dear," he said absently. Summer had a degree in art history and had once been far from stupid – but after several months with him, her aura was weak, her mind almost gone. Really, he should retire her to one of the lower zones, except that she was still so decoratively beautiful that he'd been putting it off.

The brunette – Lauren – appeared with his Evian on a small tray; Raziel shook his head at himself and took a sip. Sentimentality – he couldn't afford it. He'd make the call tomorrow and have a fresh A1 brought over immediately. For if *he* didn't deserve the highest classification of humans, then who did? Perhaps he'd get another brunette, Raziel mused. He could have a matching pair.

On the TV, a man wearing angel wings held up a

cellphone, talking excitedly. "Here at Celestial Cells we've got the best darn phones around, and every Eden resident wants one! We got *electricity* here, folks – let's enjoy it! Talk to your friends, send texts, pictures! Deals start at only a hundred and twenty-nine angel credits – so you be nice to those angels and get your new phone *today!*" He winked broadly at the camera.

Raziel yawned and flicked to the other channel. The news came on, a pair of coiffed humans sitting behind a desk. There was no investigative reporting any more; the "news" was simply them reading stories provided by Raziel.

The male newscaster beamed. "Today we're delighted to announce the openings of three new Edens: Cincinnati, Detroit and Omaha. Praise the angels!"

A film clip came on showing the opening of Omaha Eden. "I'm so happy," said a tearful woman to the camera; behind her, people whooped and cheered. "We've been living in a refugee camp for months, and the angels took real good care of us – but *this!* Oh, it's just too good to be true!"

Pride warmed Raziel at the sight of the crowds streaming into the made-over city. It wasn't easy to remake a city into an Eden, but he'd done it. And now five more Edens were scheduled to open within the next month. He had several in Canada and South America, as well – soon he'd be ready to begin expanding into the rest of the world.

I'm getting there, Raziel thought, draining his drink. Even those few humans who hadn't succumbed yet to his Edens were slowly falling into line. He made shortwave radio broadcasts daily, bombarding anyone who was listening with tempting morsels about how easy and fulfilling life was in an Eden: far more enjoyable than squatting in dark towns with no food supply.

Lauren sat perched on the arm of his chair with her shapely legs crossed. Once the news was over, she ran a finger up his arm and said, "You missed some phone calls. Nothing important. Mostly angels wanting better classifications."

Raziel smirked. It was a familiar complaint: only a few angels now had access to whichever humans took their fancy. If they wanted to stay in his Edens, then they had to stick to the classifications they'd been assigned.

Unless they were friends of his, of course.

"I told them they'd have to talk to you," added Lauren.

"Clever girl."

"I try," she said with an arch smile. Lauren had only been with him a few weeks, and already Raziel found himself torn between wanting to indulge in her as much as possible and wanting to go easy so that she'd last longer. She'd slipped unobtrusively into the role of assistant, showing a valuable sharpness at it – in fact, the best assistant he'd had since Jonah.

The thought of his traitorous former employee brought a spark of irritation. It was just as well for Jonah that he hadn't shown his face again since the arrival of the Second Wave. Raziel would like nothing better than to watch him die slowly.

Lauren's presence was soothing, desirable. Despite his resolution, Raziel's hand strayed to stroke across her clear blue aura. He could feel its slight resistance against his fingers, as if he were moving them through water.

She caught her breath. "Oh, yes, Raziel, please," she murmured, gripping his hand. She leaned down to kiss his neck. "Please," she repeated.

He didn't need further urging. He changed to his angel form and stood before both girls, wings spread; reaching out mentally to them, he rested a hand in each of their auras and began to feed. Even with Summer's sadly depleted energy, experiencing two of them at once was intoxicating: waves of sensation that rocked through him, nourishing him.

When he'd finished, the two girls sat slumped weakly, looking awestruck, Lauren in the chair and Summer leaning against it. Raziel shifted to his human form again and smiled to himself at the picture they made.

"Come with me," he said, tugging them both up by their hands. Summer staggered as she rose; he put an arm around her. All right, so perhaps he shouldn't be doing this when the girl was so weak already – but he'd be getting rid of her tomorrow, after all.

"Oh, Raziel…I feel like my life is a fairy tale now," whispered Lauren as she got up. She snuggled against his side.

Her words seemed to echo. Raziel froze, staring at her, as an image rushed into his mind: the gently shifting branches of a long-ago willow tree, lit by the glow of his wings. A woman with wavy blonde hair, gazing up at him: *You've made my life a fairy tale.*

"Why do you say that?" he demanded.

Lauren blinked. "Well, because it *is*. When the earthquakes came, it was so terrible at first, but now I'm almost glad they happened. You've made life a fairy tale for both of us. We feel so lucky, Summer and I."

"We do, we really do," said Summer dreamily.

He was an idiot. Two beautiful girls, and he was thinking about one from nineteen years ago? Who wasn't even *alive* any more and had been catatonic for years before her death?

"Well, come on then," he said, lifting Lauren up in his arms; she squealed in delight. "Let's see if we can make the fairy tale a little more real for you both."

Later the dream that was memory came again.

Both girls had now departed. Raziel stood at his bedroom window with a sheet wrapped around himself, scowling out at the flaming Rocky Mountain sunset. The images had awakened him from what should have been a refreshing nap. He could almost hear Miranda's voice still, so soft and childlike – feel her arms around him as the two of them sank to the ground, the willow branches making a private cave.

"You know, I – I get confused sometimes now," she'd whispered.

"Do you really?" It had been cold out there; he hadn't cared. Ah, the smoothness of her neck against his lips – the delicious taste of her life energy, still pulsing through his halo.

Miranda had nodded, green eyes wide. "Since I met you, it's hard for me to think… It's like part of me is in another world, and I can't figure out where I'm supposed to be."

Hardly surprising, the amount he'd been feeding from her. Raziel had chuckled, only half listening. "First a fairy tale, now another world. I'm not very good at keeping you in the here and now, am I?"

"No, you are! Oh, Raziel, you're the only thing that does." She'd reached up to cup his cheek, swallowed hard. "The rest of my life – college, compositions, concerts – none of it matters compared to this, right now, with you."

"Shall we make the most of it then?" he'd murmured, still caressing her. "Of course, it will probably make you feel even *more* confused, so maybe we shouldn't – I seem to have that effect on humans."

As he'd known she would, Miranda had joyfully acquiesced. He remembered feeling a slight regret that her mind seemed to be dissolving so quickly – though not enough regret to make him hesitate.

Now Raziel gritted his teeth. *Why* did he keep dreaming about this? Ever since the earthquakes, Miranda had been haunting him. She was a woman he'd once enjoyed, yes – for a short while, he'd been almost obsessed with her – but now, after nearly two decades, he wouldn't even have remembered her if it hadn't been for the child she'd somehow borne.

He glared out at the mountains. Yes, the half-angel, half-human, wholly impossible *child* – who, if still alive, had the power to destroy them all, according to Paschar's vision.

No. Not after tomorrow.

In the window, his reflection showed a handsome, sensitive face with crisp black hair, whose expression was more apprehensive than he liked to admit. Raziel knew the dream would linger for days now. Seeing again Miranda's image – so like their daughter's – he pressed his forehead against the cool windowpane and swore softly. Why, out of so many human conquests, had this one young music student begun haunting him?

And why did her memory fill him with such unease that what should have been a time of triumphant anticipation instead felt dark with foreboding?

CHAPTER *Four*

ALEX KNEW THAT MOST OF the drive to Denver would have been pretty desolate anyway – crossing first the Nevada desert and then the Utah one – but the earthquakes had taken *desolate* to a whole new level. Though he longed to just floor it, in too many places there were deep potholes lurking or dramatic ripples in the asphalt – and out here there'd been only aftershocks.

It had still been enough to change the terrain for ever.

Dawn was breaking as the remains of Las Vegas came into view. The Strip had been almost totally destroyed; Alex could make out the jagged base of the Eiffel Tower and half a pyramid. Grimly, he recalled a trip he and Sam had made into Vegas, to scavenge holograph machines for training from the ruins of an angel-themed hotel. Poking around in the shattered building with his flashlight had not been an experience he'd want to repeat. Christ, there'd been *people* in there when the place went down.

Willow sat in the passenger seat, staring at the devastated city, her face tight. Alex touched her leg, glad when they left the sight behind.

Five hours after leaving the base, they reached Utah. When at last they turned east onto Highway 70, the route was transformed: fresh, smooth asphalt gleamed in the sun.

Thank god. The truck leaped forward as Alex punched down on the gas. It was a relief to be going faster, though the newly repaired road meant it was a route used by Eden staff. It'd be pretty attractive to bandits too – and a truck loaded with half a dozen full fuel containers was a prize they'd kill for.

Willow sat quietly, hugging her knees. Alex took in her expression. "Getting worse?"

She gave a tense nod. "Stronger with every mile."

Gradually the road started to climb as they entered the Rockies. Neither of them commented as refugees began appearing: straggling groups weighed down with belongings. Without fail, they stuck out their thumbs the second they spotted the truck. The hope on the tired, dusty faces gouged at Alex.

An older woman holding a little girl's hand came into view. Willow's eyes were sorrowful as she studied them. "Heading to Denver Eden," she said.

"Or Golden. It's just opened, remember?" The small town was only about ten miles from Denver. Alex shifted gears, hating what he knew would happen to everyone they were passing.

"Yeah." Willow sighed, still gazing at the woman and child. "So I guess they didn't hear the Voice of Freedom," she said softly.

Alex reached across and squeezed her hand. "No. I guess not."

For amazingly, at least one other person in the world had figured out the truth about the angels. They'd first heard the "Voice of Freedom" a few months ago, when Sam had shouted the four of them into the comms room.

"I was doing a routine check – and *listen!*" he'd said, cranking up the volume.

"*Don't trust them. The Edens are a trap – if you go into one, you'll never come out. The angels are poisonous to us, toxic as rat poison. Do you know anyone who's seen an angel? Is that person well? Or are they sick and feeble and tired...*"

They'd stood gaping in wonder. The husky voice

coming out of the speakers was androgynous – and utterly welcome.

"*This has been the Voice of Freedom,*" the broadcast finally concluded. "*I'll be on again soon. Just listen, and you'll find me.*"

Alex knew the broadcasts couldn't reach more than a handful of people – those lucky enough to have both generators and shortwave radios – but, Jesus, every little bit helped. If nothing else, it was comforting to know that the AKs weren't completely alone.

An army truck appeared: one of the transport vehicles that cruised near the Edens, picking up refugees. Alex put on a bored expression. As with the other vehicles they'd passed, the driver acknowledged them with a lift of his fingers off the wheel, obviously assuming he and Willow were Eden staff. The truck disappeared and Willow let out a breath.

Alex knew how she felt. Just being on this route made him uneasy; it was the same road he'd sped along a year ago, desperate to reach Willow before her attempt to stop the Second Wave could kill her.

As if to underline the point, they passed a fading poster of Willow tacked to a tree. Her pixieish face was smiling, her long hair Photoshopped short. The headline screamed: *WILLOW FIELDS, WANTED FOR CRIMES AGAINST THE ANGELS AND HUMANITY!*

Neither mentioned it – though they both knew the poster offered a generous reward if Willow was taken alive. Alex's jaw tightened. Yeah, he could just imagine what delights Raziel would have in store for his daughter if he ever got his hands on her. At least her shoulder-length brown hair looked nothing like the poster now.

An hour later they'd passed through the heart of the Rockies and begun the long descent towards Denver. Conversation had stopped – whatever waited was now only a dozen miles away.

All at once Willow shivered. "Alex, it feels really close. Can we go faster?"

Her voice was a taut wire. Alex slammed his foot down on the gas; their tyres shrieked as they whipped sharply around turns. Willow clutched the dash with one hand.

She was actually trembling now; risking a glance at her, Alex saw she'd gone completely white. "Oh god, stop, stop!"

"What?"

"*Stop the car!*"

Alex screeched over to the shoulder. They were at a lookout point, with pine trees in the foreground and Denver half hidden in the distance, the walled city stretching up to meet the late afternoon sky. Willow scrambled out of the cab; Alex threw on the emergency brake and followed.

She stood staring down at the city, her face twisted in frustration. "I can't see! These stupid *pine* trees—"

Alex glanced back at the truck. "Come on," he said, climbing onto the hood. Seconds later they were both perched on the roof, Willow's body tense beside his. Alex had a moment of wondering how he'd explain this if their soldier friends saw them, and then all other thought was wiped from his mind. With a cry, Willow leaped to her feet; the truck rocked slightly.

"Oh god, this is it – this is it—"

A chill came over Alex. He rose, gazing down at the city. Lifting his consciousness to view it on the ethereal level made no difference at first, it was still the same – and then the sky over Denver tore open in a vertical slash.

Alex stared. Dimly, he was aware of the massive white-domed roof of the Church of Angels cathedral just below the sight. In the sky, the slit seemed to writhe with life; through it were pink-stained clouds.

And angels.

Even from so far away, Alex could see that there were thousands, millions – hovering in a shining vortex that faced the gate between worlds like a sideways tornado, twisting and spiralling far off into the distance, spiky with wings. He gaped, lost for words.

"No," whispered Willow. He put his arm around her; she clung to him. "Something terrible – any second now—"

She broke off with a cry as the angels surged forward, starkly white against the sunset of their own world. As they poured through the gate, a sound came like the cracking of a giant whip; there was an explosion of light, searing the world into a faded reflection of itself. Alex wrapped his other arm around Willow, shielding her as a wave of energy roared past; he buried his head in her hair to hide his eyes from the burning light.

Slowly, the world returned to stillness. The only sound was the rustle of the wind through the pines.

Alex dared a look. The sky over Denver was a solid mass of angels, their ethereal bodies reeling; some were making hasty landings, gliding down into the city. Whatever had happened, they obviously hadn't expected it either. In the angels' world it was now twilight, with a single star shining. Then the gash between worlds shrank as the sky seemed to knit itself together. The star winked from view, leaving blue sky and clouds.

Alex exhaled. "Hey," he whispered, rubbing Willow's arm. "Whatever it was, it's over now."

She had her fingers pressed tightly against her forehead; after a pause, she swallowed. "I can still sense Seb – I don't think we were affected. We've always been separate from them, so I guess…" She trailed off.

"Affected? What are you talking about?"

She looked up then, her eyes wide and tearful. "You –

you don't know what that burst of energy meant, do you? You don't know what he's done."

Alex stared down at her with dread. He knew he didn't have to answer; his incomprehension had to be written all over him.

Gazing out at the angels, Willow shivered. Her tone was flat, defeated. "Alex...the angels aren't linked any more."

CHAPTER *Five*

SOMEHOW THEY WERE DRIVING AGAIN – still heading towards Denver so that they wouldn't pass the cruising army truck again too soon. It was as much thought as Alex was capable of right then.

"Not linked," he murmured at last. He gripped the wheel with clammy fingers. "Are you sure?"

Willow sat statue-still. "Yes," she said quietly. "I felt it when the energy rushed past. It's something Raziel's done on purpose, to protect them. He used the energy of the gate opening to…to sever their connection, somehow. I think some of them died when he did it. I could hear them screaming."

She crossed her arms tightly. "Anyway, they're safe now," she went on, her voice wooden. "We can still kill any one of them, but to destroy them all, we'd have to—"

"Kill them one by one," Alex finished. He saw a dirt road and took it; once out of sight, he brought them to a lurching halt. The world was battering at his skull. He clutched at his temples, squeezing his eyes shut. "Oh, *shit*. Shit, shit—"

He felt Willow slip her arm around his waist and press close. "Alex…" she whispered.

No other words followed. What could she say? There were millions of angels in the world, with millions more just arrived. Even with more AKs, to kill the creatures singly could take generations. Humanity would be destroyed by then; the angels would have moved on to leech off some other world.

God, why hadn't he attacked sooner? He'd been so positive he was right – but what if he'd done what Sam had wanted instead? They could have forgotten about recruiting new people and only picked off angels that were hunting solo. They might have done it that way.

They really might have done it.

Slowly, Alex scraped his hands down his face. Through the windshield was a piercing blue sky. The dirt road sliced through a grassy field, heading up into the mountains.

Willow took one of his hands and pressed it against

her chest. "Alex, please don't blame yourself! It's not your fault."

"Yeah? Whose fault is it?"

"No one's!" Her tone was pleading. "Fate. Life. You're an amazing leader. And if you had it to do over again, you'd make the same choice, you know you would."

He'd never been less interested in hypotheticals. He'd screwed up – end of story. And, yeah, big comfort to know that if he had it to do over again, he'd *still* screw up.

A long pause wrapped around them. There was the sound of birdsong and the faint ticking of the engine. "Should we call the others?" Willow suggested finally.

Alex pinched the bridge of his nose and didn't answer for a minute. "I can't tell them this over the phone, Willow," he said in a low voice. "I just can't."

He hated the sympathy in her green eyes. Softly, she said, "All right, but we need to let them know we're okay, at least. And that the next Wave has arrived."

"We will, but just—" He broke off and gripped her hand, not looking at her. "Just give me a minute."

How the hell was he supposed to tell the base this when they got back? Exactly what combination of words could he use to break the news to his team that their efforts had been for nothing and the world was doomed now…and all because they'd trusted him?

* * *

After calling in, all Alex wanted to do was get away from this place – head for home and get the announcement over with. Willow shook her head. "We need to get some rest first." He could see her own pained shock, her worry for him. "Neither of us has slept in over a day, Alex."

He started to argue; the thought of crashing the truck with Willow in it stopped him. He'd made enough cataclysmic mistakes already. He pulled the truck farther up the road, concealing them in a grove of trees.

Though he was sure he wouldn't be able to sleep, a bone-aching weariness claimed him once they'd spread out their sleeping bag in the back. He stripped down to his boxers and crawled thankfully into its soft haven, where he drifted off with Willow nestled against him.

He awoke abruptly several hours later, unsure where he was. Then it came back in relentless detail. The truck's windows were misty with condensation; he reached over and wiped one clean. Moonlit fields and a clear starlit sky. No sign of flying angels – those who weren't staying nearby must have already moved on. Or were in their human forms now, merging seamlessly with the rest of the population.

Except for their eyes. You could always tell an angel by its eyes.

Alex took in the peaceful landscape, seeing instead a country full of Edens – a *world* full of them, for ever, because of what he'd done. Willow was curled asleep against his chest; he absently rubbed her shoulder as his thoughts pummelled him.

But was there a chance Willow had been wrong?

His hand stilled and stopped. His heart quickened despite itself. Not that he actually believed it – Willow was an excellent psychic. But come on, wasn't it at least *possible*? Okay, so maybe the odds were only one in a million…yet that still meant there was a slim hope this wasn't true.

And if there was any hope at all, he had to know.

Alex hit the display button on the sat phone. Almost midnight. The newly opened Golden Eden was about five miles away – he could jog there, check things out, and be back by two.

Just having a plan was a relief. Alex eased his arm out from under Willow – she murmured and turned to her side. With a hasty groping in the darkness, he found his clothes and rifle. He slithered out of the sleeping bag and climbed silently to the front of the truck. He squeezed open the door.

Cool night air sent goosebumps across his chest. Alex got out and guided the door shut behind him, pressing it hard so it would latch. He yanked on his jeans and T-shirt, then crouched down quickly to tie his sneakers. As he checked his rifle, moonlight glinted on the barrel.

He could just see Willow through the window he'd wiped clear. He knew she'd be fine – no one would venture up this remote road after dark – yet for a second he found his fingers resting on the door handle. But there could be no debate, none – he had to find out, and the sooner he left, the sooner he'd be back. He let his hand drop and turned away.

When he was far enough away down the dirt road, he broke into a run.

Alex had been to Golden before: a small town high in the Rockies where tanned, perfect people shopped at specialty grocery stores. Now it had been made into an Eden to deal with the Denver overflow and a concrete wall girded it, with fresh barbed wire glinting at its top. As Alex approached from the hills, he could see new housing had been thrown up, nestling among the ten-million-dollar homes like poor relations.

Lights were still on, even at this hour – people were savouring having electricity again. Alex grimaced; many of the lights were blue and flickering. Raziel had a depressingly firm grasp of American psychology all right: offer them TV, and they'd come.

Finding a good spot was harder than he'd imagined; he was acutely aware of time ticking past and of Willow left back in the truck. Finally he settled on a hill to the north near what looked like a service entrance. He could see the dark shapes of army trucks just inside the gates.

Not many angels were out, but enough. Lying on his stomach, Alex held his rifle to his shoulder and forced himself to be patient as the creatures swooped across his crosshairs. For at least a quarter of an hour, none gave him what he needed.

Then his chance came.

A small cluster appeared, circling together. Alex began tracking them closely. "C'mon, c'mon," he whispered, his muscles relaxed even if his mind wasn't. "You can't stick together all night..."

As if overhearing, one angel peeled away from the other two; in the magnified lens, Alex could see the fiercely beautiful male face. He followed the angel as it started to dive, focusing only on the halo's pure white centre. *Not yet...not yet...now!*

The crosshairs exploded into light. As white fragments twisted in the moonlight, Alex jerked his head away from the lens and looked for the other two. There they were, still close by. Ordinarily, an angel would feel another's death intensely – react at once.

The angels kept gliding away, great wings calmly stirring at the air.

Alex lay without moving as he stared after them. It was

true then. He hadn't really believed otherwise. But now, faced with proof, for a second he wanted to just go berserk and start gunning down every angel he saw, whether it gave away his position or not.

Get a grip, Kylar, he ordered himself coldly. Dragging himself to a sitting position, Alex watched the angels still flying over the town like they owned it.

Okay, so this was it – the new reality they all had to deal with. And somehow he still had to lead his team, though he didn't even know any more where he could lead them *to*...or why. Alex got to his feet wearily, hardly caring if security cameras spotted him.

"Stay down!" hissed a voice.

Alex's head snapped towards it – and then in a burst of light, he was knocked off his feet; around him ethereal blades of grass flattened as energy howled past. He rose up on his elbows and stared dumbly at the gleaming remains of an angel.

Willow appeared through the trees, silenced pistol in hand. She dropped to her knees beside him. "It almost got you," she said. Her knuckles on her pistol were stark white in the moonlight. "We're too close for me to bring out my angel, so I had to..." She stopped, swallowed. After a pause, she added, "You forgot to change your aura."

Words had left him. "Good shot," he got out finally.

I had a good teacher, she always responded. This time she just stared at him, and he realized how upset she was. "Alex, you—"

A noise came from the nearby parking lot. "Wait," whispered Alex, putting his hand on Willow's arm. Someone was walking their way. "Get down," he muttered, and pulled Willow to the ground next to him, both of them flat on the grass.

The footsteps grew louder. The sound of a vehicle door opening. "Yeah, *there* you are," said a voice. "Knew I'd left you in here."

The door slammed shut. Alex craned a hand out for his rifle, which he'd dropped with the blast. He brought it silently across the grass towards him.

A small flare of light illuminated a man in an army uniform. The soldier strolled to the gate and leaned against it as he smoked a cigarette: a dark, lounging shadow with a red glow at its head.

The guy seemed to be staring right at them. Willow was hardly breathing. Silently, she adjusted her grip on her pistol – and at that moment, the moon came out from behind a wraith of clouds; silvery light flashed briefly on the weapon.

Alex's heart sank as the shadow straightened. "Who's there?" barked the soldier.

"Don't move unless I tell you," murmured Alex, the

words not even a whisper. Willow gave a minute nod; he could feel her tension.

The soldier stood gazing intently. Suddenly he turned and walked away. Alex didn't have a chance to relax before he heard the truck door open again; a second later the guy was back. A *click* – and then Alex winced as a beam of light illuminated them as if they were onstage.

Shit. "Run," he ordered, grabbing Willow's arm; as they scrambled to their feet he heard a voice say, "No way, it *can't* be her—"

The whir of the gate opening, the thud of their own footsteps as they lunged into the trees. "Where's the truck?" Alex gasped, ducking the black shapes of branches as they ran. Willow had to have brought it; she couldn't have caught up with him so quickly otherwise.

Her answer came in short, choppy bursts. "About half a mile away – I didn't know there was a road right here – it's as close as I thought I could get when I sensed you—"

Light swept over them, sending their running shadows into the trees ahead. "Stop!" bellowed a voice; Alex could hear feet pummelling the ground. "Stop or I'll shoot!"

He won't do it; they want to take Willow alive, thought Alex grimly.

Willow had kept up with him at first but was now lagging slightly behind. Alex dropped his pace to match hers, heard the soldier gaining on them.

"Keep going," he said, pushing Willow ahead of him. "Do *not* pay attention to what's happening to me; just go, go!"

Without waiting for her response, he spun to face the guy, lifting his rifle in the same second. He scattered the ground in front of the running soldier with a spray of bullets that spat at the earth, throwing up rapid clods of dirt. The man swore and stopped. The world burst into brightness as he trained the light directly on Alex.

Alex didn't move, still holding his rifle at the ready. He couldn't see the soldier in the glare but could hear his breathing. Up ahead, he was aware that Willow must have stopped too; he couldn't hear her running any more. *Damn it!*

"Drop your weapon and get the hell out of here," Alex ordered in a low voice.

"No way," said the guy curtly. "Neither of you are going anywhere – just give up now."

"Why, so we can be turned over to the angels?" retorted Alex. "Yeah, that sounds really appealing."

The soldier started forward; Alex sent a muffled volley of bullets through the air, slicing them back and forth. The man jerked to a halt.

"I can't see you very well with that light on me," said Alex coldly. "But I'd estimate that was about a foot over your head. Want me to lower my aim and try again?"

The voice was hard. "Believe me, you're just making things worse—" The soldier broke off with a cry; the light jerked in his grasp. Willow's angel had appeared in her most tangible form, diving straight at his face. The night plunged into darkness as the soldier dropped the flashlight; its beam bounced on the ground.

"Come on, *hurry!*" called Willow's human voice from ahead.

Alex backed away a step, still aiming his rifle as Willow's angel darted about the man, striving for his pistol. The guy kept trying to get a fix on her but couldn't; her gleaming wings were batting at him, forcing him back. *If he shoots her – if he hurts her in any way—*

Willow appeared, panting, at Alex's side; she grabbed his hand. "*Now!* She'll catch up later!"

He hated it but knew it was their only chance. They took off again, tearing through the black night hand in hand, the moon swallowed up by the trees. Willow's feet were drumming out a rhythmic beat; she stumbled briefly on a root, and Alex steadied her, neither of them stopping.

"It's not much farther," gasped out Willow. She motioned ahead. "Just up this way a little more; there's a road. I think maybe we'll be able to—"

Behind them came a rapid burst of gunfire.

Willow broke off; with an anguished cry, she staggered and sank to her knees. Alex crouched hastily beside her;

she was moaning, clutching her head with both hands.

"You're okay…you're going to be okay," he said, rubbing her wrists and hoping fervently it was true. Willow's angel could shift between the ethereal level and a more physical form – this was the first time the latter had been shot. He had no idea what it might do to the human Willow.

Already, running footsteps were heading their way again, the light jouncing through the trees. Alex grabbed Willow's pistol, then got her to her feet. She sagged against him; he could see her paleness even in the gloom. Before he could lift her into his arms, the soldier burst from the trees.

Whether by design or not, this time he held his light at an angle, so that Alex could see him now. He frowned as he took in Willow, drooping in the circle of Alex's arm.

"What's the deal with her?" he demanded.

"The deal is you made a big mistake when you hurt her," said Alex in a low voice. "Drop your weapon, or I swear to god I'll kill you."

The guy scowled and took a step forward; it all happened in seconds. Willow's angel appeared right behind him – her eyes were stunned and fixed on Willow, clearly thinking only of merging. As she passed, the soldier cursed and swung to face her, aiming his pistol.

No. He would not hurt Willow again. Without thinking,

Alex raised Willow's pistol; the guy whirled back towards him. Both weapons went off at the same time: one muffled, one echoing through the night.

It felt like a car had slammed into him. Someone cried out; he realized it had been him. Oh Christ, his arm. The pain tore at him; the world dimmed at its edges. Gritting his teeth, Alex somehow managed to stay conscious and upright, still holding Willow.

The soldier lay in a crumpled heap nearby. Alex stared blankly at him…and gradually became aware of warmth and moisture. Looking down, he saw the dark blood streaming from a hole in his bicep and understood distantly that he had to stop it. He half fell to his knees, managing to rest Willow on the ground, and then pulled off his T-shirt, the motion slow and clumsy with one hand. He felt very tired suddenly – the task ahead seemed enormous.

His right arm wouldn't lift on its own. Holding the edge of his T-shirt with his teeth, Alex got the cloth wrapped around the wound, almost passing out again as it pressed against the bullet's exit hole – the thing had gone right through him. Slowly, with teeth and his good hand, he secured the makeshift bandage.

He slumped against a tree, breathing hard, the bark pricking at his bare back. They had to get moving. He had to get Willow, and they had to get to the truck…they had to…

The next thing he knew, Willow was leaning over him, shaking him. Her voice sounded high, frightened. "Alex! Alex, please wake up – they're searching the woods."

He focused on her with an effort. At first her words made no sense; all he remembered was trying to keep her safe. "Are you okay?" he whispered. Distantly, he could hear shouts.

"I'm fine – it just knocked me out." She grasped his good arm and pulled; he saw dazedly that she was close to tears. "Come on, sweetheart, *please*. We have to go."

A dark fallen form lay nearby. Memory sliced through Alex's weariness. The shots – he'd been hit. Using the tree for leverage, he heaved himself up as Willow supported his good arm.

"Oh god, you've lost so much blood…" She fumbled quickly at his bandage, tying it tighter.

Alex gritted his teeth at the renewed pressure; he jerked his head at the soldier. "Is he—?"

"Yes," she said shortly. The shouts were closer now; Alex could see lights heading towards them through the trees. Willow glanced over her shoulder. "Alex, *come on*."

The stillness of the human form gouged at him. He gripped Willow's hand, and they took off jogging through the trees. Every step felt like his arm was being sledgehammered, but the pain helped clear his head.

"Who's searching?" he panted. "Angels?"

"No, just soldiers; they must have heard the gunfire – Oh, thank god!" They'd come out onto a hill bisected by a two-lane road; the 4 × 4 sat hidden in the shadows on the shoulder.

Willow unlocked it and threw the passenger door open, her face tightening as she turned to him. "Here, get in."

Yeah, Alex thought with grim humour, this probably wasn't his night to drive. He climbed in, breathing hard and dropping his head back. Willow sprinted around the truck and got into the driver's seat.

"Good, we're on a slope," she muttered. She put the truck in neutral; obediently, it began rolling forward as she steered it onto the road. They glided through the night, slowly picking up speed; after a few minutes, Willow twisted the key in the ignition and slammed down on the accelerator.

"Hold on," she said. "Alex, just hold on."

At first he thought she meant *hold on* because she was driving fast; then he felt the wetness on his fingers and realized that blood had soaked through the T-shirt and was coursing down his arm, warming his skin. "I'm fine," he murmured, closing his eyes. Weirdly enough, it seemed true. He felt warm, drifting.

Sometime later, the truck's lulling motion turned to a harsh lurching. Alex opened his eyes reluctantly; the headlights showed another dirt road. Willow jerked them to a stop. Turning on the cab light, she lunged into the back of the truck and pulled out the first-aid kit.

She rooted frantically through it. "What do we have, what do we have...?" Alex watched her, still feeling oddly disconnected. There was blood from his arm on her hands.

He smiled. "You should just use what you're wearing," he murmured.

Though she didn't answer, he could tell she knew what he was talking about: the time she'd been shot herself, and he'd taken off his T-shirt to bind her wound.

Relief sagged her shoulders as she pulled out a large square packet. "This says it's for binding wounds." She straddled him on the passenger's seat.

Alex tried to grin. "Hey, this is getting better and better."

Willow was close to tears. "Shut up, please just shut up! Oh god, it went right through your arm..." She stretched away to fumble in the first-aid kit again and came back with a brown plastic bottle. "Okay, this is going to hurt."

She eased off his T-shirt bandage and poured liquid over his arm. He gave a yelp as fire sizzled through him. The clarity was immediate, throbbing with pain. "What the hell is *that*?"

"Hydrogen peroxide," said Willow. She doused his wound again; Alex clenched his jaw hard. The pain was like someone gouging knives in his raw skin.

"You just poured *peroxide* on my arm?" he said when he could speak again. Twisting his head, he saw the liquid bubbling and frothing. "Jesus – I thought you loved me."

"It's all I could find," she said shortly as she tore open the white packet. "And it's better than getting your arm infected."

He wasn't sure about that but didn't argue. Willow wrapped the bandage around his arm; it was some kind of high-tech netting that stopped the bleeding in its tracks. Then she carefully strapped the whole thing in place with surgical gauze.

"I think that'll hold," she said at last. "At least it's stopped the bleeding."

Alex reached for her hand, squeezing it. "It's fine. Thank you."

"The only painkiller I saw was Tylenol," said Willow after a pause, her voice stilted. "Do you want a couple?"

Alex shook his head, gazing at the delicate angles of her face. "You know, I can never get over how beautiful you are," he said.

Her eyes were bright with tears again. "Alex, you—" She stopped short. Reaching up, she snapped off the cab's light, then lay down beside him, circling his waist with her arm.

The sudden dark was a caress. Pain still beating through him, Alex stroked Willow's hair, feeling it glide softly past his fingers. "I'm sorry," he said finally. "I had to see for myself."

"I know," she said against his chest. "When I woke up, I just knew right away where you'd gone. I didn't need to be psychic for that."

Outside the truck, Alex saw pine trees crowding the dirt road: an old logging route, probably. He wondered when the next time might be that someone would come logging here again.

Maybe never.

"Anyway, it's true," he said, staring out at the prickly, moonlit branches. "They're not linked any more."

Willow's arm tightened around him. "I know," she repeated. "But, Alex, you can't just…" She raised herself up to look at him, and Alex's heart clenched at her expression, clear in the silvery light.

Letting out a trembling breath, she touched his cheek. "I love you more than life, Alex Kylar. Do you hear me? More than life. You do *not* go off and put yourself into danger like that without even telling me."

He hadn't thought it was possible to feel worse than he already did. "I'm sorry," he said again. "I just—"

"What if I hadn't been able to sense where you were?" she interrupted fiercely. "We are a *team*, okay? Now, more than ever, we are a—"

Abruptly, she gave a sob, and Alex clutched her to him, awkward and one armed. He could feel her shoulders trembling; her effort to keep control. "When I came to and saw you there, all covered in blood…" she choked out. "Alex, I thought I'd lost you."

"You haven't lost me," he whispered into her hair. He rocked her, ignoring the pain that shot through his arm. "I'm here…I'm right here."

Finally she wiped her eyes with the heel of her hand. Her voice hoarse, she said, "Promise me that you'll never go off like that again – that if you're going to be in danger, you'll tell me. Promise. I have to know."

"I promise," Alex said quietly. He couldn't believe, now, that he'd actually left Willow alone in the truck. He touched her face, gently stroking away a stray tear. He almost felt like crying himself. "Willow – oh Christ, I'm so sorry."

She nodded, her shoulders relaxing a little. "Okay," she said at last, squeezing his hand. "Okay."

They sat silently holding each other. Finally Willow sighed and shifted back to the driver's side. "I can hardly even believe what this is going to mean for humanity," she said at last, almost to herself. "It's too terrible to… to fathom it, somehow."

"Yeah, tell me," said Alex to the ceiling.

Willow glanced at him, her green eyes sorrowful. Then, with a turn of her wrist, the truck burst into life again. Soon they were back on the highway, speeding through the Rockies with the moonlight gleaming down, the road unfurling ahead like a dark ribbon.

Somewhere in the hills around Golden, the soldier had probably been found by now. With luck, his death would be blamed on the bandits who sometimes broke into Edens to steal supplies. Alex closed his eyes as he saw again the dark, still figure.

The guy's only crime had been to do his job, and Alex had shot him – he was a "killer" in more ways than one now. He wondered whether the soldier had had a wife. Or kids, maybe, who'd have to grow up without their father now.

Neither Alex nor Willow spoke as the miles passed. Alex's wound pulsed incessantly under its bandage. He was almost glad for the pain.

CHAPTER *Six*

SEB LAY ON HIS BED reading, all too aware that what he was really doing was waiting. Though it was after two a.m., he was still half dressed.

Even without Willow's hurried call back to the base, he'd known that she was nearly home – he hadn't been able to stop himself from checking on her compulsively these last few days. His own forebodings were bad enough; sensing Willow's inner turmoil had kept him taut with worry. He had to see her as soon as she was back – make sure she was all right.

Seb grimaced and tossed the book aside. *Dios mío*,

when would this end? Exactly how long could he stay in love with a girl who thought of him only as a brother?

His gaze fell on a note from Meghan on his bedside table: *I still haven't seen this harem of yours, you faker! Love, M.*

With a small smile, Seb picked up the note and turned it over in his hands. He still wasn't sure just what he felt for Meghan...but the truth was, the relationship seemed like the only good thing in his life right now.

It had started one night about a month ago, when the group of recruits he hung out with had been talking here in his room. Most of Seb's life had been spent on the road searching for his half-angel girl; now he'd finally stayed in one place long enough to have friends. Meghan was one of them – and this time, she'd remained behind after the others had left. The sudden silence had made Seb very aware of the way she was lying across his bed, propped on her elbow. The pose that had been casual with the others around now seemed much more intimate.

Seb had stayed at the head of the bed, and they'd talked as if nothing had changed...but when their conversation hit a pause, Meghan cleared her throat. "So – can I ask you something? You don't have a girlfriend, right?"

Danger flags started waving madly. Seb kept his tone light. "No, I do. I have several."

Meghan smiled. A dark red eyebrow arched against her milky skin. "Several, huh?"

"Yes, I have a harem, actually – didn't you know? Seven girls; they stay locked in a room that only I have the key to. I keep them very happy."

"And do they keep *you* happy?"

"They keep me exhausted."

She laughed then, and Seb found himself admiring the wholehearted way she gave herself to it, throwing her head back. It was what he liked most about Meghan – the reason why, in the months he'd known her, he'd found himself seeking her out more and more: her energy made him feel happy even when he wasn't.

She grew serious again, tucking a strand of auburn hair behind her ear. "No, I was just wondering, because…well, girls flirt with you and you flirt back, but you never…" She gave an expressive shrug. "So, I was wondering why not."

Taking in the gentle rose drifting through the turquoise lights of her aura, Seb knew that Meghan was interested in more than friendship with him. If he was honest, he'd known it for a long time. "Because I'm already in love with someone," he admitted. And realized, startled, that it was the first time he'd ever told the truth about himself to anyone but Willow.

Meghan nodded slowly. "Is it Willow?"

He managed a smile. "It's obvious, yes?"

"Not very. I had a feeling, that's all." She trailed a finger over the bedcover; her mouth twisted self-mockingly. "You know, I guess I should hate her, but…I just can't."

This is why I never tell the truth, Seb thought wryly – Meghan had just plunged the conversation into far deeper waters than he wanted to navigate. He wished he could go back in time a few minutes and keep her talking about how she'd just been accepted for an apprenticeship with a San Francisco dance company before the quakes hit.

"Meghan, maybe—"

He'd been about to say, *Maybe it's time to call it a night,* but the look on her face stopped him. It held such genuine understanding – more than he'd felt from anyone in what seemed a long time.

When he didn't continue, she cleared her throat. "So, tell me to mind my own business, but…did anything ever happen between you two?"

Deflecting her with banter felt pointless now. "We kissed once," he admitted. "Last December." He scraped a hand over his stubble, remembering. "She cried afterwards and said it had been a mistake." The memory of the most wonderful moment of his life, followed swiftly by the most terrible, still had the power to hurt him.

Meghan took this in silently, without judgement. "She seems really in love with Alex," she said finally.

Seb almost laughed. "Yes. She does, doesn't she?"

Meghan's rueful smile acknowledged what this must be

like for him. There was a pause that felt weighted – then with a rustle, she shifted upwards on the bed until their heads were almost level. He could feel the warmth of her arm through his shirt.

"So, if I promise not to cry…" she said.

Seb knew what she was going to do – could have stopped her, but didn't. Resting a hand on his chest, Meghan leaned close. Her mouth was warm, giving. Seb responded without being able to help himself, his heartbeat quickening as their lips moved together, the kiss staying soft.

Meghan drew away, her cheeks pink. "Bad idea?" she asked finally.

"Yes, I'd better throw you out now." Seb meant it, though he spoke jokingly.

She looked down. Her hand found his, and she gently explored his fingers. She swallowed but didn't speak again.

And then somehow Seb found himself touching her autumn-bright hair, smoothing it away from her face. Their eyes locked and held. He knew he should pull away; instead, very softly, he stroked the corner of her mouth with his thumb. Her eyes were so blue, like pieces of sky – you could fall into them and never find your way out.

Coming to his senses, he dropped his hand. "You were right – this is a bad idea," he said. "I don't want to hurt you."

She squeezed his fingers. "Seb, look, I really care about you, and – and unless I'm crazy, it's not one-sided. I mean, the way you look at me sometimes… You do like me, don't you?"

"Like" was an inadequate word for whatever it was he'd begun to feel for Meghan these past few months. He just had no idea what the right word might be, when it wasn't "love".

"You know I do," he said roughly. "But, Meggie" – the nickname came out of nowhere; it suited her – "I can't change how I feel about Willow. I've tried."

"Okay, but – wait, wait, let me get this straight," she said, sitting up a little. "I like you, and you like me – boy/girl liking, right? Not just friends?"

He had to smile; she looked so earnest. "Yes," he admitted. Of course he was attracted to Meghan, with her leggy dancer's body and golden spray of freckles across her nose – her warm, happy energy that always seemed to soothe him, embrace him. He'd have to be devoid of all his senses not to be.

"But you're in love with someone else," Meghan went on, "who is *also* in love with someone else, and who doesn't seem likely to change her feelings anytime soon – and so you don't even want to explore this thing with me a little? See what it could be like with us?"

When she put it like that, his reluctance seemed slightly

insane. "I just don't want to hurt you, *chiquita*," he said again. The endearment came with no planning either – "*querida*" belonged to Willow.

Meghan shrugged; her blue eyes had begun to sparkle. "Hey, not so fast there, *hombre*. I could hurt *you*, you know. Maybe you'll fall madly in love with me, and I'll dump you."

"Yes, this is true." Seb was smiling now. There was a pause; he rubbed his stubble. "Wait – have we just agreed to something?"

Meghan gravely pretended to consider. "I *think* we've agreed that you should just kiss me and we'll take it from there." Then she grinned and bumped him on the chest with her fist. "Because to tell you the truth, this is kind of agonizing."

And suddenly Seb had realized that he had no desire at all to resist her any more.

Now, a month later, Seb's love for Willow remained as strong as ever – he sometimes thought he'd cheerfully barter his soul to get over her. But meanwhile, the relationship with Meghan was making him happier than anything had in a long time. She was beautiful, kind, fun to be with – she seemed to know him better than he knew himself. They'd been keeping a low profile, but he was becoming less and less interested in maintaining it.

Maybe I can fall in love with her, Seb thought, folding

the note from Meghan carefully and putting it back on his bedside table. *Maybe I really can.*

As if mocking the idea, a sudden flash of awareness told him that Willow had just returned. All other thoughts left him. Seb snapped on a T-shirt – and when he left his room, found his footsteps leading him to the medical bay. His eyebrows drew together sharply. What was going on? Willow had said she was all right.

He knocked but went in without waiting for an answer. Alex was sitting on the examination table, shirt off; a bullet wound gaped in his toned bicep. Willow stood tensely beside him. Claudia, a recruit who'd been training to be a paramedic – the closest thing to a doctor they had – was there; Alex winced as she examined his wound.

"You were lucky – it looks like a clean, through-and-through shot," she said. "I don't think you've damaged the bone."

Seb gave the injury only cursory notice; what had hit him the second he walked in was the mood. Both Willow and Alex were still reeling from something that had nothing to do with however Alex had gotten shot.

The foreboding Seb had felt for days intensified. "What's happened?" he demanded.

Alex gave a thin smile. "Might have known you'd show up." As Claudia stepped away to rummage through the supply closet, he rubbed his temples and said in a low voice, "I'll be announcing it to the others soon. The angels aren't linked any more."

At first Seb thought he hadn't heard right. "*What?*"

Willow held out her hand. "Here," she said quietly. She wasn't offering comfort, she was offering information. Seb took Willow's hand, trying to ignore the feel of it in his, and closed his eyes.

A rent in the sky – angels pouring in – an ominous sense of separateness. For an added kick in the teeth, he also saw how Alex had gotten shot: felt Willow's panic, her immense love for him.

Finally Seb let go. He opened his mouth to speak, but there were no words. Willow touched his shoulder, her eyes tormented. "I know," she said.

Maybe she did; it didn't help. Seb slumped into a chair, watching distantly as Claudia gave Alex a local anaesthetic and cleaned his injury, trimming away the mangled flesh of his exit wound. As she started stitching him up, all Seb could see was a street scene in Mexico City.

It had been Revolution Day: there'd been a *mariachi* band, dancing in the street – and an angel cruising overhead. Seb had been watching from the balcony of his hostel when he'd seen the angel choose a street girl to feed from and, without thinking, he'd sent his own angel flying out to protect her.

Only through the sheerest of luck had he managed to

destroy the angel and not be killed himself. But he'd done it. The girl had been saved – and Seb left stunned by his own willingness to risk his life.

He'd thought of her often since then: her thin face and brown eyes. Had she survived or been killed in the quakes that brought down Mexico City? He hoped she'd lived. *Madre mía,* he hoped so much that she'd lived.

Saving her had been the seed that had changed him. After a lifetime of ambivalence about the angels, it had hit Seb hard: *What they're doing here is wrong.* The knowledge that the AKs could really defeat them had kept him going for almost a year now, especially as the biggest disappointment of his life had unfolded: the realization that his half-angel girl would never want him.

Seb watched blindly as Claudia finished bandaging Alex's arm. So now there were millions *more* angels here, and the only way to kill them was to shoot them one by one? There were ninety-nine AKs. Seb had never spent much time in school, but there was nothing wrong with his basic maths.

It's over, he thought. *It's all over.*

Claudia handed Alex two small cardboard boxes. "Antibiotics – twice a day, with food. The others are painkillers; I think you're going to need them."

Alex barely glanced at the medication. "Yeah, thanks. Can you get on the intercom and announce a meeting in the dining room in ten minutes?"

Claudia blinked. "Now? It's the middle of the night."

"Yes, now," said Alex, massaging his forehead.

"Alex, you need to rest. Whatever you have to say can wait until—"

His voice was quiet but firm. "No. It can't."

Claudia opened her mouth, then took in his expression. Her reluctance clear, she left the room. A moment later, her voice came booming out: "*Attention, everyone! Please come to the dining room for a meeting in ten minutes. Repeat, please come to the dining room—*"

As the announcement continued, Willow hugged Alex's waist; he put his good arm around her. "Do you want a painkiller?" she asked.

"Not yet." Alex's blue-grey eyes met Seb's; the corner of his mouth lifted humourlessly. "Bet this is just the news you wanted to hear, huh?"

Without waiting for a response – which was good, since Seb had literally nothing to say – Alex let go of Willow and stretched across the table for his T-shirt. Then he seemed to remember. "Oh, great, it's covered in blood."

"I'll get you another one." Willow kissed him, then pitched the stained T-shirt into the trash and left the room. For once, Seb's energy didn't automatically follow after her.

Alex grimaced as he lowered himself off the table. "Don't ever get shot – it hurts like hell," he told Seb wearily. Going to the mirror above the sink, he peered at himself, then reached for a towel. He moistened it and started swabbing the blood from his face and chest.

"How?" said Seb finally. His voice was ragged. "How did the *cabrón* do it?"

"Christ knows," said Alex. "It was something to do with the gate – an energy blast when it opened. He did it with that, somehow."

Alex went silent then; he wadded up the towel and threw it hard at the dirty linens hamper. "*God damn it. How am I supposed to tell them this? What am I going to say?*"

Seb couldn't answer. Willow re-entered a moment later with a T-shirt; he watched Alex wince as she helped him into it. And for some reason, he thought about his father: the unknown angel, who for all Seb knew was still out there, feeding from unwary humans entranced by his beauty. Right now, the knowledge that someone – some *thing* – so closely related to him could be harming humanity felt like more than he could stand.

"You coming?" asked Alex from the doorway.

It took Seb a second to understand that Alex meant the meeting. He started to say no – he had no desire to hear the news a second time. Then he thought of Meghan, with her bright smile and joyous energy…and, to his faint surprise, realized that he wanted to be there for her even more than he wanted to return to his dorm and block out the world. He couldn't let her hear this alone.

"Yes, I'm coming," he said dully, and rose to his feet.

CHAPTER *Seven*

As Raziel left the Austin Eden hospital room, he closed the door gently; behind it there remained only silence. The room's inhabitant was really quite formidable when it came to resisting his attempts to…well, *encourage* talking.

He gave a considering smile as he straightened his cuffs. The game had been fascinating for months now. The patient was a worthy opponent – so weak, yet so fiercely determined. Yes, he'd be quite sorry when the occupant of room 428 was transferred to Salt Lake Eden; he'd lose his perfect distraction.

And there was much he needed to be distracted from.

He strode moodily down the hallway, his reflection wavering in the polished floor. The Separation the week before had gone as planned – and as he'd suspected, the other angels had not been happy.

Of course, they'd all known that he'd been the one to prepare the gate between dimensions, by wielding the strong, pliable energy field of their own world – which, when harnessed, was capable of amazing things on both the ethereal and physical levels. It had always amazed Raziel that none of the other angels seemed to appreciate the sheer possibilities of this. The energy field was normally used only to create works of art or things of that ilk – and when its use affected them all, it had to be done by consensus.

Needless to say, Raziel had not bothered getting a consensus.

When the Separation occurred, he had been standing in the parking lot of the Denver Church of Angels, shielding his thoughts expertly from the hundred or so angels whose presence he hadn't been able to avoid. None had guessed that he'd used the link they all shared to implant a tiny essence of each and every angel in existence, including himself, within the gate above.

As Raziel had watched the sky open and the final wave of angels begin streaming in, unease had gripped him. He'd planned this for so long – but was it really for the best?

It was too late. Just as the thought came, a thunderclap roared through him at every level. He'd been expecting it; even so, it knocked him to his knees, sent his hands flying to cover his ears as agony writhed through him. He had the confused sense that he was being ripped in two – bones cracking, sinew tearing.

And then it was over…and he was still whole, after all. He sat up, breathing hard. The low, steady thrum of other angels' life forces, thoughts, *beings,* had simply vanished from his mind, leaving it strangely quiet.

Raziel rose shakily. It had worked: that part of them that had once been linked was now irretrievably damaged by the devastating blast of energy, leaving them forever alone in their own heads. He swallowed. Why had he never realized before just how intrinsic it was, the connection to other angels?

I had no choice, he told himself dazedly as the screams began. The urge to add his own voice to the screams infuriated him.

"What have you done? Raziel, *what have you done?*"

He gasped as someone shoved him up hard against a car – Lamar, his face raw and contorted.

"Me?" Raziel managed to get out. "I assure you, this had nothing to do with—"

Lamar slammed him into the car again. "*Don't give me that!* All that fiddling around with the gate in our own world – all those times you insisted you had to go over alone – and now this! You've torn us apart!"

"Get him!"

"Kill him!"

As if by magic, Bascal and his gang had descended then; there'd been a brief but violent fracas, angels scrabbling in both human and ethereal forms, shifting to their winged selves, fighting on the ground and in the air. It hadn't taken long for Bascal's lot to subdue the shocked, panicked crowd.

Finally Raziel stood panting, a bruise on one cheek. "Will you listen to sense?" he hissed at Lamar, held in a headlock by Bascal.

"There's nothing you can say," gasped out Lamar. "No justification you could possibly—"

Raziel raised his voice, sending it ringing out over the crowd. "What if I *did* separate us? Do you realize it would only have taken the deaths of barely over a hundred more for us to destroy us all?"

Anguished faces stared back at him. Behind them, Raziel could see some of the arriving angels – stunned, making hasty landings. Others were still in the air, reeling like shot birds.

"It wasn't a decision for you to make alone!" cried someone. "You had no right!"

"I had every right," said Raziel in a low voice. "Because

that is what a leader *does*. If I'd asked you, what would you have said? *Oh, Raziel, no, no, we can't let that happen!* And then we'd be vulnerable, open to attack whenever the Angel Killers finally decide to strike! You should be on your knees *thanking* me for having the fortitude to go through with this."

"The Angel Killers?" echoed another angel. "But they're all dead!"

The patient in the Austin Eden hospital bed had flashed into Raziel's mind. "We don't know that," he said harshly. "And it doesn't matter. It just *might* occur to other humans to question what's going on here. What about that wretched Voice of Freedom? If only a handful of humans acted, we could have been exterminated – extinct! Now we're safe for ever."

The angels had visibly deflated as he spoke. Now they just looked frightened and unsure. Lamar slumped against Bascal's grip; at a signal from Raziel, the little thug loosened his hold with a smirk.

"Safe, but at what cost?" Lamar moaned. "I can't *feel* anyone. I'm just locked inside my own head! First the Council and now this – soon there won't be anything left of what makes us angels!"

For a startled moment, Raziel thought Lamar was blaming him for the Council's deaths as well, then realized he was speaking more generally. Lamar didn't know. No one could.

"Then we'll become a new breed of angels," he said in a crisp voice. "This is about survival."

Lamar's head snapped up, his eyes hard. "Survival," he repeated. "And I suppose *this* will help us survive too?" He gripped Raziel's hand. At first Raziel was too surprised to pull away, and then slow horror grew. He struggled to keep his face impassive.

The psychic link between angels had always been immediate, enhanced by physical connection. The unfamiliar silence in his head was bad enough, but *this*...

Lamar's hand was merely a hand: warm flesh coating muscle and bone. When Raziel concentrated, hard, he got a glimmer of emotion.

That was all.

He let go of the other angel's fingers. Lamar looked as sick as he felt. The angels' psychic bond was at the heart of all angelic interaction – even at its most innocuous levels, their society revolved around both psychic sharing and subterfuge. Without it, they were what? Human? *No – never,* Raziel told himself, shaken.

"As I said, we will have to become new angels," he said, his voice giving away nothing.

He shifted to his angel form and lifted into the air. For several minutes he hovered defiantly before them. And for the first time ever in a gathering of angels, no psychic undercurrents stirred. With the arriving angels, there were enough in the parking lot now to take on Bascal and his gang, had they tried – instead they stood glancing uncertainly at one another, wondering what to do, how to act in this new state of being. No one moved.

And Raziel knew that he had won.

"Spread the word among the new arrivals," he said finally. "We have room for some here in Denver Eden; the rest will need to go to Edens elsewhere. My staff at the Church have the details."

His smile was cold, insincere. "And now, if you'll excuse me."

At the hospital ward's waiting area, a pair of angels stood talking – they turned as one when Raziel approached. From their body language, they were unhappy but trying to hide it.

The room was empty apart from them; this was the restricted ward. "Anything?" asked a male angel with tousled blond hair.

Raziel shook his head. "I'm pretty certain we already have all there is to get – that's why I've decided to let Salt Lake Eden have its fun with our esteemed guest."

The male angel was named Gallad, one of Raziel's cronies of old – he'd just come across with the Third Wave. He lifted an eyebrow, as if trying to put the best face on things. "Well, you never know. Mind if I try?"

Raziel gave a sardonic bow. "Be my guest."

The angel headed off. The remaining one, a svelte dark-haired female named Therese, sank into one of the blue plastic chairs. "I still can't believe you did it," she said after a pause. "Gallad and I were just talking about it. I'll never get used to this."

This past week it had felt as if Raziel were perched on a shifting mountain of sand. It drove him mad that he couldn't sense what the other angels were feeling and thinking. They *seemed* too stunned still to band together and overthrow him – but how could he be sure? He'd ordered Bascal to keep patrols going, ready to crush any sign of dissent.

At least he could trust Gallad and Therese – as much as he could trust any angels now, which perhaps wasn't saying a lot. He sat beside her. "I had no choice," he said tersely. "I would do it again in a second. I won't be dragged down by the deaths of others."

"Or the presence of others?" Therese asked, her tone suddenly arch.

He glanced sharply at her; she gave a pointed smile. "Imagine, just a dimension away but no way to get here," she said in a soft sing-song. "They must be furious."

Raziel laughed then; he couldn't help it. When he'd separated the angels, he'd also used the energy field in their world to destroy the gate between dimensions – and made it impossible for new gates out of their world to be formed. There were still several thousand angels now trapped there, all violently opposed to Raziel. Picturing them slowly starving as the ether died had cheered him more than once this last week.

He rose, suddenly restless. "I'll see you and Gallad back at the church," he said. The two angels were thinking of moving here to Austin Eden; for now they were all staying in his church quarters.

Therese's beautiful face grew pale. "You're leaving? But—"

"Only for a while." Raziel tried to squelch his irritation – he'd noticed that many angels didn't like being left alone any more; they tended to travel in small packs or not at all.

"All right." Therese sounded forlorn.

Shoving aside the realization that he too now felt better near other angels, Raziel shifted to his angelic form and flew straight up through the ceiling. A moment later he was out in the humid Texas afternoon, soaring against grey-tinged clouds.

The sight should have soothed him: another walled city made up of neat zones. Below, the residents of Austin Eden went about their business, life energies bobbing in contentment – even those that were grey and shrunken.

Hovering overhead, Raziel felt for the energy field of this world, thankful that he could still reach it. His muscles relaxed. Yes, exactly as it should be: a faintly chaotic sense of power, nothing like the energy field at home. Then, in a flash, he sensed it again: some strong force pulsing through the field and drawing everything else to it, like an unknowing black hole. As always, the moment he became aware of it, the sensation vanished.

Raziel stared down at the crowded city. The other angels didn't seem aware of the mysterious force, though whether this was because they hadn't checked or couldn't sense it, he didn't know. And he wasn't about to ask: the last thing he needed was to give them another reason for unrest.

Something had shifted since the quakes, though: something subtle yet vital. He knew it; he felt it. He just had no idea what it was.

Feeling helpless and angry, Raziel gazed back at the hospital building as he hung in the air...and suddenly an idea came. He began to smile.

These past few days it had felt as if he were straining to hold things in his grasp – but *here* was something he could easily control. When it was time to transport their friend in room 428 to Salt Lake Eden next month, his plan would be the simplest thing in the world to engineer.

And the benefits if it worked would be...quite spectacular. *If you are still out there, my daughter, I may have a surprise for you,* he thought.

CHAPTER *Eight*

HAPPY BIRTHDAY, WILLOW AND ALEX! read the banner that stretched across one wall.

The words seemed a mockery now. I took in the banner's brightly coloured letters, remembering how Liz and I had helped make it – how much happier I'd been then.

"I can't believe people still wanted to have the party," Alex said in a low voice.

Half the sofas had been moved out of the rec room and the carpet rolled back, creating a dance floor. We'd thought it would be too big; instead it was packed with moving bodies. One was Meghan – and I almost smiled as I watched her. She was as upset over the news as anyone, but she was still teaching the other girls some kind of dance step: the Mashed Potato or something, their legs all shimmying in unison.

"I can believe it," I said slowly. "Not having it would have seemed too much like giving up. People wanted something to feel good about."

Alex sighed. "Yeah, I guess."

The silence when Alex first broke the news to everyone six days ago had been the worst sound I'd ever heard. The clamour of panicked questions that immediately followed had been a close second.

"But – what now?" a girl had blurted out, her voice rising above the rest. And everyone had gone quiet... because this was the only question that mattered.

I'd watched as Alex stood at the front of the dining room, his bandage white against his dark T-shirt. "Personally, I'm going to keep fighting," he said. "I can't do anything else. I was raised an AK; I can't sit back and do nothing while the angels are still here."

The dining room had been utterly silent as he went on: "But...the odds aren't great now. To kill the angels one by one will take – hell, I don't even know. A lifetime. Generations. And our supplies won't last for ever. We're talking hardship and constant danger – because once the angels know we're still around, they'll do their best to destroy us."

No one moved. Alex's expression was hard, almost angry. "Anyway, that's not what you signed up for. If any of you want to keep fighting, I'm in no position to talk you out of it. But if you want to try to make a new life for yourself someplace where the angels can't find you...then I don't blame you, and I wish you luck."

"So – what? You're telling us to give up?" demanded a tear-choked voice from the back.

"No," Alex had said levelly. "I'm being as honest as I can. I don't want anyone to stay thinking we have a good chance at defeating them. We don't. You could spend the rest of your life fighting without it making any difference."

Sam's face had been a dark scowl. "Yeah, well if we *don't* fight, there's no chance at all!" he'd yelled out. "Listen, Kylar, you're not the only one who gets to go down fighting. *I* signed up to keep going until the bastards are gone!"

And that had been the tide that turned it. The AKs had been stunned, some tearful – but almost unanimous in their agreement with Sam. Only seven had left. Seven, out of the ninety-four new recruits. And now... I swallowed, watching the dancers. Well, I didn't blame those who were still here for wanting to forget about it for one night.

Around Alex's wrist was tied the flat woven bracelet I'd

made him for his birthday: lavender and silver threads for my aura, blue and gold for his. He ran a finger over it. "Thanks again," he said. "This is just…" He shrugged and tried to smile. "Thank you," he repeated.

There were dark circles under his eyes – these last few days he'd been working so hard, ignoring the pain of his wound, trying desperately to plan some way forward for us.

I linked my fingers tightly through his. "It's going to be okay," I said in an undertone. "Alex, I don't know how, but somehow it will be."

He squeezed my hand. "Have I told you how incredible you look tonight?" he said after a pause.

"You're changing the subject. And, yes, several times."

"It kind of bears repeating." He looked me up and down in my jeans and black-sequinned top as if he'd never seen me before. "God, Willow. I seriously don't know what I ever did to deserve you."

I stretched up on tiptoes to kiss his lips. "Whatever it is, I'm glad you did it."

His tone brightened deliberately. "Hey, it's after midnight. Happy birthday." He pulled a folded piece of paper from his jeans pocket. His mouth twisted as he looked down at it. "It's not much. If things were normal I could – buy you something amazing, or take you out for a great meal—"

"I don't want any of that," I told him softly. "I just want you."

Alex rolled his eyes with a slight smile. "Some present; you've already got me. Anyway, happy birthday." He handed me the paper. "Don't, um…don't read it now," he added. His cheeks were flushing, even in the dim light.

I was dying to know what it was, but I nodded. "Okay." I slipped the paper into my own back pocket.

The music shifted to a slow, romantic song. Alex looked at the dance floor. "Do you want to dance?"

I hesitated, taking in how tired he seemed. "Can you?"

"Well, I'm not the best dancer in the world, but…"

"No, I mean with your arm."

He grinned then – a real grin that warmed my heart. "Yeah, I think so. I've got to try anyway, since I'm here with the most beautiful girl in the room."

One slow dance turned into another and another. Alex and I moved together on the dance floor, my arms around his neck and his good arm encircling my waist, holding me close. Distantly, I realized someone must be manipulating the music and was glad.

"I've never danced with a boy before," I whispered, running my fingers through the soft hair at the nape of his neck. It felt as if we were in a fragile soap bubble, where the real world couldn't intrude.

"Yeah, that's because the guys in Pawntucket were all

idiots." Alex kissed my neck. "Not that I'm complaining that you didn't already have a boyfriend when we met."

"Would you have minded?"

"Are you kidding? I'd have had to challenge the guy to a duel or something. Might have been kind of awkward."

I smiled and pressed closer – then noticed Alex was leaning on me more heavily than he'd been before. I pulled back. "This is hurting you."

"I'm okay."

"No, really. Why don't we go to bed?" Since he'd been on the painkillers, he'd rarely been awake past ten; I knew he must be exhausted.

"Willow, I'm fine, I promise," he said, touching my hair. "It's your birthday – we should stay up and celebrate."

"Yeah, and I'll really have a great birthday if my boyfriend collapses on the dance floor." I tugged at his hand. "Come on, I don't mind."

I could see how tempted he was, but he shook his head. "Compromise, okay? I'll go to bed if you stay up for a while."

"But I want to be with you," I said in surprise.

"Yeah, and I want you to enjoy your birthday party. Come on, stay and dance some more – give some of these other guys a chance. Please?" he added.

"All right," I said finally. "I'll stay another hour or so."

I wrapped my arms around his neck and we kissed. Alex

touched the bracelet again. "I'm never taking this off, you know," he said with a small smile.

I watched as he wove his way through the dancing couples and then disappeared through the rec room door. Despite everything, for a second I just stood there smiling after him – and then I turned to leave the dance floor.

And stopped.

Seb was leaning against the wall in the shadows; his face had a carefully neutral look as he stood on his own, drinking a beer. I knew what that look meant, though for a change I didn't think it was about me: Seb had been wearing it almost nonstop since the news. I let out a breath as our situation came crashing back.

Maybe I should go talk to him, I thought.

But before I could start towards him, Meghan had already gone over. She said something; he shook his head with a grimace and threw his beer can away. She slipped close, leaning against him in an almost-hug; she smiled and jostled him jokingly, her laughing face nearly on a level with his.

Somewhere deep down, an emotion stirred; on the surface, all I could think was, *Oh, no, she's really overstepped – now Seb's going to pull away, and she'll get hurt.*

Seb kind of half laughed as he regarded her…and then the next thing I knew, he'd buried his hands in her long auburn hair and they were kissing deeply.

I stood there stupidly as dancers moved past and the music throbbed. Meghan had both her arms wrapped around Seb; she wore a short purple dress that made her legs look endless. One of Seb's hands strayed down her spine, caressing her, holding her to him.

Suddenly I realized I was staring. I moved hastily off the dance floor. When I reached the refreshment table, I grabbed a paper plate and piled it high, thoughts spinning. *I'm just surprised, that's all,* I told myself. And this was seriously none of my business.

Except that I'd sensed Seb's love for me only the week before – and knew it was true, as much as I didn't want it to be. If he wanted to make out with someone, did he have to choose *Meghan,* who was in love with him? Seb was as psychic as I was; there was no way he was unaware of her feelings. Abruptly, I recalled the look on her face as she'd said, *Do you think you could ever fall in love with a human?*

Disappointment surged through me, with anger close behind. I would never have believed that Seb would use someone this way. I wouldn't have believed he was even capable of it.

Meghan stood leaning against Seb's chest as they watched the dancers; he had his arms around her from behind. After a few more songs, she kissed him briefly on the lips and went back to her friends. He stayed lounging against the wall with his hands in his jeans pockets – but after a moment, he glanced over in my direction.

Our eyes met. I could sense his reluctance, his brief inner battle. Finally he slowly came over, his loose chestnut curls tousled.

"Would you like to dance?" he asked.

Another slow song had started. I almost said no, then changed my mind and tossed my paper plate aside. "Yeah, okay," I said shortly.

Seb held me formally as we danced, one arm around my waist and a hand firm in mine, as if he were wearing a suit instead of faded jeans and a blue shirt that wasn't tucked in. I was acutely aware of the tingle of his aura touching mine, and it annoyed me. I'd thought I was over being physically affected by Seb.

"Happy birthday," he said. There was an ironic twinge to his voice; it was obvious I wasn't happy with him.

"Thanks," I said. "It might not be very happy for Meghan, though."

His forehead furrowed. "It's not her birthday."

"You know what I mean."

"No, I don't."

Our dancing had slowed to almost nothing, the two of us staring at each other. Other couples swayed around us: intimate shapes on the dance floor. "Okay, this is none of my business," I said finally. "But I like Meghan a lot, and

I just think…I mean, it's not fair of you to mess with her, when she—" I stopped at the look on his face.

"Mess with her?" he repeated. I felt his brief confusion over the phrase, then he got what I meant. He stopped moving, his hazel eyes hardening.

"Seb, it's just that you could have practically any girl down here to make out with, if that's what you want. But Meghan really cares about you."

"I see," he said. "And I don't care about her, is that right? I am using her heartlessly."

Look, I'm sure you don't mean to, but— I couldn't even begin the sentence; the way he was looking at me made the words dry up.

Seb swore under his breath, something dark and Spanish. He dropped hold of me and walked off, leaving me alone on the dance floor. He went through the rec room door and was gone.

When I looked, Meghan was laughing with a group of girls; she obviously hadn't seen him leave. Then it hit me. Seb running towards us down the corridor the night we'd had the premonition about the angels. Seb's room wasn't even *down* that corridor – Meghan's was. The memory of his bare chest scorched my cheeks. How long had this been going on between them?

"Hey, birthday girl, you here on your own?" Before I knew what was happening, muscular arms had scooped me up and were propelling me around the dance floor. Sam, whose worries about the angels seemed to have been drowned in a few gallons of beer.

I forced a smile and danced with him; the song was almost over anyway. When it had finished, Sam gave me a hearty kiss on the cheek, then as the music changed to "Crocodile Rock", he whooped and grabbed my hand. "Hey, this is one of my tracks!"

I detached myself, smiling and shaking my head. "Sorry, Sam – there's something I've got to do."

Somehow I knew where Seb had gone – he couldn't do away with the half-angel bond between us, no matter how hard he tried. I went unerringly to the garage. Once I was up on ground level, I said hi to the recruit on guard duty and went outside.

A clear, starry night. Seb sat on the rough ground, leaning against the building. I stopped in my tracks as I saw that he was smoking: cigarette smoke drifted up to the stars.

I sat down beside him. Seb had his knees up with his wrists resting on them; I could feel his anger at me.

"Where'd you get the cigarettes?" I asked at last.

"Sam brought a few packs in," he said shortly.

I knew the time he must have meant: a few days before Alex and I had left for Colorado, Sam had gone on a party-scavenging mission and had returned, triumphant, with beer, potato chips, pretzels – all the non-essential things we'd been missing so much.

I cleared my throat. "I thought you'd quit."

Seb shrugged and blew out a stream of smoke. I hugged my knees; I could feel the chill of the concrete behind me. "So…how long have you been seeing Meghan?"

He tapped a crumbling column of ash off his cigarette. "A month. Maybe a little longer."

"Why didn't I sense it?" The words were out before I could stop them. It just felt completely wrong that Seb and I were so detached now.

He gave me a look. "I don't know. Why didn't you sense it?"

I stared at him, a horrible thought occurring to me. "God, Seb, you're not trying to make me jealous, are you?"

He snorted. Lodging the cigarette in his mouth, he started to count off on his fingers: "So, let me see – one, I am using Meghan heartlessly. Two, I'm trying to make you jealous, but have been doing such a good job you haven't noticed. Three is – what's three? What else are you thinking about me?"

Three is that you told me you loved me less than a week ago. I didn't say it; Seb picked up on it anyway. His stubbled jaw tightened as he glared at me. "What do you want from me, Willow?" he asked in a low voice.

It wasn't the response I'd been expecting. "Seb, I just – I

think maybe you should cool it with Meghan, that's all. She's going to be hurt when you don't…" I trailed off.

"When I don't love her back? Because I already love you?"

I swallowed. "Something like that."

He shook his head, scowling as he took another puff; when he blew out the smoke, it was as if he were trying to extinguish the stars. "You know, I spent half my life looking for you," he said.

"I know that," I said, stricken. "Seb, I'm not—"

"No, listen to me. I don't want pity for that; it's just what I did. I fell in love with you before I'd ever even seen you, and—" He threw the cigarette away; it skittered across the sand, its red tip fading. "And when I find you, the girl of my dreams, the only other half-angel I've ever met…you're already in love with someone else. Maybe you'd never have fallen in love with me anyway. Maybe you would have. Whatever. You didn't want me; you only wanted to be friends."

"Not *just* friends," I whispered. "Seb, you know how much I—"

"Yes, I'm your brother," he said curtly. "You care for me very much."

I didn't know what to say. Seb turned and studied me; his hazel eyes seemed to reach down to my soul.

"That's a pretty top," he said. "You look beautiful

tonight, *querida*. But you always do. Every day. Only I can never say it, because I'm just your friend, your brother. And every night, you go into that bedroom with Alex, and you close the door—"

"Seb, you *knew* all this – I thought you were okay with it!" I burst out.

There was a long pause. "I was at first," he said, scraping a hand across his jaw. "I told myself, just being in her life is enough. But after so many months…" He shook his head and looked at me again. "Did you know that for more than a year before I met you, I never touched another girl? I couldn't – it felt like I was betraying you."

I stared in dismay, remembering a conversation we'd had when we first met – Seb's hesitation as he said, *I don't know. Always being with the wrong girl…I guess it made me feel lonelier than being by myself after a while.* Oh god, how could I have failed to connect the dots and see what he was really saying?

Seb's voice was low as he went on: "Then I met you, and we came here – and almost another year goes past, and still I never touched anyone else, not once – until Meghan. I'll be *nineteen* next month, Willow. You tell me you're going to love Alex for ever – and so, what? I'm supposed to never touch another girl again, just because I love you? Is it like a life sentence? Or do I get time off for good behaviour?"

His tone was scathing, like having boiling water flung over me. "You can touch whoever you want!" I cried. "I don't *care,* okay? It's just that Meghan really has a thing for you; you're going to hurt her if—"

"You listen to me," he interrupted. He took hold of my wrists, leaning close into my face. "*I care about Meghan. I care about her very much. She's the first human girl I've been able to really talk to, ever, in my whole life. She knows how I feel about you – I have been totally honest with her. I would not lie to her; I would not hurt her.*"

I hesitated, thrown by his unexpected nearness. "But... Seb, don't you get it? If you're not in love with Meghan, then you *will* hurt her, even if you don't mean to."

He snorted and dropped my wrists. "Am I wrong to try, then? Or would you rather I spend the rest of my life being as – as *stupidly* in love with you as I am now?" He raked a hand through his curls. "*Madre mía,* Willow," he hissed. "You know, I've heard a saying here: you can't have your cake and eat it too. Well, I'm making up a new saying: you can't refuse cake and then get upset when someone else takes it."

My cheeks heated. "That has nothing to do with— That is *not* why I said anything!"

"Yes, fine. Whatever you say, *querida.*" He rose with a smooth motion. The moonlight touched his high cheekbones as he jammed his hands in his jeans pockets and stared out at the desert. "You know, the funny thing is…as the months passed, and I saw you weren't ever going to feel the same…I thought, that's all right; there's still meaning. There's still a reason I found her: it's so I can help in this fight against the angels. Only now that's gone too. So there is no meaning anywhere. None."

Dread gripped me. "No, there *is* still meaning; there has to be! And we're going to keep fighting; we—"

"It will do no good now – and you know it," Seb interrupted coldly. Before I could protest, he pulled a small, wrapped parcel out of his pocket and tossed it onto my lap. "*Feliz cumpleaños,* Willow," he said, and disappeared back inside the building.

I sat outside in the cold desert night for a long time.

The wind had picked up; I could hear the dry rustle of sand stirring in the breeze. My cheeks still burning, I gazed down at Meghan's lucky shoes. She knew Seb was in love with me – yet she'd still smiled her bright smile; she'd still loaned me her favourite shoes.

She was so much nicer than me that it wasn't funny. Oh god, what had gotten *into* me, accusing Seb like that? Seb, who I knew so well? Of course he'd never use Meghan; I should have known it instantly.

You can't refuse cake and then get upset when someone else takes it.

That moment on the dance floor when I'd seen them kissing. For a second a chill touched me, then I shook my head in irritation. It had just been a shock, that was all. Seb had always been so adamant that he could never get involved with a human girl.

Sorry, but your cake analogy is way off, I told him in my head. I still shouldn't have accused him, though. Now he was furious with me, and I couldn't blame him.

I'll apologize tomorrow, I thought wearily. Not that it would make much difference; we hardly spoke as it was.

Suddenly I was exhausted and cold through. A deep longing for Alex pierced me; the only thing in the world I wanted was to be lying in his arms. I got to my feet and Seb's present slipped off my lap.

As I picked up the small, tightly wrapped parcel, I could sense Seb's emotions entwined with it, his love for me clear. I winced; I didn't feel up to dealing with whatever this was. I tucked it away in my pocket, unopened.

Reaching behind me, I pulled out Alex's present instead.

His quick, spiky handwriting was barely visible in the moonlight. I angled the paper to bring it into view...and as I read the lines on the page, my throat closed.

Dear Willow,

I'm not very good with words. But my grandfather wrote this for my grandmother, and it's always stuck in my head. Now it reminds me of you.

*Then, I came to you with the sound of battle ringing in
my ears – the screams of men I have known.*
Your touch made it fade.
Now, there are dark nights and sometimes darker days.
*Yet there are also your eyes. They find who I am; they
pierce through me like a lance.*
I am pinned forever in your gaze.
And speaking of forever, I do not know what will come.
*But my home is in your touch and in your eyes – and
when you laugh, it lifts my soul to the sky and reminds
me what could be.*
There is no greater universe than holding you:
Then – or now – or forever.

I love you. Today on your birthday and always.
Alex

When I slipped into our room, the bedside lamp was
still on. Alex lay asleep with the covers half thrown off his
chest. He looked so tired, even while sleeping, so vulnerable
with his bandaged arm.

The tension from the argument with Seb fell away. I
leaned against the door, taking in the rise and fall of Alex's
breathing. Wonder came over me. How could it be that

I knew Alex so intimately, that I'd seen his body so many times…and could still be so entranced by the sight of him?

Silently, I got undressed, draping my jeans and the black sequinned top over the chair. I lined Meghan's lucky shoes up carefully and brushed a smidge of dirt off one. I wanted them to be perfect when I gave them back to her tomorrow.

As I slipped on a camisole top, I could feel I was being watched. I turned; Alex lay gazing at me with his good arm propped under his head, the woven bracelet a splash of colour against his wrist.

"Just enjoying the view," he said.

I smiled and crawled into bed next to him. "How are you feeling?"

He yawned and put his arm around me. "Yeah, okay. I took another pill. Did you have a good time?"

I didn't want to even go into the conversation with Seb – Alex would say I should have minded my own business, and he'd be right. I shrugged. "Being with you is a lot better." I fell silent as I stroked his chest, gazing down at him. "I loved the poem," I said quietly.

He gave an embarrassed grimace. "I guess it was kind of a stupid present."

"It wasn't. It made me cry."

"Okay, then it was definitely a stupid present. It was supposed to make you happy."

"They were happy tears."

Alex regarded me with a small smile. "Happy tears," he repeated. "You are such a girl sometimes."

"Is that a problem?" My breath caught slightly as his hand moved down my side, caressing every rise and fall of me.

He shook his head, his eyes steady on mine. "No. That is totally not a problem." He'd eased up my camisole; though I could feel he was still in pain, he bent and kissed my exposed waist softly, lingeringly. "I meant every word, Willow," he whispered. "It was like my granddad was right inside my head – it's exactly what I feel. I couldn't get through any of this without you."

I swallowed hard and put my hand over his. His fingers were warm under mine; we wove them together as we gazed at each other. If holding me was greater than any universe…then so was looking into his eyes.

"Don't worry," I said. "You'll never have to."

CHAPTER *Nine*

As the weeks passed, Alex kept himself and the others as busy as possible. He didn't know what else to do. Thankfully, there was a lot to occupy his thoughts: the daily running of the base, the continued training of the AKs. Tearing down the old Salt Lake Eden set took several days, and Alex relished the mindless work as he and the others pulled out nails and stacked planks of wood.

The fact that they needed more raw materials for new sets was a relief too. He and some of the other guys went to the ruins of Vegas, where they spent a few days scavenging building supplies. As they sifted through ruins and dragged out salvageable pieces, the autumn sun beat down – sometimes hot enough for them to peel off their shirts. The work was hard and dusty, and Alex buried himself in it, refusing to dwell on the reason why additional training sets were necessary.

Brief excitement came when a trio of angels appeared over the almost-intact Caesar's Palace, gliding in a triangular hunting pattern. Alex got two, and either Seb or Sam got the other, and everyone cheered, clapping them on the shoulders. And though Alex knew better, for a second he felt a sense of hard satisfaction.

As if three angels out of millions even made a difference.

"Come on," he said finally, turning away. Quarters crunched under his foot from a shattered slot machine. "Let's get back to work."

When they returned to the base, they built a new set: a forest simulation, this time. They all stayed up one night cutting out leaf shapes and painting them in the training room, until it looked like every autumn tree in the world had shed its leaves on the floor.

"Looking good," Willow said, pressing briefly against him. She wore an old sweatshirt and had a smudge of paint on her nose.

Alex nodded. "Yeah, it'll be a realistic set."

She glanced up at him, started to say something, and

broke off. Finally she just squeezed his hand and went back to painting.

He caught Willow watching him sometimes now, and knew that she was worried about him. Apart from when they'd seen the Third Wave arrive, he'd kept silent about his fears, even to her.

What was there to say? The world was screwed.

Alex struggled grimly against that deep-down conviction, against the nagging inner voice that said that if he were any kind of a leader at all, he'd know when to quit – just go start a settlement high up in the mountains somewhere. Jesus, what was wrong with him, that even *now* he had to keep a war going against the angels? But the stupid thing was, the other AKs still trusted him…and still wanted to fight.

He sighed, rubbing the back of his neck. It was late November, after midnight, and he was in the empty rec room with his laptop and a long-cold mug of coffee. Tiredly, he brought up a Word document filled with his notes. If they were to have anything more than a suicidal chance at this, they had to get camps established all across the country: small teams that recruited and trained people themselves, then splintered off to do the same thing again, over and over, until there were hundreds of sniper groups fighting the angels.

In the base's office, they'd found details of another

facility in the Sawtooth Mountains of Idaho – smaller than here and too remote to be of much use. The teams would somehow have to source their own shelters, along with food and ammunition, and this current group of eighty-seven would need a lot more training. Not to mention survival skills, if they were to have any hope of existing in the wild.

Alex added these thoughts to his notes, though it felt like a waste of time. Yeah, sending everyone out to set up more AK camps was great in theory…but once Raziel realized the Angel Killers were still around, he'd annihilate them.

Alex stared blindly at his laptop, imagining small inexperienced groups being systematically decimated by the angels. He let out a breath and rested his forehead on his fists. He *knew* his team; he'd worked with every one of them. How the hell was he supposed to send them off to die?

But how could he just let the angels take over?

Alex looked up as Seb appeared in the rec room doorway. Seb stopped short. "Ah. Sorry," he said. "I didn't know anyone was here."

"It's okay, c'mon in." Alex pushed the laptop away, glad to stop looking at it.

Seb dropped into a nearby armchair; his feet were bare. Glancing at him, Alex held back a slight smile. "Go ahead and smoke – that's what you came in for, right?"

Seb quirked an eyebrow but didn't deny it. He produced a battered red and white pack and dug a lighter from his jeans pocket. "Last pack," he commented as he tapped out a cigarette.

"So you'll be quitting again? Yeah, I've heard that one before."

Seb shrugged and settled back, blowing out a stream of smoke. "Meghan hates the smell anyway. She threw me out."

It was a relief to have something else to think about – even if it was Seb's love life. "She's a nice girl," said Alex.

Seb nodded. "Yes, I think so too."

They sat in silence, Seb occasionally turning his head to blow smoke over his shoulder. Finally he looked down at his cigarette and cleared his throat. "So, I've been thinking…maybe Meghan and I will go away."

Alex had been trying to rouse himself enough to go to bed; now he straightened. "What – seriously?"

Slowly, Seb ground out the cigarette in a saucer someone had left behind. "I don't think there's anything we can do now to stop the angels, *amigo*."

Hearing his own worst fears put into words, all that came to Alex's mind was, *Yeah, I don't blame you.* But he said nothing.

Seb sat playing with the ground-out cigarette. "If I thought there was any kind of chance, I'd stay for ever. Now, though…" He shrugged.

"What about Willow?" asked Alex finally. Ever since the two half-angels had met, Alex had been forced to accept Seb's presence in his girlfriend's life as a given.

Seb's mouth twisted; he snorted slightly. In a low voice, he said, "I keep thinking it will someday get better, you know. That I'll get over her and not care so much, but—" He broke off, his expression more vulnerable than Alex had ever seen it. He tossed the cigarette butt back onto the saucer.

"Anyway, I'm still her brother if she ever needs me," he said tiredly. "But I want to really try with Meghan. And… here isn't the best place, not with Willow here too."

Watching Seb as he looked down at the table, sympathy stirred within Alex. Christ, how had it happened that he and Seb had actually become friends? But somewhere along the line, they had.

"Look, don't go," he said finally. "I know what you mean about the angels – I was just sitting here thinking almost the same thing. But even if we don't have a chance now, you've got to keep training people in the aura work – if they're not proficient in it, they'll die."

Seb didn't answer, but Alex could sense the argument had hit home – Seb had sometimes spent up to twelve hours a day training recruits, with no complaints.

"And come on, this place is big enough that you can avoid Willow, isn't it?" Alex went on. "What if I changed your teaching schedules, so that you don't work together any more? You'd hardly ever see each other."

Seb plucked at a loose thread on his jeans. "I don't know," he said finally. "It might help, but..."

"Does Meghan want to go?"

"I haven't asked her," Seb admitted. He met Alex's gaze and smiled slightly. "Why are you arguing for me to stay? If I could take your girlfriend away from you, I'd still do it."

"Dude, if you could take my girlfriend away from me, you'd have done it a year ago. Let me make the change, okay?" Alex scanned Seb's face, his voice lowering in intensity. "Come on, man, I need you here – I've got to give them all the best chance I can before I send them out there."

Seb blew out a breath. "All right," he said. "I'll stay for now." After a pause the corner of his mouth lifted. "I didn't want to leave the hot showers anyway. It's the real reason I'm staying, you know."

"Yeah, you see? Massive perks."

Seb lit another cigarette and smoked it with one foot up on the chair. And as Alex thought about the day to come and all the days after that – while above, humanity became cattle for ever, because of him – for the first time in his life he was tempted to light up too.

He shut down the laptop and rose. "Don't think too hard," he said.

Seb gave a small smile. "No. You either."

Fat chance, thought Alex – and then the pager clipped to his jeans waistband burst into life. "Alex, could you get up here?" said Heather's worried voice.

He grabbed the pager. "What's going on?"

"I'm not sure. There's a truck coming."

"*What?*" Alex and Seb exchanged a startled glance, Seb lurching forward to stub out his cigarette and scrambling to his feet.

They took off at a run, pausing only to duck into the armoury and grab a couple of pistols. When they reached the small room above ground, Heather was hunched over one of the monitors; her gaze flew tensely to theirs.

"It looks like an Eden vehicle," she said. "The driver's gotten out and is heading for the gate. There's only one of them, but they've got a gun."

Doing a quick scan, Alex felt only human energy. With Seb close behind, he bolted for the door and slapped at the switch to turn on the outside light.

"*Okay, hold it right there,*" he warned as he flung the door open, aiming his pistol. He froze and the blood slowly drained from his face.

Kara stood at the chain-link fence, blinking in the sudden light.

"Alex?" she said hoarsely. The exotic beauty of her face was hidden under purplish swollen bruises. One hand clutched the fence as if holding on for dear life.

"Oh Jesus," whispered Alex. He started to rush towards the gate, then glanced at Seb. "She's not—?"

Seb shook his head, staring. "No. She doesn't have angel burn."

When Alex threw open the gate, Kara stumbled into his arms; he held her tightly, his thoughts reeling. "Kara, what's happened?" he said. Her once-toned body felt far too thin, like a fragile bird.

Kara was shivering, as if overwhelmed by cold. Finally she drew back, and Alex's stomach knotted with helpless anger – her face was even worse than he'd thought. One eye was puffed closed, her lip bloodied and swollen, her perfect nose broken.

"It…it wasn't the easiest journey, getting here," she mumbled. "I…" She trailed off, swaying on her feet.

"Explain later." Alex put his arm around her; she sagged against him. "Where are your keys?" He took them from her unresisting hand and tossed them to Seb. "Get her truck in here, okay?"

Seb looked down at the keys; his mouth twisted wryly. "Ah – I can't drive, *amigo*."

"What? Fine, tell Heather to call someone up. And come down to the infirmary with us; I need you to read her hand and see what you can get." Now that the first shock of seeing Kara alive was over, Alex's main concern was whether whoever had beaten her up was still coming after her, about to discover their base.

They'd almost reached the door; Kara stiffened and stopped short. "No," she said. "No readings. Just – no more, all right?"

Her voice shook, and unease stirred through Alex – what the hell had happened to her? He glanced at Seb and could see the half-angel scanning her aura more thoroughly, picking up who knew what from it.

"Okay, don't worry," Alex said. He got Kara inside and punched the button for the elevator. "Just tell me, is anyone following you?"

Kara had slumped against his shoulder again; blearily, she shook her head. Her short black hair, always so sleek against her scalp, was longer now, unkempt. And her nails… Alex's chest tightened as he saw that they were ragged and broken, with no sign of the jaunty pink polish she used to wear.

They got her down to the medical bay. In response to Alex's page, Claudia arrived; she looked at Kara in surprise. "Who…?" she started to say.

"She's an AK from the Mexico City group," Alex said tersely. "I'll explain later."

"All right, let me clean up her face and see what I can do for her nose," said Claudia. "Any other injuries?"

"I think I've got a broken rib," Kara murmured.

She was lying on the examination table, her good eye closed. In her jeans and old T-shirt, she looked almost skeletal.

As Claudia started to work, Seb took Alex's arm and drew him aside. "She's been around angels," he said. "I can feel their energy in her aura – not angel burn, but they've been near to her. For a long time, I think."

Somehow Alex wasn't surprised. He gazed at Kara. "I can't believe she's still alive," he said softly. "It's been almost a year; what's been going on?"

It didn't seem likely he'd find out anytime soon. Though sitting up now, Kara looked dead to the world as Claudia dabbed at her face – hardly even reacting when the paramedic adjusted her broken nose with a quick motion and then set it with tape.

They didn't have an X-ray machine. As Claudia gently examined Kara's ribs, Alex winced to see how sharply each was outlined beneath Kara's mocha skin. Not to mention the bruising – it looked like someone had used her for a punching bag.

"Think it's just a fracture…at least there shouldn't be any danger of it puncturing the lung there," Claudia muttered. "I hope." Finally she nodded. "Okay, I think that's it – you look really dehydrated, though. Let's get you into bed and onto a drip."

She brought out a green hospital gown. "Here," she

said, placing it on Kara's lap. "There's a bathroom just there, if you want to get changed."

The gown slithered to the floor as Kara eased herself off the table, clutching its edge for support. "No, I'll keep my own clothes."

Claudia blinked. "But you need to rest. You won't be very comfortable if—"

"I said no."

Claudia looked at Alex; he shrugged. "Forget it. Let's just get her into bed."

There were three hospital beds in an adjacent room. Claudia drew back the covers of one, and Alex helped Kara into it; she sank against the pillows. Then as Claudia readied an IV drip, Kara's good eye flew to Alex's in alarm.

"It's just to get you hydrated again; it's all right," he said. Kara swallowed and nodded. She made no protest as Claudia eased the needle into her forearm and taped it into place.

"Okay," said Claudia, holding a hypodermic up to the light as she filled it. She reached for Kara's arm again. "I've got something here that will help you sleep—"

Kara's thin hand shot out and grabbed her wrist; Claudia gave a startled squeak. "Touch me with that thing, and I'll stab you in the neck with it," said Kara in a low voice.

Alex had lunged at her first movement; he gripped

Kara's wrist hard. Finger by finger, she let go of Claudia. "Trust me, you don't even want to try it," he said. "Do *not* threaten my team, now or ever again. Claudia, you'd better go. Thanks for your help – I'll call you if we need you."

She nodded, still pale. Seb stood leaning against the doorway; she brushed against him as she hurried out.

"I should go too," Seb said, straightening.

There was a chair beside Kara's bedside; Alex dropped into it. Kara had collapsed back against the bedding, her good eye closed again. "I'd better sit with her for a while," said Alex, rubbing a hand over his face. "But, yeah, you go on to bed."

Seb shook his head as he glanced at Kara. "It's not that. She doesn't want me here. Goodnight, *amigo.*"

Before Alex could respond, Seb had slipped out, silent as a ghost. Alex looked at Kara with a frown. Since arriving she'd hardly acknowledged Seb's presence, but now he saw her relax a little. At the sound of the outer door closing, she turned her head to look at him, twisting at the sheet's hem with a fretful hand.

"Willow's here too, isn't she?" she asked. "Alex, how can you bear to have them around? How?"

Alex's jaw tightened. He seriously thought the question of whether half-angels could be trusted should have been settled a year ago, when Willow and Seb had almost died trying to halt the attack on the Seraphic Council. His instant anger faded slightly as he took in Kara's bruises again.

"Look, I don't know what you've been through, but you're way off base," he said. "I'd trust Seb with my life, and Willow... Christ, Willow *is* my life."

Alarmingly, Kara seemed close to tears. "The whole time he was standing there... Oh god, his energy is so similar to theirs that it makes me sick. And for you to actually *be* with one of them – for you to—" She broke off, her thin frame shuddering.

Alex started to reply, then stopped short. This so wasn't about Willow and Seb. He reached for her hand, held it between both of his. "What's happened, Kara?"

She swallowed. "I've been in an Eden."

Alex's spine stiffened – he should have guessed. "Where's Brendan?" he asked after a pause. "Is he alive too?"

Kara was staring up at the ceiling; as she shook her head, a single tear ran down her swollen cheek. "No. When we were trying to get out of Mexico City, the quake hit. The van crashed, and he was injured – really badly – internal stuff. I managed to steal another car, and we got out. I kept telling him to hold on, kept thinking he might make it... Finally we got into Texas, and there was a makeshift hospital set up for people who'd been injured in the Houston quake. He died there. He hadn't even been conscious most of the trip."

Alex let out a long breath, remembering Brendan – his shock of reddish hair; his wiry body and incessant talking. Incongruously, he thought how weird it must have been, to have travelled so many miles with Brendan without hearing him talk the whole time.

Kara wiped her cheek. "Then before I could leave the hospital, some soldiers came and said they were taking everyone to a refugee camp. I didn't want to attract attention by saying no; I thought I could escape on the way. But I couldn't. They took my gun, and once we were at the camp, we were watched every second." She gave a bitter laugh. "The others were just happy to be someplace with food and electricity. They couldn't see all the angels – all the feeding that was going on, day and night. After three months, almost everyone in the place had angel burn."

Alex's veins chilled. "How did you avoid it?"

Kara looked haunted. "I don't know. They tried. They kept coming down to – to choose me, and I'd see them looking so beautiful and feel their minds linking with mine…" She gave a convulsive shudder.

"And then what?" Alex asked intensely. "They just gave up and flew away again?"

"Yeah." Kara let out a strangled laugh. "Maybe I don't taste so good."

Alex's thoughts were whirling. It sounded as if Kara had been marshalled – something an angel named Nate had told him about. Before the Seraphic Council had executed them all, there'd been a group of angels sympathetic to humans. They'd been trying to marshal as many people as they could: place a small bit of resistance in human auras, making them unpalatable to angels.

But Kara would have realized. It wasn't something an angel could do without being noticed.

His attention snapped back as Kara started talking again, her voice thick and halting: "Anyway, I kept trying to escape – never managed it. Then they moved us all into Austin Eden."

She let out a shuddering breath. "Things were kind of chaotic in the refugee camp, but once we got to the Eden... Alex, you wouldn't believe how *organized* that place is. It's the same in all of them, I guess. They've got different sectors, and the one you're assigned to determines how often you're allowed to be fed from. Because, like, if you've got a skill the angels need – say you're an electrician or something – then they don't want you to get too weak, so they keep track..."

She went into a sudden coughing fit, and Alex rose hastily to get her a glass of water. She drank it with his arm around her, holding her up. The news about the sectors was something they'd long suspected, from reading between the lines of shortwave news broadcasts. He wished to hell they'd been wrong.

"Thanks," Kara mumbled, dropping back against the pillows. "Of course, they don't *say* all that – but if you don't have angel burn and can see what's going on, it's obvious." She gave a humourless laugh. "They put me in A1. Guess I should have been flattered – only the young, good-looking people with fresh, pretty auras went there. I mean, we were *popular* with the angels. Not that anyone ever stayed in A1 very long…" Kara's throat moved, her brown eyes lost in that other time.

"So yeah, it didn't take them long to notice that none of the angels could feed from me. I guess I piqued their interest a little. I spent the last seven months in Austin locked in a hospital room while the angels tried to figure me out."

"What – you mean examining you?" Cold crept across Alex's scalp. His eyes flew to Kara's left shirtsleeve – underneath, there lay an AK tattoo identical to his own. Once, the angels might not have known what the letters stood for; they sure as hell did now.

"Don't worry, I got rid of it before I even got to Austin," Kara said wearily. She lifted the sleeve of her faded T-shirt, and Alex winced – where her tattoo had been was now a series of long, jagged scars.

"Oh Christ, Kara…" He couldn't say any more.

She dropped the sleeve. "I had to. People know who the AKs are now, after what happened in Mexico City – they hate all of us. I did it with a piece of metal I found and managed to keep it hidden until it healed a little. Not that it made any difference once they put me in the hospital. Raziel knew it was me."

"*Raziel?*"

Her mouth was a bitter line. "Yeah. Your girlfriend's father. He kept coming all the way down from Denver to poke and prod at me himself." She shuddered. "Alex, how you can even stand touching her, when—"

"Shut it," he said sharply. "She's nothing like them, and you know it."

"Fine. Whatever." Kara wiped her eyes. "So, yeah, ol' Raz was pretty interested in what makes me tick…because I guess it's more than me just not being tasty to them. They can't – they can't seem to read me."

Alex's eyes narrowed in confusion. "What are you talking about?"

"They couldn't read me. It drove them crazy. Drove *him* crazy, especially. For weeks – months – if it wasn't him, it was one of the others. They strapped me down so I couldn't struggle and they'd hold my hand, and I could *feel* their minds creeping into mine – so cold and slimy – over and over…" She choked to a stop.

Oh Jesus. Alex rubbed a fist against his forehead. He guessed he couldn't blame her for hating anything that reminded her of the angels.

"They were trying to find out about us, weren't they?" he said. "Whether Willow's still alive or not."

"Yeah." Kara swallowed hard. "I told them you were all dead, killed in the Mexico City quake. It was true, for all I knew – I just didn't want them to get anything about the base here, no matter what. Finally they started on more... physical methods."

Alex's fist was still tight. With his other hand, he gently touched Kara's bruised cheek. "This?"

Without the dramatic make-up she used to wear, her beaten face looked young and exposed. "No, that was after I escaped – there was a bandit I stole the truck from. He didn't want to give it up, but I was pretty desperate – believe me, I gave as good as I got. The angels are...subtler than that. You don't want to know, okay?"

Taking in the slight quiver of her mouth, Alex knew she was probably right. With a bitter anger, he longed to destroy every angel who'd touched her.

"Anyway, they'll be pissed off that I escaped," Kara said, triumph clear in her tone. "Since they couldn't get anything from me, they were going to use me at the Salt Lake Eden founding celebration. Like, look who we caught! What do you think we should do with her, oh noble Salt Lake Eden people?"

Alex could just imagine: it would have been like a scene from ancient Rome, with them tossing Kara to the Church of Angels' lions. A silence stretched out between them. From the clock on the wall, Alex saw that it was after two in the morning.

"How did you get away?" he asked.

She shook her head; he could see how exhausted she was. "It doesn't matter – it was while they were transporting me to Salt Lake Eden. But, Alex, listen: there's something I haven't told you." She groped for his hand again; he enfolded hers in his own.

"What?" he urged.

Kara shut her good eye for a moment; finally she opened it again. "Before they put me in the hospital, I managed to get out of A1 a few times and tried to escape – once I made it as far as the lowest sector in the city, where they keep people who are in really bad shape. And, Alex – Cully was there. I was with him when he died. He knew something."

CHAPTER *Ten*

AT THE NAME OF HIS old mentor, Alex straightened slowly. Cully had been the best Angel Killer he'd ever known – practically a father to him. The news that Cully's angel burn had finally killed him was almost a relief; Cull would have hated what he'd become.

"What do you mean, 'he knew something'?" Alex asked.

Kara fumbled in her jeans pocket and produced a cellphone. "Here," she said, handing it to him. "I managed to hide it. Have you got a charger?"

The phone was identical to Alex's – he'd bought them

both the previous December. "Yeah, I've got one," he said, staring down at the silver case. "What's on it? A video?"

Kara nodded, her gaze sorrowful. She knew what Cully had meant to him. "He was ranting pretty badly, and he kept mentioning you. Alex, he was worried – he kept saying, 'We can't let him figure it out'."

Alex tucked the phone into his own pocket. Obviously, Cully had realized the deaths of a few angels could destroy them all. *Don't worry, Cull; I screwed that one up good,* he thought. *The angels are totally safe now, for ever.*

"You think you know what it is," Kara said, watching him.

"Yeah," he admitted. "And it's all over." He told her what had happened. The words tasted bitter.

Kara swallowed but thankfully didn't comment. "I don't know, Al...what Cully was saying didn't seem related to the angels being linked or not. He kept talking about Martin too."

Alex frowned. "Dad?"

"Yeah. Something about an idea that Martin had had... I couldn't make head or tail of it. Just watch. Maybe it'll help, somehow." Her eyes fluttered closed then, her bruised face gaunt.

Frankly, Alex doubted it – his dad had been pretty out of it those last few years before he died. He sat studying Kara for a long moment, his emotions jumbled.

"Listen to me," he said finally. "If you're staying, then I don't want to hear a single word about Willow and Seb. They're part of the team – end of story."

Her good eye reluctantly opened. "I know," she said after a pause. "It's just a gut reaction; I can't help it. But I'll keep it to myself."

Alex realized that was probably the best he was going to get from her. Maybe when what she'd been through had faded a little, she'd come around. Unfortunately, she had all the time in the world to do so now, with no end to any of this in sight.

He rose. "Get some sleep, okay?"

Kara lay watching him, her muscles tense. "You'll watch the video?"

"Yeah, I'll watch it." At the door, Alex paused. "Hey – I'm really glad you made it," he said.

Kara's smile was a ghost of smiles he remembered. "Me too."

The temptation to go crawl into bed beside Willow, forgetting the whole world as he drew her into his arms, was almost overwhelming. The weight of the phone in his jeans pocket wouldn't let him do it.

Alex headed for the comms room instead, where he'd stowed all their old phones in a cabinet. After he'd plugged in Kara's cell, he sat with his thumb hesitating over the buttons. He wasn't looking forward to seeing Cully near death. At least the last time he'd encountered Cull, the man had looked in perfect health, even if he was feverishly devoted to the angels.

Finally Alex started the video. The quality was grainy; Cully was lying on a cot in what looked like a crowded warehouse, packed with other sick people.

Alex grimaced, unsurprised that this was how the angels treated their followers when they neared death. He wouldn't have recognized the spindly man on the cot – until he saw Cully's eyes: the vivid blue of a Georgia sky.

Kara's voice was just audible. "Hey, I didn't catch all that, Cull. Can you tell me again, straight from the top?"

Cully was turning his head restlessly. His voice was still deep, with a southern resonance. "You've got to stop Alex from doing it – you've got to. He's smart; he'll figure it out…"

And then Alex stopped noticing anything except the words Cully was saying. The video was just over a minute long. When it finished, he slumped back against the office chair. His heart clubbed against his ribs as he stared down at the phone.

Jesus. No way. This could not be true; there was just no way.

Finally, in a daze, he reached for the phone and hit the *Play* button once more. As Cully's monologue filled the small room again, Alex wasn't surprised that Kara hadn't understood what he was talking about – it was all half-finished phrases, allusions to things that only Alex and his brother, Jake, had known. Along with their dad, whose insane idea it had been to start with.

But if what Cully had said was true…maybe it wasn't so insane after all.

Alex listened tautly. Cull's voice was clear, despite the background noise of groans and people talking. "It can be done, like Martin always said. I took over where he left off, back at the camp. I had to. Couldn't help myself; I didn't care what might happen. Took me so long, and I got so close – then I got sick and ended up here."

It all made perfect sense to Alex…and the part that had made the hairs at the back of his neck prickle had even more effect this time. Cully, his head rolling feverishly, said: "I just *left* it there. You've got to tell the angels, Kara; they've got to go fix it so it's not there any more. If Alex finds it, he could do what Martin was planning – it's really possible, I'm sure of it now. He was always better with the energy work than anyone else. We gotta keep him away or it could all be over – the angels gone for ever…"

Alex stared at the now-still screen; an image of Cully's face, slightly blurred, gazed back. A memory came: himself and Jake having dinner with their father. Martin was pointing his fork at them.

"Mark my words – this will be what finally defeats them. Nothing we're doing *here* will do any good."

Jake had winked at Alex out of their father's vision. "Yeah, but, Dad, even if you ever finish this thing, won't the burst of energy just kill you the second you try to go through? Kinda like, I dunno…a giant bug zapper?" His voice was innocent.

Alex had been fourteen; black humour when dealing with their father had become standard operating procedure. He'd snorted, trying unsuccessfully to turn it into a cough. Their father's latest idea was deranged on so many levels that you had to either laugh or go crazy yourself.

Fortunately, Martin had been too busy glaring at Jake to notice. "Don't be ridiculous," he'd snapped. "I'm telling you, I just need to be in their world for a *few minutes,* and I can defeat them! What I sensed was definite—"

It had been more than Alex could take. "Dad, come on," he'd protested, putting down his fork. "It doesn't matter what you sensed; there's no way you could get over there in the first place! The angels can change to their ethereal forms when they cross. If *we* tried to go through, it would just kill us. You know that! You're the one who told *me* that."

His words were a spark setting off a powder keg. When Martin finally released them, Jake had been seething.

"Next time you start arguing with him, I'm going to

strangle you both," he'd grumbled on their way back to the dorm. "Why do you bother? He'll never listen."

Their footsteps were steady on the cement. Alex shrugged testily. "Because it would just be suicide. Can you imagine the burst of energy if he tried it? This whole place would blow sky-high."

Jake had given him a look of exaggerated patience. "No it wouldn't, because – listen carefully, little brother – the idea that he could ever make his own gate is *a complete freaking delusion.*"

Now his brother's words seemed to reach across time and space to find Alex again.

"Maybe it wasn't a delusion after all, Jake," he murmured, touching the phone's smooth casing. Because, unbelievably, it sounded as if Cully had nearly finished what Martin had started.

The thought brought a chill. Of course, there was always the chance that Cully had gone crazy with angel burn; maybe nothing he'd said could be trusted. Yet somehow Alex doubted it. The last time he'd seen Cull, the man had been as sane as anyone, apart from his devotion to the angels.

Alex massaged his suddenly pounding temples and tried to recall a time when Cully had been wrong. He couldn't.

John Cullpepper had been a slow-talking southerner with a quick, sharp mind; when it came to angels especially, no one in the world had known more than Cull.

And he'd thought Martin's plan to defeat them was really possible.

On the screen, Cully's blue eyes seemed locked on Alex's. As Alex gazed down at his old mentor, he knew that the plan's feasibility was only part of it – because what he'd told his father was true. Cully had known, too: *I didn't care what might happen.*

If Alex tried this, the attempt to get there would probably kill him.

He sat motionless for a long time.

He wasn't afraid of death – he'd been raised knowing he could lose his life every time he went on a hunt. If anything, he was surprised to still be alive at nineteen. This, though – to deliberately take odds that he knew were likely to kill him – Alex let out a breath. Yeah, this felt pretty different.

He touched the bracelet Willow had given him, unconsciously tracing its strands. He wanted to live – and to actually do this thing would be insanity. Yet underneath everything was a lake of deep, pure relief. Finally, there was something he could try that might fix what he'd broken in the world – some *action* he could take, instead of just training other people to go out and die.

If Cully was right, this was their only hope.

Alex knew then that he'd decided. It was worth any odds. *I don't have a choice, Cull, do I?* he thought grimly. Ironic, that Cully had shown him a possible solution when he'd been trying his best not to.

At long last, Alex straightened. His muscles felt heavy. A glance at the clock showed it was three thirty in the morning – he'd been in here over an hour. He started to return Kara's phone to his pocket, then stopped mid-motion. No. Bad idea. He stowed the phone in the cabinet and locked the door.

As Alex shut up the comms room, he knew that the sooner he left for New Mexico, the better. If this thing was possible, then he wanted to move fast, before the angels did any more damage. And more than that…the longer he hung around here thinking about the probable outcome, the harder it would be to go. The only thing he'd ever wanted for himself was a life with Willow.

Willow. He went still as the promise he'd made came back: that he wouldn't put himself into danger without telling her. Dread touched him, and he swallowed. Danger – yeah, this probably qualified. Oh, Christ, how could he tell her this and then make himself walk away from her? Imagining the look on her face, he knew that dying would be easier.

Slowly, Alex started back to their bedroom. His

footsteps echoed in the empty corridor. *I have to tell her the truth,* he thought. *I promised her.*

But with every step, he was aware of Kara's phone locked in the cabinet, becoming further away by the second...and deep down, he realized he'd left it there for a reason.

CHAPTER *Eleven*

I AWOKE FROM TANGLED DREAMS to find the desk light on, its neck pushed down low. I blinked as I propped myself up on my elbows, wondering whether I was still dreaming. Alex was moving around the room wearing only his jeans, his hair damp as if he'd just taken a shower.

He had one of the small nylon backpacks from the supply closet, and he was packing it.

"Alex?" I glanced at the clock. It wasn't even four in the morning. "What's going on?"

"Hey." He came over and sat beside me. "It's, um... been kind of an eventful night. Kara's here."

"*Kara?*" I sat up straight. "You mean – she's still alive? But *how*? Is she okay?"

He took my hand and looked down, playing with my fingers. "She was in an Eden. Something's happened to her – I think she's been marshalled somehow."

Images of what he'd seen swirled through me. I caught my breath at the sight of Kara's bruised face. "Oh god, she's *not* okay."

Alex detached his hand from mine and cleared his throat. "No, she's fine – just pretty beaten up. And she's been through a hell of a lot." Briefly, he told me what had happened. My mouth tightened at the mention of my father. Oh, poor Kara.

"Brendan's dead," Alex added after a pause. "He was fatally injured in the Mexico City quake."

Sorrow stirred through me, though I'd already grieved for both Brendan and Kara months ago. Wordlessly, I touched Alex's arm, rubbing his tattoo.

He still sat looking down, the muscles of his torso firm even though he was relaxed. Or was he? Studying him more closely, I became aware of a faint feeling of tension, and I glanced again at the backpack, gaping open. A folded T-shirt lay on top and a couple of spare magazines for his pistol.

I slowly dropped my hand. "So…what does all of this have to do with you going somewhere?"

Alex got up from the bed, and if it had been anyone else, I'd have said that he was moving to avoid looking at me. "Kara's brought some new information," he said as he picked up his camouflage trousers. "I've got to go check something out at the old AK camp."

"You mean you're going to New Mexico?" I shoved back the covers and scrambled to the bottom of the bed. I took the trousers from him and put them aside. "Hey, stop packing for a second. What new information? About the angels?"

"Yeah. It's probably nothing, though."

"Well…what did Kara say?"

Alex's blue-grey eyes met mine. I had the fleeting sense that the moment was poised on a knife's edge. Then he let out a small breath. "It's…something my dad was working on years ago, that's all."

He stopped, and I opened my mouth to say, *Yes, but what?* Then he turned away and went on: "It was, um – kind of to do with the earth's energy field. I always thought it was crazy. But if he was right, then…" He shrugged.

"The earth's energy field," I repeated blankly.

"Well, not really. It's complicated – I don't have time to explain."

"Cully," I said suddenly. The name had just popped into my head; I frowned as I tried to put the pieces together. "Did Kara see Cully? Is this coming from him?"

Alex had gone to the desk to get his pistol; when I spoke, he stopped in his tracks. His shoulders flexed as he propped his hands on the desk. "Willow, listen – don't try to get it, all right? It's better if no one but me knows some of this."

"Whoa, whoa." I went quickly to him. Sliding a hand across the smooth warmth of his back, I leaned around to look into his face. "Alex, what's going on?"

"Nothing, it's – just a precaution," he said, squeezing my hand briefly and releasing it. "I don't think anything will happen here while I'm gone, but if it does, none of you would be able to tell the angels any details. Just…trust me and leave it alone, okay?"

I didn't know what to say. He'd gone back to packing; his dark hair was half-dry now, looking soft at the edges. "Is this something dangerous?" I asked at last.

His gaze stayed on the backpack as he put the camouflage trousers in. He shook his head. "No. Nothing I can't handle."

I fell silent, thinking about the promise he'd made. I almost said something, but then he looked up and I saw the expression in his eyes. He hadn't forgotten; I could tell.

If he were putting himself in danger, he'd tell me.

There was a long pause. Finally I nodded reluctantly. "All right. But – well, why don't I come with you? Or Sam, or Seb, or *someone*?"

Alex fastened the backpack. "No, it – makes more sense if I go alone. There's no reason to take anyone else away from training the team, when I can do this myself."

He paused and touched my hair then, gently fingering a wavy strand. As if thinking about something else, he said, "Willow, look – this is just something I need to do. I mean, it's probably nothing, but if it *is* something, then…"

He didn't go on, though I sensed in a rush how important this could be – and knew that whatever objections I had weren't going to make any difference.

The words didn't want to come out. "So…when are you leaving?" I asked finally.

"Now. I just need to tell the others. I'm leaving Sam in charge while I'm gone – is that okay with you?"

"Yeah, good call." I rubbed my arms, still hardly able to believe we were having this conversation. "How long will you be gone, exactly?"

Alex's eyes met mine. For a second I thought he was going to say something, then he turned away and tightened a strap on the backpack, yanking it taut. "However long it takes, I guess."

However long what takes? With an effort, I bit the question back.

I watched as Alex pulled on a blue T-shirt and then reached into our closet for his leather jacket, scavenged almost a year ago from an abandoned store in Phoenix.

He shrugged into it, and for a second I was reminded of when I'd first met him – he'd been driving a black Porsche and wearing a jacket just like this one. Even then, back when we'd hated each other, I'd thought he was the best-looking boy I'd ever seen.

Once we'd gotten the others up, Liz and Sam were as stunned by the news that Kara was here as by Alex leaving. Only Seb seemed unsurprised; I saw him give Alex a sharp look.

"Look, Al, I seriously don't like this—" Sam was saying as we walked down the corridor towards the garage. Outside, I knew it wasn't even dawn yet; the rest of the base was still asleep.

"Wait a sec; I'll just grab a sat phone," interrupted Alex as we came to the comms room. He ducked inside and was out again a few moments later. I had the brief sense that he'd stuffed more than just a sat phone into his jeans pocket.

Alex was walking a little ahead, fielding a barrage of questions from Sam.

"Did you know about this?" Liz whispered.

I shook my head, still gazing at Alex. Without trying, I was aware that there was something buried in his mind; that he was consciously piling other thoughts on top. I crossed my arms tight, resisting the urge to look further. He'd asked me to trust him and I did, but…what was going on?

Alex grabbed some food and a rifle, and then, all too soon, we were in the garage and he was loading up one of the 4 × 4s. He shook hands with Sam and Seb, gave Liz a brief hug. "Okay, I'll check in when I can, but try not to worry if you don't hear from me."

Like the night Alex and I had gone to Colorado, Sam was in his pyjamas, his broad face a scowl. "Yeah, we'll just throw a party. Bud, all this secret squirrel stuff is *not* reassuring."

Seb hadn't said much, though his hazel eyes were troubled. He said something to Alex in low, urgent Spanish; Alex shook his head. "*No, pero gracias, amigo,*" he replied in an undertone – and I knew Seb must have asked, as I had, whether he could go along.

"Look, if – I mean, it won't, but if anything happens—" Alex broke off, jiggling the keys in his hand. "Sam, you're in charge, but the others are allowed to mutiny if you do anything stupid," he said, his voice abruptly curt. "Seriously, just keep on training everyone, all right? If what I'm checking on doesn't pan out, that's all we can do. There are plans on my laptop I've been working on; Willow knows the password."

Sam's eyebrows lowered. "Alex, what the hell—"

"It'll be fine." Alex glanced at me, then back at the others. "Let us have some privacy, okay? Take care, you guys."

The others left with backward glances. I gripped my

arms, leaning against the truck as silence settled around us. "Alex, this is— I mean, I'm still trying to figure out what's even going on here."

Alex stood motionless. Then he shook his head as if chasing a thought away. His voice was rough. "Yeah, I know. I'll tell you everything later. I'd better get going now, though."

He stepped close and stroked my hair back with both hands – and though our kisses had meant many things before, this one was somehow different. I wrapped my arms around his neck, kissing him back as hard as I could; then we just held each other, his head buried against my shoulder.

"Hey, I'll be checking up on you," I tried to joke as he finally pulled away. "I mean, like, every second."

His throat moved slightly. "I know," he said. He gave a crooked smile and touched my cheek. Slowly, his fingers trailed down to my neck.

"You are my life, you know that?" he said in a low voice. "You always have been, from the second I met you."

He swung himself up into the truck before I could answer, not looking at me. "Get the elevator for me, will you?" he said. "I'll be back as soon as I can."

But as I moved to press the button, I froze in place. For a second, I literally couldn't make myself do it – it felt as if I'd be sending Alex to his doom.

I glanced back, drinking in his face, the beautiful shape

of his mouth as he fiddled with the truck's controls. *It's okay,* I told myself. *He said that he wouldn't put himself in danger again without telling me. He promised.*

I squared my shoulders…and pressed the button. As the elevator door slid open, Alex looked up and started the engine. "Be careful," I said, lifting my voice over the noise of the truck.

He nodded, drove the 4 × 4 into the elevator, and then hooked his arm over the seat, twisting around to look back at me. Our eyes met and locked as the door slid shut, slowly slicing him from view.

It closed.

As the machinery rumbled, moving upwards, that feeling of dread swept over me again, stronger than before. But I had to trust that he knew what he was doing.

I looked up as Seb entered the garage, his hands shoved into his back pockets. "I, uh…heard the elevator," he said. "Are you all right?"

"Yeah, I guess," I said. I could sense Alex above, the garage door rising for him as the outside gate slid open. Another second, and he'd be gone.

Unable to help myself, I connected quickly with my angel. Spreading my ethereal wings, I shot up through the elevator shaft, bursting up out of the building like a swimmer emerging from water. There were still stars overheard, with the rosy tinge of dawn in the east.

Alex's truck was making its way down the dirt road. From this height, it looked like a toy. I hovered as I watched the truck grow smaller, longing to fly after him but sensing the intensity of his purpose – and his grim conviction that he'd do whatever it took to come back to me again.

He turned onto the main road and the truck was devoured by darkness.

Seb was still standing beside my human form as my angel merged with me again. I stared at the empty space where Alex's truck had been, feeling alone despite Seb's presence.

"What do you want, Seb?" The words came out more sharply than I'd meant.

His face drained of expression. "Nothing. Forget it." He turned to leave. I could feel that he was worried about me – and Alex too, for that matter.

I sighed and followed, stopping him with a touch on his arm. "Look, I'm sorry." I leaned against the wall, rubbing my throbbing head. "It's just…this has been a really weird night, okay?"

Seb gave a humourless smile as he propped himself next to me. "It's funny – just a few hours ago, he was convincing *me* to stay."

"A few hours ago?" I stared at him. "What more do you know about this?"

Seb shook his head. "Only what he just told us."

Then his words registered. "Wait – why was he convincing you to stay? Were you leaving?"

He shrugged. "I might still. We'll see."

I paused. "With Meghan?"

Seb nodded. And for some reason, this made what had just happened a little harder to bear. "I really like her," I said finally. "I'm happy for you, Seb. I mean it."

The look he gave me was complicated – wry and vulnerable at the same time. "Yes, thank you," he said, his tone formal. "I like her too."

Neither of us spoke for a few minutes. All I could think of was Alex, heading towards New Mexico and his father's old camp with something locked deep inside of him. I let out a breath.

Oh god, Alex, please be safe.

CHAPTER *Twelve*

BACK IN MY ROOM, GETTING a few more hours' sleep was impossible – the feeling of unease was growing by the minute. Finally I grabbed my things and went to take a shower.

I was in the same cubicle Alex and I had used once when we'd snuck in here at two in the morning to take a shower together; I always used it now if it was free. The memory of the hot water pounding down on us as we'd kissed, laughing – of his body against mine, firm and warm and slippery with soap – usually made me smile.

This time it just made the fear even stronger.

I towelled myself off; my clothes clung to my still-damp body as I wiped steam from the mirror and started to comb out my hair. My worried face gazed back at me.

This is wrong. This feels so wrong. Suddenly my hands were trembling. Kara. What exactly had she told him, to make him take off like this?

With my hair still damp, I left the shower room and headed to the infirmary.

Kara was alone when I got there, asleep in one of the hospital beds. I silently drew up a chair, pity stirring in me at the sight of her battered face. I'd never liked Kara, but I wouldn't have wished what she'd been through on anyone.

Her hand looked as thin as the rest of her. From what Alex had told me, I wasn't even sure this would work. I hesitated – and then touched her hand, very lightly, her skin papery beneath my fingers.

I'd never tried to read someone who was asleep. It was a weird sensation. Images came through, but it was like experiencing them underwater. Kara, walking through city streets with her hands in her jacket pockets. *Austin Eden,* I thought dreamily. She was trying to look casual, but I could feel her apprehension; if they caught her, she'd never get out of this place. Then we seemed to fast-forward. She was in a sort of warehouse, packed with sick people on army cots.

I hardly recognized the man Alex and I had encountered in New Mexico, but could sense Kara's sadness as she sat beside him. "Hey, Cull…you don't look so hot."

"Alex," he said urgently. "Have you seen him? I've done something – we've got to stop him—"

As I listened to what followed, my spirits fell. It was all so vague; I could sense Kara didn't understand any of it either. Then my eyes flew open as her hand jerked away.

"What the hell are you doing?" she hissed.

She lay glaring – but I could feel her fear too. Suddenly I was ashamed. "I'm sorry," I said, rubbing my palm on my jeans. "You were asleep, and I had to know what you told Alex."

"Yeah? So why not ask him?"

"Because he left. He's gone to the old AK camp."

Her good eye widened. "So there *was* something to it," she murmured. "I wasn't sure." Then she grabbed my arm. "Wait – you were able to read me? How come *you* could, when none of the angels could do it?"

I shook my head. "Alex said you must have been marshalled. Maybe it only works against full-blooded angels, or something." I cleared my throat, studying her bruises again and feeling saddened. "Anyway, I'm sorry. I didn't have any right to read you while you were asleep."

Taking in my gaze, Kara's lip curled. "You know what? Getting these was *fun* compared to dealing with your father.

Give me a good, honest fistfight any day. Now get out."

She rolled onto her side, taking the IV cord with her. Realizing I was doing more harm than good, I left.

In the main room of the infirmary, I was standing slumped against the wall, trying to still my spinning thoughts, when Sam walked in.

He peered in at Kara through the small window in the door. "Oh, man, she looks awful," he said in an undertone. "I just thought—"

"That you'd talk to her about why Alex left," I finished. "I checked; she doesn't know anything." I hesitated. "But Sam, this really doesn't feel right. I mean, I don't think I'm just being a worried girlfriend here."

He snorted. "Well, *I'm* sure as hell not being a worried girlfriend, and I don't like this at all. Not one little bit."

"So…what do we do?"

Sam made a face. "I don't know. Wait for now. See what happens."

I nodded reluctantly, because I wasn't sure what to do either.

Somehow I got through the next few hours. "He'll be fine," Liz kept saying at breakfast. "Honestly, no one's more competent than Alex."

I nudged at my oatmeal, hating the way it stuck gloppily to my spoon. "Yeah, you're right," I said, because I didn't want to give words to what I was actually feeling.

He shouldn't have gone. He shouldn't have gone.

"Willow?" said Liz softly.

I rose and picked up my tray. "It's almost time for my first class with Seb."

The room Seb and I held classes in was small; a dozen recruits sat on the floor, concentrating, with legs folded in lotus or semi-lotus positions. "Watch Willow's angel while you move through the chakra points," Seb instructed, lounging against the wall with his ankles crossed. "See how it fades and then comes back."

It was all so life-as-usual, when really nothing was. After class I found myself waiting by the door for Seb. I hadn't done this in a very long time, but he didn't look surprised.

My words tumbled out. "Seb, listen – before Alex left he started to say something about the earth's energy field. What was that about, do you have any idea?"

"The earth's energy field?" Seb repeated. I felt his sudden alarm as he reached past me to shut the door. "I don't know...unless he thinks he can use it against the angels, maybe."

The earth's energy was chaotic, untamed. Trying to harness it would be... I swallowed hard. "But that's crazy."

Seb didn't deny it. "Oh, *madre mía*, I *knew* we should have gone with him," he muttered, pressing his fists against his forehead. "I could feel that he was lying about something—"

I froze. "He was?"

Seb looked startled. "Willow, I thought you must know – that he was only lying to the rest of us! The sense of it was buried, yes, but…"

"No! He told me to trust him – he asked me not to read him!" I closed my eyes and quickly found Alex's warm, familiar presence. He was still driving; he was all right. For now.

But when I opened my eyes, dread crashed through me again like a tide. There was no way that I could just stay here and wait for his return – absolutely no way.

My heart was beating fast. "So, um – thanks," I said to Seb, backing up a step. "I've got to go now."

His face was taut with concern. He touched my arm. "Willow—"

"I've got to go." I opened the door and stepped out into the corridor – and suddenly I was running for the garage as fast as I could, my sneakers pounding against the cement.

"Willow!" I heard Seb call.

I rounded a corner and collided with Sam. "Hey, whoa!" He grabbed me by the arms. "What's going on?"

"Let me go!" I tried to shake him off; he held on tighter.

"No way, not until you tell me what's happening!"

I was almost crying. "I've got to go after him! I've *got* to. Something's wrong, Sam, really wrong!"

Seb caught up just as Sam let go of me, frowning. "Yeah," Sam said, almost to himself. He rubbed a hand over his face. "Yeah, you're right. Okay, I'm coming too."

I hadn't expected this, and the relief was enormous. With two of us driving, we could make better time. "We've got to hurry," I said. Somehow I knew Alex wouldn't take many breaks, even though he hadn't slept.

Sam nodded. "Grab what you need. Meet me in the garage in fifteen minutes."

"I'm going too," put in Seb.

"No, you're not," Sam said curtly. "We can't *all* go; who's gonna run the goddamn base?"

Seb glanced at me, his muscles tense – and my fear multiplied as I realized that he wanted to be there for me. He was afraid of what might happen if we were too late.

"Seb, you've got to stay – you've got our classes to teach, and Liz can't do everything on her own," I said in a rush, thinking I'd say anything to keep him here – anything to keep from sensing his fear the whole long drive.

He started to protest and then stopped, his eyes scanning mine. "Yes, fine," he said tightly.

All at once I felt clammy with cold. "And, Sam, listen – tell Liz not to mention to Alex that we're coming when he checks in."

Sam nodded grimly. Alex would not be thrilled if he found out. He might even deliberately try to lose us.

Whatever his reasons for not wanting us there, they weren't going to magically disappear if he heard we were on our way.

"Fifteen minutes," Sam said again.

I was already jogging down the corridor. "Make it ten," I called back.

For the rest of that day and all through the night, Sam and I took turns driving. We took the shattered Highway 93 out of Nevada, then picked up I-40 east, slicing across Arizona to New Mexico. Without discussing it, we stuck to the main roads for speed – we'd take our chances with any Eden staff we met.

From the set of Sam's jaw and the tapping of his large, blunt fingers on the wheel, I knew he was as anxious as I was. Thankfully, he wasn't the type who needed to make conversation – I couldn't have handled small talk just then. We spoke only about the route or to ask if the other wanted a drink of water.

Every half-hour or so, I checked psychically on Alex, feeling briefly soothed by his energy. He'd stopped around six p.m. to sleep for a few hours; otherwise he was on the move, though Sam and I had closed the gap and were only about half an hour behind him now. When I drove I found myself edging the speedometer higher, desperate to catch up with him – to physically grab hold and refuse to let go if I had to, so that he couldn't do whatever he was planning alone.

We entered New Mexico just before midnight. Four hours later, Albuquerque Eden rose before us with its concrete and barbed wire – and its distant packs of circling angels, their wings silver in the moonlight.

It wasn't a sight I really wanted to see, just then.

The roads worsened again as we turned off and headed south. A few hours later the rising sun lit the rugged landscape that Alex loved – the endless desert, the bare, brown mountains. We were in the southern part of the state by then, with Sam at the wheel as I stared tensely at the highway, trying to remember the turn-off for his father's old camp. Finally I spotted the dirt road.

"Here," I said quickly. "We drove about twenty miles down this way – then Alex turned off directly into the desert."

Sam glanced at me. "Can you find it?"

I nodded. Even if I hadn't remembered the road, I sensed Alex so strongly now, leading me to him like a beacon.

My fingernails gouged into my palms. We had to get there in time – we *had* to. *Alex, I don't know what you're planning, but you can't do it. Please. You're my life, too.*

CHAPTER *Thirteen*

THE LAST TIME ALEX HAD made his way across the New Mexico desert, he'd been driving a stolen car: a boatlike thing from the eighties that had bucked and shivered across the sandy soil. He'd spent the entire journey expecting the thing to overheat – that, and being seriously distracted by Willow. They hadn't so much as kissed at that point; the physical tension between them had been almost painful. He could still see exactly how she'd looked as she'd asked him a question about the camp: her green eyes large, her blonde hair tied in an untidy knot at the back of her neck.

He wondered if she'd ever forgive him.

He pushed all thoughts of her away harshly. *Maybe Cully was delusional,* he thought as the 4 × 4 trundled over unmarked desert. *But if this is true, there's got to be at least a chance I'll survive – or I wouldn't even be doing it.*

He'd made the journey in good time, given the state of some of the roads. Only about thirty hours had passed since he'd left – and now, advancing through the desert, Alex could make out the place where he'd grown up: a cluster of white cement buildings wavering in the morning sun, with low mountains rising on the horizon behind them.

Nearing the chain-link fence with its razor coils flashing at the top, he did a quick scan. No sign of life. He could have figured that out anyway: one of the gates sagged limply on its hinges, with no vehicles in sight. As the sun burned down on the silent white buildings, Alex stopped the truck, eyes narrowing as he studied them. He took out his rifle just in case, swung the backpack over one shoulder, and got out.

Small brown lizards scuttled away as he walked to the gate. He squeezed through the gap and the chain link rattled. Another memory: Willow standing at this gate, fingers hooked loosely around a metal diamond as she looked back with that pixieish smile. *I'd just really like to see where you grew up.*

Do *not* think about her again.

Though it was late November, the heat streamed down as Alex crossed the enclosure. It was the only thing that still felt familiar. The camp's unnatural silence weighed on him as he made his way past the mess hall and the dorm he and his brother had shared with a dozen other AKs.

Ahead lay the plain, square house where his father – and then later Cully – had lived. A grey roof, no shutters or frills. When he was little, he thought all houses looked like this. The first time he saw homes with door knockers and welcome mats, he hadn't been able to stop staring.

Alex reached the door and scanned again, just to make sure. Nothing. The knob was sun-warm to the touch; it didn't give when he tried to turn it.

Feeling as if he were desecrating a tomb, Alex stepped back and pressed the rifle against his shoulder. A short burst of gunfire and rapid holes appeared, obliterating the lock. He kicked the door, and it swung open.

He stepped in and groped for the light switch out of habit, but nothing happened, of course; the generators weren't on. Then he stopped short. In the semi-gloom he could see an angel staring at him – dark, burning eyes, its giant wings outspread. Adrenalin gripped him until he realized what it was.

Oh Christ, Cully, he thought sadly.

The walls were covered with drawings of angels.

They crowded every available space – watching, beckoning to him. Alex turned and found another on the back of the door; bullet holes scorched through its wing. He traced his hand over it. Cully had drawn each feather individually.

What hit him most was the utter loneliness of the place. Cully, probably sick already by then, alone out here in the desert, drawing the beautiful creatures that had destroyed him. Alex dropped his hand. "I'm glad you're dead, Cull," he said in a low voice. "You're free now."

Enough. He had to do what he'd come for. Alex crossed to the table and propped his rifle against the worn wood. With a glance at the rickety chairs, he remembered how his father would angle one sideways and sit hunched for hours, glaring as he tried to bore his way through the ether with his consciousness.

Imagining himself doing the same, Alex grimaced. He crouched on his haunches instead and studied the air in front of him. What he'd told Willow hadn't been a complete lie: Martin's idea to defeat the angels did have to do with using a world's energy field.

Just not the one in this world.

Alex moved his awareness up through his chakras and kept it poised, hovering outside of himself. As he viewed the room from the ethereal level, his pulse skipped.

He straightened in a daze as he stared. Jesus. Cully had

nearly done it all right. Where there had once been nothing, there was now a slight wavering in the air facing him, like rippling water.

Relief and dread rushed through Alex. He mentally reached out and explored the wavering. It felt like a section of flimsy paper in the midst of solid plaster. Cully must have been so damn weak, to have come this close and then stopped.

Alex let out a breath. Okay, so…it was true, then. Instinctively, he knew what had to come next.

Slowly, he cautioned himself.

He focused his awareness as tightly as possible, until it was needle-thin. The sensation brought a rush of light-headedness; he ignored it. Tracing the needle carefully over the shimmering wall, back and forth, he found a tiny section that gave more than the rest. He pushed at it, but the wall felt elastic; the needle pressed harmlessly.

Fine – let's try this another way, he thought after a frustrating few minutes. He drew back and stabbed hard.

His awareness pierced the wall. Suddenly it felt like a hurricane was shaking the tiny needle. He gritted his teeth, hanging on for dear life. *Do it now or get out,* he told himself.

He steadied himself – and began to make the needle larger.

Muscles trembling, Alex sank to the ground, eyes closed as he strained. He could sense the pinpoint growing to the size of a tennis ball…a car tyre. With his fists clenched on his thighs, he felt a sudden release of resistance that sent him sprawling to the floor.

Breathing hard, he slowly rose again, groping at the table for support as he stared. There was a hole in the air. Through it, he could see another room. A plain white wall. Where the opening ended, so did Alex's view of the room; the outer wall was still seamlessly covered with angels.

Blood pounded at his brain. The two realities danced before him. He'd actually done it.

But so far he'd only manipulated energy on the ethereal level – for his father's plan to work, he had to be physically over there. And when something tangible passed through that hole… Alex's own voice came back to him: *It'd be suicide. Can you even imagine the burst of energy if he tried it? This whole place would blow sky-high.*

Alex's gaze flickered again to the walls around him. Cully must have thought surviving this was at least possible – but, Jesus, here Alex was, surrounded by hundreds of staring angel eyes. Had this place really been the work of a sane man?

He straightened his spine. Enough of this crap. This was what he'd come for, wasn't it? Millions of angels were feeding on humanity and would go on doing it for ever unless something stopped them – everything else paled in comparison. Everything. Even his own life.

Keeping his eyes on the opening, Alex picked up his backpack and put it on. His pistol was in the holster under his trousers; he reached for the rifle and hooked it over his shoulder, ducking his head under the strap.

Then he looked down at the woven bracelet on his wrist – and unable to stop himself, touched it briefly, remembering the night Willow had given it to him: the smell of her hair, the feel of her in his arms.

He let his hand fall. He shoved the table away with a single harsh screech and backed up to the opposite wall, facing the opening. The other room still waited. Alex squared his shoulders, not taking his eyes from it.

"Okay, let's do it," he muttered.

"There!" I said, sitting up straight and pointing.

It was just like I remembered: white buildings clustered in the desert. And oh, thank god: Alex's grey 4 × 4 was parked outside the gate. I let out a breath as we drew closer, rumbling over the rough terrain. Too relieved to smile, I closed my eyes to feel what Alex was feeling – and gasped as his heightened emotions slammed into me.

"No," I whispered, gripping the dashboard. "*Sam! Stop!*"

Sam screeched to a halt. Before he'd completely stopped, I flung open the door and scrambled out, running as hard as I could. *Alex, you can't go through with whatever this is – please, you won't survive it—*

As my feet beat over the sandy ground I could feel the coolness of tears on my face. Everything had slid into slow motion: a hawk circling above, the gate ahead of me as it grew larger.

"Alex!" I screamed. "*Alex!*"

Alex stood poised, his gaze fixed on the opening. Now that the time had come, he felt only an intense determination, all other thought banished. The angels watched from the walls as the strange room sat cloaked in shadow.

Now, he thought, and started to run.

He threw himself into the air at the last possible moment, meeting the opening head-on – and as he did, he thought he heard someone call his name.

The impact was like slamming into concrete.

The explosion screamed through him as the world erupted. The route between worlds vanished. Angels were shattering into pieces, flying up into the blue sky. Alex was falling, floating, being ripped apart.

Pain…oh Jesus, the pain.

Willow…I'm sorry, he thought.

It was the last thing he knew.

CHAPTER *Fourteen*

THE GROUND TREMBLED UNDER my feet as the entire centre of the camp exploded. With a roar that shook the earth, buildings went up in a wild fountain of flame, cement, and smoke, brilliant against the blue sky.

"*No!*" I screamed.

I'd been sensing Alex's rapid heartbeat – his near-certainty that he'd die. Now, for a brief, endless flash, his agony crushed me. Blown apart, wrenched into pieces – *so much pain—*

His heart gave a last weak beat…and then stopped.

Emptiness.

Before I could take it in, a wall of air slammed into me. I was knocked flat on my back, gasping for breath – dimly aware of rubble falling all around, thumping into the sand.

Muscular arms pinned me in place. "Keep down!" Sam yelled in my ear.

"Let go!" I cried, struggling wildly. "Let *go* of me!"

Somehow I got away and was running again, sprinting as fast as I could. It had all taken only seconds; now a terrible, chilly silence lay over everything. Debris lay scattered across the desert. A billowing cloud of dust and smoke rose from the camp.

The gate was half flattened, mowed down by flying shards of concrete. I scrambled over the barbed wire and lunged across the chain-link diamonds with a clatter.

"Alex!" I shouted as I ran into the enclosure. "*Alex!*"

Dust hit me, so thick I could barely see. Eyes streaming, I kept going, stumbling over the rubble-strewn pavement to the ruined centre of the camp, a scorched crater filled with debris and dust. Smoke drifted up into the sky.

Alex's father's house was gone. So were half a dozen buildings around it.

He could still be alive, I thought frantically, dropping into the hole. After the earthquakes, some of our AKs had survived for *days* trapped in collapsed buildings. Falling to my knees, I saw what looked like part of an angel's wing drawn on a chunk of concrete – I barely noticed it as I hefted it aside, and then the piece after that, and another.

"Alex!" I called. "Please, answer me!"

As I dug, I scanned desperately. His energy always came so quickly – as if our love were an arrow leading me straight to him. Now there was nothing. I kept scanning, shaking so hard I could barely think.

Nothing. And I'd known that already...because I'd felt him die.

My mind flinched from the knowledge. "*Alex!*" I yelled again, still digging feverishly, bloodying my fingers against the dusty shards of concrete.

Slow footsteps came from behind me – the sound of someone dropping down into the crater. Then I felt Sam's hand, warm and heavy on my shoulder.

His voice was ragged. "It's no use, darlin'."

"It is – it is!"

Sam crouched next to me. His eyes were red-rimmed. "Willow. Do a scan. The only ones still alive here are us."

I shook my head hard, not even pausing as I dug. "No. No. You're doing it wrong. He's alive – he has to be."

Then I saw it. My throat thickened, words leaving me. The piece of concrete I was holding slipped from my fingers, landing with a dull scraping noise. In a daze, I stretched across the wreckage to pick up what I'd seen.

Alex's shoe.

A small moan escaped me as I turned it over in my hands – realized distantly that I was trembling. A battered once-white sneaker, now covered in dust and a streak of blood. I'd seen him put it on just yesterday, leaning over as he sat on the bed, his dark hair falling across his forehead.

An ice pick stabbed at my temples. The sense of being blown apart – his warm life-energy coming to an end. Oh god, I'd actually *felt* it.

I'd felt it.

"*No!*" The word tore painfully from my throat. I clutched the shoe to myself, hunching over it as I began to rock.

Without speaking, Sam pulled me into his arms. I dropped the shoe and clutched blindly at him, gripping his T-shirt – my hands like claws as I started to sob against his chest, my body heaving.

"I know," he choked out, his strong arms tightening around me. "I know."

After a long time, Sam helped me up and got us both back to the truck.

"What was he even doing?" I whispered hoarsely, staring at the remains of the camp. The smoke had all dispersed now and the dust had settled, as if the ruins had lain undisturbed for centuries.

In the driver's seat, Sam scraped a hand over his jaw.

I could sense he was trying to keep control. "Aw, hell, I don't know." His voice broke. "From what you said, something to do with using the earth's energy field."

I was still holding Alex's shoe, my nails gouging into the leather. "Yes, but *what*? I wouldn't have thought that was even possible!"

"I guess it wasn't," Sam said flatly.

I stared at the shattered buildings. When I spoke again, my voice was thin. "We can't just...leave him here."

Sam rubbed his forehead, looking forty-three instead of twenty-three. "There may not – be much left," he said dully. "Anyway, it'd take us weeks to sift through all that. Unless…"

I shook my head woodenly. There was nothing left of Alex's essence to latch onto.

Sam took a breath. "You know, this is…not really a bad place for him to be. He loved it here, growing up. He told me. And I think his father and brother are buried nearby."

Any moment I'd wake up and find Alex in bed next to me, pulling me into his arms – his warm lips nuzzling at my neck. I shut my eyes hard. "Yeah, they are," I said finally.

Inside, I was screaming – wordless, anguished screams, over and over. Alex was only *nineteen*. We were supposed to have a whole long life together. It wasn't supposed to be that, instead, he'd felt forced to take some insane risk that he'd lied to me about.

Suddenly, I was shaking. What had it been? What had Alex thought was *this* important? Without thinking, I grounded myself and reached out for the earth's energy field. The chaotic power roared over me as I tried to grasp hold. My angel was huddled deep inside me, stunned with grief; I felt her struggle feebly as the ethereal storm battered at us.

"Willow?" said Sam.

The force was whistling past, yanking at my aura – threatening to rip it away. *Alex, what was it? Please, I've got to know!*

"Willow!" Sam was shaking me. "Get out of it!"

With a gasp, my connection with the energy field broke. When I opened my eyes again, my cheeks were freshly damp. "I don't know what he was doing," I whispered brokenly. "I don't know how to – to fix it."

Sam was glaring at me, his eyes still red. "Christ, if *that* wasn't a damn-fool thing to do! You think we want to lose you, too?"

I didn't answer. Whatever Alex's father's plan had been, it was gone.

So was Alex.

I saw again the angels, invading our world and becoming unlinked. Alex, putting on a brave face, despite thinking it was his fault. None of this would have happened otherwise – he'd still be alive now.

The thoughts hammered relentlessly at my skull. "I'm going to Denver," I said.

Sam turned his head and stared at me. "What for?" he asked after a pause, sounding wary.

"Because I have to find Raziel."

"Willow, please start making some sense pretty damn quick, 'cause you're freaking me out."

My knuckles were white against Alex's shoe. "This is all Raziel's fault. He's the one who unlinked the angels, the one who destroyed the Council and caused the earthquakes. Sam, don't you see? It's all *him* – everything bad that happens is *him*."

"Yeah, that's probably true," Sam said harshly. "So what are you gonna do? March into his Eden and demand an apology?"

"No. I'm going to make sure he never does it again."

Sam straightened and pulled the keys out of his jeans pocket. "You're in shock," he said shortly. "I'm gettin' you home."

All at once my voice was ringing through the cab. "*What* home? I am serious, Sam – I cannot just go back and do nothing! Alex is *dead*! *Dead,* don't you get it?"

"*Yes, I get it!*" he bellowed back. "What *you* don't get is that it would be goddamn suicide!"

"I am going to Denver," I said. "You can come, or not – I don't care."

Sam gripped my arms hard. "Listen to me," he growled. "If you want to go runnin' off to Denver, fine; I can't stop you. But you would be putting the entire team in danger, and probably killing yourself in the bargain. Do you think that's what Alex would want? Do you think he's watching from somewhere right now, sayin', *Yeah, go get him, Willow!*"

Something snapped in me. "I don't care what he'd want!" I screamed. "I can't just do nothing!"

The truck was suffocating me. Somehow I got the door open and collapsed out onto the desert ground. I wrapped my arms over my head as I struggled to breathe, and felt some small part of my mind try to detach itself from this pain – from the low, keening noise I was making; the way I was rocking in place, fingernails clutching my scalp, lungs clenched tight.

Alex.

Sam came and kneeled beside me. I felt his rough hand rest on my head. "I'll tell you what you're gonna do," he said. "Just what Alex said – keep on recruiting and training people. That's the only hope humanity's got now. We need you, Willow. You can run off and get yourself killed, but it won't accomplish a goddamn thing."

Eventually I managed to sit up, trembling. Sam gripped my hand, his blue eyes intense. "Alex loved you," he said in a low voice. "He never thought you were a quitter."

I couldn't speak. All I wanted was to confront my father – blow his halo into nothing and hope he felt just a fraction of the pain that Alex had felt, that I was feeling.

But I knew Sam was right. And as I gazed at the ruins where Alex lay, something inside me hardened. I would fight the angels until the day I died, if that's what it took.

"I'm not a quitter," I said finally.

Sam put his arm around me; I leaned against his broad chest. He held me silently for a few moments, then kissed my head. "Come on, angel chick," he whispered. "There's nothing more we can do here."

We got back into the truck, and Sam started the engine. I felt as if I were made of glass – one wrong move, and I'd break. As Sam glanced back at the wreckage, his face was set in stone.

"Goodbye, bud," he murmured. "Hope to hell it was worth it."

I couldn't say goodbye to Alex. Not now, not ever. But I turned and watched the shattered remains of the camp grow smaller in the rear window, along with the sun sparkling off Alex's truck.

I watched until long after they'd vanished, and the only things still visible were the low mountains on the horizon, etched against the sky.

CHAPTER *Fifteen*

SAM CALLED AHEAD WITH THE news. When we got back to the base, Seb and Liz were in the garage, waiting. All my senses were huddled inward, but I could still feel Seb's concern – how desperate he was to help me.

"Willow…" he began hoarsely as I got out of the truck.

Deep down, I winced; I turned away without speaking. Liz had started crying as she stepped towards me. I returned her hug like an automaton.

"Come on, let's get you to bed," she said at last, wiping her cheeks. "You look exhausted."

Sam was probably a lot more exhausted than I was; he'd

refused to let me help drive on the way back. He'd been right, I guess. "I don't need help," I said faintly. "Thanks anyway."

I had to be by myself when I went into the bedroom I'd shared with Alex – it wasn't something I could face with anyone else present. Liz seemed to get it. "I'll walk you there, at least," she said.

She put her arm around me and led me out of the garage, leaving Seb standing wordlessly behind us.

Once alone in my room, silence enveloped me like a shroud. For a long time, I just lay on the bed, hugging myself. Finally, feeling like it was something I needed to do, I got up and put Alex's shoe deep in our closet, laying it gently on the floor.

When I straightened, I stood gazing at his clothes. I touched a shirt – then dropped my hand. It was freshly laundered, with nothing of him in it. But still draped over our chair was the black long-sleeved T-shirt he'd had on before he left. I picked it up and buried my face in it, breathing it in.

Alex. The smell of his shampoo, mixed with the faint odour of sweat and his own scent – warm and familiar, slightly spicy. Still holding the shirt, I sank down onto the bed again.

The room felt so empty. As I watched, the digital clock

changed from 22:07 to 22:08. Then 22:09, 22:10.

I stared, transfixed. Someone knocked on the door; I looked up blearily. "Yes?"

Liz poked her head in. "Hey," she said, edging in and shutting the door. "I know you said you wanted to be alone, but…"

I didn't reply. She hesitated, then sat down beside me on the unmade bed. The last time I'd slept between these sheets, Alex had been here. I'd been planning on washing them; now I knew that nothing on earth could make me wash away whatever essence of him still clung to the fabric.

"Willow?"

I looked up, suddenly aware that several minutes had passed. Liz's eyes were concerned. She touched my hair. "Why don't I stay here with you tonight?"

I didn't want her here – not in the bed I'd shared with Alex. I ran a hand over the shirt in my hands. "No, that's all right."

"I don't like leaving you, though."

I felt too tired to answer, unable to summon up any interest in whether she liked it or not.

22:15. 22:16. "It never stops," I murmured. Liz's eyebrows came together. I gave a dull shrug. "The clock."

"Oh." She looked blankly at it, her face wan. Finally she wrapped her arms around herself. "I still just…can't believe it."

Me neither. Pain wrenched through me. *Trust me,* he'd said. And so I had. I hadn't gone probing in his thoughts, because he'd asked me not to. What if I'd ignored him and done it anyway – could I have stopped this?

My gaze fell on the desk, to the photo of myself as a child peering up through the branches of a willow tree. And I realized that I didn't have any photos of Alex, not a single one. Why didn't I?

"He's really dead," I said finally. My voice was small, defeated. Liz's face crumpled; she pressed her head against my shoulder.

I hugged Alex's shirt as I stared at the photo – my broad smile and sparkling eyes. It was like looking at someone from a different planet.

I couldn't imagine ever being that happy again.

We held a memorial service a week later.

Liz and I planned it together: some of Alex's favourite music and people sharing stories about him. I dressed up for it, wearing the black skirt I'd tried on in Liz's room with a plain black top, and I told the story of how Alex and I had first met. I told it pretty well, I guess. People were smiling through their tears as I described how he'd barked at me, ordering me into his car.

It was so surreal. I felt like an actress playing a role:

the grieving girlfriend. I almost started laughing; I kept wanting to say, *Why are you all pretending? He can't really be dead.* And then I'd remember the feeling of the explosion thundering through me, and the truth would punch me in the stomach again.

Sam spoke, then Kara, who told a story about when Alex was fourteen. Her bruises were fading, and she'd cut her hair again; it lay sleekly against her head. As our eyes met briefly, I could sense the depth of her sadness. The fact that she'd once kissed Alex seemed so unimportant now. If I could have him back, I wouldn't care if they had a red-hot affair, as long as I could hold him again.

The one good thing was that it turned out a few of the girls had taken pictures of Alex on their phones when he wasn't looking. They printed them up on the computer in the office and gave them to me after the service. My gaze went instantly to one of Alex instructing the team: he'd been caught with a grin lighting up his strong-featured face, one eyebrow quirked.

I stared down at it. Alex. His tousled dark hair, his blue-grey eyes. And if I could look under his shirtsleeve, I'd see his AK tattoo…be able to run my hand up the firm warmth of his skin…

The girls looked at each other nervously. "Was it okay…that we did that?" faltered Chloe. "We just thought…"

I came back with a jolt. "Yes, it was okay," I said, wiping my eyes. "Very, very okay."

Soon after, Liz came over and squeezed my arm. "Are you all right?" she whispered. "You look like maybe you've had enough."

She was right; the thought of having to endure one more tearful condolence was torture. "Yeah, I have," I admitted faintly. "Can we get out of here?"

The corridor was silent as we left the rec room behind. "Back to your room?" Liz asked.

I shuddered, imagining its too-quiet emptiness. "No – not there."

"Here, then." She swung open the door to the library. My shoulders relaxed a fraction as I sank down at a table. It was quiet in here too, but that was okay – it was supposed to be quiet in a library.

"Thanks." I propped myself on my elbows, rubbing my forehead; my brown hair fell forward a little. I'd worn it loose, because Alex had always preferred it that way.

Liz's face was anxious as she sat across from me. I knew this wasn't easy for her – she wasn't exactly a nurturer – but she was trying. "Do you want anything? I could get you some tea."

"No, I'm fine." Fine – right. Neither of us said the obvious. "I just want to…not think for a while."

She started to reply, then broke off as the door opened

again. Seb came in and stood awkwardly, wearing trousers and a blue shirt. He'd shaved, I saw. His eyes were fixed on mine; there were dark circles under them.

"Willow, can we talk?" he asked.

I stared at him, wondering what there was to talk about.

"Please," he added.

Liz glanced at me; finally I shrugged. "Yes, okay."

She pushed her chair back. "Okay, well – I'll leave you alone, then." She picked up the photos of Alex. "I'll put these in your room for you."

It's okay, don't bother going, I almost said, but she'd already left, closing the door behind her. Seb sank down in her empty chair.

"Willow…oh, *dios mío,* I am so sorry." He scraped his hair back; I could see the tension in his fingers. "I wasn't sure if – if you wanted me, so I've stayed away, but I've been thinking about you every second, *querida.*"

And I hadn't thought about him at all. It was almost funny. I let out a breath. "Thanks. I know you're sorry."

Seb swallowed. "Tell me how I can help you." He started to stretch a hand towards me, then seemed to think better of it. "Willow, I know things have been strange between us, but – please let me be your brother again."

"*Let* you?" I stared at him in disbelief, not sure whether to laugh or cry. "Seb, I wasn't the one who drew away and started ignoring you."

"I know. I'm sorry," he said. "I was stupid, and wrong. I just…couldn't deal with being around you."

His hand lay clenched on the table. Looking at it, the night of the party came hurtling back: the way he'd buried his hands in Meghan's hair and kissed her. And when he had, a brief, sharp emotion had stirred. I'd told myself that I'd just been surprised…but that hadn't been it, had it?

The sudden guilt felt like it might cripple me.

"I see," I said, my voice emotionless. "But now that Alex is gone, you *can* deal with being around me?"

He flinched. "That's not what I meant," he said softly. "He was my friend, Willow."

I crossed my arms tight over my chest. "So…what? You want to look out for your friend's girlfriend, now that he's dead? That's nice of you. I'm sure Alex would appreciate it."

"Why are you—" Seb broke off in frustration. "I want to look out for you, yes. It's nothing to do with Alex; it's just what we are to each other – the link we share. Nothing ever changes that, Willow." His mouth twisted. "Not for me, at least."

"Right. And what does Meghan think about that?"

"It's not her business."

"She's your girlfriend. I think maybe it is."

Seb shook his head. "I didn't come in here to argue with

you, *querida*. I'm sorry; I'm just making things worse." He started to get up. "If you need me, I'm here. That's all I wanted to say."

"Oh, wait, so you're not going away after all?" I said, my voice so innocent that it was snide.

Seb stood very still as he regarded me, his jaw tight. "No. I am not going away," he said.

I stood up too, my head throbbing – and all I could see was the camp, blown to pieces so thoroughly that I didn't even know if there was anything of Alex left. How could I have been jealous over Seb for even a second, *how*?

I gripped the table edge; my voice shook. "If you're staying because of me – then don't bother, okay? Because I'm sorry, but the answer is no. You can't be my brother again. Not now, not ever."

I lay on my bed without moving, still fully dressed. Hours had passed – my brain felt dried out, numb. Propped onto the pillow next to me was one of the photos of Alex. I'd been staring at it for a long time.

His slow, lazy grin. The way his blue-grey eyes had lit up whenever he'd seen me. Even our occasional arguments were moments I'd give anything to have back now.

You promised, I thought bleakly. *Alex, you promised that you wouldn't put yourself in danger again without telling me.*

Were they just words? How could I love him so much and be so furious with him?

How could I be furious with him at all when he was dead? I shuddered and curled into the fetal position. Slowly, I traced my finger over his mouth in the photo.

"What happened?" I whispered.

Trying to take control of the world's energy field – it was just insane. Had he wanted to die? I rubbed my temples with cold fingers. No. Alex wouldn't do that, no matter what. But he'd done something else, hadn't he?

That emotion I'd sensed when he kissed me before he left: I hadn't been able to place it then, but I could now. It had been goodbye. Not *Goodbye, I'll see you soon* – something far more final. He'd known exactly what he was doing, and what the odds were.

And he'd told me to trust him and left anyway.

With a wordless cry, I wrenched myself up and hurled the pillow across the room. It smashed into the desk, sending the lamp clattering to the floor.

"*How could you do this to me?*" I screamed. "I wouldn't have you back now for *anything*. You lied to me; you broke your promise!"

The black shirt lay nearby; I screwed it into a ball and threw it too. It landed in a puddle of fabric. Not nearly enough. I lunged off the bed after it, started to tear it in half, and then reality hit me: *This is almost all I have left of him* – and I began to cry instead.

"I'm sorry," I sobbed, clutching the shirt to my chest. "Oh, god, Alex, of course I'd have you back – I want to die without you…"

I lay on the rough carpet and cried until there were no tears left. Finally I sat up and slumped wearily against the desk. My eyes felt gritty, swollen – my hair wild and tangled. Around me, the room was silent, the lamp still lying where it had fallen.

It would stay there until I picked it up: I lived alone now. I could rage, scream, cry all I wanted – Alex would never hear me, and he'd never come back.

CHAPTER *Sixteen*

RAZIEL GLIDED OVER THE RUINS of Chicago, his winged shadow growing larger and then smaller as mounds of rubble rose and fell beneath him. The remains of Navy Pier lay half submerged in Lake Michigan, the girders of a Ferris wheel rusting where they reared up from the water. As Raziel circled it, lyrics from the old human song went through his head: *Chicago, that toddling town...*

Scattered through the wreckage were campfires and makeshift shelters. Raziel took in a shattered Dunkin' Donuts: inside were camp beds, stacks of canned food. He'd never understood why some humans were so determined to stay in the ruins of the destroyed cities, but their energy tended to be quite delicious.

Cruising over a few people fishing with makeshift poles, he chose a man with a ponytail and an aura of vibrant blue. Scant moments later, the fishing pole had been dropped and the man was gaping up at him.

"Keith, you okay?" said someone.

Keith blinked as Raziel, sated, finally withdrew. "The angels love us," he murmured, and then began shouting, scrambling up the debris-covered bank. "Guys, you guys! We've all been wrong! We need to go to an Eden and let them take care of us—"

Raziel was already soaring away. Inspecting a new Eden being built in Joliet had given him the chance to come here and indulge, to take his mind off things: there was nothing like the energy of a free thinker. Even so, he had plans to clamp down soon on the humans who resisted his Edens – their failure to comply irked him.

Failure to comply brought Kara Mendez to mind; he scowled as the half-finished walls of the new Eden came into view.

When it had come time to transport Kara to Salt Lake Eden, Raziel had, just as he'd planned, engineered things so that she could make a run for it. For if Willow and the others *were* still alive, why not let feisty little Kara lead him to them? If they weren't, it would be simple to recapture Kara and present her to the Salt Lake hordes after all.

Except that it *hadn't* been simple – because her microchip hadn't worked.

He'd been in his Denver office when he got the news. "It *what*?" he'd asked, stunned.

"It, um…appears to have malfunctioned," repeated the miserable lackey at the other end. "She got away like you told us, but now there's no trace of her."

"How?" Raziel had demanded from between clenched teeth.

"We don't know. I promise, sir, we've had no problems at all with these chips before. It's as if she was…was *protected* from it somehow—"

He'd hung up, uninterested in pointless excuses. And scarcely an hour later, he'd authorized for that particular lackey to enter the general feeding pool. No point sheltering an imbecile.

That had been over six months ago; no sign of Kara since. Not technically a defeat – hardly anyone knew he'd had her – but it grated.

More than grated, it was unnerving: far too reminiscent of other things that seemed to be slipping from his control. There were definitely murmurs of dissent now from the other angels. Not many, perhaps, but enough to bother him, enough for him to keep Bascal's force well-maintained and ready to defend his empire at a moment's notice. Yet he did not want this to happen. For if there was civil war, then what exactly would he be left in charge of?

It won't happen – they wouldn't be that stupid, Raziel told himself, and wished he believed it. He glided into the high, peaked roof of the newly completed church and changed back to his human self. He was now in a luxurious apartment of muted blues and golds, with an office adjacent. In every Eden, they completed the church first, with special quarters for him.

He went to the bathroom and splashed water on his face. He studied himself.

Seven months after the Separation, he was finally getting used to the silence inside his head. But some angels had refused to try – the loss of their psychic connection on top of the Council members' deaths had apparently been too much.

Raziel had seen footage of one of the now-infamous "final parties": a group of over twenty angels, at first simply enjoying a lavish gathering. Then they'd all stood in a circle, their shining wings touching, and one by one had stated their names:

I am Vardan. I cannot live this way.

I am Dascar. I cannot live this way.

And at a given signal, each angel had taken a knife and reached for the halo of the angel next to them.

There'd been dozens of these suicide parties; maybe more that Raziel hadn't heard about. *Cowards,* he thought, his lip curling. He should have left them in the angels' world to rot along with the dissenters – see how they felt about being separated when they realized they were slowly dying along with the ether. They'd have been howling before he even closed the gate, just like the abandoned angels who'd opposed him had surely done.

He strode restlessly to the living room. The view featured cranes and bulldozers. No other angels yet – most stayed strictly to the completed Edens, still fearful to venture out unless in groups. When they weren't feeding, many spent their time huddled together, talking and talking – fervently sharing their every thought in an attempt to recreate psychic closeness.

"A little ironic, isn't it?" he'd snapped at Therese when he'd discovered her in one of these sessions. "Before, we spent all our time trying to *hide* our thoughts from each other."

Therese was beautiful, as all angels were, but now her eyes looked tormented. "I know you understand, Raziel… Don't act like you don't," she whispered. "You're as much an angel as any of us. Even if you pretend not to be."

"I pretend nothing – and I'm a better angel than you," he'd replied coldly. "At least I have enough pride not to wallow in this like a pig in muck."

The demoralized angels were bad enough; the ones who muttered against him – who gathered in small groups that went silent when he appeared, their eyes hard and secretive – were even worse. Raziel had new, grudging respect for the human leaders of old; how had anyone ever managed to stay in power, not having *any* idea what those around them were thinking? Without knowing who to trust?

His cellphone went off: Lauren. "Yes?" he answered tersely.

Though Lauren had lasted longer than any of his other human girls, her voice was still weaker than it used to be. "Raziel, someone named Gallad called. There's trouble in Mexico City."

He frowned. "What kind of trouble?"

"I'm not sure; it has to do with that Eden they built in Teotihuacán. He said to tell you they've found six more people like – wait, I wrote down the name." There was a pause; Raziel scowled out the window, tapping his fingers. Lauren came back.

"Like Kara Mendez," she said.

Raziel stiffened. *Mexico City. Kara was there. So was Willow.* The puzzle pieces made no sense but seemed darkly ominous.

"I'm on my way home now – call Gallad back and tell him I'll contact him very soon," Raziel ordered. The only phone network currently linked to Mexico was in Denver.

The main roads between Illinois and Colorado were new and smooth; he made the trip as quickly as possible, blasting Prokofiev all the way – his own trick for combating the inner silence. When he entered his penthouse, a sunset was touching the Rockies with fire. Lauren stood waiting, her lovely face tired but relieved.

"Oh, good, you're back," she murmured, wrapping him in a hug.

As Raziel returned it, he was disturbed to realize how natural her body felt against his – *her* body, not just any human woman's. He'd gotten far too used to Lauren.

He stepped away. "Get me the phone," he ordered.

A brief conversation later, he was no more enlightened. Near the remains of Mexico City, an Eden had been built around ancient Aztec ruins, its residents the survivors from the Mexico City quake. Gallad had moved down there some months ago – one of the few angels who knew about Kara Mendez.

"And you're sure they're like Mendez?" Raziel demanded, pacing the living room.

"Well, they're nowhere near as stoic, but they can't be fed from and don't seem affected by our touch," said Gallad, sounding uncharacteristically shaken. "I guess we can't really know if they're resistant to being read psychically, though – since *that* particular angelic skill is so feeble now."

Raziel ignored the implied criticism. "They haven't just been marshalled somehow?"

"No, it's more than that. It's not just that they're unpalatable; they *can't* be fed from. It's as if we're forcibly expelled when we try."

Just like Kara indeed. Feeling a stirring of something almost like fear, Raziel stared out at the last sliver of sun. "Who are they, anyway? Did they have any connection with the Angel Killers?"

"Not as far as we can tell. A lot of them are students; they're all fairly young. Plus there's a store clerk, a waiter – no one special."

"All right, I want this kept as quiet as possible," Raziel said finally. "Keep them isolated and study them. Figure out what's going on, do you hear me?"

"We'll try," said Gallad. "But, Raziel, what if this doesn't stop?"

"What do you mean?" he said sharply.

"You know what things are like in the angel community now. If our very food starts turning against us, so that we can't survive here..." Raziel could almost see Gallad's uneasy shrug. "It would be like...a judgement."

"Don't be ridiculous," hissed Raziel. "A judgement from *whom*? We are the only gods in this world, Gallad – and don't you forget it. Keep the humans isolated, and do away with them if studying doesn't prove useful."

"All right," Gallad said after a pause. "I hope you're right."

"Ah, little Miranda…you're beautiful, you know. Even when the confusion is all that's left, you'll still be beautiful…"

In the dimly lit room, Raziel opened his eyes and held back a curse at his own remembered words, echoing in his head. He was sleeping less and less now – and though he hated admitting it to himself, he knew this was why: to avoid the dream that still haunted him.

Damn it, Miranda was *dead* – why was this happening? He'd never cared in the least before what he'd done to her; she'd loved every second. Nor did he care now, except that the vivid dreams of the two of them under the willow tree felt as if she were seeking revenge from the grave.

Raziel swallowed, realizing that this was not all. If he checked the earth's energy field, he'd like as not also pick up that vague sense again of something unaware, yet powerful.

I'm going mad, he thought. He sat up, his fists tight. Lauren lay asleep beside him; for a moment he'd forgotten all about her. Now his eyes narrowed as he took her in. Though he had two other girls living with him – both stunning – he'd given in to the urge to just have Lauren that night. She was familiar, comforting.

His favourite.

Lauren stirred drowsily and opened her eyes. "Is everything all right?" she whispered.

Seeing again Miranda's uplifted face and vivid green eyes, Raziel scowled. *No, it isn't,* he told himself. Becoming too attached to any one human was a mistake. And *this,* at least, he could control.

He flung back the covers and crossed to the dresser, where his cellphone was; he clicked a number on speed dial. "I need an A1 removed from my apartment immediately – she's being demoted to A2," he said. Lauren gasped and sat straight up; her brown eyes locked on Raziel's as he continued: "Yes, a replacement would be good, thanks – maybe a redhead this time."

He hung up. Lauren had begun to cry. "Raziel, what did I do wrong?"

His fleeting urge to comfort her was proof that this had been long overdue. "Nothing. Everything," he said, and strode from the room.

CHAPTER *Seventeen*

FOR MONTHS I'D WAKE UP in the morning and not remember. I'd stretch my arm across the bed, drowsily looking for Alex, and touch only empty sheets. Then the truth would come back, crushing me under its weight.

Every morning for months, without fail.

I'd get up. Take a shower. Get dressed. *See, I'm functioning just like a normal person.* After a while I reached Advanced Normality and even managed to smile occasionally – though it never quite reached my eyes. People were nice; they always asked about me. *How are you doing, Willow?*

Are you all right? Over and over, until the words pounded at my skull.

No. I'm not all right.

As more months passed, I finally stopped expecting to feel Alex next to me when I woke up. Now his death was the first thing that hit me, even before conscious thought: a dark, cold emptiness, as if something had gnawed away at my insides.

There wasn't a moment of the day when I didn't miss him. I missed him in the morning, kissing me awake. I missed eating meals with him. Missed talking to him at night; seeing him walk around the bedroom wearing only a towel. His jeans lying in a heap on the floor, and the way his hair had stuck up in all directions when he first woke up.

I missed making love with him. So much that it ached.

People kept telling me it got better with time. I hated hearing that – as if *time* could magically erase what I was feeling. Finally, though, they stopped saying it. And I realized that the "time" they kept talking about had passed, and I was supposed to be over Alex by now.

Meanwhile, I kept working.

Things at the base were busier than ever. I immersed myself, tried to drown myself in activity. Destroying the angels had never seemed so important – never.

The first simulation we ran without Alex was a disaster. People were all over the place, shooting at anything that moved. Sam did his best to give direction afterwards, but he was no Alex. Gradually, though, people started settling down and getting used to Sam…and he got more used to being in charge. He began turning into a good, solid leader.

We started recruiting again, venturing into the dark towns to convince people to join us. It was tricky work; you had to be so careful who you chose to speak to. And while we brought in tiny handfuls of new AKs and trained our troops with enough skills to maybe, perhaps, keep them alive…Raziel kept gleefully announcing new Edens.

Knoxville Eden. Duluth Eden. San Antonio Eden.

Whenever I heard him urge everyone "still huddling in the cold and dark" to come to an Eden and be safe, I wanted to hit something. Safe. Right. And when they'd drained you dry, they'd just shove you in a warehouse.

The Voice of Freedom kept broadcasting too. Whoever it was had guessed a lot – they always stressed the need to break away if the angels linked with you and to carry a weapon at all times.

"*The Angel Killers were our saviours, not our enemies,*" said the husky voice. "*Go for the halo, like they did. Do anything you can to get away if you're attacked.*"

Sometimes people in dark towns had actually heard the

Voice – and it paved the way for them to listen to us. When that happened, I silently thanked the mysterious broadcaster. We were on the same team, even if we'd never met.

Sam and I spent countless hours together going over Alex's plans – and also, I guess, because of what we'd been through together. Usually he was as predictable as the tides – but once, as we were discussing what set to build next, I glanced up to find him studying me with a frown.

"Don't you ever think about anything except fighting the angels any more?" he asked suddenly.

I froze, the pen I'd been taking notes with locked in my grip. "What are you talking about?"

Sam's blue gaze raked over me. His voice was harsh. "I'm talkin' about the fact that it'd be kind of nice to see you smile again, angel chick. It's been six months, you know that? And you're still just…gone."

What's there to smile about? I nearly said. I looked down at the piece of paper I'd been writing on. Of course I knew it had been six months. I knew it down to the day, the hour. Almost the second.

"I smile," I said finally. My voice was dead. "And we're not exactly down here to have fun, remember?"

I could sense Sam's frustration that his physical strength couldn't fix this – knew how much he wanted to argue, to shout me down and force me to snap out of it. Instead he hesitated…and then reached over and awkwardly squeezed my hand.

He didn't mention it again.

Seb stayed on at the base, despite what I'd said to him. I noticed him and Meghan together sometimes – once in the rec room late at night, on a sofa in a dim corner. Seb was holding Meghan in his arms with her back against his chest, his curly head bowed against her neck. As I watched she reached up to stroke his shoulder, her love for him so clear that I felt like an intruder.

I left quickly, before they noticed I was there. To my shame, jealousy was prickling at me again – not of Meghan this time, but of both of them, for the simple fact that they could hold each other.

Great, I thought, wiping my eyes as I reached my room. Was I going to turn into some bitter old crone now, who hated seeing anyone happy? I undressed mechanically and crawled into bed – and without thinking, I reached out to my mother. It had become such a habit since Alex died. Sometimes I spent hours now curled up in the feel of her, telling her things in my mind.

Mom, this hurts so much, I thought bleakly, hugging myself. *I'd give anything if I could just hold him one more time.* But I knew she'd never answer, no matter how much

I needed her to. Neither would Alex.

As I finally drifted into an exhausted sleep, I thought, *Seb had better realize how lucky he is.*

At least we only taught one class together now – I'd told him I thought it would be more efficient if we taught separately. His mouth had twisted wryly at that, as if there was some joke I wasn't in on. "Fine, *querida* – whatever you want."

The way he said "*querida*" didn't sound like an endearment any more. I didn't care; I was just relieved to not have to see him as much – to not be reminded of my moment of jealousy on the dance floor. Whenever I did see him, we were always very polite…and his hazel eyes remained distant.

Kara had stayed on too. She was quieter than she used to be – fiercer. She helped out with simulations and in the firing range, but kept to herself. Her body was slimly muscular again, her face as exotically beautiful as before. Half the guys in the place had crushes on her. Not that any of them dared to get close.

The two of us were never going to be friends. She didn't like me, and it was mutual. But we managed to work together civilly enough – and I had the feeling that we were trying to get along for Alex's sake.

The only time she showed any vulnerability was once in the war room. I'd gone in to update the map of known

Edens but stopped short when I saw her: she was sitting at the table with a fist against her mouth, regarding the map with a hopeless expression.

She straightened. "Oh. It's you."

"Yeah, I just…" I cleared my throat. I went over to the map and started putting in new pins by way of explanation.

Saratoga Eden. Eugene Eden. Toledo Eden.

My neck prickled and I turned. Kara sat motionless, her gaze still locked on the map. Suddenly she rose and came over. She fiddled with the pin for Austin Eden as if she'd love to pull it out but didn't quite have the nerve.

"This is so stupid," she said in a low voice. "I just can't seem to leave it behind. I mean, look."

She drew out a slim wallet from her jeans pocket and flipped it open. I stared. Inside was an ID card showing the familiar image of a gleaming angel with wings outspread. In the centre was a photo of Kara's face. *Mia Sanchez, resident of Austin Eden,* said the flowing script.

"You'd think I'd never want to *see* the damn thing again." She shoved it back in her pocket. "But I can't throw it away. It's like it's a part of me…" She trailed off, staring at the flag. Her eyes were almost fearful.

I knew that later she was going to hate that she'd confided in me. I licked my lips. "You've, um…heard the latest, I guess. About the army starting to forcibly relocate entire dark towns to the Edens."

Her gaze snapped to mine. Her voice quavered. "Yeah. 'For their own safety'. Your old man's all heart, Willow."

She turned and left. I let out a breath as the door closed – and knew I wasn't the only one haunted by memories.

Even so, my "normal" act must have been getting better as time passed. One day in early summer, one of our new recruits fell into step beside me as I walked down the corridor.

"Hey," he said with a grin, holding out his hand. "I'm Grant – one of your students. I've only been here a couple of days."

I nodded, bemused, as we shook. "I know." About my age, floppy brown hair. If he'd gone to Pawntucket High, he'd have been one of the popular guys on the basketball team.

Our footsteps echoed as he walked beside me. Grant cleared his throat. "So, I'm pretty intrigued by this half-angel stuff. Are you really the only one?"

I glanced at him, my forehead furrowed. "No. There's Seb too. You've met him."

"Oh – yeah. No, I meant the only girl half-angel."

"I guess. No one really knows."

"Cool," he said, nodding slowly. "That must be amazing, to be so…unique."

I shrugged and walked faster, a little unsettled by the way his gaze stayed on me. He caught up with me easily;

this time his grin had an embarrassed tinge. "I'm not doing too great, am I? Should I start over and try to be more suave this time?"

I stopped in my tracks. "What?" I said stupidly.

Grant looked confused. "Sorry, I didn't mean...I just think you're really pretty, and I'd like to get to know you better, that's all. You're not already with someone, are you? I hadn't noticed you hanging out with anybody, so I thought..."

He trailed off when he saw the expression on my face. My throat had gone dry. *No, I'm not with someone.* I couldn't say the words – wouldn't have said them for anything. I reached up and touched my crystal pendant, gripping it hard.

"I'm sorry – I've got to go," I said roughly.

In August we sent out our first groups of AKs.

Over fifty drove away in trucks bristling with supplies, honking jubilantly as they went. I watched with grim pride, praying that they could get camps established and start sniping at the angels without being caught. That had been Alex's main concern, I knew.

I tried not to worry about it and plunged back into work. *We will destroy them,* I kept telling myself.

"How are you doing?" asked Liz. We were sitting in a

corner of the busy rec room, drinking terrible instant coffee.

I gave a tired shrug. "A little on edge since the teams left, I guess." We'd known we wouldn't hear from them; it was still unnerving as the days passed.

Liz hesitated. "Me too, but…that's not what I meant."

Hardly anyone asked me any more. Alex had been dead since *November*, so obviously I was over him, right? I looked down, twisting my coffee mug on the table.

"I don't know," I admitted. "The first few months were complete hell. Now I keep thinking that maybe I'm not doing too badly…and then it all hits me again, and it's even worse than before." I stared down at the battered white mug; finally I sighed and pushed it away.

"I miss him, Liz," I whispered. "I miss him so much."

"I know," she said softly.

For a while, neither of us spoke. Then Liz glanced up; following her gaze, I saw Meghan leaving the room. Seb had appeared in the doorway at the same time – and for a second neither seemed to know what to do. Finally Meghan sort of nodded and went past, not really looking at him.

"What's up with them?" I asked.

Liz's head whipped around as she stared at me. "Are you kidding?" she asked after a pause. "Willow, they've broken up."

"What? Since when?" I looked back at Seb; he stood talking with a group of guys. His stubbled face had that neutral look I knew so well.

Liz shook her head. "I don't know, a few weeks ago? Seriously, how can you not know this? You and Seb teach a class together!"

"Yes, but we don't..." I frowned, casting my mind back. When had I seen Seb and Meghan curled up on the sofa together? Hadn't that been just recently? No, I realized, not really. Maybe three or four months ago. And now that I thought about it, Seb had been different lately – quiet, moody. The charming Seb who flirted with all the girls was long gone.

"We don't talk much," I finished lamely.

Liz and I went quiet as Seb came over. "Willow, can I speak to you?" he asked, his voice flat. "We need to decide about our classes."

Our classes had had uneven numbers since the teams left; with more new recruits coming in, we needed to decide who was doing what. Seb had been trying to corner me about it for a couple of weeks – and suddenly I had a feeling I knew why.

I nodded, my thoughts still tumbling. "Yeah, fine. Let's go into the office; we can use the computer."

As we headed down the hallway, for the first time in a long time I was aware of just how heavy the silence felt between us. I glanced at Seb. His profile looked set in stone.

In the office, I sat down at the desk and brought up the student lists on the screen. "Do you want to pull up a chair?" I asked.

Seb rolled over a spare office chair, and I moved my own aside to make room. Once our two auras would have mingled companionably; now each was drawn in against our bodies, only touching at the edges where there was no choice. Sitting this close, though, I could smell Seb's clean, woodsy scent. It brought back so many memories of being his friend – of talking for hours. A faint wistfulness stirred through me.

Seb pulled some notes from his back pocket. His handwriting was small and precise, the words a mix of Spanish and English.

"What about the first morning class?" he said, impatiently pushing the chestnut curls off his forehead. "I think Heather and Lisa should be in yours – they don't seem to be getting it with me; they always go so far, but no further."

"Fine." I cut and pasted their names from one list to the other. "Could you take Richard, though? I think he might do better having a guy for a teacher."

We made our way through the student lists, our exchanges completely impersonal. For so many months, this had been exactly what I wanted. Now I found myself wondering if avoiding Seb had become only a habit. *Maybe,* I thought tiredly. It didn't really matter – I couldn't see things ever being the same between us after so long.

On the list for Seb's afternoon advanced class, Meghan's name seemed more brightly lit than the others. I had to bite my tongue not to ask. Finally, frowning down at the paper in his hand, Seb said, "And I think Meghan might be happier with you."

I moved her without comment. But remembering the two of them on the sofa together, anger stirred. He'd had something really good with her; it was obvious. Why hadn't he tried harder?

The thought made me coldly furious for some reason. "So maybe you and Meghan should have left here together after all," I said, still looking at the screen as I typed.

Seb had never had any problem filling in the blanks. His head snapped up, and though his hazel eyes stayed expressionless, the gold flecks in them suddenly seemed to glitter. He folded up the paper and shoved it in his jeans pocket.

"Let me tell you something," he said as he stood up. "I did not stay here because of *you.* I stayed because I promised Alex. If I hadn't, then I would have left months ago, and to hell with this place. And, yes, who knows –

maybe things would have worked out with Meghan then. Is there anything else you'd like to discuss?"

I was already regretting, deeply, that I'd said anything. "I'm sorry," I said. "It's none of my business."

"No, it isn't," said Seb, and something shrank inside of me: the chill of his voice was close to hatred. "I think we're finished now."

In October I turned nineteen.

In a moment of weakness, I let Liz talk me into throwing a party. I got dressed up and smiled, and even danced a little.

But all I could feel was the warmth of Alex's lips as they pressed against my neck – the strength of his arm around me, holding me close. *Are you kidding? I'd have had to challenge the guy to a duel or something. Might have been kind of awkward.*

When it was over I went back to my room and cried so hard that I ended up retching over the toilet.

It wasn't really a good birthday.

CHAPTER *Eighteen*

"YOU READY FOR THIS?" SAID Bascal's voice on the phone.

Raziel was in his office, going over maps for his upcoming journey to Mexico City. Annoyingly, it would take days to get there on the still-shattered roads. At least there hadn't been a major snowfall yet, though it was now late November.

"Ready for what?" he said, distracted.

"The Angel Killers are still alive."

Raziel's head snapped up. "*What?*"

"Yeah, a group have been caught near Albuquerque Eden. They attacked some angels there, but missed one.

When we went back and captured the AKs, we found a base they'd built up in the mountains."

Raziel leaned forward, his posture hunched and urgent. "What about Fields and Kylar?"

"Don't know yet – they weren't there with them, at least. But listen, boss, these people have been *trained*. Just their bad luck one got away." Bascal's voice hesitated. "There's more," he said.

Raziel frowned while Bascal spoke, blindly taking in a Tiffany lamp across the room. "Just like Kara Mendez," he murmured finally. Like Kara, and like those people in Mexico City, whose numbers kept growing. Why did this seem so inevitable?

"Yeah, exactly," said Bascal. "I can tell you one thing – from the way they were acting, *they* sure don't know we can't feed from them. Anyway, they haven't been interrogated yet – I thought you'd want to have that fun yourself."

"Yes, thanks," Raziel said grimly. "Have Albuquerque send them here. Immediately."

Raziel hadn't met a human yet who could hold up under enough pain. Apart from Kara, who was exceptional – he rather missed their little games. There was no time for such subtlety with the Albuquerque group, though.

There were seven of them; from hidden cameras, it was obvious how close-knit they were. Good. Raziel ordered two of them sacrificed immediately and made sure the others heard. Standing alone outside a door in the downstairs corridor, Raziel inspected his nails as the frantic, pleading shouts echoed and finally ended. This sort of thing was beyond crass, but necessary.

Finally he entered a room. They'd separated the AKs, and a girl – Chloe, he believed – sat huddled in the corner, crying. She flinched when she saw him.

"Do you know this girl?" he asked, holding up a photo of Willow.

Her face emptied of colour. "No, I – I've never seen her before," she stammered.

Raziel smiled. "In other words, yes, you do. Everyone knows who Willow Fields is. Your lie is rather obvious, my dear. Where is she?"

Chloe looked sick. "I mean, I know who she *is,* but I don't *know* her – not personally."

Raziel perched on a table, one foot still on the floor; he swung his other leg casually. "You heard the screams, I suppose. Tracy and Paul, I believe, were their names?"

Her face contorted and she pressed her cheek against the wall, her throat working.

"It would be such a shame if anyone else had to die," Raziel went on mildly. "Especially when this is all rather futile. We *will* find your intrepid leaders, you know. We can just do it with more deaths, or without. Which do you prefer?"

"I don't know what you're talking about," she whispered.

How tedious. Raziel held back a sigh as he took out his cellphone and dialled. "Another one," he ordered. "And I think you'd better do it in here. Chloe doesn't seem convinced yet of how serious we are."

It took two more AKs in the end; Raziel was tetchily wondering whether he'd have to start bringing in random strangers off the street next. But Chloe finally broke, sobbing out that the Angel Killers were in Nevada. She didn't know exactly where; they had an underground base in the desert north-west of Vegas, about a hundred miles out. And other groups of AKs had also been sent into the field, though she didn't know where they were either.

Raziel held back a smile. He hadn't even asked about that last part – they'd definitely made progress. He touched Chloe's face, his fingers lingering. She was really a very attractive girl.

"Well done," he said. "And now suppose you tell me why you and your friends are immune to us? Is it something the AKs did?"

She stared blankly at him, shook her head. "I… I don't—"

She wasn't lying this time – he could see her struggling

with the definition of *immune* when her little group had just been decimated. "Never mind," he said, rising to his feet. "You've done very well to tell me about your friends in Nevada, my dear. Very well indeed."

"Please don't hurt them," she whispered.

"Never," said Raziel. "Why, the very thought." He left the room and closed the door behind him; as he strode back to his office, a church official joined him.

"Well?" the man asked.

"Take care of her and the other two – no need for drama this time," said Raziel without pausing.

Back in his office, Raziel's satisfaction faded as he realized his dilemma.

As he'd long suspected, Willow was alive – *alive* – and was training new AKs. Even through his fury, Raziel felt a flash of hard pride – he'd known that no daughter of his could be vanquished so easily. But finding her might take a while, now that the angels' psychic skills were so compromised; Chloe's description could encompass hundreds of square miles.

And with all that was going on, Raziel didn't have time to undertake the search himself.

He glared down at the map of Mexico. Unbelievably, there were now almost a hundred immune humans locked away there, with more being discovered every day. Through a sense of trepidation he hardly understood, he'd put off this journey for as long as possible – but now if he didn't deal with it, word was sure to explode among the angels. For unless stopped, this immunity might just keep spreading throughout humanity, until angels were unable to feed at all.

It would be like a judgement.

Absurd. Even so, Raziel was gripped by a cold fear. The Council deaths had occurred in Mexico City, orchestrated by his own hand. What if this powerful, unknowing energy that he kept sensing was in response to that? What if the human immunities in Mexico City, in the Angel Killers, were somehow his fault?

No one can be allowed to know what I did, thought Raziel. Currently, not a single angel alive suspected that he'd been responsible for assassinating the Council. If they found out, it could be the thing to galvanize the despondent ones back into action, so that they banded together with those who already hated him – all of them united against a common enemy.

No, he had to go to Mexico City and could waste no further time about it – if there was any evidence against him to be found there, he had to suppress it. The problem of Willow would have to be solved some other way.

Bascal, he decided. Let him get a good-size gang

together and go searching in the Nevada desert for the Angel Killers, using whatever psychic powers they still had left – the little thug would enjoy doing away with them immensely.

Raziel had just reached for his phone to give the order when it rang, vibrating under his fingers. And even though he was barely psychic himself any more, he felt a sense of dread.

He hesitated, then answered. The news that came, on top of everything else, was like a punch in the throat.

Pawntucket. His daughter's hometown.

"Don't let the news leak any further," Raziel said finally; somehow he sounded in control. "I've got to go to Mexico City for a while first. I'll be in Schenectady by the tenth – we'll take care of them then for good."

When he hung up, he sat very still. His fingers closed around a plastic pen; it bent and snapped. He had a flash of the willow tree from his dream, its branches blazing in the glow from his wings. And now he remembered where the real tree had been.

The knowledge chilled him; more than ever, he had the sense that everything was slipping from his fingers – and that it was all because of Willow somehow. Raziel's jaw clenched. No. He would *not* be defeated.

He called Bascal and explained what was going on, snapping the words out. "Go to Nevada immediately and find the Angel Killers – leave no one alive," he finished. "Do you hear me? *No one.*"

The clock read 8:41.

Still hugging my pillow, I stared blearily at the numbers – then it hit me, and I swore and scrambled out of bed.

For days I'd been having unsettling dreams I could barely remember, which kept me lying awake for hours. Last night had been the worst yet. Now I'd overslept; I had less than twenty minutes to help set things up for the simulation.

I threw on jeans and a V-necked black T-shirt, then brushed my hair with quick strokes. As I did, my crystal pendant caught the light, sparkling against my skin.

Two days ago, Alex had been dead for a year.

I put the hairbrush down and hesitated, looking at my dresser drawers. I didn't do this very often. But now, though I was already running late, I pulled open the top drawer.

Tucked away under my socks and bras was a folded piece of paper.

There is no greater universe than holding you... For a change, my eyes stayed dry as I read the poem, and then Alex's message at the bottom. *I love you. Today on your birthday and always. Alex.*

"I love you, too," I whispered. I kissed my finger and

pressed it lightly against his signature. As I put the paper back into place, my hand brushed a tiny package.

Even after all this time, I'd never opened Seb's present. Suddenly curious, I unwrapped it – and found a flat beige stone about an inch long, exactly the same as a million other stones in the desert. Then I turned it over and caught my breath. The stone had a pattern, some fluke of nature: the figure of a girl with long hair and outspread wings.

An angel with no halo. Me.

I'd never thanked Seb for this; I'd just thrown it in my drawer unopened. *Seb, I'm sorry. It's beautiful,* I thought, running my thumb over the stone's smooth surface.

Sam stuck his head in. "Hey! You coming, or what?"

I shoved the stone in my pocket; a minute later, I was jogging behind Sam towards the training room. As we went through the main entrance, we were enveloped in chaos. The entire base was there – we had almost two hundred recruits now, all at different levels. That included some of our original AKs who'd taken longer with the energy work; most of them would leave in the spring.

At the centre of the massive space sprawled an earthquake-ruined city. The set's shattered buildings always made my stomach tighten. It looked way too much like an explosion site.

We were just about to start when there was a fizzling noise: the holograph machines failing. Again.

Sam groaned and went over with a guy named Eric, our computer guru. Everyone had been tensely poised; now the mood relaxed as the two of them huddled over the computer.

Suddenly I realized I was standing beside Meghan. She had on camouflage trousers and a black T-shirt, her rich auburn hair piled on top of her head.

"It's like having a fire drill back at school," she said as our eyes met. "Remember, we'd get to hang around outside for a few minutes?"

"And miss algebra if we were lucky." I felt very conscious of the stone Seb had given me, nestled in my pocket. From the corner of my eye, I could see him across the room, talking with some of his students.

I hesitated, then decided to say it. "Meghan, listen… I was really sorry to hear about you and Seb. I've wanted to tell you that for a long time."

She didn't answer for a second. Then she sighed. "Yeah. Not my smartest move ever – getting involved with a guy who's in love with someone else."

I froze; I hadn't expected her to just come out with it like that. Her voice went on, low and non-accusing. "But I couldn't help it; I just…fell so completely in love with him. I really thought that someday he'd wake up and see how amazing we were together." She snorted. "Stupid, huh?"

I licked dry lips. "So what happened?"

Meghan shrugged, her face creased with sadness. "Oh, I don't know. After Alex died, Seb was so desperate to be there for you, and…well, I guess it made how we both felt pretty obvious, even if neither of us wanted to see it. Finally it got to where being with him hurt more than it made me happy. Time to call it a day."

Oh. I cleared my throat, my cheeks on fire. "I always wondered why you didn't hate me," I admitted softly.

She glanced at me in surprise. "Why? It's not *your* fault." She gave a slightly bitter smile. "When I'm being extra-mature I know it's not his either. He never lied to me, even though sometimes I really thought that…" She trailed off, then made a face. "Oh, who knows? Seb is complicated. And not my favourite topic of conversation, to be honest."

She looked up and grinned suddenly, a real smile that lit up her face. "Hey! We've got lift-off!"

The holographic angels had appeared, hanging motionless in the air. I managed a smile too as people cheered. Deep down, I guess I'd always known that Seb wasn't over me. I still hated hearing it.

Sam clapped his hands. "Okay, y'all!" he shouted. "We start in five, four, three—"

Everything else vanished as I grabbed my rifle, checking people's auras to see who'd been caught off-guard. Then the lights snapped out, and we were plunged into battle.

As the angels started diving, I felt the familiar adrenalin rush. One swooped right at me – I got it in a single shot and then ran for the set, white fireworks exploding through the room. My heart was pounding as I crouched behind a wall and aimed; I pulled the trigger. This was the one time in my life when I felt – well, not happy, but alive again.

Then everything seemed to go into slow motion. My hands chilled, and I missed an angel entirely; its holographic body sliced through me. The buzzer signalling that I'd "died" went off as I lowered my rifle, my spine suddenly prickling. What was going on?

For a heartbeat I stood motionless, surrounded by shouts and the red pinpoints of laser rifles. Then by some instinct I looked up at the broad ceiling, shrouded in darkness.

And I knew.

Time snapped back into place. "*Attack! We're under attack!*" I yelled. I scrambled from the set; ran for the door, and switched on the lights – the room flooded with brightness. I could hear Seb calling out too now; people stood gaping at us both.

"*We're under attack!*" I shouted again, cupping my hands around my mouth. "The angels are almost here! Get a weapon – *do* something!"

I flung open the door and started sprinting towards the armoury. Oh god, I could actually *feel* them now, surging through the ground like ethereal arrows. Before I'd made it halfway down the corridor, I heard the sound of screams starting.

No! I whirled back towards the training room and saw that some of the more experienced AKs had followed me out. Sam was pounding towards me; Liz and Kara, Meghan, a dozen others.

"Don't stop, we need real guns!" bellowed Sam, charging past.

I took off running again. We reached the armoury; Sam threw it open. "Grab as many weapons as you can carry, then get back in there!"

I swung a semi-automatic rifle over each shoulder, grabbed another, and then a couple of pistols. I shoved them in my jeans waistband with a hand that somehow wasn't shaking.

It's time, I thought. *Finally, it's time.*

Meghan was pale as she loaded herself up. As Kara clicked in a magazine, I saw the scars where her tattoo used to be. I registered them in a blur as I raced from the armoury, ignoring the weight pulling at my shoulders.

Sam passed me, bristling with weapons. The screams grew louder with every step. As Sam edged open the training room door, they amplified. I gritted my teeth and followed him in – then stopped, the breath freezing in my lungs.

The room was a frenzy of angelic light. Hundreds of angels – *hundreds,* swooping, diving, tearing away life forces. Through the churning wings, I saw that at least half the AKs lay dead already, their bodies sprawled amid the fake ruins. Some of the ones left must have had real pistols on them – they were shooting frantically, aiming upwards.

It made no difference. We were hopelessly outnumbered. In a daze I saw another few AKs fall; realized that in minutes we'd all be dead.

Sam had taken only a few steps in. As the others appeared behind us, he whirled around, eyes blazing. "*Get out – evacuate!*"

Kara's chin thrust out. "No *way,* Sam!"

"Do it! Each of you, take a weapon and leave the extras – *go!*" When Kara didn't move, he tore one of the rifles from her shoulder. "What part of *get the hell out* do you not understand?" he roared into her face. Reluctantly, Kara obeyed; she and the others turned and started running back towards the garage.

"That goes for you, too, angel chick," Sam said through clenched teeth. He was loading himself up with even more rifles; suddenly I could read his thoughts as clearly as my own. He'd go down fighting. There was no way he was abandoning the rest of his team.

I stared at him in a tangle of emotions...but most of all, relief.

"No, Sam," I said quietly. I skidded one of my rifles across the floor into the fray, and then levelled the other against my shoulder as I reached within for my angel. "I'm mutinying, like Alex said. If you're going down with the ship, then I am too."

CHAPTER *Nineteen*

WHEN HE'D FIRST SENSED THE angels, Seb had gone sprinting for the holograph machines; he pulled the plug on the computerized angels and spun back towards the room. "Attack!" he shouted, adding his voice to Willow's. "Get out, you need weapons!"

The door nearest him was closer to his bedroom than the armoury – he flung it open and started to run. In his dorm he snatched up his switchblade from the dresser.

It was less than a minute before he got back, but as he entered Seb stopped in his tracks, stunned. *Dios mío*, this was slaughter. He plunged into the battle anyway; as he ducked to grab up a pistol from a fallen AK, he shoved aside the sight of the girl's empty gaze.

Suddenly panic gripped him. *Meghan.*

As Seb shot at an angel's halo, he sent his own angel soaring upwards, searching for her vivid hair. One of the creatures came at him; he battled it briefly, somehow wrenched away. Oh god, where was she? All at once he glimpsed Meghan through the main doorway, running away with Kara and some others. The human Seb let out a breath as his muscles relaxed – and then he saw that Willow was still in here.

No! Seb started battling towards her, crouching and shooting as angels came at him. His own angel shielded him, whirling away to protect the others when he could. There were vanishingly few left to protect, though those few now had weapons and were doing their best. Seb took a split second to snatch up a rifle lying on the floor; it was a relief to have the weapon's greater control.

Take that, you cabrón, he thought, blasting another angel into nothingness. There were so many, it hardly made a difference.

"Sam! Look out!" shouted Willow's voice. Seb spun and saw Sam's burly form fall in a haze of angels, his life force in tatters.

"*No!*" Willow screamed. Crying now, she stood over Sam's body, shooting again and again; remnants of angels fell like snow as her own angel fought overhead. Seb reached the two of them somehow. He took a shot and dropped to his knees beside Sam; the Texan's aura was faint, almost gone.

As Sam struggled to focus, Seb gripped his hand hard. "Get her outta here," Sam gasped, clutching his fingers. "Please, man, get her out – don't let 'em capture her."

Before Seb could reply, the light had faded from Sam's blue eyes. His hand went limp.

Seb didn't let himself feel sorrow. He rose hastily. The remaining AKs had banded together at the other end of the room, firing upwards, bringing down angels. The creatures left were attacking the tiny group in a frenzy. Through twisting wings, Seb saw the AKs start to fall, one after another. In seconds, the angels would envelop him and Willow too.

Willow started to run towards the fight. Seb grabbed her, holding her back. "No!" she cried as she struggled. "Let me go! I've got to help—"

Her angel flew at him – his own angel fended her off. The human Willow was strong for her size but no match for him; Seb got her arms pinned and half carried her towards the door as she fought. "I swear I will knock you out and put you over my shoulder if I have to," he said through gritted teeth. "*Come on.* It won't bring Alex back if you die."

She went rigid – and then seemed to crumple. Looking at the motionless Sam, the final moments of slaughter across the room, she nodded mutely. He gripped her free hand, and they ran for it.

As the door closed, the corridor went startlingly silent, the only sound the drumming of their feet. Seb took the heavy spare rifle from Willow's shoulder as they ran and slung it over his own. Both their auras were grey, shrunken.

"They'll search the base for us," Willow panted. "I don't know if they realize who we are, though – I think I got all the ones who saw my angel; they might think we're dead already."

As they passed an open storage room, Seb glimpsed a few tin cans lying on the floor: Kara and the others must have managed to grab some supplies. With luck they could still be in the garage.

Seb sent his angel to go signal that he and Willow were coming – but hadn't flown half a dozen wing strokes before he whirled mid-air, senses prickling.

A small flock of the attackers were rounding a corner behind them, their ethereal wings slicing through walls as they jetted down the corridor.

Willow had felt them too; she turned around holding her rifle, running backwards a few steps as she let loose a volley of shots. Her angel appeared and went flying off to meet them head-on.

Seb twisted backwards as he ran, jaw tight as he fired again and again. One down. Another one. He felt his angel pluck his switchblade from his jeans pocket and then jet into the fray.

Seb could sense the exact moment when the remaining angels decided to retreat for reinforcements. Willow knew it too; he could feel her alarm – there were still over a hundred angels in the base. Without speaking, they redoubled their efforts.

In the air, sparks flew as his angel's wings beat against his opponents'. A glimpse of a beautiful, furious face – a hissed oath as Seb's angel struggled his knife towards the halo. The blade sliced through, glowing white; as the angel screamed, Seb's angel was already hurtling away to another one. On the ground, Seb was still firing, running after the retreating angels to bring them down.

Willow's angel was battling another female, straining to reach its halo. A burst of shattered brilliance as she succeeded. The human Willow gasped. She stumbled and fell, her rifle clattering to the ground, and gaped upwards at where the angel had been.

The last remaining angel was watching her with a sudden frown. Seb's angel lunged at him. Their wings clashed; Seb's angel lifted his switchblade – and then stopped, stunned.

The energy he was touching felt almost like his own.

The angel hovered as they gaped at each other. On the ground, Seb froze in recognition. He had no memories of the angel who was his father...yet had no doubt that this was him.

Willow got up, looking shaken; Seb had the fleeting sense that it was from more than just the attack. "Seb, what—" She broke off as she realized.

The angel shifted to his human form. Like Seb, he wore jeans and a long-sleeved T-shirt. Still aiming his rifle, Seb stared. He'd always thought he'd gotten his high cheekbones from his mother, but he saw now they could as easily have come from his father. The angel's shapely mouth was also Seb's – the strong angle of his jaw. Only hair and eyes were different: both dark brown.

"I...didn't know there was another of you," the angel said in a strangled voice.

And just as Willow's father had taken on the English accent of one of his past victims, Seb could now hear his mother's Sonoran tones. He swallowed hard, trying not to shake.

The angel took a hesitant step forward. "Can...can I ask your name?"

He wasn't sure why he answered. "Seb," he bit out. "Sebastián."

"I'm Zaran." The angel shook his head, gazing at Seb. "I didn't know. All these years..." He trailed off. "Your mother was very beautiful," he added. "I started to really care about her. I tried to leave her alone…"

A sound came like the rushing of a wind tunnel: angels approaching, more than they could ever hold off. Seb felt Willow's urgency as she tugged at him. "Seb! We have to hurry!"

Zaran glanced over his shoulder. A sudden resolve appeared on his face; he changed back to his angel form. "Go – leave," he ordered them both. "I'll say no one's down this way." He soared off down the corridor.

Seb's hands felt hot on the rifle. All the times he'd thought about what he'd do to his father if he ever met the *cabrón,* and he'd just *stood* there? Told him his name?

"*Seb!*" Willow was pulling with both hands now. "Come on! Do *you* want to die?"

Still cursing himself, Seb turned, and he and Willow ran, faster than ever. Seconds later they skidded into the garage. No sign of Kara and the others; two of the biggest trucks were gone.

"You need to drive," Seb said shortly. Meghan had given him a few driving lessons, but he didn't trust himself right now. He punched the elevator button as Willow dived into one of the remaining trucks.

When they reached ground level, both door and gate stood gaping open. Outside, it was snowing. Willow hurtled them onto the dirt road. The snow fell in big flakes that whirled towards the windshield; twisting in his seat, Seb was relieved to see it covering their tracks. The truck's clock read 9:22. The simulation had started at nine.

All those people – almost the entire team. Seb clenched his jaw, refusing to drown in what he was feeling. Then apprehension flickered; he could sense that the angels had finished searching the base.

"Hurry – we have to hide," he said.

Willow's cheeks were white. "I know – I feel it too." She lurched them off-road and steered the truck behind a large boulder. Angling them quickly into the shadows at its base, she killed the engine. In seconds, snow coated the windshield with tiny kissing noises, hiding them.

With no warning, the low roar of an explosion came, rumbling through the ground and vibrating right up through them. The car keys jingled. Willow gave a small cry, pressing her hand against her mouth; Seb swore impotently in Spanish.

The gas storage tanks under the pumps. They'd torched them. In a psychic flash, he could actually see it: the head angel changing to his human form and smirking at the others.

Watch this – the perfect finishing touch. A lit match – a shift back to his angel self before the flame had even hit the fuel. Hemmed in by a hundred tons of stone, the explosion would have surged through the base like fiery lava, scorching everything in its path.

Dully, Seb realized that the angels had erupted up out of the ground and were soaring away through the sky now, heading east. Including his father. By the time Seb could no longer sense them, the truck's interior had grown shadowy, its windshield covered with blue-white snow.

After a long pause, Willow cleared her throat. "Maybe… maybe we should try heading north," she said in a tiny voice. "If we're lucky, Kara managed to get into the office and grab the coordinates for the Idaho base."

Seb nodded. He felt numb, frozen. "Yes. Good idea."

As it turned out, the others weren't far ahead – they'd seen the angels and also pulled off-road to hide. Willow caught up and sent her angel cruising over the lead truck to signal it was them.

There was a tense moment when Seb wondered whether Kara was going to gun the accelerator – what had just happened probably hadn't lessened her dislike of half-angels much. Then she waved a slim brown arm out the window.

The three trucks convoyed north. He and Willow had lapsed back into silence, keeping their auras distinctly separate, their thoughts just as distant. Even so, Seb was aware that Willow had locked away her anguish for now and was thinking fretfully about Pawntucket, her hometown.

He almost asked about it, then bit back the words. Willow had made it clear that she wanted nothing to do with him, not even his friendship. There were times now when Seb felt the same about her – there was a limit to how much hurt he could take from one person. Even one he was in love with.

In the truck ahead, he could just make out a rich pile of auburn hair. *Meghan.* Seb's fist tightened on his thigh. Oh god, what must she be feeling, having witnessed that slaughter? With an effort, he resisted sending his angel out to check on her – she wouldn't thank him for it.

The snow dwindled until it was only a dusting on the desert floor. Sixty miles outside the Reno ruins, they reached Fallon – more of a ghost town now than a dark town. Willow followed the others to an abandoned shopping mall. The main entrance had been shattered; Kara drove her truck right inside, and they all parked in the food court.

"What happened?" demanded Kara as everyone got out. "Are you two the only…?"

"Yes," said Seb; his voice came out harshly. He explained what had happened, aware that he'd purposefully spoken before Willow, to spare her the pain. He sensed the group's mood dampening further, their auras becoming more shrunken. Meghan stood hugging herself, a rifle hanging over one shoulder.

When he finished, Kara had gone almost grey, though her expression hadn't changed.

"Well, at least you and Willow made it," she said finally – and to give her credit, she sounded as if she meant it.

She turned to the others. "Okay, we've been here before, and the place has been pretty picked over, but you can still find some things. Go in twos and threes, keep scanning, and take whatever you need. When it starts getting dark, come back to the trucks. We'll spend the night here, then keep heading up to the Idaho base in the morning."

Surreal was an English word Seb had learned only recently. The rest of that day fitted the description. While images of slaughter screamed through his head, he went from store to store, searching. Two girls from one of his classes went with him, sticking close, and he talked to them automatically, somehow managing to smile and be comforting. Yes, what a hero.

He found a sweater in his size. The only jacket to be had was of Italian leather, dyed forest green – so fine and thin it was nearly worthless, despite its price tag.

"You look like a model," said one of the girls when he tried it on, her strained giggle striving for normalcy. Seb had never cared much about his looks; now he almost hated them.

As they started back towards the food court, he stopped short – Meghan was coming out of a nearby store with another girl. Their eyes met. Seb stood motionless.

"Seb?" said one of the girls he was with.

"Go back to the trucks – I'll meet you there," he said, not taking his gaze off Meghan.

She'd hesitated when she first saw him, then said something to the other girl and came over alone. She still wore the black T-shirt she'd had on for the simulation, now with an oversize sweater on top.

"Hi," she said faintly when she reached him.

Seeing her bright, buoyant aura so cowed made Seb ache inside. "Are you all right?" he asked. He barely stopped himself from calling her *chiquita*.

Meghan crossed her arms tight and stared down at the shopping level below, where AKs stood talking in huddled groups. "I guess. As okay as any of us." Her blue eyes were anxious as she looked back at him. "What about you, though? You were right there when Sam…when…" Her voice faltered.

Without thinking Seb moved closer, ready to take her in his arms. She stepped back, wiping her eyes. "No, don't," she ordered softly. "Nothing's changed. It just makes it harder."

"You're right," he said after an awkward pause. "I'm sorry. But, Meggie, I…" He trailed off. Everything had already been said a hundred times. Meghan knew how much he cared about her. It wasn't enough.

From her expression, she knew that he had nothing

new to say…and wasn't surprised. "I'll see you later, Seb," she said quietly. She turned and walked away.

Seb stood looking after her as she started down the stilled escalators, graceful even in her too-large clothes. A memory came of Meghan lying on his bed, watching him dress. "What's this from?" she'd asked, reaching out to touch the raised, twisting scar on his stomach.

"From when I was a pirate," he'd said with a grin. "I was very bad; they had to punish me with the whip."

"Ooh, a rebel pirate…sexy." Her auburn hair had been half falling over her face, her generous mouth smiling. Her finger traced the scar, following its curves. "What's it from really?"

When girls in the past had asked about his scars, he'd spun stories until they gave up. But as always with Meghan, Seb had found himself telling the truth: his mother's boyfriend had beaten him with a belt when he was small; the buckle had ripped open his skin. Without stitches, the wound had healed badly.

Her face had become very still. When he finished, she said nothing – but leaned over and pressed gentle lips against the scar.

"Meggie, it's all right," he'd said, crouching down and touching her hair. "I haven't thought about it for a long time." It was true, yet the tenderness of her gesture had touched him deeply.

Still gazing after Meghan, Seb took in the stray auburn tendrils curling lightly against her neck – knew by heart the smell of her shampoo, the feel of her hair as he curled a fiery strand around a finger. Pain touched him, and he looked away. Why couldn't he have fallen in love with her? It should have been so easy. But, no, it was Willow, always *Willow* – no matter what the hell he did, like a sickness he could never get rid of.

He started back to the food court, fists buried in his jacket pockets. He'd been lonely most of his life; you'd think he'd have gotten used to it by now. But these last few months, he'd reached a whole new level. Meghan had taken the sunshine with her, leaving him more taunted than ever by what he couldn't have.

It would have been better for her if she'd never met me, he told himself harshly. Meghan, of all people, deserved someone who was in love with her.

Yet it filled Seb with bitterness, somehow, to imagine anyone else having the right to hold her – to wake up next to her and see her smile.

When everyone had gathered back at the trucks, Kara passed out military-issue meals. Seb sat eating listlessly with some of his students. People ate without conversation, huddled into themselves.

Willow sat with Liz, and though he deliberately wasn't looking, Seb was aware of her – knew she was still worried about whatever had been bothering her in the truck. Even now, he wanted to go to her, do whatever he could to help.

His capacity for idiocy was apparently limitless. He shoved his half-finished meal aside.

Kara had managed to grab the shortwave radio from the base. She tuned into the Voice of Freedom, and the low voice wrapped around them: "*If soldiers come to your dark town, hide, run away, fight – do anything you can to avoid being taken to an Eden. The angels are deadly. Whatever you do, don't trust them...*"

As if they really needed to be told that, after today. Aware that people were finding comfort in the familiar voice, Seb kept his cynicism to himself. And as the broadcast continued, the thought came to him that at least one angel had shown he *could* be trusted.

Go – leave, Zaran had said. Why had the *cabrón* saved them?

Yet Seb knew exactly why; it was something he himself might have done. He'd never paid much attention to the rules, and it looked like his father didn't either. The thought wasn't pleasant. He didn't want anything in *common* with the being who'd killed his mother – so many of his friends.

Then as his gaze fell on Meghan again, Seb realized the similarity went even deeper. *I started to really care about her. I tried to leave her alone.* His father, too, had caused pain to a woman he claimed to care about. Zaran had known that Seb's mother was in love with him, known that every time they touched he was hurting her – yet still hadn't kept away.

Was his son really so much better?

CHAPTER *Twenty*

WHEN IT FINALLY GOT TOO dark to see, people had started curling up to sleep on the food court floor, using clothes as pillows. Now their slumbering shapes were dark huddles around me – no one had moved for hours. I lay gazing at the skylights in the mall's high ceiling. I could see bright stars, wisps of cloud.

It all looked so pretty. It didn't seem right.

Sam. The deaths of the others hurt too – but *Sam*. He'd been like a big brother to me. He'd been there when Alex died, held me as we cried together – forced me to see reason and keep on living.

I swallowed, remembering all our long conversations. The way he'd sometimes dropped a casual arm around my shoulders as we walked down the corridor. The keenness of his blue eyes as he'd studied me during lunch a few days ago. "You're gettin' too thin, angel chick. You gonna eat that stew, or what?" In his solid, blunt way, he'd shown me how much he cared a million different times this last year.

I'll miss you, Sam, I thought bleakly.

Him, and all the others. An all-too-familiar sorrow knifed through me. Heather. Eric. The girls who gave me the picture of Alex. That picture was gone now, along with the poem Alex had given me and the photo of myself as a little girl. I felt a pang for them, but they were only *things* – nothing compared to the people who had died.

I hugged myself as I studied the stars. And now Pawntucket would soon be destroyed too.

My muscles tensed; I thought again of fighting the female angel in the corridor. As my wings had brushed against hers, a rush of images and knowledge had come – because when she'd seen who I was, thoughts she couldn't control had popped into her mind.

The wide, quiet streets of my hometown. A sense of danger there for the angels – something they hadn't expected. Raziel would be there on the tenth, in just two weeks, and he'd crush everyone in town.

As I lay on the cold mall floor, I pictured my father

smirking as he strode through the streets of my childhood – pictured everyone I'd known there being killed. Nina, my best friend. All my old classmates.

Suddenly I couldn't stand it; I had to get some fresh air. I quietly pulled on my shoes, then grabbed up the horrible pink parka I'd found, which I'd been using as a blanket. As silently as I could, I got up and slipped away from the food court and its sleeping forms.

When I reached the mall's main entrance, I breathed deeply, feeling the cold night breeze brush my face. I pulled on the parka and leaned against the frame of a shattered window as I stared out at the parking lot.

And out of all the chaos and grief of the last twenty-four hours – no, the last year – only one thing was clear to me.

I was going to Pawntucket.

There were only twelve of us left. We had no base, no supplies. The teams we'd sent out had probably already been captured; it was how Raziel must have found us. Maybe the few of us left could keep on recruiting and even still train people somehow, but it wouldn't make any difference.

It was over…and I saw now that it always had been, from the second that Raziel unlinked the angels. No wonder Alex had felt compelled to take an insane risk.

I let out a shuddering breath. Raziel had destroyed everything in the world that I cared about. *Everything.*

Alex, blown to pieces. My mother, drifting for ever in her dreams. Sam and all my other friends. The hope I'd had, even if it had been pointless.

He wasn't going to destroy my hometown too. I'd die first.

I stiffened as I heard someone behind me. I spun and winced, throwing up my arm as light blasted me full in the face. A shadowy figure lowered the flashlight, then switched it off.

"What are you doing out here?" Kara demanded.

My shoulders sagged. "You scared me."

Kara shook her head crossly, her exotic features just visible in the moonlight. "Well, you scared me too – I woke up and heard footsteps in the mall and didn't know whose they were."

She propped herself against the window frame across from me, looking out at the parking lot. A large men's shirt hung open over her tight T-shirt; she glanced down and fiddled with one of its sleeves. "So I guess you couldn't sleep either, huh?" she said finally. "Took me for ever to drop off."

I hadn't expected sympathy. "I couldn't drop off at all," I admitted after a pause. "I just kept seeing…all of it."

"At least you were *there* for it," she said bitterly. "Running away wasn't exactly my plan."

"Sam was right, though," I said, seeing again the

moment when he fell. My throat closed, and I touched a shard of glass that hadn't fallen from the windowpane. "Kara, listen – something's happened."

Her eyes narrowed as she looked sharply at me. "Why do I have this really bad feeling that you mean *besides* angels attacking and the base getting blown up?"

"Don't worry. It's nothing that matters, probably," I said. "Except to me."

I told her what I'd seen. I couldn't tell what she was thinking. When I'd finished, she just stood there looking at me.

"Pawntucket," she said finally. "As in, Pawntucket, New York. Pawntucket, almost three thousand miles away. *That* Pawntucket?"

"Yeah, that one," I said. "I'm going there to stop Raziel."

"Oh, great plan. Do you have *any* idea how much danger that puts the rest of us in? I've got ten other people to think of here, in case you haven't noticed!"

"Sounds like you're the new lead," I said after a pause.

Kara's face was set. "Yeah. I guess I am. And *you* know where we're going. I can't allow this, Willow. If anyone caught you—"

"I won't let myself be captured," I interrupted.

"Oh, *right*. And do you really think you'd hold up against torture if the angels got hold of you? Want to look at my hand again, and see some of the things they're capable of? Some of the things *dear old dad* got off on?" Her voice shook a little.

A cloud drifted over the moon, chasing shadows over the parking lot. "Maybe I'd hold up against torture, and maybe I wouldn't," I said quietly. "That's not what I meant, Kara. I'll say it again: *I will not let myself be captured.*"

I saw realization flicker in her eyes. For a long moment we regarded each other – and then, her expression hard, she reached for her holster.

In the old AK house, Kara had locked us in the basement workout room to keep us away from the Council attack – had shoved us down the stairs and slammed the door shut without thinking twice.

My pulse skipped. I took a step backwards, ready to send my angel flying out at her. "Do not try and stop me, Kara. I mean it."

She raised a sardonic eyebrow and pulled out her pistol. She handed it to me butt-first. "Here," she said.

I stared down and took it in slow motion. Kara delved into her pocket for a spare magazine and gave me that too.

"Leave," she said intently. "Right now. The others can't know why you've gone – or where. If there's even the slightest chance that I can still do some good, keep Alex's plan going, then I've got to do it. I do not want them tempted into leaving with you – I won't let them be put into danger over this...vendetta against Raziel." Her eyes met mine, dark and burning. "But it's my vendetta too. Kill the bastard."

I nodded, my chest too tight to speak. For a second I wanted to hug her, but I knew from her expression that she wouldn't welcome it. "Thank you," I whispered.

I stuck the pistol into the back of my jeans and stepped out through the broken window. I shoved my hands in my pockets and walked quickly away across the moonlit parking lot.

I didn't look back.

I didn't have a plan; it had all happened so fast. I needed a car, as soon as possible, and I broke into a jog as I left the parking lot, swinging onto the dark, wide strip of Highway 50. I was about to send my angel out past the abandoned restaurants and furniture stores in search of a residential area – and then came to a Shell station and the dark hulks of abandoned cars. *Bingo.*

I walked briskly across the station forecourt, looking the vehicles over in the moonlight. One was a nineties-model Toyota, just like the car I'd had back home – old enough that I could hotwire it. Except that its fuel gauge had to be on empty, or it wouldn't have been abandoned. My gaze flicked to the pumps, their digital screens blank.

Okay, there had to be a tank under the pumps. Almost the second I'd thought it, I spotted the heavy metal plate that covered the filling point. *I could siphon gas out from there,* I thought – and then realized that, no, of course I couldn't; not unless I had lungs of steel.

There was a garage attached to the station; someone had forced open one of its doors. And suddenly I recalled doing maintenance on my Toyota – how I'd topped up the engine with oil.

I ducked inside, bringing out my angel for light. As she hovered, I quickly found an old oil dispensing drum and unscrewed its hand crank pump. Then I found some rubber tubing and attached it to the end with duct tape. There – that should do it, if I was lucky.

Stupidly, the pump was the easy part. It took me for ever to find a rusting Stanley knife, even longer to find an empty gallon jug to put gas in. With every second I was so conscious of the others only half a mile away. I had a feeling that Kara would be the only one who'd agree with my plan. If I didn't get out of here, there'd be endless arguments, explanations.

Back outside, the metal disc in the asphalt was so heavy that I'd have broken every bone in my hand if it had slipped – but when I started pumping, I was rewarded with a thin stream of gasoline. *Yes!* If my hands hadn't been full, I'd have punched the air.

Once the Toyota's tank was full, I slid hurriedly into the driver's seat; I put the jug with extra fuel in the passenger footwell, along with the precious pump. Then I groped under the steering column for the wires I knew were there and stripped them from their casings.

Have you considered a life of crime? A hot day in Texas. Alex, grinning over his shoulder at me as he kept watch on the road. "Believe me, I'm considering it," I muttered to his ghost.

There. I twisted the wires together and touched my foot to the gas.

Nothing happened.

When it finally hit me, I scrambled out and ran back to the garage. After the fastest battery change in history, I got back behind the wheel and shut my eyes. "Please," I whispered. I twisted the wires again.

The engine fired into life. It was the most wonderful sound in the world.

I manoeuvred my way out of the forecourt, pulled out onto the main road, and floored it. The traffic lights hung from their wires with blank, dead eyes, not even trying to hold me back – I raced through empty intersection after empty intersection.

Dawn was just streaking across the east as I left Fallon behind. All I saw in the rear-view mirror was a small cluster of buildings on the horizon – and then they winked from view. God, what were the others going to think, when they woke up and found me gone? I wished that I could have said goodbye – to Liz, especially. And Seb.

Suddenly I realized that he was the one I was running from…and when I thought of the look that would be in his hazel eyes, something unexpectedly painful stirred.

But he'd wanted to leave the base; he'd only stayed because of his promise to Alex. If he still felt he should keep it, then he'd go to Idaho with the others. If not, he'd go his own way – maybe back to Mexico.

The knowledge made me feel better; our lives had diverged a long time ago. I slid my hands back and forth on the wheel. Okay, I had to start heading east as soon as possible. Then find a road atlas and scavenge for food and water.

At the moment I was travelling towards the interstate – and thinking of Seb again, I realized this was way too obvious. I took the first exit I saw and made my way instead to Route 50 East. Perfect. I'd stay on this for a while first; then once I had a map, I'd start travelling on back roads.

As I drove down the old state highway with the dawn slowly lighting the sky, an unexpected feeling of freedom came over me. It hit me that this was the first time I'd been alone, really alone, in…god, *years*.

The heartache over what had happened would always be with me. But at the same time, to be driving alone on an empty road, watching pink fingers of dawn reach slowly across the desert – to not have to answer to anyone for anything; to know that all my choices were mine, and mine alone…

It felt as if I could breathe again.

Kara's pistol was still tucked in the back of my jeans. As I drove, I reached behind me and rested it on the passenger seat. Once I'd been so leery of guns, I could barely touch one. I still didn't like them, but they were useful sometimes. Remembering what I'd promised Kara, I glanced down, briefly noting the pistol's hard metal casing, the safety switch that was flicked on.

And as I thought about what I'd have to do if I were captured, I felt no fear at all – only an iron resolve.

CHAPTER *Twenty-one*

THE NEXT FEW DAYS WERE a white blur. Snow flurries had followed me from Nevada into Utah, and I crossed the Rockies with trepidation, tapping the brakes and eyeing the poles, some seven feet tall, that would measure the drifts when the time came. It was almost December; the first big snowfall was already late. If it came now, I'd be stuck here until spring.

I was so tired that my head felt weighted, but I kept on through the mountains. When at last the Rockies loomed up in the mirror behind me, I felt as if I could relax a little.

As I pressed on, I stopped only for quick naps under the

pink parka, grateful for it despite its lurid colour. Before I drifted off, I always reached out to my mother, just like I had so many times this last year – needing to sense her presence even if she never responded.

Mom, I don't know what's happening in Pawntucket, but I promise I'll stop it, I thought, staring up at the car's ceiling. There was no answer, but her warm energy seemed to wrap around me – and I sent a silent thank you to whoever was keeping her safe.

I had veered north around Salt Lake City Eden and headed up into Wyoming, rather than risk Colorado, my father's state. The sky soared around me. Out here, there'd been little earthquake damage, plus I had some idea where I was going now – on the second day, I'd found a road atlas in an abandoned car.

I was managing several hundred miles a day, which I prayed would be enough. The cattlemen out here were all in Raziel's pocket; they'd turn me in to the angels in a second. So I stayed on little-used roads where I saw no other people at all. Sometimes, though, I'd pass rough signs – *Green River Eden 36 mi., turn L on Hwy 191. The angels love you!* – and my skin would prickle.

Once I passed one of the old posters of myself – and realized, startled, that even if I cut my hair short and dyed it red again, I wouldn't look anything like that smiling girl. The Willow in the visor mirror had a thinner face –

eyes that had known great sorrow. In fact, I didn't really look like a *girl* at all any more. I looked like a woman.

The idea was a little unsettling…then it shifted, became part of me.

With no radio stations, the time passed in silence. Sometimes I sang as I drove, belting out all my old favourite songs; sometimes I just listened to the sound of the wheels trundling over snow.

Food wasn't too difficult. Every abandoned store I came to had at least a few canned goods left – though always things like kidney beans or stewed prunes. Never any junk food; the Cheetos and Funyuns had probably been the first things to go.

Gasoline wasn't really a problem either; it was just time-consuming. Crouching on frozen, abandoned forecourts to fiddle with a home-made pump should probably have been my least favourite thing to do as the days passed – but, actually, it gave me a feeling of satisfaction every time I did it.

After replacing a filler tank lid one morning in central Wyoming, I straightened up and gazed over snow-dusted plains. A flock of geese were flying south in a V-shape, and I watched for a moment, wondering why they'd waited so long to migrate.

And somehow, despite everything that had happened, and everything that might still be to come, I realized that I felt…peaceful.

Sun gleamed on the snowy plains. The geese grew smaller against the clear sky, and my body felt lighter suddenly, as if I could take off and fly through the air after them.

"I'll always love you, Alex," I murmured. "But I think I'm going to be all right without you. And I can't tell you how glad I am."

"Okay, this was *not* a good idea," I muttered as the tyres jolted over snow-covered ruts.

It was the third day. I'd been eyeing the smooth grey sky and getting more and more worried about a serious snowstorm – and then some intuition had made me turn off the rural highway I was on, onto this unmarked dirt road.

God, I was going to break an axle out here. But for some reason I kept on going – and after about five minutes, I saw the house. It was set well back, with a paved drive that ended abruptly where it touched the road.

I stopped the car and took in a sprawling brick ranch house with a three-car garage; a twiggy tree in the front yard looked as if it hadn't had a chance to grow yet. I did a quick scan. No one.

Making up my mind, I got out of the Toyota and checked my pistol, then stuck it in the pocket of my parka.

As I shut the car door, it sounded like a bomb going off. I walked up the drive, my footsteps the only noise. *Why am I here?* I thought.

I studied the grassless front yard: the tangled, untamed lot across the road. And then I stopped, frowning.

For a second, it had felt as if the earth's energy was reaching towards me – as if everything in the whole *world* was straining towards me, without even realizing. It was a bizarre sensation; then it was gone.

I stood very still, waiting – almost holding my breath – but nothing else happened. Finally I shook my head and turned back to the house. Right. Obviously I was lonelier than I'd thought.

Though I could have just sent my angel in to open up the place from the inside, I didn't – it felt like an intrusion somehow. Instead I tried the front door, and when that was predictably locked, walked around the side of the house, testing windows. Finally one slid open.

I don't know why climbing in through a window seemed less like breaking in, but it did – as if the house itself had granted me entry. I ducked past gold-coloured curtains and stepped down onto a hardwood floor. Then I stood staring as I tapped the snow from my shoes.

I was in a study, with a computer on a desk and a soft-looking leather sofa in one corner. I gazed at a pair of reading glasses. It felt as if I'd entered Tutankhamen's tomb. Dust lay thickly on all surfaces, and everything was undisturbed, as if whoever had lived here had just stepped out and not come back.

What had happened to them? Had soldiers taken them to an Eden?

I shivered and made my way down the shadowy, carpeted hallway until I found the kitchen: a room with a bay window looking out to a large backyard. On the counter was a coffee machine, half-full and green with mould – there was even a mug with a red lipstick print. I didn't go near it; instead I found the pantry and swung open the door.

Food. Suddenly I was ravenous – I'd only eaten odds and ends for days. Cans of soup faced me; spaghetti, stew, peanut butter, crackers. I found some plastic bags in a drawer and helped myself, plucking everything still edible off the shelves. There were whole shrink-wrapped cartons of bottled water. And Cokes – I could chill them in snow.

As I placed my "groceries" by what I assumed was the garage door, my heart skipped: there was a set of car keys hanging from a wooden pegboard.

I rose slowly, staring at them. Hardly daring to hope, I opened the door to the garage…and there, like a present for a lucky high school graduate, stood a midnight-blue Ford 4 × 4.

I swallowed, positive that this was all about to go

spectacularly wrong. But when I pressed the button on the keys, the truck's locks snicked obediently open.

Yes! My worries about the snow vanished. There were even snow chains on the wall and a real fuel can sitting on a counter. Grinning like a loon, I loaded up the truck; it still had that new-car smell. But hanging from the rear-view mirror was a laminated school photo of a boy with a brown cowlick...along with a tiny plastic angel.

"*You* can stay, Timmy," I said to the boy. He looked like a "Timmy", as if Lassie were lurking just out of view. "Not you, though," I went on, detaching the angel – and wondering if this was the answer to what had happened here.

I went back in and set the angel gently on the table. I was just about to leave when I glanced down the hallway. Wait, the bathroom – I hadn't seen so much as a box of Band-Aids in the abandoned stores.

I found a lot more than that. New packets of toothbrushes, toothpaste – oh, *yes;* I'd hadn't brushed my teeth in days. Suddenly very aware of the silence in the house, I quickly bagged up everything that might be useful. Then I glanced under the sink, and found a glossy cardboard box.

My pulse started pounding. It was even the right colour. Maybe I shouldn't; maybe it was a stupid, dangerous idea. Yet I knew there was no way I was leaving the box behind.

Definitely, I thought, adding it to my bag. *But not here.*

On my way out, I checked a hall closet and was rewarded with a sleeping bag in a nylon case; I tucked it gratefully under one arm. Okay, time to go. If I were smart I'd probably start looting through all the closets for warmer clothes, but that seemed way too personal – and I had enough.

The garage door swung open when I tugged at it, and the 4 × 4 started on the first try. I backed it down the drive and grabbed what I needed from the Toyota. "Thank you, whoever you were," I murmured once I was back in the truck. The house gave no response.

I let out a breath and glanced at the boy in the photo. "Ready, Timmy?"

And Timmy said he was.

When the snow came an hour later it wasn't as bad as I'd feared; the 4 × 4 took the inch or so of white easily. It was a relief to feel how solid and reliable it was as I travelled down the main street of the next dark town: Scottsbluff, Nebraska.

A Payless ShoeSource gaped vacantly. Festive Flowers had pots of dead plants in the window. I couldn't sense any people – this time of year, they'd probably headed south, or given up and gone to Omaha Eden.

I knew exactly what I was looking for. When I saw it, I smiled and turned right onto First, and then right again. There was a small parking lot at the back; I pulled in.

Stray snowflakes fell softly in my hair as I swung open the truck's rear door. I got out the cardboard box and one of the cartons of bottled water – and then, with my pistol safe in the pocket of my parka, I locked the truck and walked up the short flight of concrete steps to the back door.

The fading gold letters read: IMAGES SALON.

The door was locked, but this time I had no compunction about sending my angel in. In seconds, I was standing inside a supply room; through an open door was a room filled with mirrors and black curving sinks.

I found a bottle on one of the shelves: *Peroxide for hair.* The memory of Alex's reaction when I'd dressed his gunshot wound came back, and I almost smiled. "Different peroxide," I told his ghost in my head. "And it *was* the right thing to do, you know."

I stripped off my parka and V-necked top, and put on a black plastic cape. Then I settled into one of the swivelling chairs and started applying peroxide to my long, dyed brown hair, combing it through. My angel hovered overhead, casting a gentle light.

Twenty minutes, the bottle said. I watched in the mirror, observing with satisfaction as my hair grew lighter by the second. I'd hated the brown so much – it had never felt like me. When the timer went off, I rinsed out the peroxide with bottled water in one of the sinks, and then opened up the box of Clairol Summer Blonde.

Less than an hour later, I was a blonde again.

I smiled at myself in the mirror as I combed my hair out. A little darker than my natural shade, but only slightly. Oh god, the relief – I felt like myself again. This was how I wanted to be when I faced Raziel: exactly who I really was. No more hiding.

"Welcome back, Willow," I murmured.

Still smiling, I took off the plastic cape and started to fold it...and then froze at the sound of the back door opening.

Footsteps started heading through the office. I leaped to the wall and pressed flat against it. My eyes flew to my parka draped over a chair, with my pistol still in its pocket. *Damn it,* what had I been thinking? I reached for my angel, ready to send her out to grab it – and then the intruder's energy hit my senses, and my jaw dropped.

Thoughts tumbling, I stepped away from the wall just as Seb entered the room.

We stood staring at each other. Seb had on faded jeans, a grey sweater, a forest-green leather jacket. His chestnut hair was slightly damp, curling more than usual with the snow. There were flakes melting in it even now, as I watched.

Finally I cleared my throat. "I, um…thought you'd go to Idaho."

Seb's eyebrows flew up, and suddenly I realized how angry he was. "Idaho," he repeated mildly, as if considering the idea. "Yes, of course – that is exactly what I would do, when I wake up and find you gone, and Kara lying about not knowing where – and her mind full of thoughts about you facing Raziel and having to shoot yourself if you're caught. Yes, I'd go to *Idaho*. It's so obvious."

"Seb—" I broke off as it hit me that I was standing there in only my jeans and bra. My cheeks burned; I pushed past him to grab up my shirt and yank it on again. "You didn't have to come after me," I said as I flipped my wet hair out from under the collar.

"No?"

"*No.* This is something I have to do alone. I don't need your help."

"Did I say—" Seb stopped himself and shoved his damp curls back; he sank down onto one of the chairs with a laugh that held no humour at all. "Yes, I know you don't *need my help*. Do you think I see you like some delicate flower?"

"Fine, so why are you here?"

He made a strangled noise, his knuckles white as he pressed them against his eyes. I could almost hear him mentally counting to ten. "Do you really have to ask me that? Really? Willow, no matter what, I am *not capable* of going to Idaho when you're planning to get yourself killed. Stupid, I know."

"I'm not planning..." I sighed and sat down in the chair next to him. "That's not what I'm planning."

"You're planning to go face your father. In your case, I think it's the same thing."

That one was kind of hard to argue with. "Look, this is just something I have to do, all right?" I said. "I'm not going to let Raziel destroy my hometown."

"I know." Seb's voice was quiet. "I'm not trying to talk you out of it."

And he wasn't, I realized in surprise. *I don't actually want to die, you know,* I thought of telling him...but despite my moment of peace as I'd gazed out over the plains, I wasn't totally sure that was true. Disturbed, I crossed my arms over my chest.

As if in reply, Seb's gaze went to my hair. "Very pretty," he said dryly. I could tell he knew exactly why I'd done it.

I gave him a look. "So anyway, thanks for coming, but I'm fine on my own."

Seb's eyes flashed. "You haven't been listening to a word I say, have you? Please, tell me: are you *trying* to drive me crazy?"

"Since you ask, no. This doesn't actually have anything to do with *you* at all."

Deceptively calm, he said, "No, of course not. Because I'm just some guy you barely know, yes? Someone you used to teach a class with. Why should I care if you die? Go, do it, have fun." His jaw tightened. "*Dios mío,* Willow. You are the most infuriating, *blind*—" He broke off, then lapsed into a string of rapid Spanish. I had a feeling that I didn't want a translation.

He slumped against his chair, frowning; a silence fell that crackled with unspoken words. I started to snap something back – and then hesitated.

For the first time, I noticed that I wasn't the only one who'd changed these past twelve months. Seb's stubbled face looked older too – and like my eyes, his hazel ones held a year's worth of pain. Maybe even more.

It stopped me in my tracks. I cleared my throat and looked away. "Well…I guess we'd better get going, then," I said after a pause. I stood up and grabbed my parka. "I mean, since you're so determined. We've still got a long way to go."

Seb's eyes flicked to mine. He shook his head. "I was right," he said, unfolding his long legs from the chair. "You *are* trying to drive me crazy. And you do it very well."

Outside was the 4 × 4 that we'd taken from the base, parked at a skewed slant next to mine. By unspoken agreement, we were taking my truck. I clicked it open, and Seb started shifting his things over.

He didn't have much. As he tossed a length of garden hose into the back, I realized he must have been siphoning gas from abandoned cars: not a fun way to cross the country. Not to mention that I knew he wasn't an experienced driver. Guilt touched me, remembering how I'd deliberately taken a different road than he'd expect. Deep down, I guess I'd always known Seb would do this.

When we got into the truck, I put the keys in the ignition and then just sat there for a second, running my hands over the wheel. "Seb, I'm sorry," I said finally. "Kara asked me to leave without saying anything, so I did. But I should have sent my angel back to tell you."

He glanced at me, his expression unreadable.

"I promise that I didn't just…leave without thinking what it would be like for you," I went on haltingly. "I did think about it, and…it made me feel really sad. I guess that's why I told myself you'd go to Idaho. I didn't like to think…" I couldn't finish.

Seb rubbed his stubble with a thumb. "Forget it – it doesn't matter," he said finally, sounding tired. "I needed to practise my psychic skills anyway. What better way than to follow you across three states?"

It was tempting to just smile and start the truck, but I knew that more needed to be said. I cleared my throat. "There's, um…something else I need to apologize for. This whole last year, the way I've treated you…"

He went very still.

"It wasn't anything you did wrong, okay? It was because…" My cheeks were bright red. Haltingly, I explained my flash of jealousy when I'd seen him kiss Meghan at the party, so long ago now. "I hated remembering it," I finished. "Whenever I did, it – it felt as if I'd betrayed Alex."

Seb's voice was quiet. "I knew you were jealous that night," he said. "And I also knew it meant nothing; it was like…you were a child and someone had taken away your candy that you weren't eating."

I winced, but that was pretty accurate. "Anyway, I'm sorry," I said. "For all of it."

Seb hesitated. "I think you should forget how you felt, Willow – it didn't mean anything. It was just…" He shrugged; his tone took on a hint of teasing. "For so long, you must have thought I was your private property, yes? Whether you wanted me or not?"

I felt infinite gratitude for Seb's kindness, when he had every right to hate me. *Is it too late to take you up on the brother thing?* I wanted to ask. "Thank you for the stone with the angel on it," I said instead, after a moment. "It's beautiful. It's in my jeans pocket right now."

"*De nada.*" Seb's eyes had turned slightly troubled as he studied me – and all at once I remembered that I was the reason he and Meghan had broken up. I looked away and started the engine.

"So, you get to be the navigator," I said, deliberately cheerful as I leaned over to pluck the atlas from the footwell and tossed it on his lap. I started the engine. "And that's Timmy. Say hi to Timmy."

Seb raised an eyebrow at the laminated photo. "*Hola,* Timmy —*¿qué hay?* I think you've been alone too long," he added as he opened the atlas.

And despite everything, suddenly I was grinning. "Hey, that's nothing," I said as I steered us out of the parking lot. "Just wait until you hear my singing repertoire."

CHAPTER *Twenty-two*

ALMOST IMMEDIATELY, SEB AND I fell into a routine that felt comforting in its sameness: meals of canned food snatched between hours on the road. And for the first time in over a year, we talked a lot. Or at least, we joked and bantered.

"Did I tell you about when I went to visit my *ranchero* grandfather?" Seb would ask solemnly as we travelled down a remote road.

He'd never known any of his family, apart from his mother. "No, I don't think you did," I'd answer, just as deadpan. "The one who used to be a gondolier, right?"

"Yes, and he missed Venice, so he dug canals all around his ranch. He'd go out in a home-made gondola and sing opera. It used to frighten the cattle. My grandmother would beg him to stop in case they stampeded."

He was being very guarded with his emotions – I couldn't tell what he was really thinking. But I was as happy as he was to avoid discussing anything serious, because whatever waited ahead in Pawntucket was feeling darker with every mile.

I knew Seb must have sensed it too, but we didn't mention it. He made me laugh, despite my worry…and despite a wistfulness that grew in me as the days passed. Seb's presence was so completely male. Having him there made me remember all the times I'd driven with Alex – being able to just lean against his shoulder, feel him put his arm around me.

Will I ever fall in love again? I wondered suddenly. We'd veered slightly north up into South Dakota by that point, to avoid the wheat farmers who were just as much in Raziel's sway as the cattlemen. Frosty fields and clusters of bare-branched trees surrounded us.

My next thought made me sad. *Will I even get the chance?* I missed Alex and always would, but I missed just *being* with someone too. Careless touches. Being held.

Seb had gone quiet. When I glanced over, he was watching me, one sneaker propped on the dash. "Your turn," he said, his voice casual. "Is there a rule about taking too long? I think this means I should win."

"You wish," I said automatically. Had Seb caught any of that? "Okay, got it," I said after a pause. "The minister's cat is an ambidextrous, bald, cunning, delightful, easy-going, fat, *garrulous* cat."

Seb frowned. "Garrulous?"

"Talks a lot."

"*Madre mía,* you could be making half of these up and I wouldn't know. I still don't think *ambidextrous* is a word."

"It *is*. Look it up." Then I realized there probably wasn't a dictionary within a hundred miles and laughed as Seb shook his head in mock despair.

At night we could, in theory, have shared the driving and kept going, but we ended up pulling over and sleeping for a few hours instead. "You don't trust my driving," Seb observed the first night, sounding wounded.

"Frankly, no. Do *you* trust your driving?"

The first night in the truck was cold, but not too bad. On the second, though, the stars overhead were sharp and piercing. With the heater off, an icy chill gripped us.

We were parked on a dirt road in the middle of nowhere. I lay huddled in my seat with the parka draped over me; after half an hour, it was so cold that it felt like I wasn't wearing anything at all. Seb didn't look much more comfortable, curled on his side in that thin jacket.

"Um – maybe we should try the sleeping bag," I said. My teeth were chattering. "Spread it out in the back, I mean."

I could feel Seb shielding his emotions more strongly than ever, and I hated that I'd had to suggest this. Finally he gave a curt nod. "Yes, all right."

Standing outside to shift stuff around in the truck made us even colder at first. When we'd cleared a large enough space, I slid into the sleeping bag first, fully dressed. Without speaking, Seb got in too and zipped it shut, his body close against mine.

The warmth was such a relief. Inch by inch, my muscles relaxed, like I'd eased into a hot bath. My mind was a different matter. I swallowed, taken aback. I'd missed this: sleeping pressed against a warm, firm body. Oh god, I'd missed this so much.

Stop, I reminded myself shakily. *This isn't Alex.*

"Yes, this is better," Seb said at last. He was lying on his side, using his jacket for a pillow; I could feel the woven material of his sweater against my hand. "Maybe we won't be ice cubes now."

I swallowed. "That…would have been bad."

Outside I could see the shapes of the trees in the moonlight, their branches sparkling with frost. Suddenly I had the insane urge to slip my hand under Seb's sweater and touch warm skin. I bit my lip and pulled my hand close against myself, trying not to touch him at all.

It took me a long time after that, but eventually I drifted off to sleep...and dreamed about my mother. She was sitting in her old chair, her green eyes focused inward on her dreamworld – the one that had claimed her from me for as long as I could remember.

I crouched beside her, dimly aware of worn floorboards beneath my knees. I frowned as I studied her. I had the strangest feeling that she wasn't just lost in her thoughts at all, but that part of her was actually somewhere else – some tangible place. And that she wasn't alone.

"Mom?" I whispered, taking her hand.

My heart skipped as she blinked and saw me. "Willow," she murmured. And as her fingers tightened around mine, familiar images started to come: small-town streets with tree-covered mountains in the distance.

"What *about* Pawntucket, Mom?" I urged. My mother's gaze stayed locked on me; I could sense her straining to communicate even this much.

"Mom, please! Try to tell me!" I massaged her hand between both of mine. There was something I wasn't getting, something vital.

But that was all; the dream was slipping away. Another glimpse of her eyes...the pressure of her fingers, fading – and then it was gone.

"No – *no!*" I burst out.

"Willow?" whispered a voice.

I started. Seb was lying beside me, very close, his face next to mine.

"I…was having a dream," I said. I licked dry lips as I realized that Seb and I had curled up together as we'd slept; I was against his chest, and his arms were around me. He seemed to realize it at the same time. His muscles tensed and he drew away, moving the arm that was resting over my waist.

I shifted back a little too. As if nothing had happened, I went on, "Only…it didn't *feel* like a dream. It felt real."

When I told Seb about it, he was silent. His arm under my head stayed very still, his hand not touching my shoulder. "It sounds as if we're going to the right place," he said finally.

The possibility that the trouble in Pawntucket had something to do with my mother had never occurred to me. But her eyes, urging me on… I let out a breath, more determined than ever to get back to my hometown.

"Yeah, I guess we are," I said.

The silence grew heavy – and then all at once I picked up on Seb's feelings. They clutched at my throat, raw in their intensity: a deep unhappiness that felt as if it had been there for a long time…and a yearning towards me that he couldn't control.

I lay without moving, intensely aware of Seb's arm under my head – and of an answering ache within myself.

It can't be for Seb, though – can it? I thought in confusion. *It's never been him I feel this way about.*

My mouth was like cotton. "Well…goodnight," I said at last.

"Yes, goodnight," Seb echoed.

And that time, I didn't manage to get back to sleep at all.

For over a thousand years, the Aztec pyramids of Teotihuacán had existed unchanged, connected by broad stone avenues that stretched in long, sun-drenched lines. Now these thoroughfares of the ancient city were flanked by new, hastily constructed buildings; the hawkers who'd once crowded them, selling souvenirs to tourists, were gone.

So were the tourists. Instead, Teotihuacán Eden was packed with those humans who'd survived the Mexico City quake – and with the thousands of angels who'd stayed down here too.

"You've got to do something, Raziel," said Gallad in a low voice. They were standing atop the Pyramid of the Sun, overlooking the busy walled city. Just visible was the dark, fenced building where the immune were being kept. Gallad motioned angrily. "We're having to put more in there every day. They're mostly A2s – the angels in that zone are starting to go *hungry*, do you realize that?"

"I do," Raziel said, his jaw tight. In the time he'd spent here, he'd found no answers. His only comfort was that his assassination of the Council was likely to go undetected; he'd found nothing that would give him away.

But plenty to threaten his leadership, if he wasn't careful. The angels down here had been baying for blood – he'd spent nearly a week already trying to smooth things over, with no idea of whether he'd succeeded.

"You do know that some are saying this is because we're not really angels any more?" Gallad demanded. "First the deaths of the Council, then being separated. They're saying we're the walking dead, rejected by the very world that was meant to save us."

"Ridiculous," snapped Raziel. "What's happening is just a fluke. We have no proof that it's spreading." The humans affected, it turned out, had all come from the same rundown neighbourhood near the Mexico City *centro*. Their immunity could just be location-based.

The other angel's eyes were unforgiving. "We have no proof that it isn't spreading either. That's the point, Raziel. *We don't know.*"

Raziel thought of Pawntucket; with a chill, he didn't answer. What was happening in Willow's hometown was not news that he'd chosen to share with the Mexico City angels. He mentally checked off the aberrations: Kara and the other AKs. Mexico City. Pawntucket.

The only thing that linked them all was Willow.

But *how*? And what if Gallad was right, and this thing was spreading organically? The angels could all die, and his reign would be over before it had scarcely begun.

His cellphone went off, giving him an excuse to turn away from Gallad without responding. Bascal. About time. He spoke tersely: "What happened?"

"They're all dead," said Bascal with satisfaction. "And, boss, you should have seen it! What a fight – we lost over a hundred, but it was worth it. Those AKs never even had a chance."

Raziel waited, but Bascal didn't continue. The dolt. Through gritted teeth, he said, "What about Fields and Kylar?" Beside him, he saw Gallad's eyebrows fly up.

"I said *all*, didn't I?" protested Bascal's voice. "Everyone in the place is gone now, I guarantee it."

"You saw the bodies?"

"Well, not personally – but when I left, no one was alive. We took care of *that*, you bet."

Foreboding pulsed through Raziel, as well as fury with himself. How could he have been so idiotic as to leave this to Bascal? "You will go back and check again," he ordered. "If you don't have a body, you have nothing, do you hear me?"

"We already did check again. We did it days ago, only there's not much to see – we burned the place out."

"*Days* ago?" Raziel hissed. "This happened days ago, and you're only just now telling me? What have you been doing ever since – carousing with A1s in some penthouse somewhere?"

Bascal's sullen silence told him that he wasn't far off. "Well, we had a right to celebrate, didn't we?" he said finally. "This was a dangerous assignment. Lots of us died. And that reminds me, speaking of A1s—"

"Don't. Even. Say it," cautioned Raziel. "You will lose everything you already have if you don't do *exactly* what I tell you – and so will your friends, and they'll know you're the reason why. Do you understand?"

There was a long pause. "Yes, I understand," Bascal muttered at last.

"Go to Schenectady Eden at once. Take your army with you. We've got another battle ahead – but before that, I'll be debriefing everyone personally, to find out *exactly* which AKs died and which did not. I'll be there by the tenth. Do not delay."

When he hung up, Gallad was staring silently. The grey, ancient form of the Pyramid of the Moon rose up in the distance behind him. "Are you going to explain what that was about?" he asked.

"This…*thing* is happening in Pawntucket as well," admitted Raziel tensely. "Much stronger than we're seeing here. The only possible connection seems to be Willow

322

Fields. Bascal thinks she's dead, but she may have escaped."

For the first time, real fear showed in Gallad's eyes. "Fields…the one who can destroy us all," he murmured.

"No, she will not," retorted Raziel icily. "I'm leaving soon for Schenectady; it's the nearest Eden to Pawntucket. When I do, I want you to destroy every human here, and then lead the angels to join me."

Gallad's jaw dropped. "Destroy—"

"*Yes,*" barked Raziel, spinning towards him with tight fists. "We don't know what's going on, and we can't take chances. Destroy them! If you're right and it's spreading, we must contain it – otherwise we could all die!"

Gallad looked pale; Raziel could almost hear him thinking that over seventy thousand people lived in Teotihuacán Eden, with another twenty thousand in nearby refugee camps. Below, bright human auras went about their business – shopping, strolling down the long stone roads.

"I'll see to it," Gallad said finally. "But as for getting all the angels to Schenectady too—"

"Oh, they'll come," said Raziel. "Tell them we've found the cause: it's the fault of Willow Fields. We are now at war. Pawntucket is our first step towards obliterating her."

And as Raziel shifted to his angel form and flew away, he knew, ironically, that he'd found the one thing that could unite the angels under his leadership: his daughter.

CHAPTER *Twenty-three*

"IT'S THE MOST DIRECT WAY." Seb traced his finger along the map.

"I know, but I'm kind of nervous about Iowa," I admitted. It was the middle of the night, with the world dark and still around us. We'd stopped for gas at an abandoned Exxon station near the eastern South Dakota border, and now we were leaning against the truck, poring over the atlas.

Seb looked up, his hazel eyes catching the glow of my angel as she hovered to give us light. "Nervous?" he repeated.

"It's pretty populated," I explained. "All the states are now between here and New York. The chance of getting spotted by Eden staff will be a lot more likely from this point on."

I could hear the faint scrape of Seb's stubble as he rubbed his chin. "Maybe we should go up through Minnesota and into Canada instead." He turned to flatten the map against the hood. "We could cross the border right here – see? And then go north and then east again."

"Yeah, I was wondering about Canada, but we'd be cutting things pretty close. Plus the snow will be worse there." I stared down at the map with its different options. My stomach clenched when I imagined getting to Pawntucket too late to stop whatever Raziel was planning.

"Let's try Iowa," I said finally. "Do you have any feelings about it?" I wasn't getting anything; I was far too emotionally entangled.

Seb gave a *not really* grimace. "Both ways feel dangerous."

We looked at each other. Finally I shrugged, trying to hide my apprehension. "Well, if they're both dangerous… then let's at least take the fastest one, right?"

As the sun rose, at first there was little difference between Iowa and South Dakota: flat, frosty plains with occasional clusters of trees. As we drove, my thoughts kept turning uneasily to that moment of longing I'd felt towards Seb, and the fact that it was preying on my mind irritated me – it wasn't as if I didn't have enough to worry about already.

At least things were relatively back to normal between us – the morning after we'd shared the sleeping bag, we'd slipped back into banter, and last night it had been warm enough to keep to our own seats. Now, as we travelled across Iowa, we played "the minister's cat" again, though it kind of disintegrated when Seb started throwing in Spanish words and insisting they counted. Twenty questions was a failure too, when we each realized we were trying to psychically probe the other.

The whole time we were joking around, it felt as if we were waiting for something to happen.

After a few hours, we started seeing people again – groups of trudging refugees, burdened with belongings. One little girl staggered along with a cat carrier, her arms rigid under its weight. My eyes lingered on her. I longed to tell them all to pile in – but I could do nothing. *Nothing.*

No. I am *doing something,* I reminded myself. *I'm going to get rid of Raziel.*

Seb's glance held understanding. He started to say something…and then we both stiffened. Angelic energy – a lot of it and close by. Suddenly my palms were damp.

"We must be getting near an Eden," I said.

Seb already had the map open. "Mason City, maybe – it must be a new one." He flipped to the next page. "I'll find another way, so we can get off this road quickly."

I nodded tensely, scanning for angels as I drove. To one side we were hugging a rocky hill; there was a drop to the other. I rounded a bend – and slammed on the brakes, bringing us skidding to a stop.

There was a rockslide across a curve in the road. I stared in dismay. There was no way we could drive across: we'd have to take our chances off-road on the slope, or else get out and start moving stones.

Then I saw something else, just past the slope: the Eden wasn't even half a mile away, with its stark barbed-wire fence and dozens of angels circling overhead.

Seb and I exchanged a taut glance. As we got out of the truck, I was very aware of the pistol in the pocket of my parka. Going over to where the road met the slope, I gazed downward. Seb had already started bending and lifting, hefting stones out of the way.

"You know, I think maybe we could make it across the slope—" I started, and then broke off as my spine tingled. Looking up in sudden dread, I saw two armed figures step around the bend.

They sauntered towards us, machine guns at the ready – a pair of grinning men in mismatched camouflage gear. "Well, look at this," drawled one. Red hair and a broad smile. "*This* is a nice fish to catch – y'all got gas in that thing?"

Neither of us answered. Seb straightened up with his eyes narrowed, his stance deliberately relaxed. Like me, I could sense how much he wanted to bring out his angel – but just then a small pack of angels cruised overhead, wings flashing. Bringing attention to our half-angel selves right now was not a good idea.

"You want to get out of our way, bud," Redhead advised Seb. "'Cause let me tell you, shooting you and your girlfriend wouldn't bother me at all."

"Nah, Blondie's too cute to kill," smirked the other one. "She can stick around. If she's nice to us." Both men were already halfway across the rockslide, picking their way through the debris as if it was a well-known route.

My veins were ice. Without looking at each other, Seb's mind and mine touched: we couldn't let them have the truck. No matter what.

Seb's next thought came loud and clear: *I'll distract them and you run for it.*

Seb, no! I'm not leaving you.

The red-headed guy was about twenty feet away from Seb now. Still Seb stood there, not budging. The man stopped, regarding him with hard eyes. "Did you hear me? Get out of our way."

"Yes, I heard you." And deliberately, Seb reached for his

waistband. He wasn't even carrying a gun, but the man's reaction was immediate – he raised his machine gun and fired off a rapid volley of shots.

Seb fell, and I stopped breathing.

Then in a confused rush, I saw that Seb had just lunged down to grab a stone – he hurled it in almost the same motion. It hit the guy square in the stomach; as he crumpled, I snatched hold of my senses and drew my pistol. I pointed it at the second man before he could react.

"Stop!" My heart was slamming in my chest, but somehow my voice didn't shake. "Don't even think about it."

The first guy was up, panting as he aimed the machine gun at Seb. "Oh, you asked for it—"

Seb tackled him; the two went scrabbling on the rocky ground. The second guy scowled and started forward. *No.* Holding the pistol in both hands, I pulled the trigger. The man yelped as the bullet ricocheted off his weapon, almost wrenching it from his grasp.

I'd meant to hit his *arm* but had the sense not to show dismay. I clutched my pistol tightly, holding it steady. "Keep walking and I'll aim for you next time," I told him through gritted teeth.

When I risked a glance, Seb was sitting on the other guy's chest, pinning his arms with his knees – his switchblade open and pressed against the man's neck. As the blade glinted, there was nothing in his expression of the boy I knew. This was the Seb who'd grown up fighting on the streets.

"Do not make the mistake of thinking I won't cut your throat," he said in a low voice.

Redhead gulped, breathing hard.

"Drop the gun," I told the second guy, still pointing the pistol at him.

He blinked, looking from me to Seb, like, *Wait – this wasn't how it was supposed to go.*

"Do it!" cried Redhead. He looked very young suddenly; not much older than us. There was a pause – and then the second guy dropped his machine gun onto the rocks with a clatter.

"Now back away," I said.

He did so with his hands in the air. My legs felt like cotton, but I advanced quickly over the rockslide and scooped up the machine gun. Still holding his knife in place, Seb slowly reached for the other one. He grabbed it and got up, aiming it at the guy on the ground. He motioned tersely with his head. His cheek was bleeding.

"Both of you – go," he said.

Redhead half scrambled across the rocks as he ran. His friend took off after him.

Seb and I sprinted back to the truck and hurled ourselves in. My stomach was trembling. I ignored it and started the engine. A second later I'd lurched us over the slope, the world tilting alarmingly, and then I was gunning us down the road. Seb opened the window and aimed a machine gun at the two men as we passed them. They stood by the side of the road, hands up, watching us leave.

I couldn't relax even when they were no longer visible in the rear-view mirror – even when the Eden no longer was.

"That was close," I whispered. I imagined Seb falling to the ground in a roar of gunfire, bullets ripping through him. I swallowed hard. "That…that was so close."

Seb put the machine gun in the back. "Yes," he said, and I winced at the raw scrape on his cheek. Studying me, he seemed about to say something else – then he looked away and reached for the atlas. "I'll find us a different road."

I nodded, clutching the wheel. "I think we should start heading north now, towards Canada. If it's remote enough, we can stick to the highway and try to make good time." I glanced at him; my throat was dry. "Do you agree?"

Seb shrugged. "This is your trip, *querida*," he said quietly.

And I realized just how long it had been since he'd called me that. I faced forward again, my emotions in turmoil.

Now that we didn't have to avoid the farms of the Midwest, our route became more straightforward. For hours we made excellent time, flashing past lake after lake. The banter between us had gone. Almost all conversation had gone; in its place was a growing tension. I felt so aware of Seb next to me: his lean body, his energy that was so similar to mine.

By late afternoon we thought we might have crossed over into Canada, though there didn't seem to be a welcome sign any more. It had snowed recently, though, slowing us down; we had to stop and put on the chains. It seemed like a good idea anyway – the sky had turned a smooth, pearly grey.

Finally we came to a county road heading north. Definitely Canada, I saw with relief: the road sign was shaped like a shield with a crown on top.

Seb was behind the wheel when the snow really hit. He muttered something in Spanish as the flakes attacked the windshield like a swarm of bees; his leg flexed as he tapped the brakes, his forehead tensed in concentration. Already, the road was fading away into a white blur on either side. When a grey chimney swam out of the storm, Seb angled us towards it.

"I think we better stop here – it's getting dark anyway."

I nodded, feeling apprehensive. If this didn't let up soon, we'd be snowed in – maybe even for the rest of the season. I wished we could push on, but it would be suicidal.

You can't control the weather, I reminded myself harshly

as Seb pulled the truck over. Whatever happened, we'd just have to deal with it.

Through swirling flakes, I saw a large A-frame building of grey stone. A sign read: TAKETA LOUNGE AND RESTAURANT. Sinking into fresh snow up to our ankles, we grabbed our things and headed over, flakes pouring down. There was a porch area with a few rustic chairs; I shook myself off, swiping the wetness from my hair.

"Locked," Seb said as he tried the door.

I started to reach for my angel, but Seb had already gone for his own. Seconds later, he returned in a flurry. Seb grimaced. "No, there's something wrong with the lock," he muttered. He took out his switchblade and crouched down.

"I didn't know you could pick locks," I said, as he started to probe at the side of the door with his blade.

"Yes, I have many skills," he replied, his voice toneless.

The bruise on his face looked even worse now, the skin tight and sore, and I gripped my elbows hard as I gazed at it.

Seb could have died. Just like Alex.

I saw Seb fall to the ground again – heard the roar of the explosion at the AK camp. Something in me went very still as I studied Seb, his firm shoulders flexing as he worked. I could sense the unhappiness that was his constant companion – the longing he couldn't control.

And my heart ached with an answering longing, this time so strong it left me dizzy.

Seb, what are you doing to me?

"There," he muttered as the doorknob gave way. "There was something bent inside it." He stood up, flicking the blade away; he put it in his jeans pocket.

He started to reach for our things. As our eyes met, my feelings were raw – exposed. Seb froze. Face tight, he abruptly turned away and started grabbing up the bags.

I helped, feeling hot and cold at the same time. Neither of us spoke. When we went inside, we found ourselves in a lounge area: an imposing stone fireplace with a sheepskin rug stretched out in front of it and an L-shaped sofa. A huge wicker basket half full of wood sat on the hearth.

Still without speaking, Seb went behind the shadowy bar and started rummaging. He found a book of matches and crouched in front of the fireplace, starting a fire with a handful of glossy brochures for kindling. They cast a greenish glow.

Once the fire was going, he came back to the bar and leaned next to me. We both gazed across at the flames.

I cleared my throat. "That's…really good that you got a fire lit," I said. "There must be a kitchen somewhere too. Maybe we can find some pots and pans, and heat up our meal for a change. Hey, we could use plates. And real silverware."

I was babbling. I fell quiet again. Seb's profile remained motionless, etched golden in the firelight. Finally he scraped his hands over his face. When he spoke, his voice was low.

"Tell me. What I sensed outside – did I only imagine it?"

My skin felt electric. I shook my head. "No. You didn't imagine it."

Seb's eyes flew to mine. He swallowed, his expression haunted.

I wanted so badly to comfort him. I wanted so badly to comfort myself. I gently laid my hand against his hurt cheek, feeling the surface chill of his skin with the warmth underneath – the soft prickle of his stubble.

My voice wasn't even a whisper. "Seb," I said.

Our gazes held as the fire crackled. For a long moment, neither of us moved. I'd forgotten how. Then, slowly, Seb reached up and took my hand.

He lowered his head to mine; I closed my eyes as our lips met. The moment spiralled out into infinity as we tasted each other. Seb's hand moved to my head, stroked through my hair. His feelings enveloped me in a rush, rocking me; at the same time he pulled me close against him, and I wrapped my arms around him tightly, drowning in the feel of him – his mouth, hungry on mine; his tongue, warm and wet and real.

It had been so long since I'd been held this way – so long since I'd felt like this. I broke away, kissing his jaw, his cheek, his temple. "Seb, Seb," I cried, burying my face against his neck.

He clutched me to him – his lips on my hair, then pulling away to hold my head with both hands, kissing my mouth again. "It's always been you," he said fiercely between kisses. "No matter what I did – no matter what I wanted – always you."

I could never get enough of him; I wanted to climb inside him. We fell against the bar with a bump as we kissed and kissed. I could feel the pounding of Seb's heart through his sweater – or maybe it was my own. Seb's hands moved across my back; he found bare skin just above my jeans, and his touch shivered through me.

And now I could feel our angels too. As the fire cast dancing shadows around the rustic room, they'd emerged above us and were buried in each other's energy…joined so deeply that I couldn't tell where one ended and the other began.

CHAPTER *Twenty-four*

ALEX'S SHOULDERS SLUMPED AS HE spotted the stream through the trees. Oh, thank Christ – it had been two days since he'd managed to fill his water bottle. Limping on his throbbing left foot, he made his way down the muddy bank. The water felt cold on his hands and face as he scooped up handful after handful to drink.

He'd been wary of the water here at first, but he'd had no choice except to try it – and he'd found it cleaner and fresher than anything back home. The angels had no industry, no pollution. In many ways their world was a complete Eden, though just the word made Alex grimace.

He drank his fill and then refilled the plastic bottle, screwing the cap back on carefully before replacing it in his pack. Turning his attention to his foot, he drew off the tattered sock. God, his flesh looked as if it had been through a meat grinder: oozing blisters and cuts that couldn't heal. He dipped it in the stream and winced. Presumably the plants here were similar to those in his world – if he knew how, he could make himself a poultice or something. He'd have to take the survivalist class along with the rest of his team when he got home.

Because he was going to get home. End of story.

"What are you doing?" asked a morose voice.

Alex hardly looked up. "Soaking my foot."

"Oh." A man drifted into view through the trees. Sandy hair and a worried expression, clothes that had been fashionable ten years ago. "Have you seen the angels?" he asked.

"No." Alex motioned with his head. "Denver's that way." He had no idea whether the place he was heading to was called Denver here or not. It didn't matter; the ghosts never listened. This one didn't either.

"They've all gone," the man said sadly. He came around so that he was standing in the stream in front of Alex, looking deceptively substantial. The water flowed on, undisturbed by his presence.

"No, they haven't," said Alex.

"There used to be so many of them…so glorious…and now they've all gone. Their world is still beautiful, though. All the rainbows…" The man trailed off, gazing at the rainbows that only ghosts could seem to see. Then he remembered Alex and looked at him hopefully. "So do you know where the angels are? Can you help me find them?"

Alex didn't respond. Once they got going on this subject, the ghosts could keep talking for ever. He drew his foot out of the water and dried it as best he could; the sores looked no less fierce. He pulled on his sock, gritting his teeth at the pain. When he looked again, the man had vanished. There were only the trees on the opposite bank.

The "ghosts" had startled Alex at first, then intrigued him – now, after three weeks in this world, he was bored out of his skull by them. He still wasn't sure what they were. He'd never seen a ghost in his own world and thought he would have, if they really existed. Were these memories, somehow, of people the angels had fed from? Except that their thoughts, though predictable, did seem pretty rooted in the here and now. The few angels Alex had seen – flying distantly overhead, looking flagging and weak – paid the ghosts no attention at all. Definitely the best policy.

Anyway, the ghost had been right about one thing – there weren't many angels here any more; clearly almost all of them had now evacuated to the human world. *Lucky us,* thought Alex. He rose and tested his weight on his foot. It would do – it would have to; he still had at least twenty miles to go.

He touched the woven bracelet on his wrist. Willow must be out of her mind by now. *Not much longer, babe, I promise,* he thought, as he climbed up the bank. Imagining being back with her again – holding her close, seeing her smile – was what drove him to walk extra miles every day, when his throbbing foot would have preferred to rest.

Alex continued on his way, keeping as brisk a stride as he could. He was deep in the angels' equivalent of the Rockies now, with woods to either side and a soaring view of mountains whenever he reached a clearing.

In his world, this area was total wilderness. Here, the angels had apparently groomed the place to be a giant outdoor park. He was walking on a path that had once been tended, lined with small symmetrical rocks; occasionally he passed items that appeared to be artwork, though any meaning was lost on him. He studied a large globe made of steel bands, lying dented beside a marble block.

As he walked, he scanned constantly for angels. He'd seen only a handful in three weeks, but wasn't about to become careless now – not when he was so close. There were none, though he saw several more ghosts. They kept their distance, staring mournfully at him as he passed.

He kept on after dark, his heart quickening in anticipation. Denver was only a few miles away now – with luck, he could be back in his own world before morning. Then hot pain tore through his injured foot.

Alex swore; groping down, he pulled away a stick with thorns. He could hardly even *see* his foot any more, but could feel the warm blood streaming from it, soaking into the sock. He hurled the stick into the undergrowth. Stopping when he was so close felt like torture, but if he kept on he might stroll over a cliff before he even noticed.

Reluctantly, he left the path and made his way into the trees; he sank down between two of them and let out a long breath, head dropped back against the bark. His muscles were starting to sing. How far had he walked today? Twenty miles, thirty?

He took a deep, thirsty swig of water, conscious now of how hungry he was. He only had one energy bar left; he allowed himself two bites and then lay down tiredly, covering himself with his leather jacket. The ground was freezing, but at least there was no snow. Adding frostbite to his sore and bleeding foot would have just been a joke.

The smell of damp earth surrounded him; he could hear the gentle rustling of the wind. Exhausted, Alex stared into the shadows, thinking about Denver. If it was laid out like the Denver in his own world, then the gate would be near the cathedral somewhere – on the north side of town, slightly outside the city limits. So he'd circle around and, he hoped, avoid the remaining angels.

He'd learned early on that most congregated in the cities – when he'd passed Albuquerque, the place had been comparatively teeming. He didn't have a clue why the creatures no longer seemed to enjoy strolling around in their wilderness parks, but he wasn't about to argue.

As Alex finally drifted off to sleep, he touched his woven bracelet again: the colours of his aura and Willow's entwined. *Not much longer,* he vowed silently. He'd get back to her soon – or die trying.

When Alex had first opened his eyes after the blast, there hadn't been a single part of him that didn't ache.

Gazing blearily upwards, he'd seen smooth white walls that met a plain ceiling, light streaming in through a small window. Dawn. Or sunset, maybe. Ignoring the fact that he felt as if he'd been clubbed with a mallet, he slowly rose to his feet and stared around him.

Jesus, he'd made it. He was in the angels' world – though getting here had been agony like nothing he'd ever experienced. Recalling the sense of being crushed, ripped apart, Alex marvelled that he was even still alive.

The room that he'd glimpsed from his father's house was weirdly ordinary, something he wouldn't have looked at twice in his own world – about the same size as his dad's place, but all one open area. It had the feel of a disused storeroom, with a thin layer of dust and a stale scent. He couldn't see any form of lighting; apart from that, the only strange thing was a painted line of symbols on one wall – elegant squiggles and swirls that he couldn't read. A wooden crate lay on its side, empty.

Wondering briefly what angels needed to store, Alex sank down onto it, his thoughts spinning. Everything ached. He was coated with a powdery grime, and had a dozen scrapes and bruises. His left ankle was the worst: a long, shallow scratch that had clearly bled a lot; his sock was stained with red.

Sock. Suddenly he realized that he was only wearing one shoe. Alex stared down at his foot in bemusement. The shoe must have gotten blown off in the explosion.

It all rushed back. That's right; he'd seen the house go, had lost sight of this room in the blast. He must have passed through just as everything went up – he was even luckier to be alive than he'd thought.

"But what the hell, Cull," he murmured. The plain room was silent, ageless. "It *is* possible to get here."

Alarm hit as he recalled again the force of the explosion. He straightened up sharply. Speeding his consciousness up through his chakra points, he scanned the room.

The opening between the worlds was gone.

No, stay calm – he had to be imagining this. Alex got up and circled the room, examining the ether from every angle. There wasn't even the faintest ripple to show where the gate had been.

"Shit," he whispered hollowly. Dust motes glinted, stirred by his walking. How could he carry out his father's plan with no gate leading back to his own world? No, forget *that* – how the hell was he supposed to get home?

"There's got to be a way," he muttered. "The angels get through all the time – I've just got to find one of their routes, that's all."

Yeah, simple.

Alex slumped back onto the crate and slowly rubbed his hands down his face as he gazed at where the opening should have been. Okay, fine – for the time being, he was stuck here. Deal with it. Meanwhile, he'd try to do what he came here for. Maybe that would provide some answers that staring into space couldn't.

His father's idea had first been born years ago, when Martin had seen an angel crossing into the human world. He'd done a hasty scan before the entryway between dimensions had closed – and learned that the energy field of the angel world was wholly different from that of the human one. Far stronger, but also more pliable, organized – nothing like the faint but chaotic energy of home.

"It could be controlled, I'm sure of it," Martin had told

his sons. "Think of it – the energy field of an entire world at our fingertips! If we could just get over there long enough to connect with it, we could bridge it back to our own world and use it to destroy the angels!"

Remembering, Alex shook his head. Even now that he'd crossed the first hurdle, the idea still seemed insane to him. *I hope you were right about this, Cull,* he thought, closing his eyes. *Or else I'm stuck here for nothing, and then I really am going to feel like a complete idiot.*

Martin had taught both his sons how to tap into the world's energy field – something Alex hadn't bothered with in years; at home there was no reason for it. Now he carefully centred himself, planting both feet firmly on the ground. Then he lifted his consciousness and let it spread out in all directions. In his own world, this sensation made him mildly dizzy; here it brought a wave of nausea that had him pale and sweating in seconds. He paid no attention.

There, exactly as Martin had described – a sea of seething energy that roared past his senses. Yet he could tell what his dad had meant: there was an *order* to it. The sense that if you could just figure out the right key, it could be yours.

Alex felt a flicker of excitement. Cautiously, he started to delve into the energy, attempting to merge into it like Martin had taught him.

"*Ahh!*" He jerked back; the crate skidded as he crashed

onto the floor. Senses reeling, he hefted himself backwards and slumped against the wall for a minute, breathing hard. The pain had been like grabbing an electrified fence.

His next few attempts were even worse. After an hour of increasingly violent expulsions, Alex was clammy and shaking, muscles taut. "Okay, yeah, this is a real success," he muttered finally, wiping his forehead. "Oh, man, Cully. I wish you weren't dead so I could kill you."

He gripped his temples, forcing himself to face the truth: his energy was alien to that of this world; there was no way for him to breach it. His dad had been wrong. Cully had been wrong. He could observe the energy field here – that was all.

Alex sat motionless, fury and disappointment raging through him. Yeah, he'd just had to *try* this thing, hadn't he? He'd known it was insane, and now what? He wondered if Willow could sense him in this world; imagining what she'd think if she couldn't, he winced. Oh, Christ, he'd be frantic if it were her. He'd rather have died in the blast than live trapped in this world for nothing.

Alex's jaw hardened at the thought. No. He would get home again.

He did a scan to check that there was no life beyond the walls. Then he grabbed his backpack and rifle, swung them over his shoulder, and stepped out into a gentle dusk in the angels' world.

He was in an enclosure reminiscent of his father's old camp: plain white buildings that were clearly abandoned, though these were clustered around a central courtyard. There was no fence. Desert lay in all directions, startlingly like the one he knew – even the low mountains on the horizon were the same. A warm breeze stroked past.

Relieved at the similarity between worlds, Alex squinted north across the desert. With the gateway here obliterated, the one place where he knew the angels had crossed dimensions before was in Denver.

Over five hundred miles of desert and mountains, and he had no vehicle and only one shoe – but at least he had a direction to head in. It should take him a few weeks, if he was lucky and made it without being discovered.

Please try not to worry too much, babe, he thought to Willow. *I'll be home as soon as I can, I promise.*

As he headed across the dusty courtyard, its flat stones still held some of the day's warmth. Where they ended, the ground turned gritty under his shoeless foot.

Leaving the buildings silent and empty behind him, Alex started walking across the desert.

Now, three weeks later – three weeks during which his sock had rapidly disintegrated until he was limping on cuts and blisters, but still he'd refused to slow his pace; three weeks of largely harsh terrain with barely any food to keep him going – Alex had finally reached his goal.

When he'd first woken up that morning, he'd found a foxlike creature nestled asleep against him – the animals here had no fear at all. He'd smiled in slight surprise, touching the reddish-gold fur; the fox-thing had awakened with a sharp, pointed yawn and ambled off. It had seemed a good omen.

It wasn't.

Alex lay on his stomach on a grassy hill, staring down at the city below. In some ways, it looked very much like the Denver he knew – some of the buildings were even the same. He could pick out a twin to the Wells Fargo Centre with its curved apex, and something that looked like the Centre for the Performing Arts, though with a kind of crystal surface.

What wasn't the same was the size of the place. It was easily twice as big as the human Denver, extending well past the Coliseum-like building to the north that seemed to match the Church of Angels cathedral. There would be no "going around" the city to reach the place – he'd have to go straight through.

And it was full of angels.

Alex raised his rifle and peered through the magnified lens. There were no cars; the street surfaces looked cobbled, like an old European town. Scanning slowly, he saw a few angels in their human forms – always in a group, never alone – but could sense a hell of a lot more that weren't visible. He frowned as he probed the angelic energy. It felt *frightened,* almost – as if they were all huddling together somewhere for comfort.

But he could be wrong, and he had to be prepared for anything. Glancing at the sun, he grimaced. He'd have to wait until dark before he attempted this. Another delay when he was so close was galling.

"What are you doing?" asked a soft female voice.

"Checking out the city," Alex responded without looking up. He watched a flock of angels circling down below; the motion had a ritualistic sense. Was that how they fed here? If so, they didn't stay in flight very long. He waited for the ghost's next comment – maybe about how beautiful the angels were, for a change, instead of *where have they all gone?*

"You seem really familiar," she said in a puzzled tone.

Alex glanced up – and his heart stopped. A girl of around his own age sat in the grass beside him, hugging her knees to her chest; she had long blonde hair and delicately pointed features.

Willow? he thought, thunderstruck.

He sat up, staring. No, this wasn't Willow, he realized in confusion – her hair wasn't as wavy, her face slightly different. Besides, Willow hadn't been blonde in over a year.

"Who are you?" His voice was hoarse.

The way the girl's mouth pursed – like Willow's did when she was thinking about something – caught at his heart.

"I should know that," she said finally. "I'm sorry – I get confused about things sometimes. It's usually better here, but…" She shrugged and rested a cheek on her knees, studying him. Though wind stirred the grass, her hair and skirt hung motionless. Her eyes were Willow's: leaf green and slightly tilted.

"You do seem very familiar," she repeated with a frown. "I don't think I know you, though."

Maybe not, but Alex suddenly had a sinking feeling that he knew her.

"Miranda?" he said softly, hoping he was wrong.

Her face lit up, making her look more like Willow than ever. "Yes, that's me! I *do* know you."

"Kind of," Alex got out. "I…know someone you know."

His throat was dry. Jesus, was *this* what the ghosts were – the part that went missing in people with severe angel burn? Willow had described to him so many times how her mother just sat catatonic, lost in her dreams. Exactly like millions of others with minds shattered by the angels. Apparently some essential part of them had simply left the human world and come here, where the angels were from.

"I don't usually come to this city any more," Miranda was saying. "There's someplace else I like to go. But then I sensed you – and you seemed so familiar that I had to come."

"Yeah?" Alex asked dully. Should he even tell Willow about this? God, she loved her mother so much – as a child, she'd cared for Miranda alone, keeping her mental illness a secret so that no one would take her away. Would it make her feel better or worse to know that somewhere her mother wandered, eternally young and beautiful and confused?

"Yes, it's strange," Miranda went on. "It's as if…as if someone reaches out to me sometimes, and I've heard them talking about you." Looking disturbed, she cocked her head to one side, studying him. "You said you know someone I do. Is it Raziel?" Her voice softened at the name.

Alex held back a bitter laugh. "Uh – no," he said. "I mean, yeah, I do, but I don't think that's how you know me." He hesitated; did she even remember she *had* a daughter? He plucked a piece of dry grass from the ground, twisting it between his fingers.

"Do you know Willow?" he asked finally.

Miranda went still. "Willow," she repeated. "I remember once in the other world…that was when…" Her eyes became lost in time; Alex had the sudden fear that she might vanish.

"Can you see that other world now?" he asked quickly. "Is anyone there with you? Do you know where you live there?"

As he'd hoped, the questions seemed to ground Miranda; she focused on him again as she considered. "There's a lake, I think. I hear it sometimes…and Jo is there. My sister."

Alex started to ask if she knew who'd protected them – the mystery person who'd burned Joanna's house down to convince the world that the two women had died – but Miranda was still talking.

"When I sense whoever it is that's reaching out to me, that's where they're reaching – to the Miranda by the lake. But I can still hear it. Feel it. Right here," she said, touching her heart with slender fingers. She left them there, frowning.

"Wait – that someone reaching out to me – Willow!" Her eyes flew to his, as if seeking confirmation. "I have a daughter."

Alex nodded. "Yeah, you do."

"How could I have forgotten?" Miranda murmured, pressing her fingertips to her forehead. She darted him an almost frightened glance. "How old is she now?"

"Eighteen." There was so much more Alex wanted to say – *she's beautiful; you'd be so proud to know her; she makes my life worth living* – but he kept quiet, letting Miranda adjust.

"Eighteen – but—" She licked her lips. "But I'm only twenty-one."

Grey clouds were rolling in over the bruised peaks of the mountains. The breeze picked up; Alex felt cold even with his jacket. He chose his words carefully.

"The part of you that's here is still twenty-one. I guess you always will be. But in the other world, you're old enough to be Willow's mother."

Though Miranda's eyes stayed locked on his, he wasn't really sure how much she was taking in. The wind tugged at his hair. Miranda sat as if in a bubble of protection, hair and clothes motionless.

"I never see Raziel any more," she said finally. She nudged at a blade of grass. Her finger passed right through it. "He used to come here sometimes – I'd follow him, though he never knew."

"You mean the angels can't see you?"

Miranda gave a wistful shake of her head. "I don't know why, when we all want them to so badly…"

When Alex had first encountered the ghosts, he hadn't sensed any energy from them, though he hadn't spent much time trying. Attempting again now, he detected only a faint life energy from Miranda – just an echo, really, and more on the human world's frequency than here. Maybe they could only be seen by humans, then.

"Raziel used to come to this city sometimes," Miranda

went on, nodding downward. "But now he never does, so I go somewhere else. It's a special place, though." A fleeting smile. "I remember things there that make me happy."

"I'm glad." The words came out huskily. God, she was so much like Willow – or Willow was like her. Except Miranda seemed so much more vulnerable. Alex felt protective towards her for Willow's sake – though it was kind of late for that now.

"It makes me feel clearer, talking to you," Miranda said. Hesitantly, she continued, "In the other place – where I'm old enough to be Willow's mother – I have trouble thinking sometimes."

"I know," Alex admitted. "Willow told me."

Her face was tense, anxious. "How did I take care of her, then?"

Christ, what a question. "You did the best you could, I guess," Alex said. But remembering how Willow had told him how much she'd dreaded going to school every day and leaving her mother alone, he knew that Miranda's best hadn't been great.

She seemed to realize this too. She winced, studying her hands clasped around her knees. "I know I didn't do a very good job," she whispered. "Before I met Raziel, I wasn't like this."

"Yeah. I know that too."

"You do?" Her gaze collided with his again; she looked

away, twisting the hem of her skirt. "I – I wonder sometimes…I mean, if Raziel had something to do with…" She swallowed. "But that's crazy, isn't it?"

Her voice was pleading, though Alex couldn't tell what she wanted to hear. "It's not crazy," he said. "You're not the only person who's felt confused after meeting an angel. All the others here are the same. Plenty of people back home too. It's…kind of a side effect." He'd never described angel burn so mildly in his life.

Miranda didn't respond directly, though Alex had a feeling she'd understood. She gazed down at the city. "Is Willow all right?"

"Yeah, she's fine."

"How do you know her? You haven't said – or have you?"

"I'm a friend of hers." Explaining that Willow had had a serious boyfriend for over a year, when Miranda hadn't even remembered that she *had* a daughter just a few minutes ago, seemed a bit much.

"She's on her way to Pawntucket," Miranda offered after a pause.

Alex straightened abruptly. "She's *what*?"

"Pawntucket," repeated Miranda. "We lived there for a long time. And it's where…" She looked down; her cheeks tinged as she cleared her throat. "Anyway, she's going there."

He'd thought Miranda was fairly lucid; now he was starting to doubt it. "Are you sure?"

"Oh, yes," she said. "I can feel it. It's something to do with Raziel – I think maybe he's going there too." She gave a crooked smile. "See, I told you that talking to you made me feel clearer."

Pawntucket, thought Alex dazedly. Why the hell would Willow be going there if Raziel was? What sort of trap was he building?

A light rain had started. "She's been very sad, you know," added Miranda, unaffected by the weather. "For a long time."

"Yeah?" murmured Alex, still distracted by Pawntucket – and then the words sank in. Oh Christ, that must mean that she couldn't sense him here; she must think he was dead. His heart wrenched in his chest as he imagined her going through that.

Alex started to ask how she was and then stopped, alarmed to see Miranda looking faint around the edges again. Her form and voice wavered as she said, "All these people who are confused... Maybe – maybe it would be better if that hadn't happened to them. I mean... even if that meant they couldn't see how beautiful the angels are."

Alex watched her sharply. Keeping his voice casual, he said, "That's what Willow thinks too. So do I. A lot of us are trying to make it so that people aren't confused by the angels any more."

To his relief, Miranda turned more substantial again. "You are?"

"Yeah." Alex swiped his hand through his hair; it was heavy with damp. "That's why I'm here. I was trying to use the energy field to defeat them. It didn't work, though. Now I'm just trying to get home."

Solid once more, Miranda crinkled her nose at him. "*You* were trying to use the angels' energy field? But that's impossible."

Great – it was obvious even to a confused, drifting ghost. "Thanks, I found that out," he said dryly.

"Because you're human," Miranda explained earnestly, as if pleased to be able to help. "The energy field here is very strong, but very exact. You can *sense* things with it, but you can't use it like the angels do unless you belong here – it wouldn't let you." After a pause, she said thoughtfully, "Willow could, though."

The world felt suddenly electric. Of course: *Willow*, with her half-angel energy. Alex propped his weight on one hand, leaning close to Miranda.

"There's another half-angel in our world too," he said intensely. "Could he help her?"

"Does he have someone here?"

Alex frowned, not seeing the relevance. But Seb's

mother was dead, and as far as Alex knew, there was no one else Seb had ever been close to with angel burn. He shook his head. "No. He's alone."

"I don't think so, then," Miranda said, her voice musing. "Because trying it would be such a jolt, you see. But I'm here for Willow, and she has someone in her own world who she could mentally hold on to there, doesn't she?"

"Yeah," said Alex faintly, sinking back into place on the wet grass. "Yeah, she does."

Willow: Paschar's vision that she was the one who could destroy the angels – her, and no one else. This was how. Oh Jesus, *this was how.*

It was full-out raining now, pattering down on Alex's head and jacket. Looking at the city, he saw how dark and shadowy it had become and made a sudden decision. "I've got to go now," he said, standing up.

Miranda blinked. "Go?"

"Yeah – back to my own world, so I can tell Willow about this. If she tries it, then you'll help her, right?"

Miranda frowned; her next words rocked him. "Of course, but...do you really know how to get back? I thought Raziel was the only one who knew that, now that he's destroyed all the gates."

* * *

The rain beat down, bouncing manically off the cobblestones; the clouds had blackened so that it was almost as dark as night. Having shifted his aura to angelic silver, Alex kept to the shadows as he made his way to the Coliseum, gritting his teeth as his injured foot struggled with the cobblestones.

At ground level this Denver looked a lot less like the city he knew. There were no traffic lights – no sidewalks or signs. Abstract sculptures rose from strange places: the middle of the street or sprouting from the sides of buildings.

Miranda walked beside him, exactly Willow's height: the top of her head reached just past his chin. "Please don't tell Raziel I'm helping you get home," she said again, her voice anxious. "He's the only one who's supposed to know about the gate – he might be angry if he found out I followed him."

"Don't worry, I won't tell him," Alex muttered. A block down, he'd just spotted a group of angels in their human forms. He kept walking, minimizing his limp. He'd hidden the rifle under his clothes, but just his backpack was probably conspicuous enough.

The angels disappeared around a corner; Alex relaxed slightly. "Raziel and I aren't exactly friends," he clarified.

From what Miranda had said, Alex doubted Raziel had many friends here either. Doing another scan, he sensed again that the angels were sticking fearfully together – and now their seething, hopeless anger also came through.

No, not many friends at all.

At last the Coliseum's curved white exterior came into view. The pale wall gleaming through the rain was the most beautiful thing Alex had ever seen. He'd made it – after three weeks, he'd finally made it.

"It's inside," Miranda said, gazing at the building with apprehension.

The downpour intensified, falling in solid sheets. Alex jogged across the slick cobblestones towards the Coliseum, pain lashing him with every step.

Miranda kept pace with no visible effort. "Can you tell me what Willow's like?" she asked hesitantly. "I mean, I know what she was like as a child, but…"

Alex panted out a response. "She's the most amazing… beautiful girl in the world. Kind…smart – everything. You couldn't ask for a better daughter, not ever."

Suddenly his senses tingled in alarm. Alex veered sharply left, but it was too late: an angel, also running, had emerged from a side street. They collided with a solid thump and the squelch of wet clothes.

"Oh, beg your pardon—" started the angel, and then he stared into Alex's streaming face. "Wait, I don't know you. You're not an—"

As the angel broke off, gaping, Alex was already running

again, pounding the cobblestones as fast as he could – there was no way he could fake his way out of this one, none.

The Coliseum grew steadily closer, but crippling pain slowed him down. Miranda had vanished. Footfalls sped after him – more than one pair, gaining on him. *Shit.* Alex unstrapped his rifle from under his jacket and whirled to face them, standing his ground.

The angel had been joined by at least ten others. They stopped a few feet away, out of breath, their faces hard. "You're human," said the first one. Black hair, dark eyes. "How did you get into our world? How?"

"I don't know – it was a mistake." The rifle was propped and ready on Alex's shoulder.

"Why don't I believe you?" spat the angel as he stepped forward, rain streaming down his hair. "You know a way in, so you know a way out. *How?* We're dying here."

Alex backed away a step, still holding the rifle on them. "Yeah, so you want to come to my world and make sure humans die instead. Not a chance." He wasn't without sympathy for the angels – trapping them here had been pretty cold-blooded, even for Raziel – but his sympathy stopped short of letting them join the soul-suckers in his own dimension.

The angels moved towards him with no warning: half of them lunged forward in their human forms; the others shifted to their angelic selves and swooped fiercely at him. Two went high, ready to dive; Alex aimed at the lead one – large and ghostly in the rain – centred on its halo, and shot, then got the second angel just as the human ones tackled him.

Pieces of light fell like confetti as Alex went crashing down. His rifle hit the ground with a clatter as someone wrenched it away from him. "Tell us!" hissed the dark-haired angel, cracking Alex's head against the cobblestones. "Talk!"

The pain spurred him on. He jackknifed upwards and swung hard, connecting with the angel's damp cheekbone. His head got slammed into the cobblestones again in response; someone else kicked his ribs. Alex threw punches wildly, not caring what he hit: blood spurting, the crunch of cartilage as he flattened an angel's nose. He knew he was outnumbered but didn't care; he was *not* giving up now, not when he was so close to getting home—

In a blur, Alex saw an angel standing on the fringe, staring at the drifting fragments of light. It let out a sudden wail of agony. "He's killed Ganziel and Larmont! We didn't even feel it!"

His words seemed to sap all will from the angels.

The dark-haired one on Alex's chest went still, gazing upwards in horror. The remainder who'd been in angelic form had reverted to human again. They stood shuddering as a group and regarded Alex with wide, frightened eyes.

For the first time ever, Alex felt a fleeting urge to apologize for shooting an angel. He didn't give in to it. He heaved the dark-haired angel off him, then scrambled to his feet and ran.

The rain was still pelting down. Alex ducked down a side street adjacent to the Coliseum, then another one and another – desperate to lose the angels before they figured out where he was going. Though he scanned continuously, he could sense no sign of them. Had they given up?

No way in hell, he thought grimly. *They've just gone to get all the others.*

Finally Alex doubled back. Breathing hard, he pressed flat against a building and peered around it at the Coliseum's high white walls.

A side entrance lay directly across the street. Alex glanced the other way, hating how open this area was. At least the Coliseum seemed empty – he had a feeling the place hadn't been used in a while.

"You're hurt," Miranda said with concern, suddenly appearing next to him. "Your head's bleeding…" She reached out to touch it; her fingers tingled lightly against his scalp.

He let out a breath, deeply glad to see her again: this wraith who was somehow all that was left of Willow's mother's mind. "I'm fine – I'm going to make a run for it. You can still show me how to get through, right?"

She nodded, and Alex took off. To his relief, the door was unlocked. He slipped quickly through it.

Inside it was cool, dimly lit. He was in a long, plain corridor that reminded him again, strongly, of the Denver Church of Angels – it was exactly like the hallway he'd gone careening down to reach Willow when she'd attempted to stop the Second Wave.

Miranda was beside him again. "This way," she said, starting silently down the corridor. "It's different from how the other gates were – Raziel's the only one who can sense it's there." They came to another door; she waited as Alex opened it.

"But what about the timings?" she asked suddenly, peering up at him.

"What timings?" Alex put his hand on the pistol under his waistband as they entered an open space larger than two football fields, blindingly bright. Tens of thousands of seats wrapped around it; overhead, a high, arched ceiling seemed both transparent and solid – one moment plain white, the next showing dark clouds still spitting down rain.

Alex's jaw tightened. Was it like that from the outside? All the angels had to do was fly over, and they'd figure out he was here in two seconds.

They were on a broad, raised platform. Though everything looked sleekly modern, there was a sense of immense age.

"Raziel always worries about the timings," Miranda explained. "I mean, he did the last few times he was here. I thought it must be hard to get them right."

Alex shook his head; he didn't have a clue what she was talking about. "I'll just have to take my chances."

He saw to his alarm that his foot was bleeding; he'd left a smudged red trail all the way across the platform. He quickly shrugged out of his jacket and yanked off his damp T-shirt, ignoring the jab of bruised ribs. He bent down hastily, mopping up the blood, and then wrapped the shirt around his foot. He wasn't going to lead them right to the gate, not if he could help it.

"All right, well…" Miranda bit her lip, and Alex realized she was reluctant to give away Raziel's secret. She motioned towards a large twisting sculpture near the edge of the platform. "It's very small, right under that first curve. Like a keyhole, but smaller."

Alex lifted his consciousness through his chakras and probed. Apprehension touched him. "I can't feel it."

"No, I told you – Raziel keeps it hidden. But it's there."

Alex took her word for it; he didn't have a choice. Pinpointing his consciousness again, just like he'd done all those weeks ago in his father's house, he plunged it, needle-like, under the sculpture's silver curve. Not the right place. He tried again. Not there either.

Suddenly Alex's senses jolted with the dark feel of angel energy close by. They'd found him, hundreds of them – and judging from the distance, they were only a block away, heading straight for the Coliseum's rear entrance.

Forcing himself to stay focused, Alex kept trying, aware of the seconds rushing past. The angels had almost reached the door now. He wasn't going to make it.

He ignored the thought; at the same moment, he found a slight give in the ether. *There.* He shoved his consciousness through; this time the energy on the other side felt calm – homelike. Working fast, he started widening the hole.

He could feel that Raziel's gate was much more efficient than Cully's; to his relief, he had it open in seconds. Through it he could see only darkness.

He heard the distant sound of shouting. The angels were through the Coliseum door, streaming down the long hallway – they'd be here any moment. Alex turned quickly to Miranda, not knowing how to say thank you. He didn't try. He reached for her hands; his own went through them, but he held on anyway, letting her tingling energy rush through him.

"You asked who I am," he said hurriedly. "My name's Alex; I'm in love with your daughter. And I promise you

– I swear to you – I will make her happy for the rest of her life."

Miranda looked close to tears, insubstantial at the edges again. "Thank you, Alex," she whispered. "And when she tries to link with the energy field – she needs to do it in Pawntucket. There's a place there where she can get through. It's—"

Alex's head jerked up as shouts reverberated just on the other side of the door.

"I've got to go," he said in a rush. "You'd better go too, just in case." He hastily kissed Miranda's fading cheek, his lips brushing air – and then hurled himself through the opening.

Alex's muscles were tight, ready for the same screaming agony as last time. It didn't come. In a smooth, seamless motion, he was suddenly lying on a floor in the darkness, wincing only at the pain in his ribs. Silence – the gate had closed once more to a tiny pinprick behind him.

He sat up slowly, listening to the hard beating of his heart. There was no other sound. Why had it been so much easier coming through from the angels' world? Maybe it was just that Cully hadn't really known what he was doing.

Whatever; Alex wasn't complaining. As he struggled to

his feet, he could see a faint light: plastic runners darting along the floor. He was in the Denver Church of Angels cathedral, in an alcove formed by two pillars near the main doors. Down below, past aisles and aisles of seats, was where Willow had attempted to stop the Second Wave.

Willow. He let out a breath, hardly able to believe that he was really back – that with luck, he'd see her again in just a few days. Then, remembering what Miranda had said about Willow going to Pawntucket, he frowned, urgency pulsing through him.

A green *Exit* sign cast a glow over two tall silver doors. A trip alarm sat on top of them, its electronic eyes gleaming. Alex reached into his pocket for his penknife and craned upwards, slicing neatly through the alarm's wire.

He swung open the door and stepped outside. Broad white steps shone in the moonlight. Faint unease stirred in Alex as he jogged down them, disregarding his injured foot. Moonlight? It hadn't even been dark yet when he'd left the angels' world. From out of nowhere came the memory of when the Third Wave had arrived – the glimpse of twilight through the gate while here it had been afternoon.

Raziel always worries about the timings now, Miranda had said.

Okay, so time in the angels' world was a few hours off from their own. Interesting, but not hugely relevant. He had to steal a car and get to Pawntucket as soon as possible.

He'd head north-east, he decided, to the main highway. There'd be plenty of Eden staff driving along that route – he'd steal a vehicle from one if it was the last thing he ever did.

Hang on, babe, I'm on my way, he thought as he jogged across the dark parking lot. Pawntucket was almost two thousand miles away, across uncertain roads. But he'd get there, no matter what… And when he did, he knew that no power on earth would ever separate him from Willow again.

CHAPTER *Twenty-five*

THE 4 × 4 TRUNDLED steadily over the empty road.

When we'd left the lodge three mornings ago, I'd felt beyond relieved to see the blue skies overhead. Only about six inches of snow lay on the ground. The truck could handle that, if the good weather held.

Two weeks, I kept thinking. Mentally counting back, I'd left the shopping mall nine days ago. If the angel I'd fought in the base corridor had been accurate, we still had five days before Raziel attacked.

It didn't make me feel any more relaxed, even though we'd crossed the New York border that morning – and with luck, would be in Pawntucket in just four or five hours. I sat curled tensely in the passenger seat as Seb drove, staring out at the pointed, white-covered fir trees. It was so serene, like driving through a Christmas card.

The atmosphere inside the truck was quiet too, though not exactly serene. Seb and I were only speaking when we had to. I kept thinking of all the things I wanted to say and then biting them back. I didn't want to argue any more.

The kiss between us had...not been a good idea.

At first, it had seemed perfect. We'd been propped against the bar, holding each other tight, our mouths hot and searching. I'd felt drunk with sensation as I caressed Seb's warm back beneath his T-shirt, thinking, *Oh god, I've missed this – please don't stop, Seb, don't stop.* Above, our angels had explored each other too, just as they had the time we'd kissed in Tepito: a dizzying burst of energy as their winged forms met and merged.

And then it happened.

Our psychic link had faded some with our distance this past year. But now, with our angels' energies so entwined, there were suddenly no secrets at all.

A girl with long auburn hair. The warmth of her smile – the sound of her laughter.

As images and knowledge swept through me, I stiffened. So did Seb; I think we both pulled away at the same moment. I stared at him in dismay, my pulse still hammering from the kiss, trying to get my head around what I'd sensed.

And then I saw that Seb was staring at me in the same way.

"What?" I whispered, swallowing.

The corner of his mouth lifted. There was no humour to it. "You are not ready for this," he said. "So I think we had better forget it."

It was the last thing I'd expected. "What? Seb, I *am*! It's been over a year now. I—"

"It doesn't matter; you're still not over Alex." He turned away and scooped up the sleeping bag, starting stiffly towards the fireplace.

Suddenly angry, I rushed after him and grabbed his arm. "Look, I'll *always* love Alex – I never said I didn't! But that's got nothing to do with—"

He whirled towards me. "It's got everything to do with it! He's all you want. You don't want me at all."

"That's…I…" I trailed off, feeling cold.

"The whole time—" Seb hurled the sleeping bag onto the sofa, hard. "How could I have been so *stupid*? I should have known that you just wanted a – a *substituto*."

"I *didn't* just want a substitute! Seb, I really care about you!"

"Not like that, and you know it," he snapped back. "You've been feeling lonely – and then when I got hurt, it

372

reminded you too much of when Alex died. You wanted *someone* – and lucky me, I was here!" He spread his arms out.

My voice was faint. "There was more to it than that."

"No. There was not," he said flatly. "My angel was part of yours, Willow – I *know*."

I stood trembling, awash with shame as I realized he was right: it was really Alex I'd been longing for. I'd completely used Seb, even if I hadn't meant to. Anger of my own followed. It was a lot easier than facing what I'd done…and the fact that I was nowhere near over Alex after all.

I crossed my arms tightly. "Yes, well – speaking of kissing one person and wanting another one, how about you?"

"*Me?*"

"Yes! You're not the only one who got something psychically, all right? You're in love with Meghan; you have been for months!"

Seb's jaw dropped; his look of surprise was almost comical. "What are you talking about? I love *you* – I always have."

My temper faded as we stared at each other. I shook my head. "No, Seb," I said quietly. "You did once, but now it's just a – a habit, a memory. It's Meghan you're in love with; you've just been so hung up on me that you couldn't see it."

His smile was hard. "I can see very well, *querida* – and you're all I've ever wanted. Believe me, I wish it wasn't true."

"But it isn't! Seb, I *know;* my angel was part of yours too. You've got me all built up in your mind like some kind of dream girl – that's all it is."

Dark anger clouded Seb's face. "Let me tell you something," he said. "I have sensed you since I was *six*. For fourteen years, I have loved you – since before I even knew what the word meant. You want Alex instead of me? Fine, I'm used to it. But do *not* tell me who I love."

My voice rose in frustration. "Oh god, Seb, at least be honest with yourself! Why do you think you've been so unhappy these last few months? You're miserable without Meghan! You love her so much that she's like an ache inside of you—"

Seb looked as if he could have happily throttled me. Brushing past, he strode to the bar again. "Why don't we eat and take a break from this very fascinating conversation?"

I blew out a breath. "Yes, why don't we? Since you're not listening to a word I say."

It was the first hot meal we'd had in days. I don't think either of us enjoyed it much. We sat at opposite ends of the sheepskin rug, eating in silence. The adrenalin from the argument had faded and now I just felt desolate.

Alex.

My throat tightened. Remembering my moment of peace gazing over the plains, I wanted to cry. I should have known by now: grief took three steps forward and two steps back. I longed for Alex so much that it hurt – and I was so tired of hurting. Dull fury at him stirred, that he was still putting me through this even after a year.

Seb had found some red wine behind the bar; he'd offered me a glass with a sardonic lift of his eyebrows. Now he sat drinking from his own glass, moodily contemplating the fire.

I stared down at my wine's red glow. "Seb, look, I—"

He drained his glass. "Whatever you are going to say, I can live without it."

Stung, I said, "I just wanted to tell you I'm sorry. I promise I didn't mean to use you."

Seb regarded me coolly, his eyes dark brown in the firelight. "Do you want the sofa or the rug?"

"It doesn't matter."

"Then get up; you're on my bed."

Fine. I rose and went over to the sofa, where I snaked the sleeping bag out of its case. A few minutes later I was wrapped in its warmth, gazing into the fire.

The only sounds were the flames snapping and the faint whistle of the storm from outside. Seb had rolled himself up in the sheepskin rug; he lay with his hands linked under his head, glaring up at the ceiling.

I cleared my throat. "Listen, um…if it turns out that we can get out of here tomorrow, I'd like you to take the first car we can hotwire and go to Idaho."

In a swift motion, Seb had propped himself up on one elbow. "What are you talking about?"

I shrugged, unable to meet his eyes. "I just don't think it makes much sense for us both to be here, that's all. One of us should go back and tell the others what's happening."

Seb snorted, his gaze raking over me. "Did I say you are blind? What you really are is *transparente*. No, Willow. I am not going to Idaho, no matter who you think I'm in love with."

My hand twisted hard at the sleeping bag. "Seb, *please*! We don't know what's going to happen in Pawntucket, and I need to know you're safe, at least – that you have a chance to be happy."

"Ah, yes. Because you know what would make me happy."

I was close to tears. "I *do*! Look, I know you don't believe me yet, but you can still be with the person you love – and I can never have that again, not ever! Please don't throw it away! If you come with me, you'll probably die."

His jaw hardened. "I am coming, Willow. There is nothing you can say to stop me."

"But—"

Suddenly his voice was low, furious. "Listen to me! This isn't just about saving your town any more. Something big is going to happen there – for the whole world. Since your psychic powers are so wonderful, do *not* tell me you don't sense it."

The moment froze: Seb with his chestnut curls tousled, the shadowy room around us. "Yes," I admitted finally. "I've been feeling it too. For days now."

He gave a hard, cynical smile and flopped back down onto the floor. "So it's decided, yes? This is my fight too. Trust me, I would be here no matter what I feel for you."

I didn't bother mentioning Meghan this time. He'd thought it was me for so long – he just couldn't see it yet.

Neither of us spoke again. I lay staring into the fire. And thinking about what might lie ahead, I swallowed... and hoped that Seb would have a chance to realize the truth for himself.

Now, three days later, Seb and I took turns driving through the snow-dusted Adirondacks. I gazed out the windshield as the familiar mountains glided past, trying to ignore the growing certainty that whatever waited ahead would impact on the whole world – but was going to be especially awful for me, personally.

When I wasn't worrying about Pawntucket, I was

aching for Alex. I felt utterly flattened, lonelier than I'd been in months. I'd thought I was moving on…and now this. As we drove, I reached for my mother, hugging the familiar feel of her close. Then I gently let go, glad for once that she wasn't actually here.

By noon we'd reached the foothills north of Pawntucket.

I stopped the truck, and Seb and I got out. My hometown spread out below us like a picture postcard, so normal-looking that it made my skin prickle. Except that it was totally silent – I could sense only a handful of people.

Was Nina one? And did she, like the rest of the world, think I was a terrorist? Suddenly I remembered the time we drove down to New York City to see a concert – the way Nina and I had danced in the crowd. The thought of her turning against me made my stomach clench.

"So, I guess we'd better go check it out," I said finally. Seb nodded.

As I opened the car door again, I stiffened, the keys gouging into my palm. It was that same weird sensation I'd felt at the abandoned house – as if I were the centre of the world, with everything straining towards me.

They all need me, I thought dazedly. And then blinked, wondering what that even meant.

Before I could ask Seb if he'd felt it too, his eyes narrowed. He stood with one arm on top of the open passenger door, gazing to the south-east. "Angels," he said.

When I sensed what he was picking up my breath caught. Angels – thousands of them – about thirty miles away. They were gathering, waiting; so many we could feel it even from this distance.

I glanced at Seb. "Schenectady's an Eden now. They must be there."

He threw himself into the truck. "Come – we'd better hurry."

The familiar road was way worse than I remembered, but I went as fast as I could around potholes. Then as the first houses began to appear, I saw that things weren't so normal in Pawntucket after all. A huge oak tree lay completely uprooted, and houses stood at weird slants, roofs and porches buckling.

Earthquake damage. I hadn't realized until now that Pawntucket had had any tremors. I licked my lips, suddenly more apprehensive than ever. "Maybe we should stop and let our angels check things out," I said.

"Yes, good," Seb said shortly – and I knew that no matter how angry he still was, he would die to protect me, as I would do for him. I pulled off the road, and a heartbeat later our angels were flying over Pawntucket.

In the air I stared down in dismay. Some buildings looked almost normal; others leaned in all directions – walls crushed, front porches falling off. A Victorian house

I'd always liked looked as if a giant's fist had smashed down on it. One whole street had been razed to rubble; more trees lay on their sides, roots exposed.

Everything was so quiet. Where were the people? Gliding in the cold air, I turned on one wing and headed towards the centre of town with Seb beside me. From the old-fashioned town square, I saw the brick tower of the town hall. At least *it* looked intact.

Then as we flew over the square, figures appeared out of nowhere; they ran across the street and darted out of view. I stared after them. Wait, I *knew* them – knew all of them.

The bells of the town hall started pealing. "Attack!" shouted a voice.

But they shouldn't be able to see us! I thought – and then bullets were slicing past. I jerked backwards, wings flapping; Seb darted in front of me. *Seb, no!* I thought at him.

"They don't have halos!" someone cried in frustration.

"Don't let them get away!" yelled someone else.

Gunfire rained around us. Seb and I went high and started flying quickly back to the truck. The human Seb and I were already hurtling towards the centre of town, as fast as I could drive over the damaged streets. *Come on, come on,* I thought fervently as our angels sped towards us.

More people had appeared with guns, and another

bullet whined past as we flew. Our angels reached the truck, diving straight through the windshield into our human forms.

"Maybe we should go the other way now," Seb said dryly, eyeing the approaching mob.

I stopped the truck with a lurch. "No!" I gasped. "I know them – and they're fighting the angels, so they're on our side." I scrambled out before Seb could respond; I heard him swear.

"Stop! *Stop!*" I cried as a dozen people thundered towards us. "It's me – Willow!"

Scott Mason, former football star of Pawntucket High, was at the front of the pack. He jogged to a halt, holding a rifle. His once-broad form was leaner now, his brown hair longer.

"*Willow?*" he repeated, his voice rising in disbelief.

The group gaped at us. Seb had gotten out too and was holding one of the machine guns, his mouth grim – and I knew he didn't trust my former classmates not to attack again.

Because everyone who'd come after us was someone I'd gone to Pawntucket High with. Scott, still wearing his purple and white letterman jacket. A girl with long auburn hair named Rachel – we'd taken freshman biology together. No sign of Nina, though.

Scott had raised his rifle against his shoulder, pointing

it at us. "If you're really Willow, what the hell was up with those angels?" he snapped.

I swallowed. "They're – they're part of us. We're both half-angel."

Someone at the rear had peeled off and was heading at a run back towards town. I watched nervously, wondering if she was going for reinforcements.

Scott snorted. "Yeah, you're *supposedly* half-angel – who are you really?"

I stared at him. "What? Come on, Scott, don't you recognize me?"

"Those angels flew right inside you!" he barked. "The Willow we knew is on *our* side – I'm not taking any chances." Scott had always been expert with a football; he didn't look any less so with a rifle as he stepped closer.

"Stay. Back." Seb's voice was a razor blade. "My angel can survive without me. If you shoot, he will grab the machine gun and fire on you all."

The bluff worked. Scott lowered his rifle a fraction, his handsome face cautious.

"But I *am* on your side!" I cried. "I've been fighting the angels for years – we both have."

"Yeah, that's exactly what you would say, isn't it?" he demanded.

"But the half-angel thing can't be *true*, can it?" protested Rachel, stepping closer. "I thought it was just a story!"

How had they already known I was half-angel? Before I could respond, a dark-haired guy said, "Either way, that doesn't mean this is her! After two years? And *now*, after this morning?"

"Way too convenient," put in someone else.

"Of *course* it's really me!" I exclaimed. "Rachel – remember how crazy we made Mr. Kovak in biology? We refused to dissect frogs, remember? And, Scott, you flunked sophomore English – Coach Campbell was furious at you."

"Angels are psychic," muttered someone darkly.

"*I'm* psychic, remember?" But it was clear that nothing I said or did would convince them. "We're here to help!" I said anyway, raising my voice. "Pawntucket's about to come under attack—"

"*Attack?*" Scott hissed. "You've led them right to us, haven't you?"

"No! You've got to listen—"

Scott snapped the rifle to his shoulder again; with no hesitation, Seb let loose a burst of machine-gun fire, scattering it at his feet. As Scott jumped back, I stood breathing hard, my mind spinning. This could *not* be happening.

"Stop!" shouted a new voice. Running footsteps were heading towards us. "*Stop!*"

A guy wearing an old duffle coat and a grey thermal cap came sprinting up, with the girl who'd taken off before and someone else a few paces behind. Panting, the guy glanced at me and then the crowd, his expression incredulous. "What are you *doing*? This is Willow!"

"You don't know what happened!" Scott said hotly. "She—"

"Yeah, Leslie told us," broke in the new guy. Average height, a boyish face. "And it's still Willow! She's half-angel, remember? I *told* you that."

I stared, wondering who this was and how he knew me – and then suddenly the figure who'd been bringing up the rear propelled herself into my arms. "Willow! It's you; it's really you—"

Nina. Tears jumped to my eyes. I forgot everything else as I held her tightly, weak with relief that she hadn't believed the terrorist stories after all.

She pulled back, swiping at her eyes. "Oh, god, I can't believe you're here!"

"Me neither," I said faintly. Nina was an inch taller than me, with golden-brown hair that used to be straightened paper-flat. Now it framed her cute, snub-nosed face in a bob, making her brownish-green eyes look even larger.

Scott still held his rifle half at the ready. "Yeah, but – come on, *that's* not how being a half-angel works, is it?" he sputtered. "An angel flying right inside you?"

My neck warmed. I felt so self-conscious, confirming to all my old classmates that I wasn't completely human.

Steadily, I said, "Well, that's how it works in our case, and we're the only half-angels that we know about. Our angels are part of us."

Nina's gaze widened as she glanced from me to Seb – but to my amazement, she didn't look disbelieving. More than her hair must have changed in two years.

"Listen, if Jonah and Nina are sure it's her, that's good enough for me," Rachel said firmly.

The murmurs of assent relaxed my spine a little, and then it hit me: *Jonah?* I turned and gaped at the newcomer as memories of the Denver Church of Angels whirled past. No way – it couldn't be. Then mentally, I put him into a grey suit with an angelic blue tie; his gentle brown eyes were just the same.

It was really him.

"Yeah, we're sure," Jonah was saying. "Come on, Scott, put your gun down. All of you."

Though his voice was mild, everyone obeyed. I stood staring, trying to take this in. "But – what are you doing *here*?" I blurted out.

Jonah glanced at me with an embarrassed smile. "Hi," he said belatedly, stepping forward and offering his hand. "It's great to see you again, Willow. I mean, it really is."

I shook his hand in a daze. "You too," I said softly. Our hands stayed gripped longer than necessary; suddenly my throat was tight. Jonah had been Raziel's assistant. He'd risked his life to help us try to stop the Second Wave.

I let go. "Um – this is my friend Seb. Sebastián Carrera. Seb, this is Nina Bergmann, and Jonah…I'm sorry, I don't know your last name."

"Fisk." Jonah extended his hand to Seb. I saw him glance at the empty truck and dreaded the question I knew would follow: *Where's Alex?*

"Listen – we're here for a reason," I said hurriedly. "Pawntucket's in danger; Raziel plans to attack in five days. At least, I hope we've still got five days."

Jonah stared at the mention of his former employer. "Raziel's going to attack *here?*"

Nina gripped my arm. "Quick, tell us everything!"

I told them what I'd gotten from the angel in the corridor. "Something's happening here that the angels weren't expecting," I finished in a rush. "Something they feel threatened by."

Jonah looked pale. "Yeah…yeah, I guess maybe there is."

Scott's jaw had turned to stone. "Oh, man, only five days – and the others are out checking the food stores! We've got to get them back so we can start *planning,* do something! Town hall, right? One hour!"

He and the others took off at a run, leaving only Nina and Jonah. "Shouldn't we go too?" Nina asked anxiously.

Jonah still looked pretty shaken, but his voice was

steady. "Scott's got people to help him. And besides—" He glanced at Seb and me, his fists moving in his coat pockets. "We've got to talk," he said intently. "I need to find out what the Angel Killers have been doing and tell you what's been going on here. You, um…probably need to hear about it, Willow."

Suddenly I had a terrible feeling that Jonah had a tendency towards understatement. "Yes, all right." I glanced back at the truck. "Should we move this? It's kind of out in the open."

Nina nodded, giving it a worried glance. "Most of us live at the elementary school now – on Birch, remember? You can park it under the covered walkway there, so it's not visible from the air. Jonah and I will meet you over at the town hall."

Not visible from the air – I couldn't believe the way sceptical Nina was taking all this in her stride. Two years ago she would have poured scorn on the very idea that angels really existed.

I shoved my questions away for the time being and started back to the truck. "Okay. Meet you there."

As Seb and I drove to the school, a weighted silence settled down on us again. I glanced at his familiar profile and cleared my throat.

"Seb, look, I know you're still angry at me…but do you think we could just pretend everything's okay for the next few days?" I managed a smile. "If we actually survive this, you can go right back to not talking to me, I promise."

He gave a quiet snort. Finally he shook his head. "You are the most infuriating person I have ever met," he said tiredly. "But, yes, you are right."

We'd reached the squat brick building of the Neil Armstrong Elementary School by then – I rocked us onto the sidewalk and parked under the covered walkway at the front. As Seb and I got out, our eyes met. He still looked irritated, but the corner of his mouth lifted a fraction.

"Friends?" I said.

He made a face. "No, I don't think that's the right word." He pulled out his rifle from the back and slung it over one shoulder. "Even when I want to strangle you, you know, it doesn't matter. We are still…" He stopped with a weary shrug.

My chest felt tight as I nodded, understanding. The bond we shared would always be there, like a deep river connecting us. Whether we wanted it to be or not.

As Seb and I walked down the familiar streets, I couldn't stop staring. The fact that some homes were okay made the damaged ones look even worse. In the town square, half the buildings were sagging – broken windows, smashed-in walls. The drugstore had collapsed completely.

At the square's centre, the town hall rose up from a snowy lawn, its tall brick structure stolid and unchanged. Nina and Jonah stood waiting on its front steps. They had their arms around each other; when they saw us, they stepped apart.

I blinked. Oh. So...apparently Nina didn't have a thing for Scott Mason any more.

As we joined them, I bit my lip and glanced back towards the square. "I didn't know you had such bad tremors here," I said. Stupid comment. But I hated to see Pawntucket so slumped and defeated.

Nina nodded, studying the square with sad eyes. "We keep meaning to rebuild, but..." She sighed.

"I guess it hasn't really been a priority," Jonah said quietly. "One day, I hope. But come on, let's get inside." His eyes met mine. "We've got a lot to talk about."

CHAPTER *Twenty-six*

I'D ONLY BEEN IN THE town hall twice – once on a field trip in third grade and once to pay a parking ticket when I was sixteen. It smelled just the same, like dust and lemon cleaning polish. Jonah led us to a room on the ground floor. At one end was a battered-looking desk with a shortwave radio; at the other, a fireplace.

Jonah crouched in front of it, feeding the small blaze with scraps of wood. "Sorry it's so cold in here," he said. "The town's only got one generator – we save it for the service station and heating the school at night."

It felt strange that Jonah knew more about my

hometown than I did now. I glanced at Nina, still hardly able to believe I was here. "How are you?" I asked her quietly. "I mean – how has everything been?"

"Bizarre," she said with a tight smile. "These last two years have definitely not been normal. Not for you either, I guess." She hesitated. "So did you *know* you were half-angel? Or what?"

I shook my head. "Not until I was sixteen – it was that day I followed Beth to the Church of Angels, actually." It was also the day I'd first met Alex. At the image of him falling into step beside me as we walked through the parking lot, I stopped short and looked away. "It's, um… a long story."

Nina studied me with a frown, looking exactly the way she'd always looked when I'd tried to evade something. Thankfully, this time she didn't pursue it.

"Are you sure your name is really Fisk and not Freedom?" Seb asked Jonah from beside the desk.

Relieved to have something else to think about, I followed his gaze – and saw scrawled notes on a yellow legal pad beside the shortwave. A puzzle piece slipped into place.

"You're the Voice of Freedom!" I burst out.

Jonah's cheeks reddened as he straightened. He briefly pulled off his cap and ran a hand over his head – his dark hair was close-cropped now, the curls gone. "Um, yeah… I guess you could say that."

I felt a sudden fierce pride that the Voice of Freedom was coming from Pawntucket. "We listen to you all the time," I said fervently. "People hear you – they tell us so in dark towns, when we go in to recruit."

Jonah's eyebrows shot up. "*Really?* That is so good to hear. Sometimes it feels like I'm just broadcasting into nothing."

"No, you're definitely making a difference. Don't give up, not ever," I said – and then winced, remembering the angels gathering in Schenectady.

A tense silence fell. Finally Jonah poured water from a plastic bottle into an old-fashioned kettle and hooked it over the fire. As we all settled near the hearth, he glanced at Nina. "So, where should we start?"

"How about with why you're in Pawntucket?" I tried to smile. "I think you're literally the last person I expected to see here."

Jonah had to be in his early twenties, but his quick, embarrassed grin made him look about eighteen. "Actually, I came looking for you."

"*Me?* Why?"

"Well, you and Alex," he clarified. When I didn't respond, he went on. "See, after the Second Wave arrived, I – I guess I didn't deal with it very well." He made a face as he traced a pattern on the faded carpet. "I mean... everything I'd ever believed in was gone. Everything. And we hadn't managed to stop them, and—" He broke off. Nina's expression had softened as she watched him.

Finally Jonah let out a breath. "Anyway, after a while I realized I could do something about it, if I could just find you two. I knew you'd still be fighting; I wanted to join you. But the only place I knew about where you and Alex might come to was here." He hesitated, looking up. "Listen, I hope I'm not saying the wrong thing, but – where *is* Alex?"

I tensed. I'd never had to say it out loud before; everyone at the base had already known. The words came out harshly. "He's dead. He died over a year ago."

Jonah closed his eyes tight, as if he'd almost been expecting this. "I'm sorry," he said. "I would have liked to have known him better."

"Oh, Willow," whispered Nina – and I knew Jonah must have told her about me and Alex being a couple. She leaned over and squeezed my hand. "Are…are you okay?"

For a second I couldn't help gripping her fingers. "I'm fine," I said. I quickly let go of her, hating the fact that tears were threatening. It had been a *year.* "Fine," I repeated.

Nina still looked stricken; Jonah's gentle brown gaze was full of concern. Seb cleared his throat. "Willow and Alex went down to Mexico City after they escaped from Denver," he said. "Willow had a dream that took them there."

He told Jonah and Nina everything – the assassination of the Council, our base in Nevada, the recent angel attack. He explained it all far more succinctly than I could have. It made me sad to listen, though. For over two years, we'd tried so hard, hoped so much – and we'd just had failure after failure.

Nina and Jonah both looked dazed when he'd finished. "Wow," Jonah said finally, pushing his cap back a little. "Well, nothing as important as *that's* been happening here. Though something pretty strange has been going on."

He glanced at me and seemed reluctant to continue. Instead he stretched on his knees to hook the kettle off the fire. He poured us each a mug of tea, his boyish face intent. "Sorry, no milk. We've got sugar, though."

"No, it's gone," Nina said, hugging a knee to her chest.

Jonah settled back beside her. "Oh, well. Sorry, no sugar, either. Anyway, I got to Pawntucket and found out that you weren't here, Willow. But then I met Nina."

Nina gave a small smile as they exchanged a glance. "Yeah, we were both outside your aunt's old house. I mean…where it used to be."

I stiffened, remembering the news footage: the shimmering wall of fire that had devoured the house, with a garden gnome glowing like a weird fire spirit in the front yard. "What were you doing there?"

Nina shook her head. "I don't know; I just…went there

sometimes. I really missed you after you left." She ran a finger over her mug as she went on: "So one day there was this guy lurking around, and it was Jonah. We got to talking, and I thought he was crazy at first. I mean, he was telling me angels were real and feeding from humans, and *you* were half-angel and trying to defeat them – believe me, I made an excuse to get away from him pretty fast."

Jonah smiled slightly. "And here I thought it was just my personality."

"It was. I thought you were cute, but certifiable." Nina swallowed. "But…then all this other stuff started happening, and I realized he was right."

"What stuff?" Seb asked sharply.

"Well, things got pretty weird as soon as Willow left." Nina glanced at me. "Right after, we had police all over the place, asking questions – and then there was all that about you running away with a secret boyfriend, which I *knew* wasn't true. I – well, I was scared."

"I wanted to call you so many times," I said softly. "It just wasn't safe."

She nodded, her eyes bright. "I know that now. Anyway, things just got even weirder after that, with everyone convinced you were a terrorist. Which made even less sense than the secret boyfriend. And then the quakes…" She sighed. "Oh god, it was horrible. No power except for one tiny generator, the middle of winter—"

"Why didn't you go to Schenectady Eden?" I asked. "I mean, I'm glad you didn't, but I haven't seen *any* populated dark towns this far north."

"Most people did. I stayed because…well, because of the angels." Nina shook her head. "It's crazy, huh? I would never have believed that *anything* like that could be true. But after you left, I'd see people just – looking up into the air with these empty smiles. And then afterwards they'd go join the Church. It was like everyone was turning into a Stepford wife." She bit her lip. "But then after the quakes hit…it all changed."

"We've, um – sort of got a theory," Jonah said. "We think maybe the earthquakes affected people here in ways they weren't aware of. Like, woke them up, on some level."

I stared at him. Nina took a deep breath. "Willow, a few days after the quakes, I saw Mrs. Baxter standing in front of Drake's Diner, staring up at the sky – only this time I could see what was happening. I *saw* the angel, saw it feeding from her. It was so…" She trailed off with a convulsive shudder.

"I know," I whispered, remembering the first time I'd seen someone being fed from by an angel. It wasn't a sight that left you.

Nina started to say something else and hesitated, looking pained.

"The next week, Nina's parents went to the refugee

camp outside of Schenectady," put in Jonah softly, touching her hand. "They're probably residents of the Eden now."

If they were still alive at all. I winced, remembering her nice, normal parents – how much I used to envy her having them. "Oh god, Nina, I'm so sorry."

"Yeah," she said at last, her eyes full of an old sorrow. "I begged them not to go, but they didn't believe me. They tried to make *me* go, but by then everyone who's here now had seen what was going on too. We all kind of…banded together, I guess, and refused." She gazed down, playing with Jonah's fingers.

"Nina, that's—"

She took a deep breath. "Wait, there's more. We didn't realize it until the first time an angel tried to feed from one of us, but – well, it's like we're immune. They try to feed and then hiss and back off. It's even gotten to where we can see them *coming* now, as if our senses are sharpening all the time."

I stared at her, my thoughts in chaos. "How many of you are there?" I asked finally.

"Almost two hundred," she said. "Pretty much everyone you had a class with at Pawntucket High. Which, um…" She glanced at Jonah.

He put his mug down. "Willow, this is just a theory, okay? The thing is, we think the quakes had something to do with what's happening – but we think *you* might, too."

"*Me?*" I gaped at them. "I wasn't even here!"

Nina's voice was low. "Yes, but the people who became immune after the quakes had all spent a lot of time around you. We've gone over and over possible links, and you're the only one that makes any—"

"Oh, right!" I let out a short, gasping laugh. "So I'm, like, secretly marshalling everyone from thousands of miles away, even though I wouldn't know how if I tried? Yes, that's reasonable."

Jonah's face was troubled. "No, actually we think it's the opposite," he said. "That people who knew you are somehow connecting to your energy and marshalling themselves."

We were speaking different languages. "But that doesn't make any sense. There's nothing about me that could help them do that."

"Jonah says the angels think you're the one who can defeat them," pointed out Nina. "So there must be *something* special about you."

I hated this conversation. "The only thing special about me is that I'm half-angel – and so is Seb, so what does *that* do to your theory? Besides, if this is true, then everyone I know should be immune, and they aren't!"

Seb had been sitting quietly through all this, missing nothing. "What about Kara?" he asked.

I froze. "What about her?"

"Kara is an AK," Seb explained to Nina and Jonah. "And she, too, is immune. We don't know that the others aren't," he added, looking at me. "During the battle, the angels weren't trying to feed; they were only trying to kill."

I shook my head dumbly. "Seb, no – this is just too strange. There's no way it can be true."

He shrugged. "I don't know... I'm thinking now of how attached everyone in the base was to you. I'd feel it, sometimes – as if everyone's energy was reaching towards you. I thought it was just – that they liked you, you know? But..." He fell silent.

I'd felt the same thing. Oh god, I'd felt the same thing. My blood chilled. Whatever was going on couldn't really be to do with *me*, could it?

"Okay, but even if this is true...it doesn't change anything," I said finally. "Because if the only people this happens to are ones who've spent time around me – well, I can't spend time around the whole world, can I? The angels will still win in the end."

"It must mean *something*." Nina's voice was tight with frustration. "If you could just find a way to harness this thing—"

"How?"

"I don't know; you're the one who can defeat them!"

"Don't you think I've racked my brains for two years

now, trying to figure out what I could do? There's nothing! I'm just *me,* Nina, not Supergirl."

There was a long pause. Nina blew out a breath and stared down at her tea. Jonah's eyes were kind but disappointed – and I realized with a jolt that they'd been hoping I was the answer. From Seb's wry smile, I knew that he, at least, hadn't believed for a second that we'd avoid a fight with the angels.

I didn't believe it either.

"I'm sorry," I said to Nina and Jonah. "I'd give anything if I knew how to defeat them. But if you're looking for a saviour, you'd better look somewhere else."

The room grew warmer as the fire took hold; finally Jonah started to speak again. The rest of his story didn't take long. He'd come here looking for me and Alex, and found a dark town full of people who were immune to the angels. With Jonah's knowledge, they started training themselves and bringing their attackers down.

It had taken a long time for the angels to figure out what was going on. Once the Edens got under way, they didn't come here often – and when they did, their small groups were decimated by dozens of fighters, leaving no trace.

"But a few months ago, we started going out after

them," Jonah said. "At a raid on Schenectady Eden recently, one of our fighters got killed. Or at least that's what we thought. Now, though..." He shook his head. "It looks like he might have still been alive and got captured."

Seb's eyes narrowed. "Why do you think this?"

"Just before dawn this morning, we found a group of angels in their human forms, prowling around town." Jonah glanced at me. "That's, um – why everyone was kind of on edge when you got here. The angels tried to fly away, and we got them all, but it was like they were scoping the place out. And now, with an attack coming..." Jonah swallowed. "I've got a really bad feeling our fighter, Chris, told them everything about us."

I nodded. "The angels know," I said in a soft voice. "They definitely know."

"And it will be more than just an attack that comes, I think," Seb said, shooting me a glance.

He was right; we had to tell them. I cleared my throat. "Look – Seb and I both feel like whatever's going to happen here will be major."

Nina stared. "Major how?"

"I don't know. Affecting the whole world, somehow." I paused and looked down at my mug of lukewarm tea. "You and the others could always evacuate," I said. "The army that's gathering is massive – I'm not sure how much of a chance we actually have."

"I'm not leaving," Jonah said, his jaw tensing. "This is my home now; I don't have another one. I've run away from them once – I won't do it again."

Nina's face was set. "I don't want to leave either. The others will feel the same." She gave me a sharp look. "You didn't come here just to tell us to leave, did you?"

"No." I hesitated, but knew there was no going back. "I came to face Raziel and get rid of him for good."

Jonah's expression darkened. I could sense him remembering how much he'd once revered his angel-employer.

"Raziel?" he repeated.

"He's my father," I said levelly. "And I'm not going to let him destroy what's left of Pawntucket and live."

CHAPTER *Twenty-seven*

THE MAIN OFFICE IN THE town hall was piled high with scavenged goods. Ignoring the thought of all the people these things had belonged to, Seb sifted quickly through the clothes. He was wearing just his jeans, his skin still damp from a hasty wash with chilly water. Scott the football hero hadn't returned yet with the others, though they'd be back any second.

Footsteps echoed in the marble hallway. Seb glanced up; Willow's voice floated in – she was talking to Nina. He stood motionless as their footsteps faded – then shook his head and snapped on a T-shirt.

Though he would never have thought it possible, kissing Willow again had at least done one thing for him: the thought of trying again with her, ever, held no appeal at all. He couldn't believe it had happened *again* – to be kissing her, then find out it was Alex she wanted. And this time it had killed something vital in him. Even if Willow came to him now, totally over Alex, and said she wanted him – he'd tell her no and he knew it.

There was a mirror propped against one wall. Seb stopped and stared at himself, frowning, as the momentousness of this hit him.

Dios mío…it was really true. He'd finally had enough.

In a daze, Seb sank down onto a desk. Searching his emotions, he found only a deep sense of caring for Willow. He loved her, yes; he always would – but *in* love with her? No.

After sixteen years of thinking himself in love with Willow, he'd at last come out the other side. Yet the sadness was still there, so ingrained within him that he could feel it in every cell.

Willow's frustrated voice came back to him: *At least be honest with yourself! Why do you think you've been so unhappy these last few months?*

The ghost of the argument still infuriated him. To go from kissing Willow to being told that he wasn't really in love with her at all—

Deep down, his angel stirred. *But you're not.*

Seb's jaw clenched as, from out of nowhere, he remembered when Meghan had taught him to drive: the way she'd laughed when he'd stalled them with a lurch, sending her auburn hair swinging forward. Suddenly his chest felt hollow. He clutched the back of his head and sat hunched over, almost wanting to punch something.

And then glanced up, startled, as Jonah stepped in.

An awkward silence. "Hi," Jonah said, shifting his weight. "I just wanted to see if you were finding everything all right."

"Yes, thanks." Seb got up and yanked on his sweater, confused by the vehemence of his emotions. What was wrong with him, anyway?

Jonah came in and leaned against the desk. His jean-clad form was tautly thin, like a runner's. "So you're from Mexico?" he asked. "My family went to Puerto Vallarta on vacation once."

Seb had been several times, hoping to spot his half-angel girl in the sunburned crowds. "Very pretty," he said non-committally. "The beach is nice."

Jonah smiled slightly. "I guess it's not the real Mexico."

Images swarmed in: the traffic of the *Distrito Federal*, with its shouting street vendors; the grinning skull of *Santa Muerte*; the danger that lay down a wrong street – the chaotic beauty down another. And the large brown eyes of a too-thin street girl as he grabbed her, told her to *Run, niña!*

"No, the real Mexico is impossible to explain," Seb said finally. "It's better to go where the tourists go. Enjoy the sun."

"I grew up in Utah – I got plenty of sun there. I'd rather see what's real." Jonah nudged at the floor with a scuffed sneaker. "I've got kind of an aversion to things that aren't, ever since I left the Church."

Voices approached outside; Jonah straightened. "Scott's back." He cleared his throat, glancing at Seb. "You know, I've never been in a battle before."

"I don't recommend them," Seb said in a low voice. "But we have a warning this time, at least."

Jonah's face might have been boyish; his thoughtful dark eyes were not – and Seb realized that at some point he'd already faced what was, for him, the worst thing imaginable.

"Yeah, I hope that makes a difference," Jonah said quietly. "But if it doesn't—" He shoved his hands in his pockets. "As long as Nina's safe I don't care what happens to me. There are some things worth dying for."

When Seb and Jonah entered the room with the shortwave radio, Scott and a dozen others were already there, including Willow. Scott had a map of Pawntucket spread out on the desk. He glanced up as Seb and Jonah came in.

"I've got the others out scavenging," he said. "Wood, nails, stuff like that, so we can build fortifications."

Seb nodded. "Yes, this sounds good."

"And listen, sorry about before. We had some angels sneaking around here this morning, and—"

"Jonah told us," put in Willow. "We probably wouldn't have been very welcoming either."

For the first time in two years, Seb realized that he didn't have to stop his aura from straining towards Willow's. She'd been about to say something else; her eyes widened. She turned quickly towards him – and he knew that she knew.

Looking somewhat stunned, Willow shook herself. "So, um – what kind of fortifications?" she asked.

As everyone pressed around the table, Seb found himself next to a tall, leggy girl with long auburn hair. He did a double take, and she glanced at him, eyebrows up.

It was only Rachel – that girl he'd seen earlier. Seb tore his gaze away, gritting his teeth as he realized: when he'd seen her, hope had leaped within him like a flame.

Damn Willow, anyway, with her stupid certainty. He was *not* in love with Meghan. Because if he was, that would mean he was the biggest idiot in existence…and had lost the girl who meant more to him than anything.

Scott was drawing something beside the map. "Okay, the angels always come in from the air; they like to attack from height. So I think we need ladders on all the intact buildings, and footholds on the roofs, like this. All around the square, so that fighters have a clear shot at them."

"What about these streets?" Seb asked sharply, pointing to the lower part of the map. "You have to protect more than just the centre, or they'll destroy you."

"But we've only got five days," Rachel protested. Her eyes were the same sky-blue as Meghan's.

"You are *lucky* to have five days," Seb snapped. She reddened and looked away, and he hated himself.

"I'm sorry," he said after a pause.

"No, you're right," Jonah said quietly. "Scott, what about—" He broke off at the sound of running footsteps.

"Jonah!" called a voice. "*Jonah!*"

Jonah leaped for the door; he flung it open just as a guy with blond hair reached it. "There's a pack of angels circling overhead," he panted.

Everyone reacted instantly. Less than a minute later, Seb found himself with his rifle in hand, running close to the buildings lining the square with a guy named David. The town hall bells rang out as angels soared far above.

"This way!" David led him into the bank with its dark, abandoned teller stations. "It's one of the tallest buildings left – there's a good view from the top—" David gasped as they pounded up the concrete stairs.

They emerged in an office that had clearly been used for defence before: two metal tables lay overturned, forming a shield, and the glass had been broken out of its windows.

Seb peered out. The dozen or so angels were just circling, too high up to shoot at. He could sense the frustration of other fighters scattered throughout the town.

Finally, after a few long, tense moments, the angels started descending. David snapped his gun into position; Seb's hand flew out to stop him. "No, wait," he said, staring upwards. "I don't think—"

Gunfire sounded from elsewhere; one of the angels exploded into brightness. Seb held back a curse as more gunfire, more destroyed angels followed – he had a sudden feeling that this was not a good idea. *Don't bring your angel out,* he thought fervently to Willow, though he knew she was too far away to hear. *Don't let them know we're here.*

As we'd all run outside, everyone had split off in different directions; Scott had gripped my arm to keep me with him. "You any good with a gun?" he demanded as we flattened ourselves against the remains of the hardware store.

I'd already brought out my pistol. "Not bad," I said, eyeing the bright forms overhead.

Then I stiffened, every sense tingling. "Wait!" I gasped. "We've got to go this way." I'd already taken a few steps further south.

Scott flung me a hurried glance. "What?"

Sudden urgency took my breath away. I had to get there – *had* to. I started running down the street; Scott caught up and grabbed my arm again. "Willow, what are you doing?"

Gunfire had started. "Come *on*!" I cried.

"What's going on?"

I wrenched away; I wanted to kick him. "I don't know, but I'm *psychic*, remember?"

Scott looked alarmed; he dropped my arm, and we took off. I caught glimpses of the others as we ran – felt them crouched behind buildings, firing upwards. *Stop shooting!* I wanted to yell, but my pounding pulse drove me forward, to the streets heading south out of town.

When we reached them, the view opened up and we saw the angels again, only five left now, high up in the sky as they flew off towards Schenectady Eden. "*Damn it,*" muttered Scott. "If the angels didn't know about us before, they sure will now."

"They knew," I said. We were at the top of Orchid, looking south. I stared at a fallen tree lying across the street. "That wasn't there before, was it?"

"No, we blocked off the main roads when we got back. Is there a reason we're here, Willow?"

Then we both heard it: an engine heading our way.

Scott swore and pulled me around the side of a house; he peered out. "Okay, you were right," he said. "Just like in high school. You know, everyone only called you Queen Weird because it was so spooky how accurate your readings were."

I crouched down and stared out from under his arm. The street was still empty; the sound of the engine was growing closer. Over the sudden hammering of my pulse, I said, "Yeah, Nina used to tell me I was ruining my chances with the popular crowd."

"None of that crap matters any more," Scott said shortly. "We're all glad you're back, Willow. We've been hoping you'd come."

A truck cruised into view: a blue 4 × 4 that looked like an Eden vehicle. As it reached the barricade, it stopped. Someone got out; the door slammed.

"Only one," Scott said, fingering his rifle. "What is he, can you tell? Human or angel?"

I'd forgotten to scan, because all I could do was stare. The guy who'd gotten out had dark hair...and was wearing faded jeans and a leather jacket. My heart skipped so hard it was painful. Oh god, when would I stop seeing Alex everywhere?

"Willow?" said Scott from a distance. "Is he okay?"

The dark-haired guy had firm shoulders, slim hips. A rifle was slung over his back. As I watched, he shoved a hand through his hair in a motion so familiar it clutched at my soul.

Suddenly I was shaking. I did a scan...and as the familiar energy hit me, the world stopped.

"Alex?" I whispered.

CHAPTER *Twenty-eight*

I KNEW THAT IT COULDN'T be him. It couldn't be. But my heart didn't care.

"*Alex!*" I screamed, and it was as if I'd woken myself out of a trance. I lunged out from behind the house and started running as hard as I could, snow flying with every step as my feet pummelled the ground.

The boy's head snapped up. "Willow!" he shouted.

In seconds he'd vaulted over the tree and was running towards me. This was a dream – it couldn't be true.

When we reached each other, I threw myself into his arms. He caught me up hard, swinging me around in a circle. *Alex*. With a sob I clung to his neck, breathing him in.

"Oh god, I missed you – I missed you so much—" He gripped my head, scattering kisses across my face. As he clutched me close again, I pressed tight against him, tears starting down my cheeks. Warm flesh…his leather jacket… his T-shirt, smelling of dust and sweat. If I loosened my hold, I'd wake up to find he'd vanished, the same as after a hundred dreams.

My shoulders were shaking. "Hey, hey…" whispered Alex against my hair. "Oh, babe, don't cry – I'm back now. Everything's okay."

I couldn't answer. I just held on, trembling. He was *real*.

"Oh, man! Are you Alex *Kylar*?"

I felt Alex keep one arm around me as he stretched out his hand to someone. "Yeah, who are you?"

"Scott Mason. Wow, this is just a complete honour. I can't believe you're really here—"

"Look, you've got problems," broke in Alex. "I waited until the scouts were gone so they wouldn't see me. Did you know you've got, like, three thousand angels waiting to attack just thirty miles away?"

My blood was pounding through my brain. I pulled away slightly, staring up at the strong lines of Alex's face. It was more tanned than I recalled, his eyes looking very blue. This couldn't be happening. Could not.

Scott had gone pale. "Scouts?"

"Yeah, what did you think?"

"I – I don't know, but – we had some other angels this morning, kind of sneaking around town…"

Alex grimaced. "Let me guess; you killed them all. So they sent some others and stayed high this time, and found out you've got an alarm system and a bunch of sharpshooters in town. Nice one."

Scott licked his lips. "Okay, but…they probably already knew that. One of our fighters got captured a few weeks ago."

"It's usually not a great idea to confirm their info," Alex said dryly. "But at least they might assume you don't know about the attack and think they can catch you unaware. You *did* already know about it, right?"

"Yeah, we're busy planning right now – hey, you can help! A bunch of us are at the town hall…"

The world was tilting – I was sliding off its edge. Why wasn't Scott surprised that Alex was still alive? But he hadn't known he was dead. Which was real? Did Alex die, or not? Maybe this whole last year had just been a bad dream.

Alex glanced down at me then; his face creased in concern. "You go on," he told Scott without looking at him. "We'll catch up."

Once Scott had left, Alex held me close. "I was so afraid of this," he whispered. "Willow, you thought I'd died, didn't you?"

"I—" My voice was faint.

Alex drew back to brush away my tears. Then he paused. My hair had tumbled down as I ran, and I saw him taking it in – felt his surprise.

I grasped his hand before he could speak. He still wore the woven bracelet I'd given him, bright against his tanned wrist. "How are you alive?" I choked out. "*How?*"

His brow furrowed. "What do you mean?"

Somehow I managed to put coherent sentences together. "That day – the day that you left – Sam and I went after you. When we reached the New Mexico camp, the entire centre exploded. There was nothing left."

The blood drained from Alex's face. "You were *there* for that?"

"Alex, I felt it…I felt you die…"

The memory was like my soul being shredded. Alex wrapped his arms around me again. "Oh god, Willow, I am so sorry," he said, his voice fervent. "I've been in the angels' world. That's why you couldn't sense me."

"The angels' world?" I repeated in a daze. "But – why didn't you tell me that's what you were doing?"

"Because—" His throat moved as he swallowed. "Because I was pretty sure that just the attempt to get there would kill me," he said roughly. "I don't think I could have forced myself to go otherwise."

I stared at him, trying to get the words to make sense.

He clasped my hands between his, his skin warm, familiar. "Willow, I'm sorry. I know what these last few weeks must have been like for you. God, if it was you, I'd—"

"*Weeks?*" I interrupted. Suddenly my heart was battering at my chest. "Wait, wait – is that what you said?"

"Yeah. Over three weeks…" Alex trailed off, taking in my long blonde hair again. When he'd left, my hair was still brown, just past my shoulders.

His face paled.

We stared at each other. *Three weeks.* The year of grief, bleak and sharp as winter, rose up in a grey crest and threatened to drown me. "Alex, no," I got out finally. "It… it was longer."

He touched a strand of my hair and stroked it slowly down its length. When he spoke again his voice was thick with dread. "How long?"

"Over a year."

He shook his head. "No," he breathed. "No way."

"It's true. You've been gone exactly one year and eleven days."

For a second Alex looked as if he might pass out. "The Edens," he murmured, pressing his hands to his temples. His knuckles were white. "I kept seeing all these new Edens on my way here – I didn't get how we could have missed so many, back at the base…"

I couldn't respond. Alex gave a short, disbelieving

laugh. "Jesus, I can't – I can't even get my head around this—" His fist tightened. With his other hand, he gently cupped my cheek, his touch so familiar that it hurt.

"You thought I was dead all this time," he whispered.

I wanted to hug him; I wanted to hit him. Hugging won. With a moan, I wrapped my arms around his waist and pressed close. He held me tight – I felt his lips brush my head. "I am never leaving you again," he said in a low voice. "Willow, I swear it."

"*Alex!*" called someone.

We pulled apart as Seb jogged to a halt beside us; Nina and Jonah stopped behind him, looking blank with surprise. Seb stood gaping, his cheeks white. "Scott told us, but…but how…" he stammered.

"I was in the angels' world," Alex said, holding out his hand to Seb. "For only a few weeks, I thought."

For a long moment, Seb stayed motionless, staring dumbly. "You're really alive," he murmured at last.

Suddenly a broad grin split his face. "You're alive!" he shouted, ignoring Alex's hand and pulling him into a back-slapping hug. "Ah, you *cabrón,* I could kill you for this – but it's so good to see you again, *mi amigo.*"

"Thanks. You too." Alex's voice was gruff as they drew apart.

Nina glanced at me, eyes wide. "Is this really—?"

I gave a small nod. "This is Alex…my boyfriend." I tried

to laugh; a sort of gasp came out. "He's alive after all. Alex, this is Nina. You remember, I—"

"Hey, yeah – Willow's told me a lot about you." He extended his hand.

Nina looked lost for words as she shook it. "Well, I – I hope to hear a lot about you too."

Jonah offered his own hand. "You probably don't even remember me, but—"

"Jonah?" broke in Alex. "Yeah, I remember. What are you doing *here*?"

Jonah and Seb helped Alex drag the tree away so he could get his truck through; as they did, Jonah gave him a quick rundown on what had been happening. Alex stopped in his tracks. "Immune to the angels?" he said sharply. "Why?"

My eyes begged Jonah not to go into their strange theory about me. I couldn't deal with it right now, not on top of everything else. "It's...kind of a long story," Jonah said, glancing at me. "Maybe we should get back and start planning first."

Alex's blue-grey eyes found mine and held them. And I knew that planning an attack was the last thing on the planet he wanted to be doing. "Yeah," he said tersely. "I guess we'd better."

* * *

We parked at the elementary school and walked to the square. Alex had on a pair of old work boots that I'd never seen before. He wove his fingers through mine, his dark hair falling across his forehead, just the same as always.

"Willow, listen, I've got to talk to you when we have a minute," he said in an undertone. "I found out something in the angels' world that – well, we've got to talk."

Every time I looked at him, it was like worlds colliding, reality turned upside down. Just the feel of his fingers against mine was indescribable. I wanted to be alone with him so badly it hurt.

I nodded, still reeling. "Yes, um – talking would be good."

We made our way through crowds of people hanging out on the snowy front lawn of the town hall: all my old Pawntucket High classmates. I could sense their tension over the scouting angels – then their excitement at seeing Alex and me.

"Go, Angel Killers!" shouted someone, and there were actually cheers.

Part of me was sure this was a dream. When we reached the room with the shortwave radio, everyone was relieved by Alex's presence but not really surprised. No one but Nina and Jonah had known he'd died.

No, he didn't die, I corrected myself, gazing at Alex's face as he studied the map. He'd been alive this whole time.

It had all just…been a mistake.

Scott was briefing Alex on their defence strategy. I could feel Alex's forced concentration – his desire to get me on my own. "Yeah, attacking from the roofs is good, but it leaves your vanguard fighters pretty exposed," he said. "What you should also have are bombs you can detonate from the ground."

"*Bombs?*" Scott stared. "Uh…we don't exactly have that kind of technology."

"Yeah, you do – bombs are easy." Alex started drawing on the side of the map, his hand moving in quick, sure strokes. "Look: this is a nail bomb."

He described how to make it; the materials were all commonplace. "You put it on a roof, then shoot at it from the ground as the angels appear. The nails will explode thirty feet up in the air, like bullets – any that hit a halo will take an angel out."

Excitement crackled through the room. "Oh, *yes,*" Rachel cried. "We have definitely got nails here!"

"I can help with the bombs." Seb seemed to be avoiding looking at her. "At the *reformatorio,* a boy there taught us how to make them."

"Will five days be enough for all this, though?" Nina put in anxiously.

Alex's eyebrows shot up; he tossed the pen aside. "Five days, with scouts here just an hour ago? No way. We'll be lucky as hell to get two."

"But…" Nina glanced at me in alarm.

The dreamlike feeling had turned nightmarish. There was no way Pawntucket could prepare that fast. "We were supposed to have five more days," I faltered.

"I've got some information that might help, with luck." Alex's eyes met mine. Without looking away, he said, "You guys go and get started." Then he seemed to catch himself. "Sorry, I'm not trying to take over – I'm just used to being in charge."

Scott barked out a laugh. "Dude, you are *Alex Kylar.* I think I speak for everyone here when I say: *Please* take over."

Alex smiled thinly. "Okay, if you all agree. Jonah, you and Scott tell everyone what the plan is, then get started fortifying the houses and making the bombs; we don't have any time to lose. Willow…I've got to talk to you. Alone."

CHAPTER *Twenty-nine*

RAZIEL HAD ARRIVED IN SCHENECTADY Eden earlier than planned – and though his church quarters here were as luxurious as all his others, he found it impossible to relax; this particular church was too full of associations. It had been here where Willow and her assassin boyfriend had first met. Here, too, where Paschar had died, blasted into oblivion by Kylar's bullet on the front steps.

I don't believe in omens, Raziel reminded himself darkly.

He was sitting in his church office, going over the list of angels who'd accompanied Bascal on the Nevada attack. Part of him wanted to strike against Pawntucket immediately, especially given the scouts' report. Caution made him wait. It all came down to Willow, somehow – who had almost certainly slipped through the net in Nevada.

One of the angels on this list knew how. And when Raziel had finished with them, they'd be begging to share all they knew.

A knock came. Raziel frowned to see Bascal come in – late, of course. The little thug looked disgustingly pleased with himself, despite his utter failure to do away with Fields and Kylar.

"Everyone's here," Bascal said, sprawling in a lushly upholstered chair. "Over five thousand. The place won't support them much longer – but then we'll be attacking soon, right?"

"When I'm ready," muttered Raziel, going back to the list. He shoved it across to Bascal. "Who do you think?"

Bascal leaned forward; without asking, he plucked a silver pen from the desk. "Not these guys," he said, crossing names off. "They were all part of the main attack. But some went looking for other AKs while we finished up in the training room."

A map of the base lay on the desk; Raziel tapped his lower lip as he studied it. "Did you search down these corridors? Especially this one." He indicated the route to the garage. Maddeningly, Bascal hadn't taken an inventory of the vehicles in the place before he'd torched it.

Bascal nodded. "Six or seven did, but most of them were killed. Zaran's the only one who made it back – he says that corridor was empty."

Zaran. Raziel's dark gaze narrowed. Not someone he knew well, though Zaran was one of the angels who'd also enjoyed human energy, back before all angelkind came here. Unusually private, even for an angel – when they'd all been linked, the joke had been that you couldn't even get the weather from Zaran's thoughts.

"You know, I think I'd like to have a little chat with Zaran," mused Raziel.

Bascal's eyes glinted. "*That* guy, huh? You know, I never did like him. He's sneaky."

"Go get him," Raziel ordered. "Don't let him know what's going on – and bring some backup."

"Will do." Bascal rose; as he turned to leave, he paused and reached into his pocket. "Oh – almost forgot. Present for you." He tossed a small framed picture onto Raziel's desk with a clatter.

Raziel stiffened with unpleasant surprise. Willow as a small child, smiling up through the branches of a weeping willow tree. "Where did you get this?"

Bascal grinned. "At the base – found it in one of the bedrooms that wasn't destroyed. Thought you might want it. Spoil of war and all that."

A willow tree. *The* willow tree, presumably: it would

have been just like Miranda to take her there. "Thank you so much," Raziel said with distaste. "Anything else?"

Bascal pulled out a folded piece of paper and handed it over. "Kinda sweet, huh?" he sneered. "Wouldn't have thought Kylar was the poetic type."

Raziel opened out the well-worn page. *My home is in your touch and in your eyes…* He made a face. "No, quite," he said, tossing it aside. It was the photo that kept drawing him; his daughter's joyful smile was mesmerizing.

"We've got a date with Zaran," he reminded Bascal. The other angel saluted ironically.

Once he'd left, Raziel leaned back in his chair. The office around him was decorated in quiet good taste: golds and browns; leather and soft fabrics. He scarcely noticed it. He picked up the photo, studying Willow's face with an intense frown. So like her mother.

He shook his head. He couldn't believe now that he'd ever been so smitten by a human woman; the week Miranda had spent away from college with her grandparents had dragged into infinity, so that he'd actually travelled up from New York City to this backwater region just to savour her again. That must have been the time it happened, since she'd been so revoltingly sentimental as to name the child "Willow".

The photo's appearance *now* of all times was unnerving. It forcibly brought back his dreams of Miranda – her face, gazing up at him. *You know, I'm often confused now…*

Raziel's teeth gritted. *The dreams mean nothing,* he reminded himself. Miranda was dead; before that she'd been catatonic. She could not be haunting him.

Their child was a different matter.

"You were wise to run, my daughter," Raziel murmured to the blonde, smiling girl. He stroked a finger over the frame. "But you can't run fast enough. I'll find you very soon – you, and whatever powers you're hiding."

CHAPTER *Thirty*

ALEX AND I WENT TO an empty room on the town hall's chilly second floor. As soon as he shut the door behind us, I let out a shaky breath and wrapped my arms around him.

"Whatever this is, can it wait just a few minutes?" I said hoarsely against his leather jacket.

His voice was rough too. "Yeah – that's an excellent idea." His arms enfolded me; he dropped his head down to my shoulder. I pressed close, listening to his steady heartbeat under my cheek.

"I still can't believe this," I said finally. I drew back and wiped my eyes. "Oh god, Alex, to actually have you back again…" I couldn't finish; I'd start crying for real.

"I know. It must have been—" Alex broke off as he studied me. "You look different," he said softly. He stroked his knuckle across my cheekbone. "Your face and your eyes."

I thought of the grief that had lodged in my throat these past twelve months, making it hard to eat, giving me hollowed-out cheekbones. My reflection in the truck's rear-view mirror on the way here: my eyes showing a year's worth of pain.

And Alex's voice when he'd left: *Trust me.*

An emotion stirred that I didn't want to analyze. I pushed it away and tried to smile. "Just another year older, that's all."

He nodded slowly. "Yeah…I guess that's it." He kissed me; I shut my eyes as his warm lips touched mine. Then he sighed and rubbed my arms. "You know, all I want to do is hold you for about the next week, but…"

"I know." I could sense his apprehension over whatever he had to tell me – and suddenly recalled my premonition that whatever happened in Pawntucket would be especially awful for me. I could have done without remembering that, right then.

There was a metal table with folding chairs; we sat down. Alex took my hand. "See, my dad's idea was that the energy field in the angels' world could be used to destroy them," he said. "Cully thought it was possible, so I had to try it – even though getting there seemed suicidal. That's why I didn't tell you. Just imagining the look on your face…"

The look on my face. I thought of this last year again and couldn't respond.

Alex sat gazing down, playing with my fingers. "Anyway, the blast destroyed the gate, and then I wasn't able to connect with the energy field anyway – I was just stuck. So I went to Denver to try and find another way back home, and…that's when it happened."

"When what happened?"

He took a breath. "Willow, I met your mother in the angels' world."

The words slammed into me. My spine jerked away from the seat. "You *what*?"

"Yeah," he said softly. "Humans who have severe angel burn are like ghosts there. Their physical bodies still exist here in our world, but their minds just…go wandering with the angels." He gave a sad smile, his thumb rubbing my palm. "She's beautiful. She looks just like you. She's been, like – frozen in time at twenty-one."

Alex described his encounter with my mother as I sat stunned, drinking in every word. "She asked about you," he said. "She wanted to know everything. And…she wished she'd been a better mother."

"She did the best she could," I said fiercely, swiping at sudden tears. "I always knew that – even as a little girl."

Alex squeezed my hand hard. "She helped me escape," he said quietly after a pause. "And, Willow…" He hesitated. "She said *you* could be the one to link to the energy field in the angels' world."

I straightened, staring. "Me?"

"You're half angel, half human. You can straddle the two worlds and use their energy field to destroy them. I'm pretty sure that's what Paschar's vision meant."

Was Paschar's vision really true, then? I shook my head in a daze. "But, Alex, the immunity to the angels that's happening here…Jonah thinks *that* has something to do with me too." Quickly, I told him what Jonah had said. "None of this makes any sense!"

"Maybe it does."

My hand in his went cold. "How?"

Alex shrugged. "The quakes were the most catastrophic event our world's ever known – on the ethereal level too. What if, afterwards, humanity started trying to heal itself? Maybe people are unconsciously reaching out to the one thing that could save them from the angels."

"Me, in other words," I said in disbelief.

"Yeah, maybe. Except the only ones who can manage it are those who've been around you and know what your energy feels like."

I remembered standing above Pawntucket with Seb – that strange sensation of the whole world straining towards me. "Fine, but that doesn't explain what it is about *me* that lets them all marshal themselves! Why not Seb?"

Alex's gaze was level. "Because he's not the one who could save them. To be able to connect with the angel world's energy field, you'll need a link there to ground you, and you've got your mother. A piece of her energy is there – you connect to it every time you reach out to her."

I opened my mouth; at first nothing came out. "So you're saying that Paschar was right," I said finally. "I really *am* the one who can destroy them."

I could sense Alex's fears for me. "Yeah, I guess that's what I'm saying," he said shortly. "And that means we've got to hold the angels back, no matter what. Miranda said that you need to try from Pawntucket – there must be a gate here you can still get through. If the angels destroy it, that's our last chance gone for ever."

My brain felt numb. We'd hoped to defeat them so many times. But oh, god, if this was true… I pressed my fingers against my temples. "Did Mom say where the gate was?"

"No, she didn't get a chance."

"Well, she didn't get out much, so…maybe it's somewhere in Aunt Jo's house?" The idea was bizarre, but no more so than anything else today.

Alex got up. "Okay, let's check it out. If we're lucky, we can find it fast and do this before the angels even get here." Then he stopped. "Wait, I haven't had a chance to ask – how are things back at the base?"

My chest went tight. I saw Sam fall again – heard the screams of almost two hundred AKs. The news would devastate Alex. And what good would telling him now do, with thousands of angels about to attack?

I rose too, and ducked my head as I zipped my parka. "They're all fine." I glanced up and managed a smile. "We've been recruiting new people, training them... Everyone's fine."

Alex looked relieved. He touched my hair. "Good. When we have time, I want to hear everything that's been going on, okay?"

That strange emotion flickered again like a dull flame. Remembering how I'd cried myself to sleep at night in the bed we'd shared, I almost said, *I don't think you really want to know, Alex.*

I swallowed – and instead of speaking, just hugged him hard.

He was alive. That was all that mattered.

At my Aunt Jo's old house, I was bracing myself for a black, burned-out shell – instead there was only a vacant lot and a driveway that led to nothing. I couldn't stop staring. It was like no one had ever lived there at all.

We searched the ethereal plane for hours. Nothing – and when I reached out to ask Mom where she'd meant, her energy was as warm and unresponsive as ever. I tried reading Alex too…and though the image of my mother that was in his mind brought tears to my eyes, I didn't get anything new.

When it became too dark to search, we went and helped with the fortifications. People were working by torchlight, doing everything they could to prepare the houses for the fighters. We pounded in nails and climbed up and down chilly ladders until my limbs felt numb.

Finally, sometime after midnight, Alex gave an order for people to start grabbing food and sleeping in shifts, and we headed back to the school. As Alex drove, he rested one hand on my thigh; the feel of it brought back a thousand memories. I kept glancing over, taking in his strong profile.

I felt that if I stopped looking at him, he'd vanish.

When we got out of the truck, we saw a tired-looking cluster heading towards us: Jonah and Nina, with Seb, Scott and Rachel. "My group will keep making nail bombs in here tonight," Seb was saying.

"They know how to make them now?" Alex asked sharply. When Seb nodded, he said, "Good – we need you for something else tomorrow. We've got to start searching the town at the crack of dawn."

He explained what he'd found out in the angels' world – and the mood shifted abruptly to excitement. Jonah's eyes widened. "You mean we could actually *defeat* them?"

For the past few hours, I'd managed to blank out the fact that the fate of the world apparently depended on me after all. I cleared my throat as we all headed inside the school. "Maybe," I said. "If I can figure out what to do when we find this place."

When – okay, more like *if.* It looked as if the gate between worlds could be anywhere in town. Finding it could take days – and we didn't have many left. I tried not to think about it.

It was weird being back in the elementary school again after so long, with its bright posters now all in shadow: the school's single long corridor was lit with Coleman lanterns.

"We don't turn on the lights at night," Nina explained. "Just the heat."

Looking distracted, Rachel tucked back an auburn strand of hair. "The kitchen's probably the best place for us to make the bombs, once the others get here," she told Seb.

"Yes, fine," he said shortly. He turned to Scott. "Will you show me where that is?"

As they headed off, Rachel bit her lip. "Wow, he really doesn't like me, does he?"

I'd sensed how tightly Seb was holding his emotions in check. "It's not you," I said, gazing after him. "You just remind him of someone, that's all."

Alex stood studying a bulletin board; he glanced at me. "You're kidding. He's finally fallen for Meghan?"

Suddenly I remembered Seb's lips on mine, only days ago. My cheeks heated – though I wasn't sure *why;* it wasn't as if I'd had a clue that my boyfriend was still alive. Remembering why I hadn't known, that odd emotion stirred again.

"Kind of," I said, managing a smile.

Then, taking in the weary set of Alex's shoulders, my heart twisted; everything else faded away. Alex was *here.* It was every dream I'd ever had since I thought he'd died.

I touched his arm, stroking it gently. "You look really tired."

He rubbed his eyes. "Yeah, I am," he admitted. "I'm about ready to crash, if Seb doesn't need any help."

"We'll let you know if he does," Jonah said. "Do you want something to eat first? We've got canned stuff, or more canned stuff."

Alex smiled slightly. "Thanks, I'll pass."

"I'm not hungry either," I said – and then realized what that meant: Alex and I would be going to bed now. My heartbeat quickened. Suddenly I felt like I was sixteen again and had never even held hands with a boy.

Nina took my arm. "Come on, I'll show you where the sleeping bags and stuff are." As the two of us headed down the corridor, she lowered her voice. "Willow, this is all so weird. Are you okay?"

I looked back at Alex, savouring the sight of him. He stood talking to Jonah and Rachel with his hands stuck in his back pockets – a pose I'd seen him in a thousand times.

"Better than okay," I said quietly.

Nina shook her head. "It's so unbelievable. I mean, *I'm* still stunned, and I don't even know him." She grinned suddenly. "Oh, and he's gorgeous, by the way. But then, so's Seb. Are you just, like, surrounded by hot guys now?"

I rolled my eyes. "Seb and I are just friends, Nina." But remembering what I'd sensed earlier, a tiny pang struck me. I'd wanted Seb to get over me for two years – but knowing that he actually *had* felt a little strange.

Nina opened up a supply closet and started pulling out sleeping bags and pillows; I moved to help her. "So, you and Jonah, huh?"

Her voice held a smile. "Yeah. For almost a year now. Jonah says he fell in love with me right when we first met – I was so fierce and suspicious, he said. For a long time we were just friends, though. Then when he started doing the Voice of Freedom, we did a lot of travelling together – he has to broadcast from all over, so he won't get caught – and one day we were broadcasting from the woods, and I looked at him sitting there with the sun shining on his face, his expression so intense…and I just knew."

A weary-looking group passed on their way to the lunchroom. I smiled automatically as people said, "Hi, Willow," and "Oh, man, it is so good to have you back!" – and tried to ignore the awe in their eyes.

"I was never this popular in high school," I muttered to Nina.

She shrugged. "I know, but I guess you've become kind of a hero here – you and Alex both. Besides—" She broke off, studying me.

"Besides what?" I said uncomfortably.

"Well…you *are* one, aren't you? I mean, it's you who we're all counting on."

I had no idea what to say to that. Just then I heard Alex and the others approaching. Nina glanced back and cleared her throat. "Listen, um – if you two want some privacy tonight, no one sleeps in the gym this time of year."

My lips had gone desert-dry. "Yeah, privacy is probably good."

She hesitated. "And…well, here." She opened the closet again and pointed. "See that big cardboard box? Our own personal Planned Parenthood." She gave me an impish look. "It's amazing what you can find when you scavenge a whole town."

I was saved from answering; Alex and the others were

walking up. "And we've got guards posted, right?" Alex was saying.

Jonah nodded. "All over town. They can alert us in minutes if the attack comes."

"Okay, sleep with your gun next to you. All of you. Spread the word."

As Jonah and Rachel continued down the corridor, Nina fell into step beside them; I saw Jonah link his fingers through hers. "Goodnight," Nina called over her shoulder.

"Hey, you," Alex said softly once we were alone.

He looked just like I'd remembered every second of this past year – every plane and angle of his face was exactly as I'd recalled. I swallowed, trying not to shake.

"Hey," I whispered back.

Alex stroked my upper arms; even through my parka, I could feel the warmth of his fingers. "Willow, I—" he started, and then looked up as more people passed.

"*Alex Kylar*," I heard one whisper. Breathless hellos, eyes shining.

Once they'd passed, Alex gave me a wry look. "It's not going to be like this all night, is it? I just want to be alone with you for a few hours."

I could feel my angel stirring, but I ignored her – because right then being alone with Alex was all that I wanted too. "Nina says the gym's private," I offered.

That slow grin I'd dreamed of so many times spread

across Alex's face. "Yeah?" He kissed me lightly, then grabbed up the sleeping bags and pillows. "Let's go."

The gym's shadows melted away as we entered with a lantern: a broad, cold space with a small stage at one end. Alex jumped on the stage with a light leap. "Look – we can close the curtains. It'll be warmer that way too."

I went and joined him. He was on his knees, opening up the sleeping bags – and as I kneeled to help him, our eyes met. I paused mid-motion; we both went still. Finally Alex reached out and ran a gentle hand over my hair.

"I still can't believe it, you know," he said in a low voice. His thumb caressed my cheekbone. "Christ, I've missed a whole year of your life."

A raw yearning for him rocked through me. I longed to reach for him – but all at once the shadows, the stage, came together in a surreal dream. If I moved, I'd wake up…and I couldn't bear even the thought of that.

He murmured my name and kissed me. When he'd first come back, his kisses had been quick, frantic – this one was so long and deep that I felt myself dissolve into nothing. *Alex.* His smell – his taste. With a sudden moan, I pressed close, wrapping my arms around him, kissing him back for all I was worth.

"I love you," I gasped. "Alex, I missed you so much – every day—"

"I love you too – I thought about you every second—"

Somehow our jackets came off; they fell to the stage with a rustle. I ran my hands under his T-shirt, needing to feel him; still kissing me, Alex pulled away slightly to yank the shirt over his head.

He reached for me again. "Wait," I whispered. I sank back onto my heels and drank him in: the way the lantern's glow played on the muscles of his chest; the look in his eyes as he gazed back at me.

I slowly reached out and glided my fingers over his smooth torso. I shivered at the familiar warmth. I hadn't forgotten, not any of it. I traced the letters of his AK tattoo, then leaned over to press my lips against them. I felt drunk on him; I could never get enough.

"Oh god, Willow," he whispered roughly. I felt his lips on my head, my cheek, his hand under my shirt, caressing over my ribcage, going upwards—

I pulled away, breathing hard. "Stop," I said.

He paused, his eyes surprised. "Stop?"

I could feel my angel stirring again – that weird sensation of looseness that came when we weren't in accord. She wasn't happy about something, but right then I wasn't too interested in finding out what.

"Yes – stop." I picked up Alex's T-shirt; as I handed it to him, I kissed him lingeringly. "Put that back on," I whispered. "There's a cardboard box out in the closet that you need to go check out."

* * *

When I woke a few hours later, I was curled in Alex's arms; his breathing was slow and steady. For a few heartbeats, my drowsy brain thought we were back at the base. *Do we have a simulation today?* I thought, nestling closer to him. *Hope we haven't overslept.*

Then I remembered.

I froze, my eyes abruptly wide open. We'd closed the stage curtains and were in total darkness; I had no idea what time it was. I sat up, hugging a blanket tight around myself – so aware of the warm sleeping form next to me. And even though I *knew* now that this was real...I still had to check.

I brought out my angel, and the stage exploded into ethereal light. Alex lay with one arm up on his pillow. The three weeks of stubble on his jaw was only a shadow; the light from my angel picked out every hair.

Three weeks, I thought, staring at him. Twenty-one days – that was all this had been in Alex's life.

The emotion that had been tugging at me since he returned came again, stronger than ever. I could feel my angel's disquiet. I touched my forehead as it started to pound – and that's when the thought I'd been trying to avoid hit me with sickening clarity.

There had been no reason for me to go through this last year. None. If Alex had just told me the truth...if I'd known there was a chance that he was still alive in the angels' world...

It wouldn't have made any difference; you still wouldn't have known for sure, I told myself dazedly.

It would have made the difference between hope and despair, and I knew it.

I felt dizzy suddenly – all I wanted was to slam this away again as hard as I could. Beside me, Alex stirred. He reached out and rubbed my arm. "Hey," he murmured. "Everything okay?"

"Fine," I got out. "Couldn't sleep."

He tugged at me. "Come back, you're too far away."

I felt like a clenched fist. I lay down beside him again; he wrapped his arms around my waist and kissed my shoulder. I sensed him doing a scan and realizing: "Your angel's out."

"Yes, um..." I closed my eyes hard, willing this to go away. "I just wanted to see you. Make sure you're real."

Alex lifted his energy above his crown chakra and took in my angel. "She's more beautiful than ever, you know," he said. "So are you." He touched my hair, fingering a blonde strand.

"I like this," he said. "You were gorgeous as a redhead and a brunette too, but – this is who you are."

I cleared my throat. Somehow my voice sounded normal. "That's...why I did it. I wanted to be me again when I faced Raziel."

Alex glanced at the closed curtains. "Speaking of that – any idea what time it is?"

I sent my angel soaring up briefly through the roof: icy air and piercing stars. "Still early," I said as she returned. "I don't think we've been asleep very long."

"Okay, let's at least try to get another hour." Then Alex really looked at me. "Are you sure you're all right? You seem so tense."

Alex, so close that I could feel his body's warmth even where we weren't touching – it was everything I'd longed for, so why was I *feeling* like this? "I'm fine," I said after a pause. "It must just still be the shock, or something."

He sighed. "Yeah. I'm still dealing with that myself." Keeping one arm around me, he rolled onto his back, gazing at my angel. "A year," he murmured. "Jesus, you're nineteen now. We're the same age."

I fell silent, remembering my nineteenth birthday party. How I'd cried so hard that I'd thrown up. Then my gaze fell on the battered work boots lying nearby; Alex had said he'd scavenged them from a dark town.

The explosion at the camp thundered through me again: my voice screaming Alex's name, my fingers bleeding as I clawed at shards of concrete, the way I'd cradled his shoe as I sobbed.

All because he hadn't wanted to see the look on my face.

Alex touched my cheek. "Oh god, babe," he said softly.

"I can't even imagine what this last year has been like for you."

A great, dark wave was cresting inside me. "It…wasn't much fun," I said thinly. "I mean, obviously. But I got through it."

He raised my hand to his lips and kissed my palm. "I'll make it up to you, somehow," he said. "I swear it, Willow. All that matters now is that we're together again."

I'll make it up to you. I went very still. For a moment I almost felt short of breath. Had he actually just said that? For him to even think it was *possible*…

He'd put me through hell, and he didn't even know it.

Alex settled back with his arms around me. I could feel that he thought I just didn't want to talk about it yet. "So what's been happening back at the base?" he asked. He smiled slightly. "How did Seb finally come to his senses about Meghan, anyway? Last time I talked to him, he wasn't even close."

And he looked so relaxed that suddenly I hated him.

"I don't know," I said, my voice tightly controlled. "I guess maybe it was when the two of us were kissing a few days ago."

Alex's expression drained. He propped himself up on one elbow, staring at me. "You were kissing Seb," he repeated.

"Yeah, we had to take shelter on the way here." Who was this person talking, with her hard, deliberate tone?

"It was this really romantic setting – a fireplace, a sheepskin rug – and we just fell into each other's arms. It was so passionate – we couldn't get enough of each other. I've never—"

Hurt anger had come over Alex's face. "Fine, I get the picture! You totally wanted Seb. So what happened?"

I longed to tell him that we'd spent a night of wild passion on the sheepskin rug. Instead my voice shook as I snapped: "*Nothing!* Because Seb sensed I was still in love with you, that I was using him without even meaning to! And I sensed he's in love with Meghan."

Alex lay staring at me. Feeling ashamed and small suddenly, I looked down at the sleeping bag, tracing its seam. "He, um…hasn't really figured that part out for himself yet. I think that's why he's being so rude to—"

"What the hell was *that* about?" Alex interrupted. He gripped my bare shoulder. "Let me get this straight: you're telling me nothing else happened, because you're still in love with me."

I swallowed. "That's…pretty much what I'm saying, yes."

"Great – so was there a particular reason you had to tell me that the two of you were all over each other? What a romantic *setting* it was?"

"I thought you'd want to know," I said levelly.

Alex snorted. "Yeah, I'm overjoyed – thanks for sharing.

Jesus, Willow! Seb's my friend, and right now I want to—"
He stopped abruptly; finally he let out a breath and rubbed
a hand over his face.

"Look," he said. "I don't even know where any of this
came from. I don't want to argue, all right? I get that you
must be upset over what's happened, but—"

Something like a laugh choked out of me. "*Upset?* You
told me to trust you and I thought you were dead for a
year. But hey, you're back now, so it's all good."

"I *had to go.* I didn't tell you the truth because—" Alex
cut himself off, looking frustrated. "Oh, what's the point?
You already know all of this. It doesn't seem to make any
difference."

He glanced at my angel's gleaming form, his jaw tight.
"Do you mind? I've got to get some sleep. Unless you've
got any more revelations you'd like to throw at me. Hey,
throw them really hard, all right? Bonus points if you
knock me out."

I didn't tell him about the base. At least I didn't do that:
I didn't use it as a weapon against him, even though I was
so angry and hurt myself that I was trembling.

"No," I said finally. "No more revelations." And I
brought my angel back to me, and the stage fell into
darkness.

CHAPTER *Thirty-one*

"I STILL CAN'T BELIEVE YOU'RE really Alex Kylar." Scott
stood propped against the sink next to Alex; he'd just come
into the school on his break. It was nearly dawn – a lantern
lit the shadowy boy's bathroom.

"Yeah, I really am," Alex said dryly. He stood clad in his
jeans as he quickly shaved. The second it was light enough,
he, Willow and Seb would start searching for the gate.

"Man, you must have seen so much action. How many
angels have you brought down?"

"I stopped keeping track."

"What was your last count?"

Would this guy never shut up? "Over a thousand." Alex's tone was terse.

His reflection looked back steadily from the mirror as if the argument with Willow hadn't happened. But when he'd woken up, her stiffness had brought it back in excruciating detail. They'd dressed in silence.

Scott whistled. "That is just…epic."

"Not epic enough – they're still around," Alex said curtly. There were other guys in the restroom too; to Alex's annoyance, they were listening. Great, just what he needed.

He glanced up as Seb walked in.

The other sinks were in use; Scott reluctantly stood up. Seb poured a bucket of steaming water into the basin and hastily stripped off his T-shirt. "Morning," he said to Alex.

"Morning," Alex muttered back. He knew he didn't have much right to mind about the kiss – Christ, they'd both thought he was dead. But leaping straight to acceptance was a little beyond him. He had to fight the urge to slam Seb up against a wall.

Scott was eyeing the *AK* on Alex's bicep. "I am seriously getting one of those tattoos if we survive this thing. And, dude, is that a *bullet* wound?"

Alex didn't bother answering. After a few more attempts, Scott gave up and left. One by one the others filtered out too, until only Seb was there. Alex glanced at him as he swiped his face dry.

"Willow told me," he said.

Seb had been frowning as if there was something on his mind. He glanced up. "Told you what?"

Alex looked at him without speaking.

"Oh." Slowly, Seb rinsed the soap from under his arms. "*Amigo,* it wasn't anything," he said, sounding tired. "It was a mistake; we both knew it right away."

"Yeah, she told me that too."

"Did she tell you the rest?" Seb pulled his T-shirt back on; his loose curls appeared. "I'm not in love with her any more," he said quietly. "I care about her as a friend – that's all."

Any other time, the news would have been welcome. Now Alex's muscles stayed tight; he snapped on his own T-shirt. "No, she kept that one to herself. But, hey, it's good to go out on a high – I heard you couldn't get enough of each other."

Seb looked taken aback. "She said that?"

"Oh, yeah. I've got a lot to compete with, apparently. Even if you're not in the running any more."

Seb's high-cheekboned face looked conflicted. "This last year has been very bad for her," he said finally. "But I know she still loves you. The kiss meant nothing, I promise."

Deep down, Alex knew it wasn't really the kiss that bothered him. Well, okay, it did, but he'd get over it.

What hurt was how much Willow had wanted to cause him pain.

It was easier to snap back, "Yeah? So why don't I go make out with Meghan for a while, and you can see how meaningless you think *that* is."

Seb stiffened. "What does she have to do with this?"

"She's the one you're in love with, right?"

Seb's expression had turned murderous. "I said it was nothing, and I meant it," he said with icy control. "Do you want me to make up something different? Or are we finished?"

"Yeah, we're finished," Alex said in a low voice. He glanced at the window. "It's almost dawn. Outside in five minutes."

That day and the next passed in a daze of scanning. Taking the southern side of town, Alex searched for the gate to the angels' world everywhere he could think of. As he worked, he kept passing people hammering up on roofs – and even if he *wasn't* psychic, he could feel the tension gripping the town. He worked as fast as he could, urgency pounding through him. But by late afternoon of the second day, he'd only covered about ten blocks.

It wasn't nearly enough.

"Any luck?" called a voice. Jonah, standing on a ladder

built against the side of a house. Alex went over, and Jonah hopped to the frosty ground.

"Not yet," Alex said. "I don't know how the others are doing today, though." It wasn't true – if either had found something, he was sure they'd have come to tell him.

Jonah's brown eyes didn't look as if they missed much. "You don't think you're going to find it in time now, do you?" he asked after a beat.

The air bit coldly at Alex's face. "No," he admitted.

Jonah nodded slowly as he took in what this meant. Finally he let out a breath and glanced up the home-made ladder. "Want to come take a look? This one's done; I was just checking it."

Alex climbed up; the roof was covered with wooden rods nailed at neat intervals. He braced his way up them to the apex. Below, he could see a few streets of houses with bombs attached to their roofs – and then frost-covered fields, with the sunset streaking above. The dying sun was the same red that Willow's hair used to be.

During these last two days, their exchanges had been perfunctory; mostly he'd caught only glimpses of her. Each time he'd seen her, she'd been searching intently – and when dark had come the night before, she'd helped the builders just as fervently. Finally, around one o'clock in the morning, he'd seen her heading off towards the school with

Nina, so tired-looking that he wanted to go after them and take her in his arms.

But he didn't know what to say – what to do. This cold, angry Willow was nothing like the girl he thought he knew. He hated what had happened as much as she did, but he couldn't make it *un*happen. What exactly did she want from him?

This is just unreal, he thought as he gazed out at the fields. Gone for three weeks, then back to find a year had passed…and his girlfriend acting like a stranger.

Jonah joined him, shoving his grey cap back as they looked towards Schenectady. "Part of me wishes the angels would just attack and get it over with," he said in an undertone.

Alex nodded. For the hundredth time, he wondered what the hell was taking Raziel so long.

"It won't be much longer," he said grimly.

Jonah was still gazing towards the Eden. "You know, the only real faith I ever had was in the angels. To lose that was—" He broke off. "But there are still things I believe in," he added after a moment.

He glanced at Alex. "Remember when we first met? You pulled a gun on me. I thought you were actually going to use it."

Alex smiled slightly. He'd been carrying the wounded Willow out of the Denver Church of Angels, with no time to spare before the frenzied crowd turned on her again. "I would have, if you'd tried to stop me."

"At first I was surprised that you're younger than me, but then I thought – no, he's older than I'll ever be. These last couple of years, though…" Jonah lifted a shoulder. "I don't know. Maybe I've caught up with you."

"Yeah," said Alex. "Fighting angels will do that to you."

They went back down from the roof; Jonah swung himself onto the ladder first. Alex was just about to follow – then stopped mid-motion. There was Willow, searching the next street over.

She hadn't seen him; she was walking with her gaze fixed in concentration. And suddenly, as he watched, Alex's throat went tight.

There'd always been a kind of lightness to Willow, even in their worst moments: the sense that unhappiness wasn't her natural state; that soon she'd be back to her usual serene self. But the way she was walking now, hugging her elbows so tightly…how could he have missed it before?

She looked as if she'd never smiled at all. As if any lightness in her had been buried by months of sorrow.

Willow glanced up and saw him then. She started over; Alex climbed down and hopped to the ground beside Jonah. "Any luck?" she asked as she drew near.

"Nothing," Alex said. "You?"

She shook her head, glancing up and down the street in frustration. "No, nothing."

She was too thin, Alex realized suddenly. Oh Christ, that's why her face looked so different. He'd noticed her thinness the other night, of course, but they'd both had other things on their minds. Now it hit him hard: Willow was naturally slim. If she was thinner, it was because she wasn't eating enough.

She looked as if she hadn't eaten enough for a long time.

Even with Jonah standing there, Alex couldn't help himself: hesitantly, he touched her shoulder. "Willow…" he started.

She glanced at him and then away, her mouth tightening unhappily. "I'd better keep searching while there's still a little light." She turned and walked off, still holding her arms. Her small figure in its jeans and parka passed between the houses and was gone.

Alex stood staring after her, Miranda's words echoing: *She's been very sad for a long time.* He had a terrible feeling now that this had been the understatement of the century. And he'd *known* that. Jesus, if it had been him, and he'd thought Willow was dead—

Yeah, he'd known it with his head. But he hadn't let himself think about the reality much, had he?

Alex scraped a hand over his face, aware of Jonah's

quiet, non-judgemental gaze. "Come on," he said at last. "We'd better go start helping the builders."

"We won't find it now." Willow sat clutching her head. "There's just no way. We can't have enough time left."

It was hours later; Alex was sitting at a table in the school lunchroom, poring over the map with her and Seb. The lantern cast a mocking glow on all the places they'd marked off. Not even half the town yet, and nothing. Around them a few subdued groups sat eating. Awareness was rife now: soon they'd be battling thousands of angels.

Alex massaged his eyes. "Both of you, try to get a little sleep," he ordered. "The attack could come any time now."

"There must be something else we can—" Seb broke off as Rachel appeared.

"Seb, could you come look at the way we've placed these last few bombs?"

Seb's face had gone expressionless. He shoved his chair back without looking at her. "Yes, fine."

Once he'd gone, Willow cleared her throat. "So, I'm going to sleep with Nina again tonight," she said after a pause.

That hurt, though he should have expected it. As she rose, Alex also got up and touched her arm. "Willow, wait. We've got to talk."

Her face had turned stiff with pain. "Not now," she said, drawing away. "I'm sorry, Alex; I just can't. These last few days, all I can think is…"

"What?" he asked softly, his hand still reaching towards her.

She started to say something, then shook her head. "No. I'm not going to do this. I'd only say things I'd regret."

She left the lunchroom. Alex started to go after her; some instinct warned him to leave her alone. He sank back down, resting his forehead on his fists.

Once he'd started noticing how much Willow had changed, he hadn't been able to stop. She seemed to get headaches now; several times tonight he'd seen her massaging her head. And her eyes looked so sad – and he didn't think it was just because things were so tense right now. No, her eyes had the look of someone who hadn't really smiled in over a year.

What have I done to her? he thought.

"Hey." Scott Mason in his letterman's jacket, swinging himself into the chair opposite. He dug into a bowl of stew with a spoon. "So how does all this compare with the old days of the AKs? What was it like when—"

Alex got up and left. Ignoring everyone he passed, he pushed open the school's front door and started walking, following the sound of hammers. Within ten minutes, he

157

was up on a roof in the torchlit town square; it was a relief to be working instead of thinking.

He glanced up as someone else appeared: Seb, his expression stormy. Without speaking, he started hammering too.

When there was a pause, Alex glanced over. "You know, it's not Rachel's fault she looks like Meghan. So stop taking it out on her."

Seb lined another dowel into place. "Why should I care who she looks like?"

"Just knock off the bad mood around her. And I thought I told you to get some sleep."

Seb hammered without answering, slamming the nail in as if he hated it. Alex didn't push the point. He and Seb kept working, moving across the roof; when they finished that building, they moved on to the next.

Finally Alex felt a hand on his arm. A guy named Mark, raising his voice over the sound of tools. "You two haven't had a break yet. You said no excuses, remember?"

Alex scraped a tired hand over his eyes. It had to be almost three in the morning. "Yeah," he said at last. He glanced at Seb. "Same for you."

Seb looked as if he was going to protest but didn't. They left in silence.

The sound of activity faded as their footsteps echoed down the street. A question was pounding through Alex's brain. He didn't want to ask it, but he had to. He jammed his hands in his jacket pockets.

"Look, I've got to know – what was it like for Willow?" He glanced over at Seb. "After I left. Was it as bad as I think?"

Seb's face in the moonlight was still dark with his own problems. Finally he sighed. "Worse," he said.

Alex swallowed. "Were you…able to do anything for her?" There'd been times when he'd resented Seb and Willow's closeness; now he hoped fervently that they'd become closer than ever.

Seb shook his head. "She wouldn't let anyone near. She did her work; said what she was supposed to say. But she was just…a zombie."

Alex's throat tightened as he pictured it. *I'll make it up to you,* he'd told her. It may have been the stupidest thing he'd ever said. He could never make it up to her, not if he spent his whole life trying.

"Then during the attack…" Seb looked down at his feet as they walked. "I think she really wanted to die. I almost couldn't get her out."

Alex stared; his steps stilled. "What attack?"

Seb stopped with a quick, surprised glance. He closed his eyes. "Oh, *dios mío,* she hasn't told you."

Alex grabbed his arm. "Told me what? What's happened at the base?"

Seb's eyes were reluctant. "There was an angel attack about two weeks ago," he said at last. "Almost everyone was killed."

Alex stood stunned as Seb told him the details: how the angels had struck with no warning during a training session; how Sam had died and Willow had tried to run into the final fray.

"I had to fight with her to get her out," Seb finished. "She was kicking, struggling – she wanted to die with them. No, she just…wanted to die."

Alex had one hand over his eyes, pummelled by every word. "I should have been there," he said roughly.

He sensed rather than saw Seb's shrug. "There was nothing you could have done."

"I should have been there anyway – they were my team," Alex snapped. He dropped his hand…but couldn't force away the image of Willow standing over Sam's body, crying and shooting at the angels. Or of the others, almost all dead.

The world was icy and silent – the sky overhead brilliant with stars. "They were my team," Alex repeated finally. The words tasted like dust.

CHAPTER *Thirty-two*

"AND THEN WHAT HAPPENED?" RAZIEL asked, his tone conversational. He stood propped against the desk in the Schenectady Church of Angels office, idly cleaning his fingernails with a letter opener. "Do not lie to me again, Zaran."

The dark-haired angel sat clutching his temples, visibly trembling. He'd been sitting there for over two days – since just after Raziel had arrived, in fact. All that time without feeding, for to shift into his angel form would make him vulnerable.

He wasn't handling it very well.

"I'm not lying," he gasped. "Nothing happened. I flew down the corridor, and no one was there, so I flew back to tell the others."

"Mmm, yes, so you keep saying." Raziel motioned to Bascal, who stood waiting by the door with two other goons. "You know, I'm feeling rather peckish," he confided. "What about you?"

"Sure am," said Bascal with a leer. "Want me to call for a couple of A1s?"

"Delightful." Raziel noted with satisfaction how pale Zaran had become at the mention of food – angels, unlike humans, could not go for very long without partaking of sustenance. Zaran's aura had been shuddering for hours, its edges a vivid, painful blue.

Raziel straightened up and stretched as Bascal headed out. "You know, it *is* funny how all roads keep leading back to you," he said. "Willow Fields did not die; I'd stake my own life on it. And the entrances she was nearest to could only be reached by the corridor you say you flew down. So where did she go?"

"I don't know – I told you!"

Idly, Raziel picked up the small photo Bascal had given him. "Such a pretty girl," he mused. "You must have thought it a shame that she had to die."

"I didn't think—" Zaran broke off. Raziel raised an eyebrow and smiled.

Low murmurs came from the outer room as Bascal returned. He'd left the office door slightly ajar behind him; through it they could see a starry-eyed pair of humans – and then silence came as Bascal fed. His halo pulsed brightly through the crack in the door.

Raziel had enacted this little performance several times already with Zaran; this time it could truly be called a success. The high-cheekboned angel sat staring as Bascal fed, his aura shaking with weakness and fatigue. "I – no, I didn't—"

"Didn't what?" Raziel asked gently.

"Didn't think of *her*! I didn't—" With a moan, Zaran buried his face in his hands. "All right," he whispered raggedly. "I saw them – saw them both. Her and the other half-angel."

"And you let them go," hissed Raziel.

"It was just the spur of the moment – it was the other half-angel, you see. He…he's my son. I didn't want him to be hurt."

Ah. The mystery of Seb's parentage finally revealed itself. "How fascinating," Raziel said coldly. "And how quaint of you to feel such a human emotion. What about Kylar?"

"He wasn't there." Zaran's eyes were still fixed on Bascal; his fingers gripped the chair's arms. "That's everything. Let me feed now – promise you won't hurt me if I do."

"Oh, but I don't think it *is* everything. What aren't you telling me?"

Zaran shot him a wretched look. His face was pale, clammy with sweat.

"I know there's something, you see," Raziel said softly. "I may not be very psychic any more, but I've become quite, quite adept at body language. Yours is very revealing right now."

Zaran sat frozen. His throat moved.

Without taking his gaze off him, Raziel called, "Bascal, I don't think I'm hungry after all. Take the humans away, will you?"

"No!" burst out Zaran. "All right. Willow fell in front of me during the fight, right after she beat Margen. And the expression on her face – I think she got something psychically from Margen before she killed her."

Electricity surged through Raziel. Margen had been one of the few angels to know about Pawntucket. Willow knew, then, that he planned to destroy her hometown.

And that meant, unless he was very much mistaken, that she was in Pawntucket right now.

Raziel smiled. Suddenly he felt almost friendly towards Zaran – the wait before the attack had been well worth it. "Why don't you go and feed?" he suggested gently. "Go on – we won't hurt you."

Zaran didn't move at first, his expression an agony of

disbelief and desperation. Finally, with a weak lunge, he bolted out the door. A moment later, light from his angel form poured in through the office doorway.

Raziel nodded at Bascal's two goons; they straightened and slipped into the other room. There was a blaze of light as they, too, shifted – then winged shadows struggling briefly on the wall. A broken-off scream from Zaran. A moment later, drifting pieces of light glinted at the corner of Raziel's vision.

"Goodbye, Zaran," he said, carefully placing the photo back on the desk. "It was a pleasure knowing you."

A few hours later Raziel was still in his office, eyes narrowed in thought as he leaned back in his leather chair. The information was even better than he'd first thought.

Pawntucket, with Willow leading them, would be preparing for the attack, of course. It didn't matter; they'd be crushed in moments. Yet now that it came down to it, merely killing the girl seemed anticlimactic…especially since the quakes seemed to have awakened such a power in her over human auras.

Raziel had no doubt now that the Mexico City anomaly was because of Willow: people who she'd merely lived near, perhaps, or whose auras she'd brushed against on the street. The sheer *power* that implied – not to mention the energy shift he'd been sensing in the world. If that was linked to her too, and he could get her to harness it…what couldn't he do?

Yet to do that, he'd need to control her.

Raziel's gaze fell on the photo of Willow again. He narrowed his eyes at the smiling girl. "You're a worthy opponent, but I am more so," he murmured, touching the brass frame. "And I will get what I need from you."

A knock came; he glanced at the clock. Almost three in the morning. "Yes?" he called with a frown.

A human church official peered in. "Sorry to disturb you, sir. But there's a woman here to see you."

"At this hour?"

The man shifted uncomfortably. "She says she's been travelling for several days, down from the Adirondacks, with no car. And that it's urgent. She says…" He took a breath. "She says that the fate of the angels depends on it."

Raziel's eyebrows shot up. "Send her in," he said after a pause.

A moment later a thin woman with a pursed mouth entered. Everything about her looked faded – nondescript hair, pale skin. She gulped when she saw him.

"Sir, it's – it's an honour," she gasped. "When I came here, I never dreamed I'd see *you*. Why, I thought you were in Denver Eden!"

Raziel rose, crossing to a sideboard. "Yes, quite. And you are...?"

"Joanna Fields."

He'd been about to pour himself a glass of water; he froze mid-motion. "Willow Fields's aunt," he said.

There was a mirror over the sideboard; he saw her expression darken. "That's not my fault. *You* know that, sir. Miranda and I have nothing to do with that girl."

He was glad he wasn't facing her; he wasn't able to keep the stunned surprise from his face. He finished pouring his water and turned, leaning against a low table.

"Miranda?" he enquired blandly.

"Yes, my sister." Joanna started to sit down and hesitated. "I'm sorry – may I?"

"By all means." He remained where he was, playing with the glass. "Suppose you remind me of the circumstances surrounding your and Miranda's – er – continued existence," he said. "I find myself fuzzy on the details."

"Our – oh, of course." Joanna sat up straight. "*Well,* you see, it all started when Willow ran away with that secret boyfriend of hers. He must have been a terrorist: a terrible influence. She was always strange, that girl, but never malicious, do you know what I mean?"

Joanna went on breathlessly, not waiting for his response. "Then when Willow tried to blow up the cathedral in

Denver – oh, it was just horrible. Reporters knocking at my door, demanding comments day and night. I told them I deplored what Willow had done and that she was no niece of mine any more, but it never satisfied them. So of course when the angel came to see us, at first I thought she was one of *them*."

Raziel swirled the water around in his glass. "The angel," he repeated in a neutral tone.

Joanna nodded eagerly. "Yes. Well, *you* know, sir – she said that you'd sent her. Oh, she was the most glorious creature! She explained that we were in danger, and that she'd take us away where no one could harm us. That's why my house was burned down, so everyone would think we'd died. Then she took us to a cabin hidden up in the Adirondacks. She thought of everything."

Rage was building within Raziel; it was difficult to keep from squeezing his crystal tumbler into pieces. "How enterprising of her," he said. "May I ask the name of this paragon?"

Joanna blinked at "paragon". "She said her name was Paschar."

For a second, shock jolted Raziel; an even greater fury followed. Oh, someone thought they were very clever, all right – and he had a feeling he knew who.

Raziel shifted to his angel self. Joanna had been about to say something else; her mouth dropped open as he approached, wings outspread, the light from his ethereal form bleaching out her features.

"I think perhaps I need more information," he said, and buried his hands in her aura.

Though he found her energy distasteful, he fed deeply. It was, he'd found, the one thing that enhanced what little psychic ability he had left. As Joanna's life force flowed into him, Raziel closed his eyes, scanning through her thoughts like shuffling cards.

An angel with pale blonde hair and dark eyes appeared – a crystal smile. *Charmeine,* thought Raziel grimly, unsurprised. They'd always had a strong psychic connection; she'd obviously realized he was Willow's father and squirrelled Miranda away somewhere, to use when the revelation would be the most damaging to him. Just like her to have had all her bases covered.

Raziel shimmered back to his human form with a smirk. Ironic that Charmeine's machinations had now delivered Miranda right into his hands. *Foiled again, my dear,* he thought, seeing again the moment of Charmeine's death.

"So beautiful," murmured Joanna, gazing into space. "Almost as beautiful as when Paschar touched me."

"Thank you." Raziel leaned against the desk. "Well, I think I'm up-to-date now," he said, falsely cheery. "Why did you come to see me?"

Joanna stared at him; her aura was now a murky grey.

Raziel wondered if he'd overdone it, and then she roused herself and sat up weakly. "Well, I – I know we were supposed to wait until the angels came for us, but... something's happened. You see, Miranda's been talking."

Raziel's eyes narrowed. "Go on."

Joanna swallowed. "Usually she just sits in her chair and dreams. But last week she started speaking – as if she were talking to someone I couldn't see."

"Last week?" Raziel said sharply.

Joanna flushed. "It took time to find someone who could stay with Miranda – and of course I couldn't trust anyone else to come here with this message. I didn't like the sound of what she was saying at all. It – it sounded *traitorous.*"

Raziel struggled to keep his voice controlled. "What was she saying?"

"I wrote it down afterwards, so I wouldn't forget." Joanna fumbled in her handbag; she handed him a folded piece of paper anxiously.

Raziel's eyebrows rose as he scanned the neatly written passage:

Miranda seemed to be talking to someone. At the very end, she said his name: Alex. They seemed to be planning something. Miranda said it might be better if people weren't confused by the angels any more. She sounded like she was somewhere else, because she talked about the "Miranda by the lake" and said that wasn't her. She mentioned a gate and said that Raziel was the only one who knew it was there, but that she could show it to this Alex to help him get home. And that when Willow tried to link to the "energy field", she'd need to do it in Pawntucket.

Shock and understanding roared through Raziel. Some part of Miranda was still cognizant, and existed in the angels' world. And *Kylar* had been there with her. *How?* How had he gotten across to their world?

Enraged, Raziel resisted the urge to crumple the paper into a tiny ball. He'd destroyed all the known gates – yet if this information was accurate, he'd missed something vital. His plan to gain control of Willow flashed back to him. Yes, and none too soon, if she knew how to use the angelic energy field. If he didn't act quickly, she'd destroy them all.

Fortunately, his next move would not be one she'd expect.

Raziel folded the paper and ran his fingernail sharply along its crease. "Where did you say Miranda is being kept again?"

Joanna had been studying the photo of Willow on his desk, her mouth tight with disapproval. She looked up. "We're in a cabin maybe a hundred miles from here, right up in the mountains – on one of those remote lakes that doesn't even have a name. And I don't mean to complain, but it's *very* difficult to get to, I'm afraid. The roads are—"

"Perhaps you would wait in the outer office," interrupted Raziel, reaching for his cell.

"Oh! Yes, of course." She got up hastily.

Raziel was already hitting a button on speed dial. A voice answered.

"It's time," Raziel said as Joanna disappeared through the door. He reached for the photo of Willow and tapped it against the desk.

Bascal sounded instantly awake. "For the attack?"

"Precisely." Raziel glanced at the clock: 3.17. "It's to begin at six a.m. exactly. I want that town decimated. There's a gate there; find it and destroy it – spare no one except the girl. She's to be captured *alive,* unless she gets to the gate and tries to open it. Kill her immediately in that case."

"Oh?" Bascal's voice was wary.

"She can control our world's energy field," snapped Raziel. "It's what Paschar's vision meant."

Bascal's tone turned deadly. "Don't worry. She won't get away with it."

Raziel was still holding the photo of Willow as he hung up. He gave a hard smile as he studied the girl's radiant face. *Oh, I've got a surprise for you, my daughter,* he thought. *I've finally found the way to control you.*

CHAPTER *Thirty-three*

IN A WAY, MY FIFTH-GRADE classroom was exactly like I remembered: the battered paperbacks on top of the art supply cupboard, the whiteboard at the front of the room. Someone had written *Pawntucket Tigers STILL Know How to Roar!* on it – with a drawing of a tiger attacking an angel.

But all the desks were gone. Sleeping bags clustered on the carpet, as if this were a giant slumber party. I lay in one without moving, fists pressed against my forehead as I tried scanning the town mentally, street by street.

I'd done this a hundred times now, and there was

nothing – but was that because I couldn't find the gate this way, or because there wasn't anything to sense? *Mom, where is it?* I pleaded. No answer.

"Are you awake?" Nina whispered from the next sleeping bag.

I swallowed hard and opened my eyes. "Yeah."

"I can't sleep either," she said softly. "Do you think Alex would mind if we got back to work early?"

It doesn't matter if he minds or not, I wanted to say; I stopped myself. Searching the town these last two days had given me far too much time to think about Alex: relentless thoughts had pounded at my skull until I was sick of them, battered by them.

"Yes, I think he'd mind," I said finally.

I could feel Nina trying to decide whether to say something about Alex and me; I was relieved when she didn't. She cleared her throat. "So, I've been wondering something. You know how you told me last night that you and Seb can teach people to manipulate their auras?"

I nodded. "I know, but there's no time for that here – it takes people months to learn aura work."

"Okay, but...can't *you* do it?"

I frowned as I turned my head towards her. "What do you mean?"

Her voice was hesitant. "Well, if everyone's energy really *is* reaching out for you, then couldn't you sort of...I don't know; use that to grab hold of all our auras when the angels attack? If you could make them really small, so that the angels can't catch hold…"

She trailed off when I didn't answer. "Forget it." She tried to laugh. "Grasping at Straws 101."

"No, wait!" I was remembering once when Seb and I'd been under attack. He'd done the same thing: grasped both our auras and drawn them so close to our bodies they couldn't be seen.

Could I do it – on such a major scale?

"I don't know," I said slowly. "I – I guess it's possible." All at once my heart was pounding. I reached out with my mind…but found that I didn't even know where to begin. How was I supposed to grasp hold of a whole town?

A few frustrating minutes later I opened my eyes. "Did it work?" Nina whispered.

I hated the catch of hope in her voice; it was bad enough that my own hope had faded. "No. I'm sorry."

Suddenly I couldn't stand it any more – I unzipped the sleeping bag and slid out. I still had my clothes on; I started pulling on my shoes.

"Nina, look – go be with Jonah, okay? Please. I want you to." I'd seen them in the corridor together earlier – Jonah touching Nina's face. The look in both their eyes had been so uncomplicated it had wrenched my heart.

Nina sat up. "What about you?"

"I've got to get some fresh air. Maybe try scanning some more."

"But it's freezing out!"

"I know, but I've got to do *something*. And, Nina, don't you see? This might be the last night you and Jonah have." I grabbed my parka – and before Nina could protest any more, I squeezed her hand tightly and left.

The school playground was ghostly in the moonlight. As I sat in one of the swings, I nudged at the frosty ground with my toe, twirling slightly in place.

Though I was cold through, I didn't get up. Scanning the town mentally hadn't helped. Neither had trying to grasp hold of everyone's auras again, though I'd tried it until my mind felt like a damp rag.

Now there was nothing left that I could attempt before the attack came. And it would be soon now; I could feel it.

We're all going to die, I thought.

I looked up, imagining the sky covered in angels with Raziel at their head. *If I die, he will too,* I vowed to myself. Without the gate, our last chance to defeat the angels might be gone – but I'd manage *that* much, at least.

My spine was straight, but I felt so tired: a weariness that had nothing to do with lack of sleep. I was just about to go help with the fortifications again when I heard footsteps. I looked up in surprise.

Alex appeared out of the shadows and stood in front of me, hands buried in his jacket pockets. "Hi," he said.

"Hi," I said back after a pause.

Alex came and sat down in the next swing. He rubbed the bridge of his nose. "You didn't tell me about the base," he said quietly.

His face in the moonlight was just as I'd imagined a thousand times. What I'd never imagined was this feeling inside of myself.

I cleared my throat. "No. I thought it'd be better to wait until after whatever happens."

Alex sighed and dropped his hand. "Yeah…you were probably right. Willow, look, I—" He broke off, as if thinking better of it. "Have you been out here scanning?" he asked at last.

Why was I yearning for his arms around me even now? "Yes," I admitted. "Not that it's made any difference."

He shook his head a little as he studied me. "God, you look so much like your mother," he murmured. "Except you're even more beautiful." Then his forehead creased. "Wait a minute," he said slowly. "Your mother. I wonder—"

At the feel of his sudden excitement, my own pulse leaped. "What?"

He leaned forward, elbows on knees. "Willow, listen!

There was a faint energy to your mother, and when I left the angels' world, I held her hands – kissed her cheek. So maybe if you try contacting her again, I could be a link for you to reach her."

I recalled the dim, heart-wrenching sense of her energy that I'd picked up from reading Alex. "But how would that work?" I said blankly. "It was *you* touching her, not me. And she was fading already by then—"

"Just try it! What have we got to lose?" He held his hand out to me, palm up – and I was flung back to the day we'd first met. He'd offered me his hand in just that same way.

I nodded stiffly. "All right." As I turned towards Alex, the swing's chains twisted above me. I took his hand – and pushed my emotions away.

Reaching out, I found my mother's energy quickly but knew I couldn't communicate: this was the mother in my own world. Concentrating on Alex's hand – on the same warm skin that had touched some forgotten essence of her – I reached even further.

Mom? Are you there somewhere?

I asked the question over and over. The minutes passed. Just as I was ready to give up, suddenly the sense swept over me that I was travelling someplace both very far and very near. Oh god, she was so close – closer than I ever could have imagined.

Willow?

It was more sensation than word. But she was *there* – she knew me. The same elation rushed in that I'd felt as a little girl, on those rare, glorious days when my mother had actually seen me.

"Mom," I whispered. I felt Alex's hand tighten in mine.

Words didn't seem possible across the worlds; it didn't matter. My energy was merging with my mother's as completely as Seb's and mine did sometimes. I sat frozen in wonder as images came: me when I was little, before she'd drifted away completely. And such an overwhelming sense of love. For this one moment, I hadn't lost my mother at all: she was still there, just like I'd always longed for.

I wanted it to last for ever – knew we didn't have time. *Mom, where's the gate into the angels' world?* I thought. *Please, we have to know!*

I sensed her straining to tell me. Another image: shifting green curtains, stirred by the wind. I frowned in confusion.

I don't understand, I thought. *Is it in someone's house? Whose?*

But already, she was starting to fade – just like in the dream I'd had on the journey here. "No!" I cried in alarm. "Oh, Mom, wait – please don't go—"

It was as if we were clinging to each other in a

windstorm, pulled apart inch by inch. A last sense of love – of frustration – and she was gone.

"Mom," I whispered raggedly. I opened my eyes; realized my cheeks were damp with tears. "We – we communicated," I said, swiping at them with my hand. "She tried to tell me, but I couldn't…" I trailed off as my throat tightened. *Mom.*

Alex drew me towards him, swing and all; he wrapped his arms around me tight. A sob escaped me. "She knew who I was," I choked out against his chest. "Oh god, Alex, she really knew who I was…"

"I know," he whispered into my hair. "She loves you so much – she wanted to know all about you."

I shut my eyes hard and for a moment just pressed close to him, listening to the quiet thudding of both our hearts – and then I remembered lying on the scratchy carpet of our bedroom, crying until there were no tears left.

It felt as if I'd been punched. I winced and drew back.

"Willow, no, *stop* – please don't pull away." Alex clutched my hands. "Listen to me," he said intensely. "I get it, okay? I swear to you, I get it. What you went through—" His Adam's apple moved; his eyes were suddenly bright as he touched my hair. "I can never make it up to you. Never, no matter what I do. I'm sorry – oh Christ, I am so sorry. But please don't push me away."

"Don't, just – *don't.*" I pressed my fingers against

suddenly pounding temples. "I told you I can't do this now, Alex."

His voice was steady. "The attack could come any time. We could die with this still between us – is that what you want?"

And suddenly the rage that had been building for three days burst through like a tsunami.

My head snapped up. "You are kidding me," I said. "Are you *really* sitting there lecturing me on things I should do before I die? *You?* I suppose you had a – a checklist, didn't you, before *you* took off?"

"Willow—"

"Where on the list was telling me I was your life? Number three, maybe? Because *one* was obviously lying to me, and *two* must have been to remember to pack your gun—"

"Willow!" He gripped my arms. "Don't do this," he said quietly.

"Why not? Because you don't feel like hearing it? Because you *get it* now, so we can just forget all about it?"

"That is not what I meant!" Frustration darkened his features. "Look, I know I deserve this, but at least get it right. I wanted to tell you the truth—"

I jumped to my feet; my voice rose in a shout: "If you wanted to tell me, then why *didn't* you, you coward? It was just easier for you to go and get killed than be honest with me!"

"Yes!" he yelled back; the word echoed across the playground. "Yes, okay? I was wrong. What else can I say? I'd do anything if I could undo this last year for you, but I can't; we're stuck with it!"

"We?"

His eyes flashed as he also stood up. "Yeah, *we*! Or don't you think this is affecting me too? What, do you think I'm enjoying this?"

The words came out low and deadly. "Let me tell you something – you think you 'get it'? You don't have a clue. I loved you so completely, Alex. Part of me died with you that day, and I have never gotten her back."

Alex swallowed hard. He stood staring at me. "*Loved*," he said softly.

"What?"

"You said you 'loved me so completely'. Does that mean you don't any more?"

I hugged myself. The way I felt now was just a mess. Love. Hate. Anger. Sorrow.

"I...can't even answer that."

"Willow—" He started to touch my arm; I jerked away, furious and close to tears.

"Stop it! Stop touching me like you've got a *right* to! You don't any more; you gave it up when you disappeared for a year!"

Alex's face in the silvery light looked carved from stone

– his hands clenched into fists. "What about the other night?" he demanded in a low voice. "You told me you loved me then, remember? And you sure as hell acted like you did."

Something snapped. "*It doesn't matter!*" I screamed. "Don't you understand? It doesn't *matter* what I feel for you – because every time I look at you, all I can think about is crying myself to sleep at night! Even if I love you, I might as well hate you – because *that's what it feels like!*"

My voice rang through the night. Alex stood very still, his eyes locked on mine – his expression full of pain. "All right. I understand," he said finally, his tone unnaturally level. "But I love you, and that will never change. Even if you hate me until the day you die."

Shuddering, I gripped my face with both hands, breathing hard. It felt as if everything was caving in on me at once: Alex, the thwarted communication with Mom, Raziel about to attack.

Mom. Raziel.

It hit me hard, knocking everything else out of my mind – out of the whole world. I gasped, my eyes widening. "Oh god, of course," I whispered. "I've got to go to Schenectady Eden."

"*What?*"

I'd already turned away; Alex lunged after me and grabbed my arm. "Tell me what's going on, Willow!"

I was desperate to leave; the words rushed out. "Don't you see? *Raziel knew Mom.* I've got to read him, somehow; it's the only way we might find the gate."

"Are you *insane*?" Alex demanded. "Schenectady is full of thousands of angels! And you want to just wander in and read Raziel?"

"Have you got a better idea?"

"You'll be killed," he said flatly.

"And if I don't go, we'll *all* be killed!"

His jaw was tight. "All right, I'm coming with you."

"What?" It was the last thing I wanted. "Alex, no – you need to stay here."

Anger leaped across his face. "Jesus, Willow! If you think I'm going to just *sit* here while you head off to Schenectady—" He stopped short, glaring at me. "Maybe you didn't hear me before, but I love you. You're stuck with me."

There was no time to argue. "Fine," I said, and we headed to the walkway where the trucks were parked.

CHAPTER *Thirty-four*

THE DRIVE TO SCHENECTADY ONLY took half an hour. Alex sat without speaking as I drove, rubbing his chin with his knuckle as he stared out at the empty highway. I longed to have a radio to switch on – anything to battle the quiet. Anything to take my mind off what I'd shouted.

But every word I'd said was true.

Finally I saw the familiar billboard, its silver letters sparkling in the headlights: *THE ANGELS CAN SAVE YOU! CHURCH OF ANGELS SCHENECTADY, EXIT 8.* A mile later I spun the steering wheel.

Alex looked at me for the first time since we'd set off.

"How do you know he's there?"

"He always stays at the church," I answered tightly. Two years ago Raziel and I had had a psychic link. I knew far more about my father than I wanted to.

The energy of thousands of angels prickled at me like the air before a storm. Up ahead, the glow of Schenectady Eden drowned out the stars. Before I'd travelled even another half-mile, I saw the stark barbed-wire fence that enclosed the Church of Angels and the rest of Schenectady.

I pulled over to the shoulder under some trees and killed the engine. Staring at the fence, I said, "I guess we'd better walk from here on out."

Alex was checking his rifle; he slid the bolt home without looking at me. "Unless you plan on driving right through the main gate. Hey, *that'd* get Raziel's attention."

I didn't answer. We got out and started to walk. I'd rarely been this close to an Eden before; my every instinct was screaming at me to get away, not stroll right up to it.

Street lights up ahead shone on the church and blocks of new apartment buildings – mostly dark, with one or two lights on here and there.

The fence sliced right across the road. As we got closer, we ducked into a field to the side. "Keep low," Alex said curtly.

Following his lead, I lay on my stomach and we started edging forward, squirming on our elbows across the hard, frosty ground. Alex looked as if he'd done this a million times. Maybe he had, back before we met, when he was still stalking angels one by one.

When we reached the fence, Alex swung his rifle off his back and brought the telescopic lens to his eye. "Guard coming – he's human," he murmured; a second later I saw the shadowy figure for myself.

We stayed very still as he patrolled not ten feet away. The second the footfalls faded, Alex hissed, "*Now* – just like on the Torre Mayor."

I knew exactly what he meant. My angel soared out of me; I shifted to my most tangible form. Alex put his arms around me, and my angel grasped hold of us both. In a sudden dizzying arc of wings and light, she flew us up over the barbed wire and down again on the other side.

She merged with me again; Alex and I were already running for the shadows hugging the nearest building. When we reached their cover, we slowed to a quick walk, heading towards the church.

"Let's hope they only patrol the borders," Alex muttered. "I don't really want to shoot anyone tonight."

I couldn't answer. I was picking up human energy now, packed in densely all around me: a deep love for the angels but also waves of weakness – sickness. No one in this section of the Eden had been well for a long time.

I guess these aren't the essential people, I thought bitterly.

Kara had said the angels fed only lightly from those who kept the Edens going, like plumbers and doctors. The others were just cattle on a farm.

There were no angels hunting overhead. Their energy was distant and incredibly condensed, and when I scanned, my blood chilled: a few miles away, the angels had all gathered in one place.

"Do you feel that?" I whispered urgently.

Alex's expression had been grim ever since he'd had to put his arms around me. Now I felt his jolt of alarm. "Oh, *shit* – they're preparing to attack." We broke into a run, our footsteps pounding in unison.

The church sat alone on its vast lawn just as I remembered; its high, vaulted roof gleamed in the moonlight. The stairs leading up to it lay still and silent. A hasty scan – and to my relief, there was still one angel up on the second floor. *Raziel,* I thought, exploring the energy briefly.

Though I was desperate to hurry, we slowed to a brisk walk again, skirting the edge of the parking lot. Despite myself, memories were crashing in: this was where Alex and I had first met. Where I'd first turned around and seen him heading towards me – noticed how he moved like an athlete, so confident in his own body.

Where I'd first seen his eyes and could hardly look away.

Alex was a shadow beside me as we crept around the

side of the church, winter-dry grass rustling under our feet. We found a side door and glanced at each other.

"The whole place will be wired," Alex whispered. "Check for alarms."

I nodded stiffly. My angel shivered out and glided through the metal door. I was in a corridor, made ghostly by my own ethereal light. Trying not to think about the fact that Raziel was just a floor above and could sense me if he tried, I cruised hastily through the building, searching.

When I found the security office, a man was slumped, dozing, in front of the control panel. I rested my ethereal hand on his and concentrated. That strange, underwater sensation came again, like when I'd read Kara. After a few seconds, I quickly jabbed in a sequence of numbers, praying I'd gotten it right.

A small green light began to flash. Up in the corner of the ceiling, the light on the security camera died.

Thank god. I flew back in a frenzy; a moment later Alex and I were inside, rushing down the hallway. As we pushed open the door at the end, we entered the airy vastness of the church: snowy marble that gleamed in the moonlight; ornate stained glass; the pulpit shaped like a pair of angel wings.

No. I was not going to think about how Alex had saved my life by getting me out of this place.

A doorway at the side led to a flight of stairs. The lights

were on here; when we reached the top, Alex swung his rifle off his shoulder and held it ready under one arm. He quietly pushed open the stairwell door.

I had my pistol out as we made our way down a long, plush corridor with low lighting. I scanned feverishly. My spine stiffened. There – Raziel was behind that door at the end.

I kept my eyes on it as we advanced, my pulse beating hard. This had to work. If I couldn't find out where the gate was; if we couldn't get back to Pawntucket before the attack… I took a breath. No. Failure was not an option.

Then as we neared the door, I stopped short, senses prickling: our presence had been discovered. My hand flew to Alex's arm, halting him. He glanced at me – and then the hallway exploded into radiance as a glorious winged creature burst through the wall at us, snarling with fury.

It wasn't Raziel.

Jaw tight, Alex snapped the rifle to his shoulder and fired; the silenced shot thudded through my brain. I stood staring dumbly at the drifting leaves of light. And of course *now* I could sense that this angel's energy had felt similar to my father's, but that was all. How could I have been so stupid, *how?*

Trying not to panic, I glanced in the direction of the gathered angels. "He must be with them. Alex, we've got to get over there, fast!"

He grabbed my arm. "No, wait – you said Raziel always stays in the church. So we can get to his things."

"*Why?* It's him I need!"

Our voices were low, fierce. "Because we're here now, and you get details from objects sometimes, and it's worth a try! If you *do* get something, then we might actually have a shot at surviving long enough to use it!"

I felt desperate with indecision, the seconds ticking past. If we made the wrong choice...

"Okay," I said hurriedly.

We opened the door the angel had come through. A richly decorated office with a living area. Definitely Raziel's quarters; the angel must have been a guard. My brow furrowed with sudden intuition as I looked at the sofa. I quickly went over and touched one of the cushions.

Faint residual energy clung to the fabric. My face slackened. No way. Aunt Jo, *here?*

"Willow, come see this, quick!" Alex called.

Confused, I rushed into the inner office. Alex nodded tersely at the desk. "Look."

I stared at a piece of paper so familiar that it stole my breath. *There is no greater universe than holding you...*

I snatched it up and folded it again, hating that Raziel had seen this, that he'd touched it. As I tucked the poem in my jeans pocket, I couldn't meet Alex's steady gaze. "I – I guess they got it from my room after the attack."

"That's not all they got," he said quietly.

And that's when I saw the photo.

As I gazed at myself as a little girl, a deep foreboding turned my skin clammy. I started to shake. Because somehow…I knew exactly what I was going to get even before I picked the photo up.

The small brass frame felt cool in my hand as I held it. Raziel's energy swept me, sickening in its strength. He'd touched this for several minutes – he'd been thinking so intently – I swallowed as thoughts, images, knowledge whirled past.

Aunt Jo *had* been here; she had angel burn. She and Mom had been hidden up in the Adirondacks all this time, not even a hundred miles away. She'd told Raziel everything.

His voice as he gave an order on his cell: *It's to begin at six a.m. exactly. I want that town decimated.* Then he'd turned off his phone and smiled, looking down at my photo.

Not taking his eyes from it, he'd lifted his voice and called out: *Suppose you come along and show me where this place is, Joanna? I rather fancy paying Miranda a visit.*

No! But that was all, no matter how hard I clutched the frame – no matter how much I willed more information to come.

"Willow?" Alex's voice was distant.

I opened my eyes. My fingers were stiff, the frame's corners gouging into my palm. "Oh my god," I whispered.

"Raziel knows where Mom is; he's on his way there now – and the attack's due to start at six! What *time* is it?"

"Five-thirteen," said Alex, glancing at a clock. He took hold of my shoulders. "What do you mean, he knows where your mother is?" he said urgently. "How?"

I quickly told him what I'd seen. "I can't let him hurt her—" But I had no idea where Mom was. The Adirondacks were huge. Frantically, I tried to scan Aunt Jo's thoughts, but we'd never been close; all I got was her awe at Raziel's presence.

Trembling, I looked down at the photo again. At the willow tree.

Long strands of green that looked like curtains, shifting in the wind. My mother's voice the day she'd taken the picture: *It's a special tree. Someday I'll tell you the story of why you're named after it.*

Alex's grip tightened on my arms. "What else have you seen?"

I felt dizzy. "I – I think I know where the gate is. It's the willow tree in the photo. It's not in Pawntucket. It's in Murray Park, a few miles outside it."

We stood staring at each other as we both realized: there was only one option, and it didn't include saving my mother's life.

Somehow I shoved away my anguish. "I've got to get there," I said. "I've got to try to link with the energy from the angels' world while I still can, while Mom is still – there."

Alex nodded, the muscles in his arms rigid. "Come on, let's get the hell out of here."

CHAPTER *Thirty-five*

ALEX GLANCED IN THE REAR-VIEW mirror every few seconds as he drove them back to Pawntucket. How fast could angels fly – ninety miles an hour? More? He was taking no chances. They were already going well over a hundred, but he edged the speedometer up higher.

Willow sat tensely. The expression on her face tore at him. Her mother. Oh Jesus, not her mother – and not like this, with him and Willow so helpless to do anything. *Hasn't she been through enough already?* he thought savagely.

Suddenly he was hurtled back to the time after his brother died. He'd spent months expecting to see Jake around every corner, had dreamed of him almost every night. When the CIA had taken over the operation of his father's camp barely a month later, Alex had hit the road gratefully, not wanting to interact with anyone – not wanting to care about anyone ever again.

Willow had brought him back to life.

The drive to Pawntucket seemed to take both years and scant minutes. A few miles from the turn-off, Alex glanced at Willow. "Where's this park?"

Her face was like a statue's. "On the other side of town, on Route 16."

The dashboard clock read 5:44. "Once we get into town, you take the truck – I'll help with the attack," Alex said. "We've got to keep the angels away from you. They'll sense what you're doing otherwise and kill you."

Willow's face paled, but she didn't argue.

"Look," he said harshly, downshifting onto the exit. "I know this isn't the best time, but it's the only time we've got. Give me a clue what I'm fighting for here, Willow. Am I just trying to save the world? Or is there a chance for us?"

She winced. "Alex—"

"Check out the clock," he bit out. "I could die in sixteen minutes."

Willow looked at him then; he could see her reluctance. "I don't know," she said in a quiet voice. "I meant everything I said, Alex. I can't go from grieving you to being your girlfriend again like nothing happened. I just can't. I feel so—" She broke off, closing her eyes hard.

"I don't know what I want if we survive this," she said finally. "All I know is that right now…it's not you."

It felt as if his soul were being ripped out. He wanted to argue, point out that, yes, she was angry at him and had a right to be – but was she really going to throw everything away?

Except he knew that, to her, it felt as if he'd thrown it away already.

A jumble of sensations came: the look of her in the morning, hair rumpled, green eyes smiling. The feel of her in his arms, sending his pulse soaring. Talking with her for hours – exchanging a look with her across a room, their eyes a private world.

They were in the outskirts of Pawntucket by then; Alex went as fast as he could down the damaged streets. When he finally responded, he hated what came out – but it was the only thing he could do.

"You can find me if you want to, right?"

Willow's brow creased. "Psychically, you mean? Yes, of course. If you're still in this dimension, that is," she added somewhat bitterly.

His didn't look at her. His voice was low and controlled. "Okay, then. If we live through this, then once I know you're all right, I'll leave. If you want me, you can come and find me."

Willow started to say something and stopped. She nodded, her expression pained.

As they neared the square Alex leaned on the horn, blasting it non-stop. People scrambled down roofs to run towards him. He lurched to a halt in front of the diner. Up above, someone had started ringing the town hall bells; the peals were urgent, echoing.

He and Willow got out; as she rushed round to his side to get in, he couldn't help himself – he gripped her face and kissed her hard. "I will always love you, no matter what," he said fiercely. "*Do not die.*"

As the truck sped off, Alex could see people racing into the square from all directions. Seb came sprinting from the school; he had the machine guns with him and a rifle over his shoulder.

As the bells died to nothing, Jonah came tearing down the town hall steps. "Is – is this it?" he panted out.

Alex nodded grimly. "Yeah. This is it." He leaped up onto an old pickup truck; the snowy truck bed rocked. Two hundred tense faces stared up at him. He refused to think about the slaughter at the base.

"Okay, listen up!" he called out through cupped hands.

"We have *got* to stop the angels from getting past us. We found the gate; Willow's on her way there now, and they'll kill her if they realize."

He could sense the crowd's sudden hope at the news and was brutally glad that he had that much to offer them, at least. Because Christ, they were going to need all the help they could get.

He glanced hurriedly at the tower clock. "They'll be here in eleven minutes. I need three buffer zones. The south-east end of town is the first one – who was going to set off the nail bombs on the outskirts?" About seventy people raised their hands. "Good – wait until the angels are in range, then the second you set off your bomb, run for one of the fortified houses; take them out as they come. *Go!*"

The group raced off, disappearing away into the streets to the south. "Who are the best shots left?" called Alex. To his relief, no one wasted time being modest; about forty hands rose.

"You guys are the third buffer zone, streets north of the square – *do not* let the angels get past you. Take the machine guns with you. Hurry!"

Beside the truck, Seb held up the machine guns. Two of the AKs snatched them away as the group took off running.

With their footsteps still echoing, Alex said to those remaining, "Okay, the second buffer zone is right here.

Take cover and set off the nail bombs when you first see the angels; once the bombs go off, get up onto the roofs if you can – otherwise use the square; you'll need as clear a shot as possible. That's it – *go!*"

Alex jumped down from the truck as people started darting off. Seb was heading towards the third buffer zone; Alex grabbed the half-angel's arm. "No, stay here – you and I will take the angels as they cross the square, then join the third zone." Seb nodded.

Jonah's face was apprehensive but determined. "I'm not fighting," he said in a rush. "I'm going to take the shortwave up into the tower and broadcast this – let the world know what's happening."

Nina still stood nearby; her eyes widened. "Up in the *tower?*" she echoed. "But I thought you'd be with the fighters on the ground!"

"I'm not a good shot and you know it," Jonah said tightly. "But I *can* do this, and people need to know what's going on."

She looked close to tears. "No! You'll be the first thing the angels see when they come over the square – they'll go right for you—"

"We do *not* have time for this," Alex cut in savagely. "Jonah, if that's what you're doing, then for Chrissake hurry!"

With an agonized look at Nina, Jonah turned to go.

Alex grabbed his wrist. "And do a good job," he added in a low voice. "I want the Voice of Freedom to tell this exactly like it is."

Nina flung herself at Jonah suddenly, hugging him tight. "Oh god, be careful."

"I'm sorry," he said as he clutched her to him. "I have to do this—" He kissed her hard, then ran off towards the town hall. Nina struggled to compose herself and then raced off too, her footfalls echoing.

In the sudden silence, Alex and Seb ran for the doorway of Drake's Diner. A garish painted mallard still flew on the glass door. *Drake's – the best in town!* read the cheery lettering.

The square was utterly still, with shadowy figures pressed in every doorway. Alex's eyes flicked up to the clock. Two minutes. Scanning, he could feel the great angelic force heading their way now, and his skin crawled at its sheer size. Even more than he'd thought – there must be five thousand. Christ, how long would the first buffer zone be able to hold that back?

And how many people were about to die?

Seb seemed to pick up on this. "You've done all you can," he said, still gazing out at the square. "And you did well, with only minutes to prepare them."

Things had been slightly strained between him and Seb since that morning in the boys' bathroom; it seemed stupid now. "Listen, stay alive during this, okay?" Alex said, glancing at Seb's profile.

Seb gave a dry smile. "Yes, look who's talking."

They fell silent then as the first explosions came from the south-east – blast after thundering blast. As the sound of gunfire started, Alex stood poised, watching the sky above the square. The rifle in his hands felt cool, ready.

"Here we go," he muttered, and then shot Seb a look. "Can you sense her? Is she okay?"

Seb had his rifle pressed against his shoulder, his stubbled face intent. He paused, then nodded. "She hasn't gotten through to the angels' world yet."

Be careful, babe, thought Alex. *Please, be careful.* And then flashing white wings and angry, glorious faces appeared over the square, and there was no more time for thought.

CHAPTER *Thirty-six*

MURRAY PARK SAT ON A hill north of Pawntucket. I screeched to a halt in the empty parking lot; the picnic benches looked damp and abandoned.

The whole drive there, I'd had my consciousness linked with Mom's, terrified that any second I'd sense Raziel with her. So far, he hadn't arrived. What I couldn't let myself think about at all was Alex's final kiss, his lips almost harsh against mine.

A hiking trail snaked away into the trees. I raced down it, old snow crunching under my feet as my breath came in short, icy puffs. When I'd lived in Pawntucket, I hadn't come here much; I'd sort of saved it for special occasions, when I wanted to feel close to Mom. But the willow tree was just as I remembered, beside a small frozen pond. Its draping branches were empty of leaves now, wreathed in frost like crystal curtains.

The hill dropped away to one side. Below, Pawntucket was laid out like a toy town. As I reached the tree, I froze. In the distance I could see angels coming, spreading across the sky in a solid sheet of white. My breath caught. So many of them!

Alex, I thought wildly. And Seb, Nina and Jonah, everybody else. There was no way they could defend against that, none.

No, I thought, staring down at the town. This couldn't happen. It just couldn't.

There was no time to try and protect everyone's auras again; I did it anyway. I quickly shut my eyes and this time didn't let myself think at all. I just stretched my energy out as wide as I could, as if it were a huge blanket.

Wide – wider. The sensation was bizarre, as if at any second my energy would fray into pieces. But it didn't – it just kept expanding, getting thinner. Slowly, my heart beating hard, I draped it down over Pawntucket.

The dizzying sense of two hundred different auras hit me; I could feel them all craning towards me in return. My teeth clenched as I tried to grab hold, shrink them down

– it was like trying to juggle too many balls at once. I was trembling; I'd never be able to hold this, even if I'd managed to get them all.

The sound of distant explosions started. No more time. Breathing hard, I opened my eyes – and stared as angels jerked backwards in the air like shot wildfowl; others exploded like fireworks, with thousands more coming up behind.

Please, please, let me have done some good, I thought frantically – and ran for the tree.

As I ducked through its branches, the smell of damp earth enveloped me. Forcing myself to ignore the gunfire, I took a deep breath to steady myself. With one hand, I reached out and touched the tree's bark – felt its slight roughness. Then I lifted up through my chakras and studied the air in front of me.

At first I couldn't see anything and was horror-struck. Maybe I'd gotten this wrong. *Stop. Calm. Look again.* And this time, ghostly in the predawn light, I saw the gate just as Alex had described: a small patch of air like rippling water.

Limp with relief, I quickly explored it psychically. Not quite complete yet – the ether felt thin, insubstantial, as if I could flick my finger through. Suddenly my heart leaped so hard it was painful: I could feel my mother's spirit right on the other side.

Mom, I'm here! I thought wildly. I craned my energy towards hers; it was as if we were each touching a pane of glass from opposite sides. Warmth started to build: a gentle swirling that was melting away the fabric between worlds.

Suddenly I saw myself twelve years ago, standing in the sunshine, only feet from this very spot – my mother, smiling and taking my photo: *It's a special tree. Someday I'll tell you the story of why you're named after it.*

"Mom, I know," I whispered as other images started to come.

Raziel had met with her here – I'd been conceived here. The barrier between worlds was so thin in this place because her spirit had spent years just a hair's breadth away, yearning for the angel she'd been in love with. My throat clenched as I saw her looking young, beautiful – her green eyes full of awe.

Raziel had known exactly what he was doing to her and he hadn't cared.

Then I caught my breath – my connection with my mother's physical self had strengthened too. All at once I could see everything: Mom was sitting in an armchair in what looked like a lake house, her blonde hair soft around her face.

"Mom!" I cried aloud.

"She's in here," said Aunt Jo's voice.

My heart froze. *No!* With a sense of loving regret, my

mother's spirit in the other world drew quickly away. A second later I could feel her again – still in the angels' world, but now just beside her physical self.

I trebled my efforts, directing my will at the thin spot between worlds. A tiny hole appeared – I seized hold, began prising it open. A rush of energy came, tugging at me; I gasped at its ferocity.

In the lake house, my mother had come out of her daze and was frowning at the door in confusion. "Mom, don't just sit there – *run!*" I pleaded.

But she didn't hear me. She'd never heard me, no matter how hard I'd tried.

Raziel entered slowly, footsteps echoing. He wore a rain-flecked jacket; his black hair was mussed from the wind. He smiled.

"Hello, Miranda," he said.

"Stay away from her," I whispered raggedly. The hole between worlds was larger now; I could see another willow tree. On the ethereal level, its leaves were shifting prisms that caught the light.

Raziel crossed to my mother, his tread deliberate against the floorboards. His eyes stayed fixed on hers with a small, considering smile. "Why, Miranda, this is just like old times, isn't it?"

And he shifted to his angel form and plunged his hands into her aura.

"*No!*" I shouted. The hole wavered – somehow I managed to hang on and keep going. Raziel was instantly aware of me; his thoughts came crawling into my mind:

Hello, daughter. I'm glad you're here – it makes things so much easier.

Mom's energy was growing weaker by the second. I struggled to hide my panic. *Leave her alone!* I thought back fiercely. In front of me, the hole between worlds was almost large enough now.

He ignored me. *Perhaps it has escaped your notice, but your town is under attack,* he said. *And, look – I seem to have your mother too.*

A breeze shifted the willow's long strands. Between its frosty branches, I could see Pawntucket; the angels were like a blizzard swirling over it. Gunfire was still sounding.

I'm afraid I can't stop the attack, now that it's started, Raziel said, and actually had the nerve to sound regretful. *Such a pity, but I hope it makes an effective point – that I am not to be trifled with.*

My mother's aura was shrinking, crumpling as Raziel fed. Bile rose in my throat; I could tell he was relishing the taste of her again after all these years.

Stop it! You'll kill her!

Yes, that would be a shame, wouldn't it? Especially after the deaths of so many of your friends. But, you know, I think there's a way we could stop such a terrible thing from happening.

He kept feeding. My mother's smile was gentle, her body limp and sagging. Oh god, she couldn't take much more of this. Why did I have to be seeing it – why? With a sob, I managed not to shout out, *Anything! Just stop hurting her!* – and stepped into the breach between worlds.

I reached for the angelic energy field; it surged untamed around me. With the gate open, it was like standing in a howling wind tunnel – yet it was nothing like what Alex had described. The energy of the human world felt natural to me, and so did this.

I couldn't take hold of it, though. It was too much – too *big*. With a gasp, I craned for my mother's essence in the angels' world and grabbed hold; felt her grounding me. And in my own world, there was only one person, wasn't there? Even now. I reached for Alex and hung on tightly.

It strikes me that we don't need to be on opposite sides, Raziel mused. *You have something I want, you see. And I have something* you *want – your mother's life. The perfect symbiotic relationship.*

The churning energy calmed a little. I could sense patterns to it now: there were worlds within worlds here, power beyond belief. It felt as if I had to learn a new language in seconds. Even anchored, if I didn't do this right, it would kill me.

What do you want from me? I asked to buy time as I frantically scanned the energy, looking for the key.

Somewhere deep down, my soul was being kicked with jackboots. Mom…Mom…

Ah, good girl – you're seeing sense, Raziel murmured. *I do admire you, you know, Willow. There is much of me in you.*

Just talk, I snapped.

You have the power to manipulate people's energy, he said, all friendliness gone. *I want that power. It's rather inconvenient for us angels that humans are so damaged by our touch. We don't want* that *to happen, you know.*

Get to the point. Bracing myself, I took hold of the angelic energy; it was like grabbing a hurricane. I stifled a cry and clutched harder to the people I loved most – felt them holding me fast in both worlds.

I want you to manipulate the humans' energy so that angels can feed without harming them. They'll still adore us, but with no lasting damage. In return, I will spare your mother's life – and your own.

I could feel his confidence that I'd do anything to save my mother. I stood caught between worlds as I took in her face with its dreamy smile – and thought of all the times I'd crouched beside her chair, talking gently to her, trying to bring her back to me. But some part of her still existed in the angels' world. If Raziel spared her, I could contact her whenever I wanted.

I'd have a mother.

You're tempted, aren't you? Raziel said softly. He'd

stopped feeding, though his angelic hands remained in Mom's life force. *It would be the best way, you know. You don't want to commit genocide, Willow – I know you. This way, both angels and humans are happy. For we do make humans happy. No matter what you might think of us, our touch brings happiness.*

A cold wind stirred the willow tree in both worlds. I stood shaking, my face damp with tears as the energy of two worlds surged around me.

Could he actually be right? What would happen if I took the angels away from everyone? Destroyed the only real hope humanity had ever known, even if it had been slowly killing them?

And I must admit, I've wanted to know you for some time, Raziel went on, and I knew he was sincere for a change. *We could rule together, Willow. You'd have a mother and a father.*

A flicker of protest came from my mother's spirit – too weak to form words, but enough to snap my attention back to what mattered. Down below, the sound of gunfire still raged; the angels were churning over the town like hungry seagulls. The battle at the base came back: Sam, falling in a haze of angels; the deaths of almost two hundred people in minutes. Oh god, and I was actually standing here thinking of *bargaining* with Raziel!

I plunged completely into the angelic energy field. The real world dimmed at the edges – I was the centre of a seething ocean. It felt as if I no longer had a body; I was pure energy. I merged with the ocean, became one with it…and started to direct it.

From far away, Raziel's voice sharpened in suspicion. *What are you doing?*

Your happiness is poison, I said. Like a toreador swirling a giant cape, I manoeuvred the angelic energy towards my own world. The gap between worlds widened with a roar.

The power would have been intoxicating, but holding onto those I loved kept me grounded. Even if I was the only person in existence who could do this, I was still just me – and it was all I wanted to be.

With the energy field of a whole dimension at my command, I started to link it with the earth's. A howling shudder began that I sensed rather than heard.

Raziel's voice halted me in my tracks. *Stop or your mother will die.*

She still sat in her chair – and though I knew she couldn't see me, her green eyes seemed to meet mine. On the verge of everything, with power surging through my fingertips, I hesitated. My heart was being shredded.

Raziel moved his fingers back and forth in Mom's life force, making the dying grey of her aura swirl. *Think carefully, Willow. Do you really want to kill your mother?*

And suddenly I was shaking too hard to stand. With a sob, I staggered and then fell to my knees, clutching at the willow's trunk. I couldn't do this – couldn't watch my mother die. *Please, no – I'll do anything you want,* I started to say – and then Mom's spirit stirred again.

I felt a wave of love, and then heard her voice clearly for the first time. *This is my choice. I love you, Willow.*

My heart quickened – from the cabin by the lake, her gaze *was* meeting mine; I wasn't imagining it. She smiled, her lips curving gently upwards. Then, with a weary sigh, she closed her eyes and settled more deeply into her chair. I could sense her giving in to the damage Raziel had inflicted.

"*Mom – no!*" I gasped.

So softly I almost didn't hear, she said, *You know what you have to do.* As her body slumped, her blonde hair feathered across one cheek. Her aura faded, its grey lights slowly flickering to nothing.

She was gone.

I felt a flash of Raziel's fury, then the connection vanished. For a second the energy of the angels' world bucked wildly, but I was immersed in it enough now that it was part of me – I could still control it, even without Mom's support.

And she was right: suddenly I knew exactly what I had to do. With tears streaming down my face, I got back to my feet. Standing half in the angels' world and half in my own, I linked the two energies and dived into them.

Raging power. But what had once been chaos could now be tamed. I held onto Alex more tightly, feeling his love for me.

I closed my eyes and began.

The sky was a seething mass of angels.

When they'd first appeared over the square, Seb had started shooting at the nail bombs automatically, trying to ignore the panicked screams. As the bombs went off one after another, nails spewed into the air like glittering fountains; the angels' wings writhed as they jerked back. In seconds, fragments of perished angels were drifting down like sun-kissed snow.

How many dead? thought Seb tensely, still shooting. Over a hundred, maybe?

But there were thousands more. As the last of the bombs went off, Seb's fellow fighters darted out into the square, firing upwards; others raced for the ladders leading to the roofs.

Seb sent his own angel out. A girl slipped and fell; as an angel swarmed in for the kill, Seb dived to block him. He and the snarling angel battled briefly, wings colliding with sparks. There was gunfire, and the angel vanished in a burst of light.

The girl scrambled up and ran, still firing into the sky

– and Seb registered her aura. A second ago it had looked normal; now it had shrunk close to her body. It flickered, growing larger and then small again.

Abruptly, Seb's attention snapped back to the battle – his angelic body darted aside as a spray of bullets tore past, and his human self shot another angel, catching it as it went high.

Alex was firing like a machine, his finger barely pausing on the trigger. Then he glanced across the square and clapped Seb's arm. "Come on – they're heading north."

They broke cover from the diner and ran, firing upwards. Seb caught a glimpse of Jonah up in the town hall tower, talking urgently into a mic – and then a group of angels converged on him in a frenzy. Seb's heart sank; he slowed down as he shot at them, but Jonah had vanished in a haze of wings.

Seb and Alex plunged into the streets north of the square; all around, Seb could see auras doing that same flickering. He winced as an angel managed to grab hold of one and rip it away – the fighter fell. But nearby, another angel veered off with a furious screech as an aura shrank to nothing. *Willow?* Seb thought, dazed.

Quickly, he checked on her again; the energy roaring through her tingled at his scalp. She'd opened the gate, then. *You can do it,* querida, he thought as he and Alex ran, footsteps pounding as they tried to get ahead of the angels. *Just keep going – you can do it.*

The street took them to a residential neighbourhood. Alex paused, scanning the sky. Over the centre of town it was still a churning white, the angels now behind them and heading their way.

"We need to get onto a roof, fast," Alex said. "*Damn it, these houses aren't fortified – how are you at climbing?*"

"I was a thief, remember?"

Alex nodded tensely. "Okay, take one of these; I'll go a few streets over. Just *hold them back*, no matter what."

Seb had no intention of doing anything else. He could sense that the angels were looking for Willow – and just then the air started to throb with the force of what she was doing. Seb swore; it wouldn't be long now before they realized and took off past the town to stop her.

As Alex raced off, other fighters came pouring into the street; Seb shouted out hasty instructions as the first few angels appeared. He quickly chose a house and started towards it – and then a flurry of action caught his gaze.

A tall girl with long auburn hair, sprinting for the houses. She turned and shot at an angel; nothing happened. It dived – her aura was low but not low enough—

With no thought, Seb went hurtling towards her; he tackled her to the ground just as his own angel swooped to defend them. He could feel her heartbeat crashing against his, and then his human self rolled off her, firing upwards. The angel burst into light and vanished.

For a second Seb lay breathing hard. *Don't scare me like that,* chiquita – *I thought I'd lost you.* And then he realized that of course the girl beside him wasn't Meghan at all.

Rachel scrambled to her feet. "Thank you!" she gasped. "I ran out of cartridges – I thought I was going to die—"

Stunned, Seb got up too. He swallowed hard and glanced behind him. The first few angels, dead now, had been ahead of the others; just behind were a thousand more.

The sight galvanized him. "Hurry! Take cover!"

As Rachel ran off, Seb leaped up onto a window sill; after a quick scramble, he gripped the rough, sloped surface of the roof and pulled himself onto it. Other fighters had gotten onto roofs too; they waited tensely in position all up and down the street.

The angels hit in a rush, turning the sky white even with their depleted numbers. The roof was slick with frost. Seb crouched beside the chimney, bracing himself against it as he shot again and again. More shooting came from the houses nearby – the air was full of confetti, of flashing wings that dived straight at him.

Seb pivoted himself frantically around the chimney as he shot, his feet sometimes slipping a few inches, his angel protecting his back. His jaw was tight. He couldn't think now about what had just happened; he only knew he felt a raging sorrow inside, a fury at his own stupidity that made him want to tear apart every angel he saw with his bare hands.

Then, for a moment, everything seemed to hang suspended, even the angels. A sense of gathering power grew. Above, the sky lightened to an ominous white; to the north, a swirling vortex had appeared, an angry eye peering down from the heavens.

In the physical world, everything had gone still; on the ethereal level, it felt as if Seb were standing in the path of an oncoming train. The angels seemed to realize all at once what was happening; with roars of rage they began streaming to the north, ignoring the fighters now in their hurry to get to Willow.

Swearing, Seb swivelled around the chimney, firing at the angels as they passed. One of them grabbed for his flickering life force but missed as Seb's angel quickly shielded him.

Then a burst of gunfire came from across the street, tearing through his angel's ethereal body. Seb cried out, twisting in agony. At the same moment, the corner of the chimney exploded into flying fragments of brick.

It was like being hit by a truck. Dimly, Seb knew he was slipping down the slick roof – he was falling. The ground slammed into him.

He couldn't move. Dios mío, *the pain* – he was broken.

Meggie, he thought in a daze. *Oh, my love, please forgive me. I was so stupid – so blind...*

His thoughts faded until there was only blackness. Seb lay without moving, his curls damp with blood and melting snow.

At the moment when the world seemed to still, Alex cursed harshly – he had a feeling he knew exactly what was coming next. He scrambled down from the house where he'd been shooting and took off at a run, charging through the streets of Pawntucket as the first faint swirls of the vortex appeared.

He passed a fallen fighter: a girl holding one of the machine guns. Shoving aside his feelings, he snatched up the weapon and kept going, his footsteps thudding through his brain. Somehow he managed to pull ahead of the angels.

In less than a minute, he'd gone beyond the third buffer zone. The streets lay empty. As an ethereal wind began to howl, Alex chose a house on the edge of town and flung himself at it, scaling it quickly. Too late, he realized it was one that had been made unstable by the quakes – the wood creaked alarmingly under his feet – but there was no time to change.

As he hefted himself onto the roof, he caught a glimpse

of snowy fields beyond the edge of town – and the hill on the horizon where the girl he loved was fighting for everything they believed in. The vortex moved above her like a pale, swirling bruise.

Hang on, babe, you can do it, he thought hurriedly – then braced himself against the chimney and spun to face the town. He could just see other fighters heading this way, knew they wouldn't get here in time. Because coming right towards him was a raging river of white, as a thousand angels bore down.

Alex set his jaw; he swung his rifle over his back and raised the machine gun to his shoulder. "You are *not* getting past me," he muttered down the barrel. "Try to touch her and you die."

As the first angels came into range, Alex started shooting, picking off halos – he swept from left to right, then back again, seeing nothing but the gleaming circles. Angels exploded with furious screams; wings seemed to tangle and churn in a maelstrom of white.

The angels at the front burst out in all directions – some went high, some tried to veer around. "Don't even think it," murmured Alex.

He shot at a pale blur off to the side; whipped the weapon around to get another; shot at a third with no pause. A fourth, a fifth…twenty…fifty shards of light rained down as he fired, not bothering to check if he'd missed or not. They *would not* reach Willow – there was no other option.

The angels behind hurtled towards him in a steady stream. When Alex had shot the machine gun dry, he swung the rifle into position; he moved mechanically across the halos again, firing over and over. The falling light was a blizzard now. Angels darted out from its depths.

Alex somehow held them off again and again – but they were advancing steadily; he felt his control slipping – and suddenly they were on him in full, screaming force.

Shit. He flung himself onto the cold, frosty roof; with an outraged groan, it buckled under him. As he struggled to hold on, a hundred angels surged around him, all straining for his life force. He couldn't shoot the rifle single-handed; he swore and let the weapon drop – briefly considered letting himself fall, too, though the floor below him was gone.

No. If he was going to die, he'd go out fighting. And though he could barely see through the haze of wings, Alex reached in his waistband for his pistol.

CHAPTER *Thirty-seven*

I STOOD POISED BETWEEN TWO WORLDS.

It felt as if my hair were crackling with electricity. The energy surged through me – that of the angelic world strengthening our own, rushing out over the planet. In both dimensions, willow branches stirred in the cold wind as I rode the energy's crest…and used it to reach out to all humanity.

Millions of people. Billions. Lives, names, images flashed past too quickly to take in: damaged with angel burn, undamaged, young, old, of every colour and creed. Slowly, as the power increased even more, my arms spread out from my sides. My angel lifted up out of me and hovered above, bright and shining.

Let me help you, I thought, and didn't even know where the words had come from. *Please. It's time.*

I stood caught in the hurricane between worlds; I was the centre of everything. I felt detached, focused – even though I somehow knew that Raziel was racing towards me, his wings eating up the miles as he was carried along by the surging energy. Even though I knew that in my hometown below, a thousand angels had started heading my way.

It didn't matter. Because now it wasn't only those who'd once been near me whose energy was straining towards me – it was all humanity's. And this time I was taking control, doing exactly what needed to be done.

The energy seethed across the earth, leaping from person to person. It felt as if dazzling light was streaming out from my fingertips – though when I risked a dazed glance, my hands looked the same as always. Dizzying swathes of information were roaring past – knowledge of every person on the planet. Blurred images of spiral ladders: the building blocks of humankind, morphing and shifting under my direction along with the very earth itself – the boundaries of our dimension.

In the angelic world, an enraged crowd of angels had gathered, kept at bay by the swirling power. And though I was shifting things in their world too…I knew it wasn't me they wanted.

My outspread arms began to shake as the energy force whipped around the planet again and again, using me as a conduit. I cried out as its raging power almost knocked me off my feet; I couldn't control this for much longer…

My angel quickly took the bulk of it on herself. The powerful force screamed past, howling through both her ethereal body and my physical one – if I moved even an eyelash now, I'd be torn to shreds. I gritted my teeth, trembling, as oceans raged and lashed at me. I could feel my angel being battered – hurt – yet still she stayed in place. Oh god, how much longer? I couldn't hold on – I couldn't—

And then…it was done.

I let out a gasping breath. Somehow I knew not to break the connection yet. Instead, I gradually let the power recede: the angelic energy field was still connected with our own, but it was more placid now. My angel crept feebly inside me.

The last vestiges of power still sizzled around me, holding back the angels in the other world. The massive army from town hadn't reached me yet and I dimly wondered why. If they had, there'd been enough of them to break through – they'd have killed me in seconds.

But another angel had arrived.

I opened my eyes and saw Raziel standing just outside the bare branches of the willow tree, his face contorted in fury. My muscles shuddered with exhaustion as we regarded each other. I knew that the second I dropped hold of the energy, he'd try to kill me. Because he knew exactly what I'd done – I'd made sure that every angel in existence knew.

"*How dare you?*" he hissed.

"There are lots of other gates now," I said levelly. "I've opened them all around the world. They'll close in a minute – and when they do, they'll draw every angel here right back through them. You're never coming back here again."

Around us, the willow branches rustled – the same branches that had moved around him and my mother that winter night twenty years ago. Raziel's eyes burned into mine.

"I had an empire here – an empire!" he spat. "A minute will be more than enough time to kill you, my darling daughter. And I plan to do it with my bare hands."

His bare hands. The same ones that had plunged so eagerly into my mother's life force. My spine turned to steel.

"You know, you were right," I told him quietly. "Genocide isn't something I'm capable of. But patricide… I think I can live with that."

I dropped the energy and stepped away from the gate.

With a quick shift to his angel form, Raziel lunged at me – and then jerked back with a yelp as the river of attacking angels surged through from the other world. I could feel their rage that they'd been stranded, left to die. Raziel disappeared under a frenzy of wings; the willow's ethereal branches churned, while the physical willow tree shifted gently, stirred only by the breeze.

Below, I could see the army of angels now, their bodies shining as they neared the park. I still couldn't turn away from the melee before me. My arms prickled as Raziel screamed – a high, terrible sound that was cut short. Then snowy fragments came drifting on the air, glinting as they caught the light…like the rainbows my mother had loved so much.

I let out a long, ragged breath.

"Goodbye, Father," I said.

The words had barely left my mouth when the gate's surface churned and yawned open. I jogged a few hasty steps back. An immense rushing noise came, like the ocean crashing over a ship.

And then the gate started to do exactly what I'd designed it to.

The angels who'd attacked Raziel vanished first, the

energy reeling in their bright, struggling bodies almost lazily; then it picked up speed, and the angels who'd been surging towards me from Pawntucket were drawn through in a panicked tumble of wings. Angelic screams, glimpses of stunned, frightened faces.

The noise grew deafening, a roar that shook the ground, as the gate pulled them in faster and faster – I fell to my knees, crying out and clapping my hands over my ears. I couldn't even see angels any more: just a sparkling river of light that led into the willow tree as thousands were drawn through, from miles away.

But I could sense their despair – their certainty that what had happened here was a judgement on them. In their gamble with our world, they'd lost almost everything that had made them angels.

When it was all over, there was silence.

I rose slowly, staring at the willow tree, with its shimmering, frosty branches. Ice skirted the edge of the pond; above, a few patches of blue were showing through the clouds. It all looked just the same. As if the last half-hour had never happened at all.

Then, with a chill, I realized something *had* changed. *My angel.* Oh god, the way the energy had battered so fiercely at her – I reached for her in a panic. In my mind's eye, I could see her: my radiant, winged twin. Her head was bowed…and one of her wings lay crumpled and useless at her side.

"No," I whispered, gently reaching out to her. Our hands touched with a soft glow as her eyes met mine. They were sad, resigned – and in a daze I knew that this was not an injury that could be healed.

Angrily, I wiped away tears. No – no, this couldn't be true. I switched my consciousness to hers, longing to sense that everything was all right. Instead it felt as if my ethereal body were bound down by tethers, unable to break free.

My angel couldn't fly any more.

I stood motionless beside the tree, trying to take it in. She'd never leave my body again – never lift away and send me soaring through the stars. At first I'd spent so long hating my angel self, wanting her to go away for ever. Yet now that she'd been diminished, it felt as if part of me had been chopped off.

The willow tree shifted gently in the breeze as I gazed at the spot where I'd been conceived – the place where the angels had disappeared, for ever. After what seemed a long time, I felt my shoulders straighten a little.

If this was the price I had to pay, then okay – I can live with it, I thought finally.

I turned and made my way back down the hiking trail, listening to the tread of my footsteps against the snow and damp earth. And somehow, despite Mom, despite my angel…I felt strangely at peace. Already what had happened felt like a dream, yet at the same time everything was so clear now, as if the world were brand-new. I tipped my head back as I walked, gazing at the frost sparkling on the pine trees.

When I reached the parking lot, my truck was still there. I got in and started the engine – and glanced at the picture of Timmy.

"Let's go home, kid," I murmured.

CHAPTER *Thirty-eight*

MY DREAMY FEELING OF PEACE evaporated the second I pulled out onto the highway. *Alex.* I couldn't sense him any more – at some point I'd lost the connection. As I drove, I hastily scanned.

Nothing. I took a deep breath and tried again, reaching for the strong, familiar sense of him.

Panic clutched me. It wasn't there.

No, that wasn't it – confusedly, I realized that I didn't *know* whether his energy was there or not. Whenever I tried to send my consciousness out of myself, nothing happened.

As the truth hit me, my hands went cold on the steering

wheel. The road suddenly looked strange, off-kilter. Apparently my angel hadn't been the only thing damaged by the ethereal storm that had raged through me. I was still psychic; I could feel it…but on nowhere near the same level.

I swallowed hard; I couldn't even begin to process this yet. *Alex is okay,* I told myself harshly. *He's got to be.*

As I drove into the town, people were cheering, waving their weapons. They shouted my name as they saw me, pounding on the hood of the truck as I passed. My heart quickened as I brought their auras into view. They lay flat and flickering against their bodies. Oh my god – had I actually done it?

I sped the rest of the way to the square, looking for Alex at every turn. There was no sign of him.

When I got to the town hall, people were gathering in front of it; jubilant shouts filled the air. As I jumped out, I saw Nina and Jonah holding each other tightly on the lawn, his dark head against her golden-brown one. They spotted me and came running over; I met them halfway.

Nina and I embraced. She was crying. "Oh, Willow, you did it! We saw them all sweeping away through the sky, and then they vanished—"

"Is everyone okay?" I gasped.

She gulped and wiped her eyes as we drew apart. "No. We're still counting, but we've lost eight so far."

My chest turned to ice. Then Nina named some of my old classmates – no one I'd known well, but I could put faces to all the names. One was a girl I'd shared notes with in English class.

"Eight people," I murmured, my throat tight. "But I thought—" I stared at the shouting crowd, their auras still flush with their bodies. Slowly, I let go, and watched them all return back to normal.

"I thought I'd saved everyone," I said in a small voice.

Jonah touched my hand, his brown eyes intense. "Willow, you saved so many," he said. "You saved *me,* for that matter – I had five on me at once, but they couldn't grab hold." When I didn't respond, he added, "We all would have died, you know. Just like the attack at your base."

"And you know what else?" Nina said, her expression fierce. "We are going to have the celebration to end all celebrations today – because the angels are *gone,* and that's what we've all been fighting for."

Wrestling with pain, triumph, confusion, I hugged her again, unable to speak. Then I pulled away. "Have you seen Alex?" I asked urgently.

Jonah shook his head. "I got a glimpse of him during the battle. He was up on a roof at the far end of town, holding off – well, an entire army of angels. He must've killed hundreds."

Alex. He'd been the reason why the army hadn't reached me in time – the reason I was still alive. "Is…is he all right?" I got out.

"I don't know. I lost sight of him—"

"Jonah!" shouted an urgent voice. Rachel came panting up. "It's Seb. We found him behind one of the houses – he looks pretty bad."

My heart gave a sickening lurch. Following Rachel's gaze, I saw a small knot of people carrying someone on a makeshift stretcher. The next second I was running across the square as fast as I could, with Nina and Jonah right behind.

A girl I hardly recognized was crying. "I didn't mean to! I was trying to hit the angel attacking him—"

I skidded to a stop on the damp ground and fell to my knees. Seb lay with his head to one side, not moving. A dark bruise stained the left side of his face. Blood was everywhere – in his curls, mixing with the stubble on his face, staining his green jacket.

"Seb – no." I gripped his hand; it felt cold. With my other hand, I touched his face, trying not to shake. "Seb, *please.*"

Rachel was pale. "He was up on a roof – he got hit with shrapnel from a chimney and fell off. We know you're not supposed to move someone who's injured, but…but we couldn't just leave him…"

I couldn't take my eyes off Seb's face. "I have to get him to Schenectady," I said in a rush. "He needs a doctor."

Nina stared at me. "But Schenectady's an Eden! Even if the angels are gone now, won't—"

"It'll be fine," I said shortly. I was certain of it, though I couldn't begin to explain why just then. The girl who'd shot at Seb was still crying. Resisting the urge to slap her, I jumped up and fumbled in my pocket for my keys.

Nina and Jonah looked at each other. Nina said, "Okay, I'll come with you—"

"Willow!"

My head jerked up. Alex was running across the square towards me. The relief was too deep to fathom – I held back a moan as he reached me and swung me into his arms. "You're all right," he whispered against my hair. "Oh, thank Christ, you're all right."

Suddenly it felt as if I'd forgiven him everything – all I wanted was to wrap my arms tight around him in return. Confusion reeled through me. Shakily, I pulled away, hugging myself and avoiding the sudden hurt in his eyes.

"I'm fine, but – but Seb isn't," I said. "We're taking him to the hospital."

Alex crouched hastily beside him. "Oh, shit, man – I told you to stay alive," he muttered. He pressed two fingers under Seb's jaw. "His pulse is weak. I hope this looks worse than it is."

We loaded Seb gently into the back of my truck, trying to keep him as steady as possible. Alex took the keys from me without asking, and I crawled in beside Seb. Nina got into the front, asking, "Do you know how to get to Schenectady?"

Alex's gaze met mine in the rear-view mirror; he had a scratch over one eye. "Yeah, I've been there," he said. "You'll have to give me directions to the hospital, though."

As we headed out of Pawntucket and onto I-90, Seb's hazel eyes flickered open. "Meggie?" he whispered.

My heart broke for him. I rubbed his hand between both of mine. "No, it's Willow," I said softly. "But you're going to be with Meggie, Seb. I promise."

He gave a groan as the truck lurched around a curve, and seemed to pass out again. My throat clutched as I held his hand tightly. The two of us had taken so many wrong turns together these past two years. But he was the brother I'd never had – and I hadn't had him in my life for nearly long enough.

Nina twisted around in her seat, her eyes wide. "Willow, what *happened* up there, anyway?"

I swallowed hard and stroked back Seb's curls. And, still staring down at him, I explained.

I'd used the energy field to alter everyone on the planet. It was now impossible for angels to feed from humanity. And though I couldn't change it if someone had been physically hurt by the angels...I'd taken away people's delusions about them. I'd tried to do it as gently as possible, but the whole world knew the truth now, and that the invaders were gone for ever. I'd managed to heal the ether in the angels' world a little; it might last long enough now for them to figure out a different way to save themselves.

But they couldn't get back here again – ever. I'd sealed off our dimension for good.

As I finished talking, Alex was staring at me in the rear-view mirror. When he faced forward again, his expression was dazed.

"So it's really over," he murmured finally.

Silence fell; I could see him and Nina trying to come to grips with all this. It still felt dreamlike to me: nowhere near as real as Seb's hand, cold in mine.

Or Alex's dark, tousled hair as he sat in the driver's seat. I swallowed. "What happened with you?" I asked. "Jonah said he saw you up on a roof holding off hundreds."

Alex shrugged, still looking stunned. "Yeah, trying to. When they finally got past, I thought I was dead, but they couldn't get hold of my aura." His eyes met mine again. "Was that you?"

I nodded. I was so overwhelmed by what he'd done that my voice came out too formally: "Thank you. If you hadn't held them back, I never could have done it."

I saw his flash of hurt. "Christ, Willow, you don't have to *thank* me."

None of us spoke again. When we got to Schenectady Eden, the main gates were open – there was already a flow of traffic heading out. Crowds of people stood just outside in small clusters, talking intently; some were crying. No one paid any attention as we drove through.

When Schenectady Hospital came into view, we pulled up to the ER and a pair of attendants came racing out with a clattering gurney. "Here," I cried, sliding open the door to the back.

A few minutes later, we were all sitting in a crowded waiting room. Seb had been taken away down a long corridor. A nurse came over and held out a clipboard. "I know everything's kind of upside down at the minute, but could you fill this out for us?"

I stared blankly at the form, not even able to take it in just then. Alex was sitting across from me; he leaned over and took it. "He's not an Eden resident," he said, scanning the sheet.

The nurse tried to smile; underneath it she looked as flattened with shock as everyone else. "That's all right… I guess none of us are any more, are we? Just do the best you can."

CHAPTER *Thirty-nine*

WE SAT IN SILENCE. I kept glancing down the hallway, worried about Seb – wishing I was able to send my angel to see what was going on.

The room was full of dazed, weary-looking people. I saw a woman in the corner clutching a Church of Angels pendant and crying silently, tears streaming down her face. Pressing my fingers against my head, I hoped I'd done the right thing – that humanity would find its way forward.

Nina was flicking through a magazine called *Eden Now*. Alex frowned up at the TV that hung from the wall. Bizarrely, an old episode of *Cheers* was playing.

"Nothing on the news yet," he said finally, almost to himself.

I shook my head. "No. I guess it'll take time for people to organize themselves."

Our gaze met; my cheeks heated and I glanced away. Alex had been keeping his distance from me for hours now. I knew he thought this was what I wanted...only I wasn't sure if it was any more.

Mom, I'm so confused, I thought miserably.

Even without looking at Alex, I was so aware of him: the curve of his dark eyebrows, the sense of easy strength as he leaned back in his chair. All I wanted was to sit beside him and feel him put his arm around me. But it didn't make any sense. How could my anger have just evaporated?

But you know *why,* piped up a tiny voice inside me.

I went very still as those minutes at the willow tree rushed back in vivid detail...and now I was able to take it all in. When I'd clung tight to Alex's grounding energy, I'd seen him with so much clarity, right down to his soul. Leaving me when he'd thought he was going to die had been the hardest thing he'd ever done. His decision hadn't been perfect, not by a long shot. But he'd done the best he could.

I sat frozen in my seat, recalling how I'd touched every person on the planet: explored the rich tapestry of all their frailties, hopes, strengths...their humanity.

Oh, god, of course I could forgive Alex – I already had. After seeing all that, how could I not forgive someone who'd struggled with such a terrible choice, and would now give anything – *anything* – if he could somehow change the outcome?

Especially when I loved him so much it hurt?

Suddenly my eyes were full of tears. Alex wasn't looking at me; he was staring at the TV with the thoughtful frown I knew so well. Why was there a coffee table between us? Why were we in a waiting room full of people?

I cleared my throat. "Alex, um—"

Before I could ask if he'd step outside with me for a second, a doctor came into the room. "Are you with Sebastián Carrera?" she asked, crouching in front of us.

She'd pronounced his name wrong; I hardly noticed. Nodding, I sat up straight and gripped Nina's hand.

"He's okay," she said.

I let out a shivering breath. Across from me, Alex had closed his eyes in relief, shoulders slumping.

The doctor's expression held a deep sadness of her own, but her tone was compassionate. "He's got a bad concussion and a few broken ribs. We'll need to keep him overnight for observation. But his X-rays are clear, no internal cranial pressure. He's going to be fine."

Remembering how Seb had asked for Meghan, I had a sudden feeling that *fine* was relative. My half-angel awareness of him had lessened, but I could still sense his despair, and my chest tightened.

"Can I see him?" I asked.

The doctor looked at her watch.

"Please? I'm his sister."

It didn't even feel like a lie. The doctor nodded. "Just you, then, and only for a few minutes – he needs to rest."

As I got up, my eyes met Alex's. "Tell him I said hi," he said quietly. "And that I'm glad he's okay."

I nodded, feeling choked by everything I wanted to say to Alex, but this wasn't the time. I hurried after the doctor. "I won't be long," I said over my shoulder.

The doctor led me down a maze of corridors, then stopped in front of a door. "He's in here – I'll be back in five minutes." Her gaze widened as she studied me. "Wait. Aren't you—?"

I shook my head. "No," I said softly. "I just look like her."

When I pushed open the door, I found Seb lying in a bed with crisp sheets, his bruises worse than before; harsh black stitches slashed diagonally through his left eyebrow.

I sat on the bed beside him and reached for his hand. "Hi," I whispered.

Wincing, Seb turned his head on the pillow to look at me. He tried to smile, but the look in his hazel eyes was breaking my heart.

"You were right," he said.

I didn't have to ask. I squeezed his hand tightly between both of mine. "I know."

Neither of us spoke for a long moment, and then Seb let out a breath. "We defeated the angels, yes? I can feel it."

"Yes, we did it. They're really gone now – for ever."

He sagged against the bedclothes and closed his eyes. "That's good," he whispered. "Oh, that's so good."

I stroked his curls from his forehead. "Alex says hi," I added.

Seb smiled faintly, but I could feel his mind wasn't on it. "Willow, what am I going to do?"

"You mean about Meghan?"

His fingers gripped mine restlessly. "How is it possible for a man to be this stupid, *querida* – how?"

"Shh, you need to rest. Seb, it'll be okay."

He gave a shattered laugh. "Really? When we broke up, do you know what she said? That she'd wanted to tell me she loved me for so long…but never had, because she knew I wouldn't say it too."

Holding onto Seb's hand, I got a faint flash of Meghan sitting on Seb's bed, her blue eyes anguished. *I'm sorry, Seb. I just can't do it any more.*

"And I just *sat* there. I told her that, yes, I understood, I didn't want her to be unhappy – and all I could think was, *Meggie, please don't do this…*" Seb's voice faltered.

"But you know how you feel about her now! She'll see that; she'll realize."

He shook his head, closing his eyes again. "No," he said dully. "I don't think so."

Time for a change of subject. I cleared my throat, looking down at our hands. "Seb, listen. When I was manipulating the energy, it was like I had this incredible rush of knowledge, about every living thing. And...I found out more about half-angels."

His eyes flew open. "Really?" he said after a pause.

I nodded – and told him what I'd seen. Altogether, there'd been maybe a dozen half-angels throughout time; I'd sensed it in people's genes. But Seb and I had been the only ones for centuries. And I had a feeling we were the only ones ever who'd been aware of our angels.

As I spoke, I tried not to think about that other part of myself, broken inside of me. Especially as I told Seb the rest: angels weren't supposed to be able to breed with humans at all, but in a few cases of extreme angel burn, the human's system had morphed slightly, becoming receptive.

Seb and I existed solely because our mothers had been so severely damaged by our fathers.

Now it seemed like Seb's hand was comforting me, instead of the other way around. "This doesn't change anything, not really," he said after a pause. "Neither of us thought we were here because of some great love affair."

I nodded, throat tight.

Then Seb's forehead creased. "You feel different," he said suddenly.

Before I could answer, I sensed his angel reaching out for mine, and I winced and ducked my head. I hadn't wanted Seb to know yet, but of course I couldn't hide it from him.

I sat very still. As his angel touched my own, I felt him realize. He didn't speak. When I lifted my head, his eyes were bright with tears. Softly, his angel slipped inside of me, finding and cradling that wounded part of me.

Oh god, the look on his face… "I'm all right," I whispered hoarsely. "Seb, I promise you, I'm all right. Don't you see? I still *have* my angel, inside me. And I'm alive. And so are you and Alex – I have everything that matters."

I clutched his hand. "Please listen to me: you have *got* to tell Meghan how you feel. You love her – and you tried your best the whole time, and she knows that. She'll forgive you." I managed a lopsided smile. "Trust me, okay? I kind of know what I'm talking about on this one."

I saw hope battle disbelief in Seb's eyes. "Maybe you're right," he said finally.

"I am."

He smiled slightly then. "You often are," he said. "It's very irritating."

The doctor eased open the door. "Time's up," she said.

I bent and kissed his stubbled cheek. "I'll be back tomorrow when they discharge you, okay?" I lowered my voice. "And by the way, I told her I'm your sister."

He was already half asleep, his stitches stark against his eyebrow. "Then you were right again," he murmured. "Because that's what you are."

CHAPTER *Forty*

As I walked back to the waiting room, my stomach tightened with anticipation. *Alex, can I talk to you?* Nina could wait a few minutes. All I wanted was to get Alex someplace private and feel his arms around me again – press my face against his warm neck and never let him go.

When I entered the waiting room, my brow creased: his blue plastic chair was empty. Nina sat looking through a different magazine. I perched beside her and then twisted around in my seat, glancing at the restroom.

"Where's Alex?" I said.

Nina had tossed the magazine aside and was reaching for her coat. "He left."

My heart stopped. "What?" I said blankly.

She nodded at a pair of empty seats nearby. "He got a ride with those guys; they said they'd drop him off in Pawntucket so he could get his truck. He said to tell you goodbye."

She saw my expression then and stared at me, flustered. "Willow, the way he said it, I thought you knew. He made it sound like something you'd agreed on."

Once I know you're all right, I'll leave. Suddenly the world was crashing in on me. "How long ago?" I gasped.

"I don't know, maybe five minutes?"

I'd grabbed up my parka and was running before she finished talking. I darted around a crowd of people as they came in the entrance, heard someone give a startled cry. Nina was shouting behind me. "Willow! *Wait!*"

The cold air hit me as I shot through the doors. I pounded down the sidewalk, not stopping until I reached the parking lot. I craned up on my tiptoes, longing for my angel. I couldn't see him. I couldn't see him anywhere.

"Alex!" I shouted. My voice echoed over the half-empty lot. "*Alex!*"

Nina caught up with me, panting. "Willow, what—"

Where was the truck? I spotted it and started running

again; as I reached it, I whirled towards Nina. "The keys, did he give you the keys?"

She handed them over, and I lunged into the driver's seat. "Get in!" I cried. A second later we were screeching away from the parking lot.

"Willow, what is *wrong*?" Nina said loudly.

What's wrong is that I can't scan for him any more. If he leaves, I won't be able to find him – and he'll think that's what I wanted. I couldn't say the words. I knew Seb wouldn't be able to find him either; it took such a deep, multi-layered bond.

I clutched the wheel hard. "I just – I've got to find Alex."

I almost cried in frustration as we reached the main gates and got caught in a traffic jam: a river of glittering metal. It looked as if every car in Schenectady was leaving at the same time. People were carrying their belongings, heading out in droves on foot – it was like the refugees that Alex and I had once seen heading for Denver Eden in reverse.

"How many of them do you think are sick?" asked Nina in a soft voice. Over half an hour had passed.

"A lot," I said shortly as we crept forward. "But at least their minds are clear, and they'll get treatment now, once things are a little more normal again."

She looked at me. "Do you really think the world will *ever* be normal again?"

"Not really," I admitted. My hands felt clammy; I wiped them on my jeans. "I guess we'll have to…find a new normality."

Finally, *finally*, we drove through the gates. I got off the traffic-laden highway as soon as I could, taking a country road that was the scenic route. Nina set her jaw and reached for the strap on the ceiling.

"Good – now burn rubber," she said.

"Believe me, I plan to," I said as we whistled around a curve. I swung the wheel hard to avoid a pothole. *Alex, I don't want to lose you – not again.*

When we finally reached Pawntucket, I plunged into its damaged streets; they were all empty. Alex's truck had been parked in front of the elementary school – near the front door, with its bright construction-paper decorations.

My chest was clenched as I turned into the school's parking lot. The words were part prayer, part hope: *Please, Alex – please.*

His truck was gone.

"No!" I gasped.

"Try the town square – maybe he's there," Nina said urgently.

When we reached it, I lurched to a stop in front of Drake's Diner and jumped out. I couldn't see Alex's blue truck anywhere. The square was full of people, though, all gathered in front of the town hall. Someone was bashing out "We Are the Champions" on a guitar; raucous singing filled the air.

"Is Alex here?" I cried, as Jonah came running over and we got out.

He looked surprised and shook his head. "No, he came and said goodbye about twenty minutes ago."

The world stopped. Somehow I got the words out. "Do you…do you know where he went?"

"No, he didn't say." I could tell how much Jonah wished he had a different answer. "I'm really sorry."

I stood frozen in the weak winter sunshine. Twenty minutes. Oh god, I'd been so close! He could have gone in any direction, and I had no idea which one he'd choose. He was miles away now…thinking it was what I wanted.

I was too late.

Nina squeezed my arm as I stood there speechless. From the town hall lawn, loud singing was still going on. Someone had started banging on an upturned garbage can; the sound pounded at my skull.

Finally Nina cleared her throat. "Do you want to go join the party? You deserve it, Willow."

I'd never cared less about celebrating. I shook my head dully. "No. Maybe later."

Nina looked as if she was racking her brains to think of something to cheer me up. "Okay, well…I'll just go get us some Cokes or something. There's a whole stash we've been saving."

I managed a smile. "Thanks. That would be nice."

As Nina headed off towards the square, Jonah stayed beside me, propping himself against the truck. "Is Seb okay?" he asked.

I nodded. "He'll be fine."

We stood watching the party. A few people had started a snowball fight, laughing and shouting. "So…what will you do now?" Jonah said, glancing at me.

I had no idea. Remembering that serene moment when I'd gazed over the Wyoming plains, I knew that I didn't *need* Alex…but I wanted him so badly it hurt.

Even if I love you, I might as well hate you, because that's what it feels like! I shut my eyes, wincing at the memory. I might be fine on my own, but I wouldn't find peace again. How could I, when Alex thought I hated him?

And someday, I guessed he'd fall in love with someone else.

The thought brought so much pain that the celebratory scene in front of me seemed to dim at the edges. "I don't know," I answered Jonah finally. "I, um – I guess I'll stay in Pawntucket, for a while at least. It'll take a lot of work to get things back the way they were. What about you?"

Jonah's eyes were on Nina as she returned. "Yeah, I'm staying too," he said quietly. "This is my home now."

Even through my sadness, I thought how strange it was: the way the threads of life can weave destinies together like a spider's web. My brief meeting with Jonah two years ago had brought him here, to my best friend.

"Here, fresh from the snow," Nina said when she reached us, pressing an icy can into my hand.

A whoop of laughter; Scott Mason lurched past with Rachel on his shoulders. "Hey, Willow!" he cried, reversing quickly. He and Rachel both went silent; Scott held out his hand to me, suddenly serious and inarticulate. "Thank you so much," he said fervently. "You are a *hero,* you know that?"

Suddenly I knew that, no matter whatever else happened to me, I did not want a lifetime of people looking at me the way the two of them were.

"That's okay," I said as I shook his hand. "But it wasn't me, actually."

Scott blinked. "It wasn't?"

"No. I was just there when it happened. Maybe I was a catalyst or something, but…the angels' time here was just finished, I guess."

"Oh," he said, looking bewildered.

"Well, at least they're gone," Rachel put in. After a pause, she added, "Too bad Alex couldn't stay for the party. He was incredible during the fight."

Scott glared up at her, jiggling her legs. "Yeah, could

you have *been* any more obvious?" He put on a falsetto voice. "'Ooh, Alex, are you sure you can't stay?'"

I'd been leaning against the truck; now I jerked upright. "Wait – you saw Alex?"

Scott shrugged. "Yeah, on his way out of town. He asked us for directions."

Suddenly my heart was racing. "Where to?"

He looked taken aback by the urgency in my voice. "Route 16."

I caught my breath; my gaze met Nina's.

"Go!" she cried, grabbing the Coke from me and shoving me towards the truck. Because she knew as well as I did what was down that road.

I must have set new speed records as I drove out of Pawntucket; two years earlier I'd have been pulled over before I even reached the town limits. On Route 16, winter-bare trees flashed past.

Please, I thought. *Please.*

I slowed down at the brown-and-white sign: MURRAY PARK. My heart pounded as I took the turn.

At first glance the parking lot was empty, and my soul withered inside me. And then I saw it: a blue 4 × 4 sitting in the far corner. Suddenly I was trembling almost too hard to park. I rested my forehead against my fists on the steering wheel for a second. When I looked up, the truck was still there.

It was the most beautiful sight I'd ever seen.

I got out and walked quickly up the hiking trail. When I got to the clearing, I could see the willow tree – and a boy standing beside it. His hands were in his back pockets, his dark hair rumpled by the wind as he looked up at the tree's branches.

As I approached, Alex turned at the sound of my footsteps. His eyes widened in a flash of blue-grey. I stopped short as our gazes met, my mouth dry.

I saw him swallow. "I just…wanted to see it," he said finally, nodding at the tree.

"I'm glad," I said as I started to cry. "I mean, I really, really cannot tell you how glad I am."

I took another step towards him, and then I was running. Alex met me halfway and caught me up hard in his arms.

For a long time we just held each other. I clung to him, my face tight against his neck as I drank in his familiar scent – the feel of his arms around me. Finally he stroked my hair back with both hands. Without speaking, he started pressing slow kisses over my face, brushing away the tears.

His warm mouth caressed its way over my cheeks, my lips. "I thought I'd never see you again," I whispered, closing my eyes. "That years would pass – that you'd fall in love with someone else…"

Alex stopped and stared at me. "Are you crazy?" He sounded almost angry. "There will never be anyone else for me, Willow. Never. If you hadn't come after me, I'd have come back here in a few weeks – I'd have begged you on my knees."

I reached up and gripped both his hands. He rested his forehead against mine; we stood with our heads bowed. The willow tree stirred as the wind whispered around us.

"I'm sorry," I said. "Alex, I was just so angry and confused…"

"I know," he said. "I deserved it. Don't apologize."

And somehow that was all that needed to be said.

We drew apart a little, gazing at each other. I slowly felt a smile spread across my face. I just stood there, smiling. I couldn't stop.

Finally I cleared my throat. "You know, there's something I have to do," I told him gravely – and I took his head in my hands and kissed him, gliding my fingers through his dark hair.

By the fourth kiss, he was grinning. "Wait, are you sure you definitely want me back? You seem kind of indecisive."

I could feel myself grinning too. "Don't talk," I said. "Just kiss."

EPILOGUE

MY MOTHER'S BURIAL TOOK PLACE five days later. It was the day after we'd buried the Pawntucket fighters, in the same old cemetery outside of town. I'd always liked it there – it was so quiet. Some of the headstones in the cemetery had mellowed with age, and in the summer the oak trees cast a dappled shade.

There weren't many of us present. Alex and me. Nina and Jonah. A few others. Seb wasn't: he'd left to go after Meghan. We'd spoken to the Idaho AKs on the shortwave by then – Meghan was heading to Tulsa to see her family. Seb hadn't been in contact with her yet. He said you couldn't tell a girl you loved her over the radio. I closed my eyes briefly, wishing him luck as hard as I could.

Aunt Jo wasn't at the funeral either. Now that the angels were gone, she seemed much more bitter, and had stayed on at the lakeside cabin. I hoped that she could find peace.

I hoped we all could.

My grandparents were buried in the cemetery; they'd died before I was born. As everyone said a few words at my mother's graveside, I found myself studying their double headstone with its stark black letters. In a strange way it was comforting – as if they'd take care of her.

I was the last to speak. I hadn't planned what I was going to say. But I talked about how Mom used to play the guitar when I was little. How hard she'd tried to be there for me as she grew sicker, and how often she'd failed. How amazing it had been whenever she opened her eyes and really saw me.

"Mom, I wouldn't have traded you for anything," I finished softly. "So much of me is you. Thank you."

"You okay?" whispered Alex, as I went and stood beside him again.

I nodded, leaning against him as he put his arm around me. "Yeah," I murmured. "I really am."

I held his hand tightly as they lowered Mom's coffin into the cold ground. I'd dreaded this moment all my life, but now that it had come, it was impossible to feel too sad.

Mom was finally free.

In the spring, Alex and I went back to our cabin in the Sierra Nevadas.

What we'd planned as a one-month break stretched seamlessly into two. Neither of us could get enough now of simply lying on the grass, listening to the wind in the pines. Or sitting up for hours talking. Or taking our sleeping bags outside and sleeping under the stars, our bare limbs entwined.

Slowly, I was getting used to having the angel part of me so diminished. There were days when I thought it would have been easier if she'd just vanished. But then, touching her shining presence, I knew I'd rather have this little bit than nothing at all. And being at the cabin, with its total peace, was healing.

Being with Alex was healing.

One day in June, we were lying on the grass, soaking up the sun. All Alex had on was a pair of shorts; his eyes were closed, his hands folded on his tanned stomach.

"Hey, have we figured out yet if I'm an older woman or not?" I said drowsily. I was lying beside him, my head against his.

He grinned and made a lunge for me; I gave a laughing shriek as he pulled me on top of him. "I think you're just two weeks younger than me now," he said, nuzzling at my neck. "You're catching up."

"I've done all the catching up I'm ever doing." I drew a blade of grass across his perfect mouth. "You are *not* going into another dimension again. Ever."

"Oh no! How am I going to live, now that you've squelched my dream?"

"You'll manage."

There was a vibration in my shorts pocket as my cell went off. I hardly ever remembered to charge it up here – we had an extension that ran off the truck's battery. I slid off Alex and pulled the phone out. A message from Seb:

We leave tomorrow. Can't believe it's really happening. Text me and let me know you're alive. xx

I showed the text to Alex; he grinned. "Hey, so they're really doing it."

"Yep," I said, smiling at the screen. "They're really doing it."

It had been weeks after Seb left before I found out what happened with him and Meghan. Finally I'd received a letter in Pawntucket from him that had gone on for pages about his journey. I'd scanned it impatiently, knowing he'd done this to torture me.

It ended: *Then I got to Tulsa. Well, I think that's all for now. I will write again soon, and you must write to me too. I hope you and Alex are both well. Love, Seb.*

"What?!" I yelped. "Oh, Seb, you are in so much trouble—" And then I saw his postscript, in tiny letters… and a grin burst across my face.

Meggie said yes. I didn't know I could be this happy.

Seb had been busy these last few months, though. He'd never been able to get the street girl he'd once saved out of his mind – or, I suspected, the street child he'd once been himself. Now he was about to head back down to Mexico; he planned to start a centre to help street kids who'd been left even more destitute by the quakes.

And Meghan was going with him.

I texted back:

Alive and well. So excited for you both, querido. You're going to do a wonderful job. xx

I glanced at Alex as I put my phone away. "He's making me feel incredibly lazy, you know. He's been setting this up for months."

"Lazy's good – for now, anyway." Alex laced his fingers through mine. "God, Willow, if anyone deserves a break, you do."

I gazed out at the unchanging mountains. And for the hundredth time, I was glad that no one was aware of what I'd done. Even with Jonah's broadcast, all most people knew was that after the earthquakes, humanity had started spontaneously marshalling – and then the angels had "perished".

After the battle, Alex and I had stayed on in Pawntucket for a few months, helping to rebuild. The work was long and hard, but after a while the town square didn't have that defeated look any more. It made me smile every time I saw it.

People everywhere had been doing the same thing: tearing down the trappings of the Edens, fixing roads, clearing away the ruins. The Denver Church of Angels had been razed to the ground. Now, a few months on, there was electricity again, phone service, the internet. But already the world felt like a very different place, though it was too soon yet to tell what direction it was heading in.

And – I guess inevitably – there was also the small, continued existence of the Church of Angels. Even now that everyone knew the truth…some people couldn't bear to give up the beautiful creatures who'd ensnared us.

Thinking of the angels now, just a dimension away, I knew their fate was in their own hands. Paschar's vision was right: I was the one who could have destroyed them.

I'd just tried to choose a better way.

"Are you sorry?" I asked softly, turning to look at Alex. "I mean, not that the angels are gone, just…everything's so different now. Especially for you. You trained your whole life for something, and now it's over with."

Alex was still lying on his back. He shrugged, eyes half closed. "Yeah, it's weird. But I'll figure something out. Maybe I'll start a bungee-jumping business."

He could if he wanted to – now that everything was over with, Alex had been able to access his old bank account, with the funds he'd received for being an AK for years. We wouldn't be hurting for money anytime soon.

"I could definitely get into bungee jumping." I flopped down and crossed my arms on his bare chest. "Hey, if the CIA starts back up, you could always work for them again."

He opened his eyes and studied me with a slight smile. "Are you sure you're not as psychic as you used to be?" he said finally.

I blinked; I'd only been kidding. "You mean you've *heard* from them? But when?"

Alex sat up, carrying me with him. "A few days ago, when we drove down for supplies. They'd gotten my cell number somehow. It was when you went to the drugstore, remember? My phone went off, and it was them."

"Oh," I said faintly. I could guess what was coming next.

Alex's toned stomach was creased as he sat leaning forward, running a blade of grass between his fingers. "The thing is…they're starting up a paranormal intruder division. They want me to run it."

The words echoed inside me. The whole time we'd been up here together, I'd been imagining us having a quiet, peaceful life from now on – the thought of it being taken away before it had barely begun made me want to cry.

"So…I guess that would pay a lot," I said at last.

"Yeah, it sounded like they'd give me a blank cheque if I wanted it."

I cleared my throat. "And – it's what you love, right? I mean, it's what you've done your whole life; it's part of who you are. I totally understand that."

Alex looked up in surprise. "Willow, I told them no."

"You…really?"

"Yeah, of course." He snorted and tossed the grass aside. "It's just so typical of those guys. When there was an actual paranormal intrusion, Dad struggled to get *any* funding – and now that there's no intrusion whatsoever, they're throwing money at it."

I hated mentioning this, though knew I had to. "But Alex, won't you get bored eventually if you're not doing something exciting? I mean, you could probably do whatever you wanted for the CIA. Hunt terrorists or fight crime or—"

"Willow, no," Alex interrupted softly. He put his hand on my cheek. "Listen to me," he said. "I have been worrying about saving the world since I was five years old. I never had a choice, and that was okay – it was just what had to be done. But now the world's finally getting back on track; it doesn't need me any more. That means I can do—" He stopped, shaking his head with a sudden grin.

"Anything," he said.

All at once the sun shining down seemed even brighter. "You really don't want the CIA job?" I asked.

Alex looked like he was trying not to laugh. "What gave it away? Anyway, what about you? The CIA would snap you up in a second, if they knew what you'd done."

I smiled and stretched my legs out. "I think I'll pass."

We sat basking in the sunshine. A hawk was circling high overhead; the only other movement was the clouds drifting across the sky.

"You know what I'd really like to do?" Alex's blue-grey eyes had turned thoughtful.

I'd just started to brush the grass from his warm back. "No, what?"

"I'd like to travel."

I stopped mid-motion and glanced at him in surprise. "Is there even a single state you haven't seen?"

Alex nodded, leaning back on his hands as he gazed out at the mountains. "All of them. I was always on the hunt before – I never got a chance to just enjoy any of it. I'd like to see the country again and…" He shrugged, looking a little embarrassed. "Well, see exactly what it is we've saved."

I began to smile as I imagined it. I swiped the rest of the grass from his back and then slowly caressed his spine.

"You know what?" I said. "I like the sound of that. A lot."

Alex's gaze flew to mine. "Really? You want to?"

"Yeah," I said. "I think I do. We can take the truck and go all over."

He cupped his hand behind my neck and kissed me softly, then pulled me onto his lap with a grin. "Nah, let's get a couple of motorcycles. I'll teach you to ride, and you can be a biker chick. You are going to look seriously hot in leather."

I laughed and twined my arms around his neck. "Okay, deal. But you're not allowed to have one of those big biker beards, so don't even think about it."

"I can't have a beard?"

"No. Definitely not."

"Hmm. We may have to negotiate this one." Alex took a strand of my hair and tickled it across my face. For as long as I'd known Alex, he'd looked so much older than his age – weighed down with responsibility for the whole world.

Now his stormy eyes were simply…happy.

For a moment, as the breeze whispered, I thought of my mother. Alex's family. Sam. Everyone who'd fallen in battle; the groups we'd sent out; Alex's old friends who'd died years before.

And I knew that this was what we'd all been fighting for: the freedom to find joy in the world, now that we still had a world to enjoy.

My heart felt almost too full for speech. I touched Alex's face, tracing the dark arch of one eyebrow, and finally cleared my throat. "So how's this for a plan? We'll spend a few more weeks up here, then hit the road for a while. Then after that…just be together."

He took my hand and turned it over. Slowly, he kissed my palm; my pulse skipped at the feel of his summer-warm lips. Below, the mountains shone like a new dawn.

"Who said you're not as psychic any more?" Alex said softly. "You just read my mind."

ACKNOWLEDGEMENTS

No man is an island. No author is, either. *Angel Fever* was over a year in the writing, and huge thanks are due to all those who helped make it happen.

First, my editors on both coasts: Rebecca Hill and Stephanie King at Usborne in the UK, and Deborah Noyes at Candlewick in the US. *Fever* was determined to be very different from the story I'd originally planned, and without my editors to offer solutions, feedback and a keen, critical eye I would have been lost. Thank you more than I can say.

My thanks also to:

My agent Caroline Sheldon for her unwavering support and guidance. You are a rock! (And you also rock.) My lovely friends Julie Sykes and Linda Chapman for all the honest criticism, coffees, and generally keeping me sane(ish). Love to you both. Special thanks to the fabulous Julie Cohen, who had THE answer about a crucial scene. Amy Dobson and Anna Howorth at Usborne Publicity and Marketing respectively, for general awesomeness, as well as the aptly-named Tracy Miracle at Candlewick

Publicity. My brother and sister, Chuck Benson and Susan Lawrence – love you! Neil Chowney, who knew how Willow could get gasoline from a disused service station (don't try this one at home, kids!). Jean and James Vallesteros: Jean, your enthusiasm for books is inspirational, and James, your portrait of Alex and Willow makes me smile every time I see it. All of the bloggers, Facebook friends and Twitter followers who have reviewed or commented on the series, or even just tweeted to say hello – thank you! Special thanks again this time to @MarDixon, @DarkReaders and @EmpireofBooks. Thanks also to everyone who took part in the #ILoveAngelTrilogy Twitter contest, especially the winner, Christine Brenda Bernard Bolodo from Malaysia, for her great winning tweet: "It's the first novel that got me deeply engrossed into reading, took me away from reality and I just can't stop myself." And to all my readers who've loved the story and have waited, patiently or impatiently, for this final instalment – thank you so much. I hope it was worth the wait.

Last but never least, my husband. Pete, thank you for always being there, especially these last few years. The poem that "Alex's grandfather" wrote is for you. I love you.

Readers can drop me a line at the L. A. Weatherly Facebook author page, or follow me on Twitter: @LA_Weatherly

L.A.WEATHERLY

ANGEL

The only good angel is a dead angel

ANGEL

THE FIRST CAPTIVATING TALE IN
L.A. WEATHERLY'S ANGEL TRILOGY

Willow knows she's different from other girls.
And not just because she loves tinkering around with cars.
Willow has a gift. She can look into people's futures, know
their dreams, their hopes and their regrets, just by touching
them. She has no idea where she gets this power from...

But Alex does. Gorgeous, mysterious Alex knows Willow's
secret and is on a mission to stop her. The dark forces within
Willow make her dangerous – and irresistible.
In spite of himself, Alex finds he is falling in love
with his sworn enemy.

ISBN: 9781409521969

EPUB: 9781409530930

KINDLE: 9781409530947

L.A. WEATHERLY

ANGEL FIRE

Sequel to the bestselling ANGEL

ANGEL FIRE

THE SECOND STUNNING STORY IN
L.A. WEATHERLY'S ANGEL TRILOGY

Only Willow has the power to defeat the
malevolent Church of Angels, and they will stop
at nothing to destroy her. Willow isn't alone,
though. She has Alex by her side – a trained
Angel Killer and her one true love.

But Willow will always be a half-angel,
and when Alex joins forces with a group of AKs,
she's treated with mistrust and suspicion.
She's never felt more alone...until she meets Seb.
He's been searching for Willow his whole
life – because Seb is a half-angel too.

ISBN: 9781409522010
EPUB: 9781409541776
KINDLE: 9781409541783

PRAISE FOR

ANGEL

WINNER OF THE LEEDS BOOK AWARD 14-16 CATEGORY
Shortlisted for the Worcestershire Teen Book Award
Shortlisted for the Coventry Inspiration Book Award 14+
Shortlisted for the Romantic Novelists' Association YA Award

"Extremely compelling...so rich and deep and thrilling."
Liz Kessler, New York Times bestselling author

"A celestial stunner." *Lancashire Evening Post*

"It's a sin to miss a book this good!" *Girls Without a Bookshelf*

"Fantastic...beautifully written." *Dark-Readers*

"Incredibly hard to put down... If you only read one
young adult angel book, make sure it's *Angel*."
Jess Hearts Books

"Beautifully crafted, intense... Weatherly's writing
is like a dream." *Painting with Words*

"Absolutely compelling...by turns
tense, romantic, scary."
Our Book Reviews Online